❊ LONESTAR SANCTUARY ❊

COLLEEN COBLE

SWEETWATER
gap

Denise Hunter

THOMAS NELSON
Since 1798

NASHVILLE   DALLAS   MEXICO CITY   RIO DE JANEIRO   BEIJING

Lonestar Sanctuary © 2007 by Colleen Coble
Sweetwater Gap © 2008 by Denise Hunter

Published in Nashville, Tennessee, by Thomas Nelson. Thomas Nelson is a registered trademark of Thomas Nelson, Inc.

Thomas Nelson, Inc., titles may be purchased in bulk for educational, business, fund-raising, or sales promotional use. For information, please e-mail SpecialMarkets@ThomasNelson.com.

ISBN: 978-1-5955-4766-8

Printed in the United States of America

10 11 12 13 HCI 6 5 4 3 2

✵ LONESTAR SANCTUARY ✵

For my brother, Rick Rhoads,
*who should have been a cowboy
and whose strength and loving heart inspire me.*

PROLOGUE

THE RODEO CROWD, REEKING OF BEER AND PEANUTS, FINALLY REELED OFF into the night. Allie Siders heard their good-bye calls faintly through the faded cotton curtains. The twin bed sagged under her weight as she sat down and slipped off her worn cowboy boots. She smelled like horse—not a bad smell, but pungent nevertheless. A hot shower would ease her muscles, taxed with riding around barrels all day.

Her five-year-old daughter, Betsy, slept with one fist curled under her cheek in the youth cot next to Allie's bed, and Allie watched her sleep for a moment. So innocent, so beautiful.

So damaged by the blows life had dealt.

But things would get better soon. They could hardly get worse. Once Allie won the barrel-racing championship, the money would

1

come rolling in, and they'd have a better place to live than this old, broken-down trailer.

Allie dreamed of the day she and Betsy would have a real home again. They had one once upon a time, until the rough seas washed the sand castle away. But she'd find a way somehow. Betsy deserved more.

Allie slipped out of her dusty jeans and padded to the hall in her bare feet. The floors of the tiny travel trailer creaked and groaned under her weight as she tiptoed toward the bathroom. She left the door open a crack in case Betsy called out for her, though the chance was unlikely. The little girl hadn't spoken a word in nearly a year.

The tiny bathroom was spotless except for the rust stains Allie couldn't get off the worn fixtures. The Lysol she'd sprayed still lingered in the air, and she resisted the urge to sneeze.

She stared at her reflection in the mirror. The rodeo queen's smile was one that vanished with the crowds.

She went to the tub and turned on the shower. The hot spray sputtered from the rusty showerhead and struck her sore arm, soothing it, enticing her to step fully into the welcoming warmth.

Straightening, she tugged her shirt over her head. A creak like someone stepping on the weak floor came from beyond the door. She whirled in time to see it slam shut. Allie jerked her shirt back down. Gooseflesh pebbled on her arm when the creak came again.

"Yolanda, is that you?" she called.

Her friend's cheery voice didn't answer. Allie wet her lips. She was being a nervous Nellie tonight. The noise was probably the old trailer settling. Her hand gripped the bottom of her shirt again to remove it.

Something scratched at the door, and she caught her breath.

"*Aaaallieee,*" the taunting voice whispered through the door. The scrape sounded once more. "*Aaaallieee.*"

A man's voice, low and guttural, maybe even deliberately pitched so she wouldn't recognize it. A sharp edge under the low, cruel voice vibrated. That voice could cut to the bone without a weapon.

Allie took a step away from the menace, her back pushing away the wet shower curtain until water sprayed her neck. It was like a wet slap, bringing her back to what mattered most.

Betsy!

She grappled with the embrace of the wet shower curtain and managed to disentangle herself from it. She leaped to the door and grabbed the doorknob, yanking hard, but the door didn't move. With her hand on the cold metal knob, she could feel his movements on the other side.

"Let me out!" she screamed, pounding and kicking at the door.

"You want out?" He chuckled, the razor edge of his voice contrasting with the smooth laugh. "Your sister wanted out."

The room felt close, airless. Her lungs strained to pull in enough oxygen. She wanted to scream for Betsy but didn't dare call the man's attention to the fact that her daughter was in the bedroom.

"You sure you want out, Allie?" he whispered.

Terror whirled inside like a mounting tornado. She forced it deep, down to the dark place where she kept all the things she feared. For Betsy's sake she had to keep herself together.

Maybe she could get out, circle around to Betsy's window, and get to her. She spun around and ran to the bathroom window, but it was too small to allow even her tiny frame to exit. She turned back to the door and tried to open it again. It opened a crack against the force of his hand holding it to on the other side, then slammed shut before she could get it open wide enough to get her leg through.

"Let go of the door!" She tugged harder, kicked at it. Her fear morphed into a cold anger. If she could face him, she'd tear at his face with her nails. She would allow no one to hurt her baby girl.

The man's laugh—if such an evil sound could be called laughter—whispered through the door again. "Your sister was so pretty. Not nearly as pretty as you, though. Especially not now." A knife poked through the crack. "She screamed when she saw the knife. Are you going to scream, Allie?"

Allie stared at the blade slicing through the door. It wasn't true, couldn't be true. He was just trying to scare her.

Tammy had walked in on a burglar.

The knife blade danced in the crack, moving forward, then pulling back long enough to make her think he was leaving. Then it reappeared, the edge sharp and dangerous.

She pulled on the knob again. "You coward," she yelled. "Face me like a man! Quit hiding behind whispers and phone calls."

"You might faint if you saw my face," he whispered. "Just like Tammy did."

The fear tried to surge out of the box she'd stuffed it into, but Allie tightened her control. Her sister's face flashed through her mind, and sorrow welled in her eyes. Had this man really been the one? She couldn't let herself believe it.

Allie laid her head against the door. "What do you want?"

"I want you to pay," he said, his whisper harsher. "I'm going to take everything you love, just like you destroyed the things that mattered to me. What matters most to you, Allie?"

Betsy, he would take Betsy!

Allie's frantic gaze ran around the room. What could she do? Though she knew it was so late no one would be out there to hear, she ran to the window and screamed, "Help, somebody help me!" Her cries fell into the silent yard. No one answered her scream.

"Don't do that," he growled.

Allie ignored his commanding tone and raised her voice so loud it hurt her throat. "Help! Please, someone help me!"

Then she heard the sweet sound of another voice. A shout answered her, feet shuffled through the dust toward her trailer. Help was on its way. She whirled and leaped back to the door. The knife was gone. This time the knob turned easily under her fingers, and the door flew open.

The hallway was empty.

Allie bounded from the bathroom and raced across the hall. "Please, oh please, God, let Betsy be all right." She rushed into the room and saw Betsy's tousled dark curls on the pillow. "Bets?" she whispered.

Betsy stirred and rubbed her eyes, then rolled over and went back to sleep.

Allie sagged against the doorframe. Her legs trembled, and she wanted to crawl into the bed herself, pull the covers over her head like she used to when she was afraid of the boogeyman.

But this was a real-life monster.

Someone pounded on the front door hard enough to make the whole trailer shake. She tottered down the hall and threw open the door.

Her best friend, Yolanda Fleming, stepped through the door. "Allie, what's wrong?"

Allie clutched her. "He was here, in my house!" Aware she wore only her shirt and underwear, she backed down the hall. "My sister. He said he killed Tammy!"

Horror began to dawn on Yolanda's face. But even as Yolanda hugged her, Allie knew none of her friends would be able to protect her and Betsy. There was only one thing she could do.

1

HIS BOSS DROVE WITH BOTH HANDS ON THE WHEEL, SLOW AND STEADY AS A tortoise. Some days Elijah DeAngelos's attention to detail drove Rick Bailey crazy, but today wasn't one of them. He had other things to worry about.

Interstate 10 stretched out east, straight and nearly empty of traffic. Sage and creosote had greened up with the winter rains. The old man turned the steering wheel in his gnarled hands, and the truck rolled down a narrow dirt path toward a broken-down barn a quarter of a mile back.

"Look there," Rick said. His hand gripped the door handle, wishing he could wring someone's neck. The call had come in two hours ago about these horses, but he'd hoped the caller was wrong about how bad their condition was. Everyone in the area knew to call Bluebird Ranch when a horse was in danger.

The two horses, one a pinto and the other a dun, stood on the other side of a gate that hung cockeyed on its post, their heads down. They could easily have gotten out, but they didn't have the strength. The ribs of both animals showed through their rough, dull coats. They barely mustered the will to turn to look at the vehicle.

They were so far gone, it would be a battle to save them.

Rick flung open his door and strode to the trailer they'd hauled here. Opening the back, he reached in for the bucket of high-protein dog food and sweet feed, a combination of oats, steamed cracked corn, and cottonseed pellets, all covered with molasses. The quick energy would be crucial to saving the mares. He carried the mixture to the animals. Elijah followed with a bucket of water.

Rick watched the feeble horses try to feed, and he fisted his hands. If he could find the man who had starved these horses, Rick would bloody his nose. He told himself to take a few deep breaths. Getting mad wouldn't help these animals.

He stepped to the dun and ran his hand over her patchy coat, wincing at the protruding bones. "I'm not sure we can save them," he admitted.

"I fear you might be right." Elijah held the bucket of water under the pinto's lips, but the mare refused to drink.

Rick heard the sound of an engine and turned to look. "The vet's here." He stepped to meet Grady O'Sullivan. "Thanks for coming all this way." The ranch was two hours from town, and Grady was the only vet he trusted to come this far.

The large man had red hair that stuck up like Woody Woodpecker's crest. About Rick's age, his big hands and feet matched his bulk. Dressed in jeans and a T-shirt, with feet thrust into sandals, he could have been at home on the Gulf beach.

He was also the pastor of the church Rick attended. He knew more about Rick than any man except Elijah.

Grady's gaze was on the horses, and he just nodded as he got out his bag. "They look bad, Rick."

"They are." Rick followed the vet to the two mares.

The dun's front legs buckled, and she went down. Rick knelt on one side, and the vet on the other. Grady ran his hands over her, checked her eyes and mouth, then prodded her stomach.

Rick knew the verdict before the man said anything. His gut clenched in a painful spasm, and he exhaled until it released. He'd hoped to reach her sooner.

Grady shook his head. "They're too far gone. I doubt they have the strength to make the trip. This one will die in the next couple of hours. She's just been starved too long."

"What about the pinto?" Elijah asked. The other mare had managed to get down some water and a handful of sweet feed and dog food. She stood swaying, her head down.

"Maybe, but it will take a miracle," the vet said.

"Those we have had before," Elijah said.

"Do what you can, Grady," Rick pleaded. "For both of them."

The vet heaved a sigh and opened his bag. "I'll start an IV of electrolytes and add in some B_{12}. Then all we can do is pray."

Rick had already started that, and he knew the other men had as well. He watched the vet insert the IV and get the fluid going. The minutes ticked by, and he swatted at the horseflies congregating around the desperately ill mares. Squatting by the dun, he rubbed her head and neck, but half an hour later, she blew a final puff of breath into his palm, then . . . nothing.

No, no! He couldn't lose her. He blew in her nostrils and massaged her stomach, but the great chest stayed motionless. His head dropped. Pain pulsed behind his eyes. "She's gone," he said.

Feeling older than his thirty-four years, he stood and went to check on the pinto. Elijah was at her side, coaxing her into eating another handful of the high-calorie feed. "She looks a little stronger," he said.

Elijah nodded. "This one, she will make it."

"Another hour and the prognosis would have been different," Grady said. "She's a nice mare. Small, but good lines. The kids at the ranch will love her."

Rick looked back at the dun. He'd failed that one. "Can we take her home now?"

"Give her another hour and some more feed, then see how strong she is. Wait until she's not wobbly. And leave the IV in until the second bag is empty." He closed his supply case. "Call me if you need me."

"Thanks, Grady. Tell Dolly I appreciate her sparing you on your day off."

"No problem." Grady carried his bag to the car, and Rick walked with him.

Over an hour later, Rick and Elijah decided the mare was strong enough to attempt the trip. The men got her loaded into the trailer, then climbed into the truck.

"We'll have to stop and feed her a few times," Rick said.

For now Rick could be glad Elijah was a slow and careful driver. The mare couldn't handle much jarring. "How can men be so cruel?" he asked softly once they were out on I-10 again. "We see so much of this neglect. People think they want a horse but don't stop to realize how much care one requires. When they're tired of it all, they just abandon their responsibilities."

Elijah gave him a quick glance. "Somehow I do not think you are speaking of the man who did this to the horses. It brings back memories of your mother, *sí?*"

The scars on Rick's back throbbed at the word *mother*. The woman didn't deserve the title. His thoughts raced to the woman who'd scarred him. It was her fault the county had taken his brother, Chad—Rick had never found him again. If he'd had a real dad, like Elijah, and a loving mom, what might he have done with his life?

Those kinds of doubts could drive him crazy. Rick was doing what he wanted, saving the horses he loved and helping kids turn out right.

THE SUN HAD ALREADY CONVERTED THE TRAILER INTO A SAUNA, THOUGH A slight breeze relieved the heat a tad. Allie swiped away the sheen of perspiration on her forehead with the back of her hand before tossing a handful of socks into the suitcase.

"But where are you going?" Yolanda blocked the doorway.

About Allie's age, Yolanda was a pretty African-American who could ride like Dale Evans and rope like Roy Rogers. Yo would go far in the rodeo. Ice curled around Allie's veins at the realization she wouldn't be around to see it.

She glanced up from packing and forced a smile. "It's better if you don't know," she told Yolanda. "You're safer that way."

Familiar sounds and smells wafted in through the window: shouts from the stock crew, steers bellowing, the jingle of horse tack, the good scent of horse and cattle. Allie would miss the rodeo. And El Paso. Even this little trailer had come to feel like home after so many years.

Yolanda flopped onto the bed, her black cornrows bouncing on her shoulders. "I'm scared for you, girl. You'll be alone, without anyone to help you with Betsy. Let me tag along for luck."

"You're going to win the barrel race this year, Yo. I can't take that away from you. We'll be fine." Allie's purse sat on the nightstand with only a hundred dollars in it, and she prayed it would be enough to get them to the Big Bend. Yolanda would give her anything she had, but Allie couldn't ask.

It was bad enough that she had to give up her dream of winning the barrel race this year herself. She wouldn't dream of torpedoing Yo's chances as well.

"Did you talk to the cops?" Yolanda asked.

"What good would it do? The police have done nothing to stop whoever this guy is." A lump crept up her throat, but she swallowed it down and focused on her packing.

"They're trying. The guy is slick."

Allie zipped her old green suitcase closed. "I have to disappear."

The worry in Yolanda's dark eyes intensified. "I know we've gone over this before, but, girl, you have to have *some* idea who could hate you so much."

"Hernandez is the only one with something against me, and he's dead."

"What if it's someone he met in the clink?"

Allie set her suitcase on the cracked linoleum floor. "Why would someone take on his vendetta? Whoever this guy is, he's *killed* three people, Yo. That takes a lot of hatred. And I'm not waiting around for him to get to Betsy."

After her parents died when her father's plane went down, the calls started. An eerie voice taunted her on the phone, telling her he had killed her parents and would take everything she loved. She'd been sunken in despair and grief, bowed down with more than she could bear until the guy started calling.

Strangely, his calls infused her with the determination to protect the rest of her family. The threats gave her purpose.

Only one person could help her now. She hadn't wanted to go to him—not with him working for the one man she wanted to avoid—but now he was her best chance.

"How do you think Betsy will handle the change?"

Allie glanced out the open curtains to the melee going on outside. Her daughter stood on the first rung of the fence, watching the cowboys practice throwing their ropes at the stationary stands. Dust billowed from the horse's hooves. "I hope the place where I'm taking her will make her well."

Yolanda's forehead wrinkled. "Some place that will make her talk? What kind of place would that be?"

Allie wagged her finger at her friend. "Don't try to find out any more."

"What if Betsy's grandparents show up? What should I tell them?"

"The truth. That you don't know where I am. If they can't find me, they can't serve me with custody papers." She picked up her suitcase and dragged it toward the door. "I packed too much," she panted.

"Let me help." Yolanda sprang toward her.

"Just get the door."

Yolanda opened the door, and Allie dragged the bulky luggage out onto the dirt. She opened the tailgate of her old pickup and heaved it into the back with the ragtag assortment of rope, bridles, empty Pepsi cans, and old blankets.

"What if the police have questions?" Yolanda followed Allie toward the paddock. "And all your friends from church will want to know you're okay. Girl, it scares me to think about you being off on your own with no support."

"I'll call and check in occasionally. I can't let that guy find me and Betsy." Allie stepped to where Betsy stood at the fence. She scooped up her daughter and inhaled the scents of red licorice and little girl.

Betsy was all she had left of Jon. Allie would give her every possible reason to talk again. "Ready to go, Bets?"

Betsy shook her head so hard her ponytails flipped against her cheeks. She set her chin, and her lips quivered. Even the threat of leaving everything she knew and loved didn't break the wall of silence that had encased her for a year.

Allie set her on the ground and took her hand. "We'll come back for a visit. Come along, honey." Betsy's feet scuffed along the dirt, but she followed her mother to the truck.

"Call me, girl." Yolanda grabbed Allie in a tight hug.

Allie clasped Yo back, closing her eyes and imprinting the musky scent her friend wore in her memory. It would be all she'd have to hold her until they met again.

She was going into hostile territory.

"I'll call when I get there." Allie's eyes burned, and she knew she had to get out of there. Tears would upset Betsy. She got in the truck and buckled her seat belt, just a lap belt, the thing was so old. "Fasten up, Bets."

As the truck pulled away from the stockyard, Allie forced herself not to look in the rearview mirror and watch her ten-year dream dissolve in the distance.

2

BLUEBONNETS. THOUSANDS OF THEM. THE CARPET OF BLUE UNDULATED over the hills, melding into the distant haze of the mountains. Those peaks had been growing ever since she left the Del Norte Mountains behind and pressed closer to the Rio Grande.

Allie rubbed her tired eyes. Even Eddy Arnold belting out "Gonna Find Me a Bluebird" failed to energize her. Six hours on the road with the dust blowing in through the open windows had left her eyes dry and gritty.

She glanced in the rearview mirror. No other vehicles meant no pursuit. They had time to enjoy this, make a memory. She lifted her foot from the accelerator. "Look, Betsy, let's get your picture taken in the bluebonnets!"

Dark curls tied up in red holders hid Betsy's face from view. She plucked at the frayed edges of a hole in her jeans and didn't answer.

Allie would *not* allow despair to take hold. She would root it out, trample it underfoot, burn it to ash. Her daughter would talk again, laugh again, find joy again.

She forced a bit of cheerfulness into her voice. "I'll stop here and get your picture."

Something clanked in the old Ford's underbelly when she parked it at the side of the road. "Come on, sweetie," she coaxed. She hung the camera around her neck and turned to her daughter. "I'll show you the picture of me in the bluebonnets. I think I was about five at the time too."

She remembered the day so clearly. Her mother's smile, her scent. Allie's hands gripped the wheel in a spasm of agony. Nearly a year after her parents' deaths, the pain still threatened to swamp her. She shook off the memory and got out of the truck.

The sweet aroma of the thousands of flowers wafted around her. The wildflowers tossed their blue heads in the breeze and lifted their faces to the fading sunlight. How could Betsy not be moved by this place?

These hills felt like a sanctuary, a place of healing for them both.

Allie went around to the passenger door. The latch was always a bit tricky on this side, but she managed to wrench it open. Betsy's wide eyes were as blue as the wildflowers carpeting the landscape. Allie could see Jon in those eyes.

She lived for the day when those blue depths didn't hold fear. "It's okay," she said. "There's no one here."

Betsy hiked one leg out the door and looked around before she stood and put her small hand in Allie's. Allie led her into the blue-bonnets and sat her down. The flowers almost looked like hyacinths, and the fragrance was divine, the sweetness intoxicating. The flowers stood tall on bright green stalks and came up to Betsy's chest, where they contrasted with her yellow shirt. Dusk was only a few minutes away, and the lighting was perfect.

"Just a minute." Allie turned on her digital camera, a gift from her parents, and snapped several shots of Betsy sitting stone-faced in the flowers. "Smile, Betsy," she called. But of course her daughter's lips stayed straight and sober.

Allie would give anything to hear the little girl giggle again.

"Let's go, sweetie."

Betsy jumped to her feet and ran to the truck. She slammed the door shut, then got out her coloring book and crayons.

Allie inhaled the fragrance one last time and slid under the steering wheel. She twisted the key. The engine did nothing but grind. "Come on, come on," she muttered. Releasing the key, she let the engine rest a minute, then tried again. The sound of the engine softened as the battery weakened.

If she had the money, she would have gotten a new battery before she left El Paso.

"Please, please." She leaned her head against the steering wheel. They couldn't be stuck out here. It would be dark in another hour, and the ranch had to be miles away.

Her gaze went to Betsy, who was lost in coloring the bluebirds in the Cinderella picture. Betsy would freak if they were stranded in the dark. Her night terrors were bad enough without actually being in danger.

Allie tried the engine again, but the grinding slowed until all she heard was the clicking of a dead battery. The empty highway stretched out to the horizon ahead and behind. Marfa was at least twenty miles behind her. There was no one she could call for help, even if she had a cell phone.

Leaning across the seat, she unlocked her daughter's door. "Let's go for a walk, Bets. I want to get a few more shots of you in those blue-bonnets, and there's a great patch just a little ways down the road."

Betsy shook her head and locked the door. Hating to be firm, Allie bit her lip and got out of the car. She went around to the passenger door and unlocked it with her key. "Come on, it will be fun."

Betsy's lip trembled, and tears filled her eyes, but she got out and took Allie's hand in a death grip.

Allie hit the lock on the door with her other hand, and they started toward the darkening mountains. "Just a little ways farther." She'd get Betsy to go about half a mile, then they'd take some pictures, then walk some more. Once the truck was out of sight, Betsy would quit looking behind.

"Your daddy was the strongest man who ever lived," Allie said. "One time the car fell off the jack when his friend was under it, and your daddy lifted it up with his bare hands so his friend could get out."

Betsy smiled, obviously drinking in the story. For a second she looked up at her mom instead of at the ground.

Their feet made a lonely sound on the pavement. "Look at the bluebirds, Bets." Allie pointed out a flock sitting along the electrical wires along the road.

Betsy rewarded Allie with an expression of interest as she craned her neck to watch the birds. She adored all things with feathers, and Allie took her bird-watching as often as possible. Maybe if she pointed out birds along the way, she'd be able to get Betsy to walk until dark without too much coaxing.

Allie watched the bright mountain bluebirds herself a moment.

She'd once thought she found her own bluebird of happiness, but it flew away, never to be found again. Now all she could do was put one foot in front of the other and keep going. Keep Jon's memory alive for Betsy and honor the amazing man he was.

The light was beginning to fade, and the birds would be finding spots to sleep soon. Then what?

Allie quickened their pace. They had to find help. The road rose to meet them, and the steep incline ahead didn't look pleasant. She tried not to worry about how many deserted highway miles lay ahead.

"Race you to the top!" She started to let go of Betsy's hand, but the little girl clutched it more tightly and slowed her steps. "Don't want to race?"

Betsy shook her head and made a drinking motion with her hand. Allie slapped her forehead with her palm. How could she have forgotten to bring water? She had a case of bottled water in the truck, and they'd walked off and left it. Casting her gaze back, she couldn't see the truck in the gloom that was whisking away the last of the light. They'd lose even more light if they went back.

She stood in the middle of the road and tried to figure out what was the best thing to do. A road sign was just ahead. She studied the words, figuring them out in her head. Big Bend 10. Bluebird Youth Ranch was supposed to be nine miles from the national park, so maybe the road to the place would be right up ahead. They were closer than she thought. That would be faster than going back.

"There will be water at the ranch," Allie said, tugging Betsy onward. "Let's hurry."

A rumble sounded behind them, and she turned to see lights shining out of the gloom. Her initial relief dimmed as she realized how isolated they were. Maybe they should hide in the bluebonnets.

The way Betsy clutched her hand told her the little girl was frightened too. "Let's hide in the wildflowers, Bets," she whispered. "The ranch isn't far." Praying the driver was too far away to see them, she dashed toward the flowers with Betsy in tow. They hit the dirt, and without warning, a line of bumblebees flew up from their ground nest.

Right toward them.

Allie shrieked and leaped to her feet, jerking Betsy with her. The little girl's mouth opened in horror as the bees descended, but she didn't scream. Allie felt a sharp pain on her cheek and another on her arm. The loud buzzing disoriented her, but she reached for Betsy. Four or five bees clung to her top. Allie swatted them off, too intent to even flinch at the stings in her fingers.

Maybe there were some under the fabric. Allie pulled the T-shirt over Betsy's head and found two more bees clinging to the underside. She shook them off, then grabbed her daughter's hand and ran. Another bee stung her in the back of the arm, and she swiped at it, knocking it to the ground. They reached the road and left the bees behind. Silent tears rolled down Betsy's face, and she held her arm.

Allie slipped the top back onto her daughter. "Oh Bets, I'm sorry. It was my fault. Do the stings hurt?" She pulled Betsy close. The little girl wrapped her skinny arms around Allie's neck and buried her face in her chest. Allie rubbed the soft skin of the little girl's arm. The stings were already swelling.

Allie thumbed Betsy's tears away. "Let me check for stingers. There might be some left in your skin."

"I saw what happened." A man's voice came from the truck idling five feet away. "The little girl okay?"

Allie had forgotten all about the approaching vehicle. She glanced around for a stick or some kind of weapon. There was nothing. Edging her daughter behind her, she backed up.

"That was a pretty stupid thing to do." His voice went flat. The truck door opened, and a man stepped out and moved into the headlights.

Allie's nails bit into her palms, and she struggled to hold back the words she wanted to say. With the lights blinding her, she got only a brief impression of his bulk and height. Betsy sounded like she was about to hyperventilate.

"Stop, don't come any closer!" Allie edged further away. "I've got a gun." She put her hand in the pocket of her jeans like there was really something there.

He squatted near Betsy. "Are you hurt, honey? Let's go get something on those stings." His voice was surprisingly gentle.

Betsy edged her wet face around Allie's waist, and her death grip loosened. Allie stared at her daughter. She didn't trust easily, but she pulled away from Allie and stepped toward the man. Anyone who coaxed a bit of trust from Betsy deserved a second look.

"She has several stings," Allie told him. Her own fingers throbbed with stingers, but she'd get them out on her own. Putting her fingers to her mouth, she pulled one out with her teeth.

"Let me see. Come in front of the headlights." He leaned into the truck and rummaged in the glove box. Carrying a first-aid kit, he moved to the front of the vehicle. "It won't hurt," he said to Betsy, who lowered her head and moved slowly. "Show me the stings."

Betsy held out her arm without looking at him. "Looks like the stingers are still there." He pulled out his wallet and extracted a credit card, which he swept over the marks. "Got them!" He opened the kit and pulled out a can.

"Is that deodorant?" Allie asked.

"Yep. Meat tenderizer is better, but aluminum chlorohydrate reduces the effect of bee venom too." He sprayed Betsy's arms and neck. "Better?"

Betsy nodded, still not looking at him.

He stood and nodded to the north. "Was that your old rattletrap down the road? You need some help?"

"I could use a jump," she said. She kept her voice cool. Rattletrap indeed. Maybe it was, but the comment held too much contempt for her liking.

"Hop in."

Her trust would only go so far. "We'll meet you down there. Who are you, anyway?"

His sigh was loud and exasperated. "Look, lady, I'm not an ax murderer. Just get in the truck, and I'll give you my résumé later."

Betsy shrank back at his harsh voice and buried her face in Allie's waist.

Instantly, the man squatted. "I'm sorry, honey. I'm not mad." Betsy peeked at him from between her fingers, and he smiled. He stood and put his hands in his pockets. "It's not safe to walk out here by yourself. I'll let you drive my truck back and I'll walk."

"How about you ride in the back and let me drive?" Allie didn't think he'd agree, but she didn't feel right about making him walk.

If only Jon were here.

"Okay." He tossed her the keys and strode to the pickup's rear, where he put one boot onto the wheel well and vaulted into the back.

The guy was a mountain. Allie didn't like big men. They made her feel even smaller than she already was—and more inept.

She stared at the keys in her hand and forced a smile. "Let's go get our truck, Bets." She opened the driver's-side door, and Betsy climbed in, then scooted across the seat. Allie slid inside after her daughter. Nice wheels. The vehicle wasn't new, but he'd taken good care of it. Its gray interior didn't hold a speck of dirt.

She started the truck, turned around, and drove back toward her pickup. The headlights picked out the silhouette. When she reached it, she angled the man's vehicle so the headlights shone on her hood.

The man jumped out and opened the hood of his truck, then fiddled with something inside. She watched him walk around to her truck and open the driver's door. She thought she'd locked it. No, only Betsy's door, she remembered.

She got out to help. Only one boot showed under her open driver's door. The battery clicked, then he exited the vehicle.

"Lady, you're out of gas," he said with a disgusted thrust to his lip. "Don't you have any sense at all? Dragging a kid out into the middle of nowhere without gas, putting her in a nest of bumblebees, and not even taking any water with you."

He had no idea what she'd been through. Stiffening her back, she stared at the man until he looked down.

"Sorry, it's none of my business," he said.

"No, it's not. We're on our way to Bluebird Youth Ranch. Is it close?"

His head came up at the mention of the ranch. "I work at the ranch. It's just a mile down the road. We weren't expecting any visitors."

"I know. I've come a long way to talk to someone there." Two men actually, but he didn't need to know the details. If she had the nerve, she'd ask him if he knew Rick Bailey, the foreman.

The surly man stalked to his pickup and flipped down the tailgate. Tight-lipped, he stalked back with a gas can in his hand. He drained it into the gas tank, then went back to his truck. Revving his engine, he called out the window, "Try it now."

Allie ran to the truck and slid under the wheel. "Please, please start," she muttered under her breath. She cranked the engine. It ground slowly, then picked up speed and turned over. It was running so rough that the truck shook, but at least it would go.

"Come on, Bets," she called. Betsy ran to get into the passenger seat.

The man's pickup pulled away, the tires spitting sand and dust. Allie dropped the transmission into drive and followed him. The blackness of night cloaked the land as she followed him into a wide dirt lane, hard and packed from the weight of vehicles. At a distance, the lights of the house and four outbuildings shone a welcome, and Allie felt the weight of fatigue press heavier.

So this was the Bluebird Ranch. Even the name had intrigued her when her mother talked about it. A longing for home and family rose, and she squelched it. She had to stay focused.

Surely they wouldn't turn her away tonight.

The man switched off his engine and walked back to her truck. "I'll take you to Elijah. He's probably in the barn. Cupcake is about to foal. Come with me."

Grabbing Betsy's hand, Allie leaped from the truck and followed the man's long steps toward a big white barn. It had a hipped roof, and white paddocks stretched as far as she could see in the moonlight. The last building was a hangar that held a small plane.

"Who's the pilot?" she asked, pointing to the plane.

"I am. The distances are so great out here, it makes sense to fly when we can."

A border collie, tail wagging, came to meet them. The animal rose on its hind legs without touching either of them. The joyous expression of the dog's excitement brought a smile to Betsy's face.

"Nice dog." Allie said, pausing to pet the collie. "Male or female?"

"Jem's a male. Don't spoil him. He's a herd dog."

"He's gorgeous." With a last pat, she and Betsy followed the man.

The good scent of horses and hay lifted her fatigue when they stepped into the barn. The man led them to the back, where they found a short, sinewy old guy tending to a laboring horse. The bay mare was down in the straw, and the man had her head on his lap. His brown skin was leathered with age and sun, but when the dark eyes under the cowboy hat met her own, she saw a depth of love and compassion that made her feet move toward him.

This was Elijah? She tried to hide her curiosity but was unable to look away. She hadn't known he existed until her mother died.

His stare seemed a bit intense for just having met, then his gaze settled on Betsy, and his face softened even more. "Hello, *niña*. Do you like horses? We're going to have a colt soon."

Betsy nodded, her gaze locked with the old man's. Allie's hope surged. Betsy's face held more interest than she'd seen in a year. The little girl stepped forward with her hand out, then pulled it back.

"You can pet her." Elijah's voice was gentle.

Betsy knelt and touched the mare's nose. The horse blew her breath into Betsy's hand, and she scrambled back. A huge yawn erupted from her mouth.

Mr. DeAngelos nodded to the corner. "It will be a long night. There are blankets for the *niña*. You both look tired."

"Want to lay in the hay, Bets?" Allie wouldn't have minded curling up in that soft mound herself.

Betsy nodded. Allie led Betsy to the hay in the corner and sat her down with a blanket over her lap. Dust motes danced into the air when the little girl rustled in the mound. Betsy kept her gaze fastened on the horse, but her lids drooped, and Allie knew it wouldn't be long before she would be asleep. Then she could make their case to the old man.

And then she would find Rick Bailey.

Elijah glanced up at the other man. "Rick, would you get us some hot coffee? The stuff in the kitchen has been sitting there since morning, so brew some fresh."

Rick. Allie sank into the straw next to Betsy. How could Jon have told her to come to this tight-lipped man for help? The only assistance he'd give would be to escort her right out of here.

3

Rick muttered under his breath as he strode across the yard to the ranch house. Jem did his little air dance at Rick's side, then stopped at the front door when he went inside. Women like that one gave the word *mother* a bad rap. Some just weren't born with a maternal instinct.

She had only been thinking of herself.

And what was wrong with the kid? Betsy hadn't said a word. Something weird going on there, and it was likely the mom's fault. Everyone that pretty had entitlement problems anyway. She wasn't much bigger than a kid herself, and she'd probably used her tiny stature and big blue eyes to her advantage.

He was going to advise Elijah to get rid of her as soon as he could.

He stepped into the kitchen and threw together some sandwiches while the coffee brewed. He put them in a knapsack along with some apples and bottles of water. The most he would do is feed them. After pouring coffee into a thermos, he started back to the barn.

To give Elijah and the woman more time to talk, he stopped at the smaller barn to check on the horse they'd hauled back this morning. Scooping up the sweet feed mixture, he offered the mare another handful. The dull eyes looked at him, then her teeth nibbled at his palm. She was far from out of the woods.

The wind changed and brought the odor of manure to his nose. He winced as memories of another stench washed over him.

He was back in Fallujah, moving past puddles of raw sewage running in the streets. Joking with his buddy Jon and tossing pennies at the children who ran shouting and laughing beside them.

At one time, he'd thought to save the world. Right now, saving this horse would make him happy.

ELIJAH RUBBED THE MARE'S BELLY. "MY FOREMAN IS NOT AS GRUFF AS he seems."

Allie didn't believe the old man, though she wished she could. Allie glanced at Betsy. She was asleep. Now was the time.

She wet her lips. "I've come a long way to talk to you, Mr. DeAngelos."

He held up his hand. "Please, call me Elijah." He nodded to Betsy. "The *niña* has been hurt."

Allie nodded. "My name is Allie Siders, and this is my daughter, Betsy." The old man made a sudden movement, and she stopped. "Is anything wrong?"

"No, no, continue."

Was it her imagination or had he paled? She hoped he didn't have some kind of heart condition. When he didn't move, she went on. "She hasn't talked for a year. I've taken her to therapist after therapist, and there's been no change. I've tried everything I know to help her. You're my last hope." Especially now that she knew she'd rather die than ask Rick Bailey for anything.

"How did you hear about us?"

She hesitated. How could she explain without telling all? "One of your hired hands came to a rodeo I worked in El Paso. He told me about this place. I had to try it." She decided to see if she could get a reaction out of him. "I found a scrapbook about this place in my mama's things."

"Your mother? She stayed here?"

Allie nodded. "Her stage name was Anna Morgan." Something seemed to shift in the room when she said the name, but everyone reacted that way.

"The barrel racer?"

"Yes."

"She is dead now, killed in a plane crash."

Allie took a deep breath. It had been the worst day of her life. "A year ago."

Her mother had been as beautiful and flamboyant as a flamenco dancer. Her half-Hispanic blood was further diluted in Allie, who had her father's blue eyes and calm temperament. Her mother brought passion and excitement to everything she did, and Allie's life seemed to be lived in dull black and white since her mama's death.

She studied his impassive face. Did he know his Selena had changed her name and become famous? Until Allie found the scrapbook and began the research, she thought her grandparents were dead. She found no evidence the old man knew he was her grandfather.

"You are hurting too, *mujercita*. What happened to you and the *niña?*"

He'd called her "little woman," and she drew herself up to her full five foot two. "It's Betsy I'm worried about. She's been like this for a year, and I've tried everything. I don't have any money to pay you, but I'll work. I know horses. I've grown up in the rodeo. I can cook, clean, anything you need." She rushed on, certain he would refuse when he found out she had nothing.

He didn't have to know she'd sold everything—her horse, her new car. She had some pride left.

"I was once a bronco buster," Elijah said. Then his gaze shifted as the horse groaned, and the hay darkened with fluid. "Ah, our foal is coming. Sleep. There will be time to talk tomorrow."

Allie squatted beside him. "I can help you."

"Cupcake is an experienced mother. She'll do it all herself."

"I'll wait with you then." If she could show how much she knew about horses, maybe he'd find her a job. It was no secret Rick Bailey wouldn't be in favor of that. But Betsy needed Allie to do this. Though Elijah couldn't help the other things that threatened them, if he could heal Betsy, it would be enough.

Elijah lifted the mare's head enough to ease away. He stood back and watched the horse labor.

Rick came back in carrying a coffee thermos and Styrofoam cups. A knapsack was slung around his shoulder. He set the cups on a bale of hay and poured out a cup of coffee. Digging in his jeans, his hand came up with small containers of creamer. He still hadn't said a word.

"Thanks." Allie accepted two creamers and dumped them into her coffee. The aroma made her mouth water. Then the hot liquid filled her empty stomach. She'd been hoarding the last of her money to make sure Betsy had enough food and hadn't eaten herself since breakfast, part of an omelet in a greasy spoon at nine this morning. Even then, she hadn't eaten until Betsy was full.

Rick slipped the knapsack off his shoulder and unzipped it. "Turkey sandwiches," he said, handing her the sandwich wrapped in plastic. "There's fruit in here too." He handed her an apple.

Maybe he had some compassion to spare for adults after all. Allie smiled at him, but he still hadn't looked her in the eye.

"Let me see if Betsy wants some first."

"There's plenty for you both," Rick said. "And more where that came from. Let her sleep."

He was right, but Allie felt wrong to eat when her daughter might be hungry. A peek in the knapsack reassured her. There were two more sandwiches in it, and four apples. She took a cautious bite. Relishing the hot sting of horseradish on her tongue, she devoured the sandwich.

Food had never tasted so good.

She swallowed the last sweet bite of apple and looked up to find both men watching her. "Thanks," she said, clamping her lips against the explanation that pressed against her teeth.

Without a word, Rick held out another apple. She took it and squirreled it away in her backpack. Betsy might need it later. She did the same with the rest of the food. If Rick and Elijah turned down her plea for help, she and Betsy would be in desperate straits.

She settled on the hay to wait for the foal's arrival. With a full tummy, her lids drooped and her breathing eased. Maybe she'd close her eyes for just a minute.

4

"GOOD LINES," RICK SAID, EXAMINING THE WET ARRIVAL. CUPCAKE nudged the colt. The small, black foal stood on wobbly legs. He moved a few feet along her flank and nosed her belly before beginning to nurse.

Elijah grabbed a pitchfork and began to clean the wet, soiled straw out of the stall. Where did the old man get his energy? "I'll do that," Rick said. "Why don't you go on into bed? It's after two."

"Many hands make light work," Elijah said.

Rick shoveled with him. When they were done, he hung the pitchforks on a nail. "What about those two?" he asked, nodding toward the sleeping woman and girl.

The girl looked like a miniature of her mother. Fine, dark hair, blue eyes, dimples that flashed. At least the mother's dimples had flashed. Betsy hadn't smiled yet.

"You don't like Allie," Elijah observed.

"It's hard to like stupidity," Rick said. "She doesn't have an ounce of sense." He told Elijah how he'd found them fighting off bees in the bluebonnets. "And she didn't even have any water for the kid. I'll bet she did something to make the girl quit talking. Now she wants you to fix it."

"A snap judgment, Rick? You should get to know them before you point fingers."

A slow anger burned his belly. "You're going to let them stay? It's because she resembles Maria, isn't it?"

"I realize she is not my daughter, Rick. I would not be taken in so easily. And wasn't it you who just told me you weren't going to do the cooking anymore?" Elijah was smiling. "You have lost weight since Rosa left us. A woman's cooking might fatten us both up."

"For the slaughter," Rick said. "She'll steal you blind in the night."

The woman raised his hackles for some reason. For one thing, she was too pretty. He'd never seen eyes such an electric blue. In his experience, beautiful women expected pretty things handed to them. She just showed up here and expected Elijah to take her in. That whole wolfing down of the sandwich was probably an act to get Elijah's sympathy.

And it worked. Rick could see the softness in the old man's eyes. Elijah was a sucker for a sob story.

"Someone once told me the same thing about you," Elijah observed. "Trust my judgment, *hijo*."

Rick gave a grudging nod. "You made up your mind to help her when she ate her food like a starving street person."

"No, it was when she put the food away for the *niña*. You can't tell me that you were untouched by that, Rick."

He didn't want to be moved by her love for the child, but the gesture had affected him. "Yeah, I saw it too. It's the only reason I haven't thrown her out on her ear. The kid needs help."

"And so do we." Elijah went toward the door. "Let them sleep. If we wake them to move to a bed, the *niña* may have trouble getting back to sleep."

Rick followed his boss out of the barn to the ranch house. Stepping into the living room, he looked around, seeing it with fresh eyes. He couldn't remember the last time one of them had mopped the scarred wooden floors or dusted the battered furniture. Last autumn maybe?

A stale odor hung in the air as though the windows hadn't been opened in months. And maybe they hadn't. He should clean it up a little before Allie took over. But not tonight. Fatigue weighed down his legs. He'd do it in the morning.

ALLIE STOOD WATCHING THE SUN COME UP OVER THE MOUNTAINS. THE morning air made her shiver, but she couldn't go inside yet. Not while the sunrise gilded the peaks and valleys, and the air smelled like sage and creosote. Her hair still uncombed, Betsy stood beside her with their hands locked.

"You like it here, Bets?" Allie asked.

Betsy nodded and pointed. A flock of bluebirds blanketed the grass and pecked for insects.

Allie drank in the sight. If only finding the real bluebird of happiness was as easy as following a flock of birds. "I've never seen so many in one place. I wonder if this is a migration spot for them. We should ask Mr. DeAngelos."

Betsy nodded, her gaze still on the birds.

The old man had to let them stay. The bluebirds told Allie she and Betsy were in the right place. Betsy would talk again, and no one would find them here. She'd been careful to cover her tracks, and the faceless man wouldn't know where she'd gone. They would be safe here.

"I don't think they're up yet. If the door isn't locked, we'll go in and fix breakfast." Allie glanced at her watch. It was nearly seven, so the lack of lights in the house surprised her, but the men might have been up most of the night with the mare.

The thin, sandy soil felt cool under her bare feet, and she avoided the cactus in the path as she stepped toward the house.

A male voice spoke. "You made it."

Allie turned to see a fresh-faced young man. He looked like a fourteen-year-old trying to act twenty-four. A big rodeo belt buckle on his waist glinted. With his thumbs hooked in the pockets of his jeans and his cowboy hat pushed back, he stood with one worn boot on the fence rail as if posing for a documentary about cowboys.

Poor kid. If he only knew trying to make an impression on her would get him nowhere. He'd tried it at the rodeo last month, and though she hadn't caught his name, he was the one who told her about this place.

"We never introduced ourselves when we met at the rodeo." She extended a hand. "I'm Allie Siders, and this is Betsy. We came in last night."

"Like I'd forget a honey like you. I'm Charlie." He put his propped foot back on the ground, shook Allie's hand in a strong grip, then knelt in front of Betsy. "Hey kid, want to see some horses?"

Betsy buried her face in Allie's waist and didn't look at him.

"She's tired," Allie said. "Maybe later."

The young man straightened. "I made a run to Marathon after oats yesterday," he said. "When I saw that old truck parked beside the barn this morning, I wondered who had blown in while I wasn't looking."

"I don't think anyone in the house is up yet."

He nodded. "Cupcake foaled. I think the boss was up most of the night. Otherwise, there'd be breakfast on the table. I could rustle us up some grub."

"Let me do it." Allie took Betsy's hand and moved toward the house again. "I was about to try the door when you called to me."

The house looked like it had grown out of the red soil, but as she neared, she saw red dirt coated the stone face of the home. The big pillars that supported the massive porch of the two-story dwelling sported a fresh white coat of paint. The place was bigger than she'd thought at first, easily three thousand square feet.

She followed Charlie up the stone steps and across the porch to the entry.

"It's always unlocked." Charlie twisted the doorknob and pushed open the door. "Go on in."

She stepped onto an oak floor, its patina of old age as fitting as the well-worn boots on her feet. Stucco walls painted a soft green invited her in, but they were bare of any ornamentation that would have enhanced the effect of the color. Heaped under the window was a jumble of discarded socks, boots, and shoes. They gave off a pungent odor, and Betsy wrinkled her nose.

Allie took Betsy's hand and moved down the hall to the door at the end. "Is this the way to the kitchen?"

"Yep. Don't mind the mess. The housekeeper left last fall."

Mess was an understatement. As Allie moved past the living room, she caught a glimpse of a large den littered with newspapers and piles of books. Some kind of video game controller lay on a recliner, its wires stretching to the TV.

She averted her eyes and stepped through the swinging door into the kitchen. And stopped short. Had no one cleaned the kitchen since the housekeeper left?

The sink overflowed with pots and dishes. Several cupboards hung open to reveal empty shelves. Every dish in the place must be dirty.

Charlie seemed oblivious to the chaos. He went to the refrigerator and opened it. "I know we've got eggs and bacon. There's bread for toast. I think there might be hash browns in the freezer."

"I'll figure it out. First I'd better do some dishes." Allie rolled up the sleeves of her blouse and went to the sink. "I can't cook in this . . . dirt." She eyed the stove, thick with grime.

Charlie's smile was weak. "Yeah, it's bad."

"Want to dry the dishes?"

"Uh, I'll go feed the stock." He backed out of the kitchen.

THE SETTING OF THE SUN ONLY SLIGHTLY COOLED THE BRUTALITY OF THE Fallujah heat. Rick tossed his cards onto the battered wooden table. "You win," he told his best friend.

"I always win." His buddy grinned at him and began to gather up the cards. "I'm done. I need to write to my wife."

"You write to her every night." Rick's tone was sharp, but in his heart he wished he had someone to write to every night. Someone who cared if he lived or died.

His friend's smile faded. "I worry about her. What if I don't come back?"

Rick shuffled on his chair. "Don't talk like that. We're both going to get on that plane next month and fly home."

"Tomorrow's mission is dangerous, buddy. Promise you'll look out for my family—if the worst happens."

"You'll take care of them yourself." Rick stood and pushed his chair under the table. "I don't want to hear this."

"I know what will happen if I don't come home. My parents will try to get my daughter. And that can't happen. Not ever. Promise me you'll make sure."

"If I promise, will you drop it?"

"Promise me," Jon said again. "I know you're a man of your word."

"Okay, okay, I promise. Now shut up about it!"

His friend's shape began to morph. Red spots bloomed on his chest, his face grew pale and stricken. Rick saw breastbone protruding through the skin before he awakened with a start to hear an echo still lingering in his room.

I promise.

He sat up and wiped the sweat from his forehead. His heart was thumping in his chest like he'd just had a fright. He drew a few deep breaths until he got control of his racing pulse. It was over, he reminded himself.

Maybe these nightmares were going to continue until he checked on his buddy's family. This was the second dream in a week, and he always woke drenched with dread. Shaking off the effects of the dream, he climbed out of bed and pulled his clothes on.

Rick's nose twitched when he opened his bedroom door. Was that bacon? The tantalizing scent pulled him from the room and down the steps. His stomach growled, and he spared a glance at his watch. Holy cow, was it really that late? Though he'd only had about four hours sleep.

He heard banging in the kitchen. Charlie was sure loud this morning, but bless him for making breakfast. Rick stopped in the doorway and saw the tiny woman at the sink. The kitchen sparkled, even the tile underfoot. Every dish and pot was in place. Bacon sizzled in a skillet, and the eggs and hash browns looked crisp and tasty.

Allie whirled to face him. Her welcoming smile faded. Rick felt his own smile falter.

"Where's Charlie? I thought he was fixing breakfast."

"He's feeding the livestock. You're up late," she said.

He squinted at the clock on the wall. "I think it was four when we got to bed."

"Is Elijah up?"

"No, he's still out." He frowned. "You think you can win him over by cleaning the kitchen?"

Allie opened her mouth, then closed it again. That would put her in her place. Did she think she was Martha Stewart, coming in here and taking over?

She turned back to the stove. "Breakfast is ready." She ladled up a plate of food and handed it to him.

His stomach, traitor that it was, rumbled loudly in the kitchen. He took the plate without a word and sat down beside Betsy, who was finishing up her own serving of eggs and toast.

The little girl gave him a shy glance, and he tried to coax a smile from her. "Hey Betsy, have you seen the new baby?"

Betsy nodded, but the smile he wanted didn't break out. He glanced at her mom. What had she done to this kid?

"We saw him," Allie said.

Rick frowned. "You always answer for her?"

"She doesn't talk."

"She won't ever talk if you don't let her."

"I'm her mother. I think I know how to behave around her better than you do." Allie turned her back to him and turned off the burners.

Touchy. She made him tense just by being in the same room. That was the trouble with women—they came in and upset everything. He'd woken up in a good mood, and now he could tear the head off of a bear with his hands.

Betsy tugged on his hand and pointed to the door. "You want to go watch cartoons?" Rick asked. The little girl nodded. "Okay, but don't turn the TV up very loud. Let's let Elijah sleep."

The wooden chair legs scraped across the tile, and Allie settled into the chair. She wet her lips, and her eyes looked uncertain. "I thought I'd better formally introduce myself," she said. "I'm Allie Siders."

She paused as though she expected the name to mean something to him. That's when it hit, and when it did, his pulse leaped like spurred horse.

Siders. Jon's wife was named Allie. It couldn't be. The egg in his mouth formed an immovable lump.

"I'm Jon's widow," she said quietly.

Rick choked, then managed to swallow the bite of eggs. "Jon's widow?" His gaze locked with hers. Jon Siders. Even hearing the name made the grief and guilt well up like a spring. The promise he'd never kept had come here searching him out.

His promise to Jon rose up to mock him. He'd tried halfheartedly to find Jon's widow but couldn't. The Bluebird Ranch became his refuge, the safe haven where he could lick his wounds. His selfishness shamed him. Jon had sacrificed everything for him, and Rick was all too quick to abandon his promises.

Her eyes never left his face. "I know I should have called or written first, but there wasn't time." She finally looked away and cast her gaze to her plate.

The words he wanted to say locked behind the muscles of his throat. He wanted to ask her to forgive him, he wanted to ask her what she wanted, he wanted to tell her everything would be all right.

He choked back the confession of guilt and forced himself to cast a cool gaze on her face. "Why are you here?"

"Jon told me to come to you if I was ever in trouble." She said the words with an edge of reluctance.

"Are you in trouble now?" So he wasn't ready to honor that promise, even now. The responsibility loomed like a mountain.

"I'm in big trouble." She shut her mouth, then finally lifted her gaze. "I didn't even want to say anything. You've made it clear what you think of me. But I don't know where else to turn. Even if Elijah gives me a job, there's another . . . issue."

The silence echoed in the room. The words he needed to say stayed lodged behind his teeth. He had to wonder what kind of trouble would bring her clear out here to what the Mexicans called *El Despoblado,* the land of no people.

Guilt seized him in its sharp teeth. Whatever it was, he had to help. He'd promised Jon.

"Aren't you going to say something?" she whispered, finally raising her gaze to meet his.

The color had leached from her face, and her blue eyes looked murky with an emotion he couldn't name for sure. Maybe fear and grief. His own grieving had thinned until all that was left was a wisp of fog that dissipated every day.

Her revelation brought it storming back.

He wet his lips. "Jon was my best friend."

Allie smiled then. "I know. His letters from Iraq were filled with stuff about you. He loved you like a brother. I——I always wanted to thank you for trying to save him. I heard you were wounded trying to get him out."

Her blue eyes warmed then, and the gratitude in them was hard to take. He knew the truth.

"I failed him," Rick said, his voice harsh. Confession would be hard. She would hate him when she found out what really happened.

"You tried. That's all anyone could do."

"No." He pushed back from the table. "I wanted to contact you when I got back, but I couldn't find you." The silence seemed to grow louder before he finally broke it by clearing his throat and saying, "What's the trouble?"

"It would be a shorter list to tell you what's going right." She blinked rapidly. "It's been hard since Jon died, but we were doing okay. I was making the rodeo circuit in barrel racing—and doing great. I worked at the rodeo as well. Then my parents died in a plane crash, and a month ago my sister was killed. There's no one left to turn to."

Rick wasn't good at platitudes. First Jon's death, then the rest of her family. Pity stirred in his heart. "You need money?"

"No! I'm able-bodied, and I'll support us. I don't want a handout." She looked down at her hands, clasped in her lap. "Jon's parents are trying to get custody of Betsy. My world would end if I lost her." Her gaze came up to stare at him with a pleading expression. "One of your hands told me about this place, that it could help Betsy. I'd been coming here to see you anyway."

Just as Jon thought. He'd been adamant they shouldn't have a hand in raising his daughter.

"They've got grounds?" Though he framed it as a question, his tone suggested he'd have no trouble siding with someone who thought her unfit. It was hard to let go of his initial judgment of her. Elijah was right—Rick shouldn't have assumed so much.

Lifting her chin, she stared him down. "None. But they say the rodeo isn't a fit place to raise a child, especially for a single mom. They want her to have a stable home with two parents." The fire in her eyes dimmed, and her shoulders sagged. "I want that for Betsy too, but I have to make a living, and the rodeo is all I know."

He ran through all she'd said in his mind. "Do they know you've come here?"

She shook her head. "I didn't tell anyone where I was going—not even my best friend."

He forced out a question he didn't want her to answer. "What is it you want me to do?"

She spread out her hands. "I didn't know where else to turn. I thought I could hide out here, and just maybe Elijah could help Betsy the way he's helped other kids. I can't lose Betsy. I've lost everything else, but I can't lose her. But they might find me here too. I thought maybe with your contacts, you could make sure they can't get custody. I can't let them have her."

"That's true," he agreed. "Jon wouldn't want that."

She had put more faith in his ability than he possessed. He didn't have the kind of contacts that could save her from a custody suit. He stood and went to look out the window. An idea presented itself, a crazy idea. Not even Jon would expect him to go so far to help his wife and kid. His gaze lit on her old rattletrap truck. Both front tires were flat this morning.

He owed Jon his life.

No, he couldn't do it. There had to be another way. His thoughts raced, looking for a way out. A good lawyer could help. He had some cash saved. Turning, he looked at her and saw what a judge would see. A young woman with no steady means of support, dragging a kid all around the country. Put that up against two stable parents with plenty of money and a nice home, and Allie would lose.

He'd promised.

It wouldn't be forever. If he clung to that, maybe he could do it. What right did he have not to? Jon had counted on him. And, really, what would this cost him? Nothing in money. Only some time and a little inconvenience.

He went back to the table. "I made him a promise I've been too chicken to keep."

"A promise?"

"To take care of you and Betsy. I only know of one way to ensure Betsy isn't taken away from you." He hitched his thumbs into the pockets of his jeans. "If you're married and your husband adopts Betsy, his parents won't be able to touch her."

The soft pink drained from her cheeks, and her blue eyes grew enormous. "Marriage? To who?" she whispered. "Are you crazy?"

"To me. You'll have a stable home, insurance for her care, a father to replace the one she lost." He finally found the courage to look her in the eye. "I'll probably be a lousy husband, but I think I could be a good dad. A stepfather would have no trouble adopting Betsy."

She swung her head from side to side. "I can't marry you. I don't know you. Neither does Betsy."

"Think of it as a temporary thing. Once the adoption is final, we can wait a few months, then get a divorce."

"Marriage should be more than a convenient arrangement."

"Do you have a better idea?" He waited until she looked away. "I didn't think so."

She held up her hand. "Just be quiet a minute. Let me think. There has to be some other way."

He pressed his lips together and prayed she'd think of something. But he knew she wouldn't. Sometimes only the hard way worked.

ALLIE COULDN'T THINK, COULDN'T GET HER MIND AROUND RICK'S outlandish proposal. The silence had gone on between them long enough that she managed to force down her breakfast, but it was as dry as the sand outside.

She couldn't marry him. Maybe she should just run back to El Paso and take her chances. He was the exact opposite of the type of man who attracted her. The Neanderthal type was too overpowering for her taste. She liked long, slim limbs and someone who didn't tower over her like a ponderosa pine.

Even more importantly, she couldn't run the risk of anyone taking Jon's place with Betsy. The little girl was already warming up to the big man. How well did she remember her daddy? The thought of her forgetting Jon broke Allie's heart. Jon deserved whatever it took to keep his memory alive in his daughter's heart.

Elijah stepped into the room.

"Breakfast, *mujercita?*" Elijah's dark eyes drooped with fatigue, but his step was spry.

Allie pinned a smile in place. At least she and Rick didn't have to discuss it now. "Good morning, Elijah. I hope you're hungry."

"I could eat Roscoe, the big bull in the back pasture," Elijah said. He took the plate of food. His gaze swept the kitchen. "You worked hard this morning," he said. "Thank you for taking care of us bachelors. I think we would win a title for biggest slobs, *sí?*"

"My bedroom is neat," Rick said. "Too much military in me for me not to make my bed."

Allie avoided looking at Rick. "Is there anything else I can do for you today, Elijah? I thought I might clean the house if that's all right."

"I'm in need of a housekeeper since my Rosa retired," Elijah said. "Would you want the position?"

"Of course!" There. She didn't have to marry Rick. There were surely other options.

"The housekeeper takes care of the accounts too. Are you trained in this area as well perhaps?"

"I—I—no. But if you showed me, maybe I could do it." She'd always had trouble with numbers. Her eyes jumbled them up as badly as letters. But she had to try for Betsy's sake. She *would* master it. If all went well, she could save enough to replace her lost glasses.

He nodded. "Rosa lives on the other side of the ranch. You might speak with her about the duties. I must warn you, the pay is not so much. You will get room and board for you and the *niña,* and a little besides for incidentals."

"I don't care about money," Allie said. "I just want Betsy to get better."

Elijah's dark eyes touched Betsy's head. "I want this too, *mujercita.*" He glanced at Rick. "Would you object to giving us references, Allie?"

She bit her lip. If she gave references, her stalker might find out where she was. "I have good references, bu-but it would be better to keep my whereabouts quiet. Can you ask questions without identifying where the ranch is located?"

"I'll be careful with the questions," Rick said.

She would have no trouble getting a recommendation from the

rodeo. She was careful to keep her gaze averted from Rick's. "Where will Betsy and I stay? In the bunkhouse?"

"No, you may take the small suite at the top of the stairs. There are two beds in it, and it has its own bathroom. I'm afraid we have no chaperone, but with the *niña* in the same room and an old man like me in the house, no tongues should wag in town."

Gossip was the least of Allie's worries. "Could you explain to me how the ranch operates? What you do here?"

Elijah cocked a gray eyebrow. "Rick, if you would be so kind?"

Rick shrugged. "Bluebird Youth Ranch encompasses nine hundred and fifty-three acres. Elijah started with rescuing abused and neglected horses."

Allie shuddered. "I've seen some of that in the rodeo. Breaks your heart."

Rick's gaze softened. "It happens more than anyone realizes. Owners turn the horses out to pasture and abandon them. A drought comes along, and the horses starve. They suffer mostly from neglect, not mean-spiritedness. But the end result is the same."

"Do you see abused horses too?"

"Yeah. I wish we didn't, but it happens. An owner gets mad when the horse doesn't turn out to be a Flicka. Or an abuser takes his rage out on his animal rather than his wife or kids."

"Go on with the story of the ranch. Sorry I interrupted," Allie said.

"It's important to know the background. Elijah took in some foster kids back in the sixties. Some of them had been abused by their parents, and he found that the horses and children bonded in some amazing ways. They helped one another heal from past traumas. Bluebird was born out of his passion to help kids and horses."

Allie glanced at the old man. She didn't get him, not at all. How could he have such passion for this work, yet turn his own child out onto the streets? Unless her mother had lied to her.

"Who runs the ranch?"

"I'm the foreman, but I talk everything over with Elijah. We've got three hands who live in the bunkhouse. They care for the horses and cattle that roam the ranch." He nodded at Elijah. "The boss has a group counseling session with the kids every day. I take care of the inter-action between the kids and horses."

"What training do you have for that?" She didn't mean to challenge him, but it sounded like some pretty troubled kids came through here.

He didn't look at her. "I was one of those kids once. I've got a degree in social welfare."

"And I have a degree in psychology," Elijah put in. "The children are safe here."

Allie couldn't figure Rick out. She moved toward the doorway. "Thanks for the information. If you don't mind, I'll clean the house before we move our things in."

Elijah chuckled. "Mind? Rick and I will help. Right, Rick?"

Allie finally dared to look at Jon's best friend. They were going to have to talk about his proposal, but not yet.

"I'll clean the bathroom," he said.

Allie wanted to laugh, but she bit it back. The idea of the big guy on his knees, cleaning the porcelain throne, was ludicrous. But she might actually pay good money—if she had it—to see a sight like that.

5

THE BLOATED MOON SHONE IN THE WINDOW AND MADE MONSTERS OUT OF the dresser and nightstand in Allie's room. She closed her eyes against the images. There were enough monsters in her life. With all she had to do today, she'd managed to avoid considering Rick's proposal—but now that darkness had fallen, it was all she could think about.

What if he had a temper or was some kind of pervert? The possibilities of danger were enormous. He could be a serial killer for all she knew. She thumped the pillow like it was the obnoxious man's head. Okay, maybe not a serial killer. Everyone said serial killers seemed *nice,* and Rick Bailey would never answer to that description. Rude and opinionated, but not nice.

What on earth had Jon seen in Rick to recommend him so highly?

All she saw was a muscle-bound jerk who looked at her like she was a cow patty under his boots.

Still, it took guts to make an offer like that.

His solution hung out there, tantalizing and repelling at the same time. It would work, there was no doubt in her mind. Betsy would be safe from any custody suit. But what a price to pay. Allie didn't know if she had it in her to make that kind of sacrifice, even for Betsy.

There had to be another way.

She rolled onto her side and stared at the hump in the bed next to hers. Her daughter enjoyed the sleep of the innocent. Betsy's deep, easy breathing should have eased the tension humming along Allie's veins, but something was off. She strained to hear the sounds outside: the crunch of horse hooves in the paddock outside, the shuffle of cattle in the pasture, the wind chimes tinkling in the night breeze.

He couldn't have found her already. The sense of something lurking outside was her imagination. Rick's preposterous suggestion had put her out of kilter.

Though all the sounds were normal, she swung her feet out of bed and moved to the window. The breeze lifted the gauzy curtains and brushed them against her cheek with a touch as light as spiderwebs. She shivered and pushed the fabric away, but the wind blew it right back against her. Moving them out of her way, she stepped to the screen and looked down on the bucolic scene, illuminated by the moon and the security lights.

The remuda of horses stood in a corral west of the barn. Huddled together against the chill that had swept down off the mountain with the setting of the sun, they dozed on their feet. A few head of cattle lay nestled on the other side of the fence. The two trucks sat silent and empty on the far side of the barn.

Nothing stirred but the wind.

Then why did the hair on the back of Allie's neck stand out? Why did she feel if she breathed someone would hear? Something had awakened her, but nothing in the barnyard below gave any cause for concern.

Then she heard a sound that stole the oxygen from her lungs. The bloodcurdling scream pierced her eardrums.

Someone was in trouble.

In her bare feet, she leaped for the door and threw it open. The tile chilled her toes. Her feet pounded down the steps, then she was at the front door. She threw it open and stepped out onto the porch. The scream came again, and she shuddered. The poor woman was in deadly peril. Did no one else hear? Why wasn't Rick out here too? Or Elijah?

"Rick, Elijah, help!" she yelled up the steps.

Maybe they were exhausted from lack of sleep tonight. She needed a gun. Whirling, she dashed back inside and grabbed the key from the top of the gun cabinet. Twisting it in the lock, she threw open the cabinet and lifted out a shotgun. The shells were on the top shelf. She grabbed a handful, jammed two into the gun, then relocked the cabinet.

The moon illuminated the outdoor scene. The horses moved restlessly in their paddock. Their skittishness spooked her even more. The scream didn't come again, but Allie had localized it just past the big rock at the edge of the piñon grove. She stepped off the porch. Her toe slammed against a rock, and she winced.

Jem, the ranch border collie, whined and touched his nose to her hand. The warm contact strengthened her. "Come with me, Jem," she whispered, slipping her fingers under his collar. Limping, she picked up the pace. At the grove, the trees blocked out the moonlight, and she hesitated before stepping into the darkness. She should have brought a flashlight. Maybe she should wait for the men.

The unearthly scream came again. Were there ghosts in these mountains? She'd heard of the Marfa lights, the centuries-old unexplained phenomenon of lights with no apparent origin.

The men were slow. Some protectors they were.

She pointed the gun and sidled toward the trees, inhaling the scents of vegetation. "Where are you? Are you hurt?" The trees bounced her voice back in her face. There was no other sound beyond normal night noises. She stepped cautiously away from the safety of the clearing and farther into the darkness. Her own breathing sounded harsh and fast.

A twig snapped behind her. The sound of rushing steps came toward her, and she whirled to run. Before she made it two steps, someone grabbed her. In several quick moves, hard hands flipped her around, yanked the gun from her hand, and pinned her against the bark of a pine tree.

It was too dark to make out more than a hulking shape. "Let go of me," she said, jerking her arm in the man's grip.

"What do you think you're doing?" Rick's voice was a low growl.

She should have been relieved it was only him, but her terror fueled anger instead. "Get your hands off me."

His big hands lifted from her shoulders. "What in the sam hill are you doing wandering outside with a mountain lion on the prowl?"

"Mountain lion?" She clutched the fabric of her shirt in her fists. "I—I heard what I thought was a woman screaming."

"Oh brother." He grabbed her arm and hustled her back toward the porch. "You don't have any shoes on either. You want to get snake bit or stung by a scorpion?"

"Wrong time of year," she said, dragging up a bit of defiance. How stupid of her. A mountain lion. She glanced over her shoulder, expecting to see yellow eyes or a large cat springing toward them, but there was only darkness. "Wait, what about the rifle?"

"Leave it."

"We can't leave it. Betsy might find it." She jerked her arm out of his grip. "You threw it down. Where is it?"

"Feel free to get it. I don't carry a firearm. Not for any reason."

A cowboy that didn't carry a rifle? What did he do about snakes and other varmints? If only the moonlight were brighter here in the trees. She'd like to study his expression and try to determine what was behind his odd statement. His voice was as prickly as a cactus too.

She retraced their few steps and felt around on the ground for the rifle. Her hand touched stiff grass, rocks, and sand. Then her fingers settled on cold steel. She picked up the rifle and hurried back out of the tree cover, all the while expecting to feel the teeth and claws of an angry panther. When she started back to the clearing, she realized he'd followed her. At least he hadn't left her at the lion's mercy.

It was probably long gone by now, and she was being skittish for no reason. She nearly ran from the trees into the warm wash of moonlight and Rick's solid presence.

"The least you could have done was come with me," she said.

"You made enough noise to scare away a pride of lions. The cougar was long gone."

"Do you have mountain lions here often?" she asked him. The breeze, laden with the scent of pine from the piñons, touched her face.

Rick didn't reply. They stepped into the moonlight, and he stopped for a second, then took off running for the barn.

Allie darted after him. "What's wrong?" Then she saw. The gate gaped open, and the horses were out. She put on another spurt of speed, ignoring the rocks that poked her feet. A rope, she needed to help lasso them. Dodging Rick, she stepped into the barn, grabbed two ropes from the hook, and rejoined him in the paddock.

She handed him one of the ropes. "It wasn't open a little while ago. I looked down from my window and watched the horses before the scream came. The gate was closed. I'm sure of it."

"I'll check it out. But first, we'd better get those horses back." Uncoiling the rope, he walked away.

Allie followed. There were four horses out. At least she could show him she knew how to rope and ride. While she might not have a lot of skills, she'd be an asset to any ranch.

He called out the name Moonbeam, and a black horse with a gleaming white blaze turned its head to stare at him. Rick approached, and the horse snorted and backed away. The coil of rope he threw missed Moonbeam's neck, and the horse whirled to bolt.

Running her hands over the rough rope, Allie twirled it and let it go. The rope burned her palm as the loop on the end sailed through the air and settled around the horse's neck. She braced her feet, digging her bare toes into the sandy soil. Moonbeam's head came up and he snorted, but she had him.

"Come here, boy," she coaxed, pulling on the rope.

"Nice," Rick said, his voice grudging. "Where'd you learn to rope like that?"

"Rodeo. I could rope a calf by the time I was five." She ran her hands over the horse's gaunt frame. She winced at the bones poking through his rough coat. "He's so thin."

"You should have seen him when we rescued him. I didn't think he'd make it." Rick grabbed Moonbeam's rope halter when the gelding neared. "I'll put him in the barn while you lasso the next one."

Some men would have been intimidated by her superior skill. Score one for the cowboy. She spared a glance after him. He was powerfully built, with broad shoulders and muscular thighs. Very different from Jon. Maybe that was a good thing. It would ensure that she and Betsy wouldn't put him in Jon's place.

Her thoughts danced away from his preposterous suggestion again. Marriage to him terrified her.

She lassoed the next horse, Cupcake. The mare came willingly with her colt following after. They were probably skittish after hearing the mountain lion. If the big cat had gotten hold of little Frost . . . Allie shuddered.

Once all the horses were secured, she and Rick walked the fence line. "Maybe the gate failed to latch, and one of the horses pushed it open," she suggested.

"It's got a chain on it." He secured the chain and latched the padlock. "It couldn't have been accidental."

The stalker had found her. No. No, she was sure no one knew where she'd gone.

"Could Betsy have come out to see Frost?" Rick asked.

"I had trouble sleeping, and she's been asleep since her head hit the pillow." Allie followed him toward the porch.

"I'd guess it was kids, but we're so remote out here they'd have to come from Alpine or Marathon."

The explanations all fell flat. Why come here?

"Maybe campers from the Big Bend." He stretched his big frame, then folded his arms across his chest. "We didn't get a chance to finish our discussion."

She took a step back. "I—I don't know what to say. I appreciate the offer, but I just can't marry someone I don't know." The night air held a chill, and Allie told herself she was shaking only because of the temperature.

He didn't answer right away. Rick leaned his shoulder against a porch post and looked out into the star-filled sky. "Jon saw this coming," he said finally. "He said if anything happened to him that his parents would try to get Betsy. He made me promise if it happened that I'd marry you and adopt her. I guess his childhood was bad."

"I know," Allie said. The cold penetrated her bones, and her teeth began to stutter together. "Always drinking and fighting. They've got several foster kids too, so they'll look good to a judge with their pseudo-Christian mask. They go to church all the time and quote all kinds of rules, but it's all for show. They don't possess an ounce of real faith."

"Didn't Jon ever tell you what he'd asked me? He said he would."

Allie shook her head. "He only said if I was ever in trouble to come to you. Maybe he didn't want to worry me. I—I think it seems a little extreme, his solution, I mean. You've been in special ops. Surely you can pull some strings and make the problem go away."

He smiled, his white teeth catching a glint of moonlight. "No strings that could alter a custody battle. They'll find you eventually, but there would be nothing they could do if we were married and I adopted Betsy."

She studied his face, the strong planes and angles, the determined jaw. Jon said Rick was one in a million, but she couldn't imagine being tied to him for the rest of her life. Maybe it wouldn't have to be that way. "W—we would divorce once Betsy was secure?"

"If that's what you want."

Was that relief she heard in his voice? He probably didn't want this any more than she did. Maybe she wasn't his type any more than he was hers. "I'll think about it," she said, turning to flee to the safety of her room.

RICK DISMOUNTED GUNNER AND SCANNED THE FAINT MARKS IN THE DUST.
Two people, one smaller than the other, had left their tracks in the
pasture behind the barn. Maybe a man and a woman or a man and a
youth. Or the tracks could have been made before last night. He was
too tired to tell.

He shaded his eyes with his hand and let his gaze wander over the
hills around the ranch. There was no movement other than a jackrabbit darting from shrub to shrub.

"Anything, Cowboy?" Charlie asked.

"Nope." Rick dropped his hand back to his side. His gaze lingered
on Charlie's new saddle. "Nice chrome. You must have spent a year's
pay on that."

Charlie grinned. "It was worth it."

"Did you hear anything last night?"

Charlie shook his head. "I fell asleep with the TV on. The volume
was kind of high." He gestured to the tracks. "Could be illegals. I'd
guess a couple wandered through here and tried to catch a ride.
Maybe the big cat scared them off."

"Maybe." Rick wasn't buying it. "You go to rodeos. You ever see her?"

"Allie? She was working the rodeo in El Paso I went to last month.
I told her Elijah might be able to help Betsy."

"What do you know about her?"

Charlie mounted his roan mare, Freckles. "Her parents were killed
in a small plane crash about a year ago. Her mom was Anna Morgan."

Rick whistled. "I heard about that crash. It will probably be a long
time before anyone breaks Anna's record. Most barrel racing wins.
She was a phenomenal rider."

"Word was Allie had a good shot at it. I saw her in one event. She's
fast. She had a great horse. I wonder what happened to the mare?"

The men turned their horses' heads to the trail that rambled to the top of the butte. A good barrel-racing horse was worth as much as forty thousand dollars. Plus whatever she got from her parents' estate.

"So the poverty act is just that—all show." His lip curled at the memory of the way she'd wolfed down the sandwich. And he'd fallen for the act. What a sap.

Charlie shook his head. "Not according to the chute boss who told me about it. Her dad liked toys: his own plane, the best of everything. Wasn't much left after everything was sold, and she sold the horse to pay for trying to fix Betsy's problem."

Rick regretted his cynicism. Okay, maybe she wasn't just a good actress. He eyed Charlie. "You sure know a lot about it."

The kid flashed a grin toward Rick. "She's a hottie, man, in case you didn't notice. So, yeah, I watched her."

"She's a little long in the tooth for you."

"Only ten years or so. Her sister was a real looker too."

"Was?" Though Rick knew she was dead, he wanted to probe a little. Maybe Charlie had heard some rumors.

"She was murdered—about a month ago, I think. What a waste."

Rick pulled up on the reins and stopped in the trail. "What happened?" Maybe Charlie could add to what Allie had told him.

"Talk around the rodeo was it was someone who was after Allie. Hey, race you to the top." Charlie shook the reins, and Freckles leaped forward at the jingle of tack.

Rick let Charlie beat him while he pondered the information. Parents and a sister, all killed—just like she'd said, though she'd said the sister walked in on a burglar. Why would rumors be flying that the killer was after Allie? She'd said nothing about that.

But it didn't matter. He saw no way out of fulfilling his promise to

Jon. He'd been as surprised as Allie when he blurted out that marriage proposal, and ever since the words left his mouth, he'd been looking for a way to take them back.

His contacts in special ops might be able to shed some light on her situation.

Charlie turned in the saddle to look at him, and Rick waved him on. He pulled out his cell phone. Coverage was spotty on the ranch, but he'd always found good reception on this hill. Reining Gunner to a stop, Rick called up the number and waited for Brendan to answer on the other end.

"Waddell." Brendan's curt voice came over the line.

"It's Rick. You got a minute?"

"Hey, Cowboy. It depends. I've got a situation here I need you for. Tit for tat. I do your favor, you come back to work."

"You know I can't do that." Rick let the grin filter through the phone to his friend. He and Brendan never had a conversation without his ex-partner grinding that old ax. By now Brendan should know it was a lost cause.

The sound of Brendan closing a door came through the phone. "You know you miss it."

Sometimes Rick longed for the days of never knowing what country he'd be in come nightfall, but if he showed a sliver of weakness, Brendan would be all over him.

He forced derision into his voice. "What's to miss? Hard beds, crappy food, a bullet around every corner."

"It's paradise, I know. I can hear your voice break." Brendan laughed, and his voice sobered. "What can I do for you, buddy? Got cattle rustlers bothering you? Illegal drugs being smuggled across the desert?"

"Nothing so exciting. A woman and kid showed up here, Jon

Siderses widow and daughter. Her parents died in a plane crash, then her sister was murdered. Now she's asking for my help because Jon's parents are suing for custody of the daughter."

"Jon was a good man. I always wondered what happened to his family." Brendan's voice fell, and the hiss of a bad connection filled the phone line. "You going to do something about it?"

"Something like that."

"What's her name?"

"Allie. Little girl's name is Betsy." Rick debated about telling Brendan the little girl was mute. Nah, it wasn't an important detail. The names would be enough. "She seems to be in some kind of trouble. Won't talk about it. Can you see what you can find out?"

"Sure. Let me check it out. I'll get back to you by tomorrow. You sure you don't want to get in on the rescue of some hijacked tourists in Baghdad?"

"I think you can handle it by yourself," Rick said, his grin widening. "Thanks, Brendan. I owe you." He closed his phone, then called up directory assistance and had the woman dial the rodeo where Allie said she worked. Rick gave his name but was careful not to say where he was calling from. The man he talked to there told him she'd been one of his best employees for eight years, and he hated to lose her. He'd said she might have won the national barrel-racing competition as well, if she hadn't taken off.

Rick put his phone away and urged his horse on up the slope. Had he been hoping it was all a scam—that she really wasn't Jon's widow? How could he? One look at Betsy spoke a world of truth. He saw Jon in the little girl's eyes.

He had to honor his promise, but all he wanted to do was bail.

6

ALLIE STOOD ON THE PORCH AND RUBBED LOTION SMELLING OF LAVENDER into her chapped hands. The Chisos Mountains were called "sky islands" by the locals, and she'd already fallen in love with their brooding presence. They held up the sky in the distance as the cold night gave way to sunshine, warming the rocks and vegetation.

So far she'd avoided Rick this morning. She still couldn't believe she'd been stupid enough to mistake a mountain lion for a woman in trouble. What should she do about Rick's suggestion? Part of her wanted to let someone else shoulder her burdens for a little while, but they'd been with her so long, they'd become part of her. She didn't know if she could even let them go.

Through the open window she could hear Charlie talking to himself as he tried to figure out how to catch a calf that had slipped through the gate.

The door opened behind her, and Elijah stepped out. "There you are, *mujercita*. I have time to show you the books now. To my office, if you would be so kind."

The books. A ball of dread coiled in her throat. While bluffing it came easily to her, this might be more than she could fake her way through. "I should probably check on Betsy."

"The *niña* is on the back porch playing with the kittens. This will not take long. They are not difficult." Elijah beckoned her with a brown finger.

Allie swallowed her excuses and followed the old man to the office off the living room. A large, high-ceilinged space, the pale yellow walls were further warmed by the sunlight streaming in the four large windows. An oak desk dominated the center of the room. The chair's back was to the window, and the light fell on the vast expanse of the desk.

Her eyes were drawn to the ledger in the middle of the desk. It lay open, the squiggly black lines of letters and numbers crawling across its pages like scorpions. Such small text would make the job even more difficult. She'd hoped for a computer that let her make the fonts larger.

Elijah swept his arm over the chair. "Be seated, please."

Allie went around the desk and sank onto the cracked leather desk chair. She stared at the ledger. Clasping her hands in her lap, she told herself the nursery rhyme that usually calmed her:

Once I saw a little bird

Go hop, hop, hop.

So I cried, little bird,

Will you stop, stop, stop?

And I was going to the window

To say, how do you do?

When he shook his little tail

And away he flew.

Something about the cadence stole her flustered feelings away. She eased back in the chair and listened to the singsong in her head until her confidence surged again.

It was only numbers in a book. She would work hard and learn.

Elijah stood beside her. A stack of bills lay in a wire tray on the desk, and he took the first one. "This is the electric bill." He ran a gnarled finger down the rows to stop on the third line down. "You find the month by going across." He moved his finger in a vertical direction to the third column. "This is the February bill, so it is to be written down here. Very easy, much as you have likely done in your private affairs."

Allie clamped her teeth against the hysterical laughter rising in her throat. If he only knew what a mess her private affairs were.

When she didn't pick up the pencil, Elijah did it. "I'll show you." He carefully inscribed the date and some numbers in the boxes.

She forced herself to look at the page, trying not to feel sick at the way the black text jiggled on the white paper. She squinted and managed to make out one entry. "Your electric bill is over five hundred dollars?"

"It costs money to run the pumps for water for the livestock, for showers when we have a bunkhouse full of children."

"How do you pay for all this?"

He smiled. "I made much money in my younger days as a child psychologist in Houston. The ranch, we bought when our daughter was a baby, but we did not come to live here until she was a teenager."

His face grew pensive. "This was maybe not so good a choice. My wife, she was very frugal. I have enough for many years to come. The agencies who send the children, they also provide some income."

"When is our next group coming? How does it all work?"

"Sometimes we have a group come for a month or two, sometimes a larger group for just a day. Right now, the crew is remodeling the bunkhouse, so we have none. But a few rooms are done, and we will take a handful later today." He went toward the door. "You look, *sí*? I will get us coffee."

The stack of bills seemed huge. Her head already ached from looking at just one page of the black numbers on white paper. She should confess her condition and get it over with. Sitting back in the chair, she glanced around the room until her gaze settled on the picture of a young woman.

It almost could have been her.

She stood and picked it up, running her fingers over the cool glass. The woman was younger than Allie, and her eyes were brown instead of blue, but she had the same high cheekbones and full lips. The same dark hair. Who was she?

She heard Elijah coming and put the picture back on the bookshelf. He arrived at the doorway as she turned around. Caught.

"That was my granddaughter, Maria."

"Was?"

"Ten years now she has been in her grave. A riding accident when she was twenty-five."

"I'm sorry."

"You have the look of her, *sí*?"

"I noticed. Was that why you stared when you first saw me?"

"It is so." He turned to the door. "I will leave you to your work."

"Could I use the phone to call my friend in El Paso and let her know I arrived safely?"

"*Sí*, of course. Anytime you wish." He closed the door behind him.

Allie looked at the picture again. Maria would have been her cousin. Her mother had always told Allie she was an only child. So who were Maria's parents? The thought she might still have family filled her with a sense of purpose and rightness about coming here.

Allie went back to the chair, picked up the phone, and dialed Yo's cell phone number. Her friend answered almost at once. "Yo, it's me."

"Allie, I've been so worried. Are you okay, girl?"

The chair squeaked as Allie leaned back, glancing at her nails. She'd managed not to bite them for three days, but the polish looked terrible. "I'm fine. Got here in one piece. How's everything? How are you riding today?"

"I am all that, girlfriend," Yo crowed. "Ran just over 14.7 seconds today."

"Oh great, Yo. You're going to win this year!" Allie pulled polish remover from her purse and began to remove the chipped polish. The pungent sting of the chemical reminded her that her chance at the title was a thing of the past.

"As long as I don't bite it."

"You won't. You'll do great."

"I miss you, girl."

Allie closed her eyes and wished she could be back where she belonged. "I miss you too, Yo. Listen, I need your advice." She started to bite her nails, then yanked her fingers from her mouth. Her mother always used to say a lady didn't bite her nails.

"Like I'm the one to ask." Yo's voice held a smile. "What's up?"

"I've had someone offer to help me make sure I don't lose Betsy.

It's a friend of Jon's. He says if I'm married and he adopts Betsy, she'll be safe from Jon's parents."

"Uh-uh, no way, girl. You don't go marrying no stranger." Yo's voice rose.

"He was Jon's best friend. I—I think I trust him, Yo. And it would only be for a year or so. Just until Betsy is safe." Was she actually arguing *for* the idea?

"What kind of lesson is that teaching Betsy? You marrying then divorcing for convenience's sake. And she'll be yanked from pillar to post."

Allie winced. "I'll take care of her."

Yolanda sighed. "Allie, you don't know this guy. He could be an ax murderer or something."

Allie grinned, remembering how Rick had said he wasn't an ax murderer when she'd been afraid to get in the truck. "He's not like that, Yo."

"Hmm, do I hear some interest, girl?"

"Not hardly. He's a big guy, all muscle and testosterone. Not at all like Jon."

"That's not a bad thing. It's not good to try to find a Jon look-alike."

"Now who's pulling for the idea? Not interested."

"Because he's not like Jon? Honey, you've got to let him go sometime. He's dead. I know it's harsh to say it, but you've got to face it. You're still young. I want you to find someone else and love again."

"I'll never love anyone like I loved Jon. And I don't want Betsy to put someone else in her daddy's place."

Yo sighed. "Girl, she can't remember him by now. Kids forget."

"She *won't* forget," Allie said fiercely. "I won't let her."

"Time has a way of smoothing out the bumps. You wouldn't want

Betsy to grieve forever. I don't want you to, either. You've got to trust again, Allie. Let go of that ironclad control."

Allie pressed her lips together. Yo didn't understand. She hadn't gone through the losses Allie had suffered. She turned to glance out the window. "I've got a job, Yo. Doing bookwork and housekeeping."

"Bookwork? Your specialty." Yolanda's chuckle lightened her poke at Allie's problem.

"Ironic, isn't it?"

"So why marry this dude? You've got a job, a place to stay."

"I thought about that. But it's a room in a ranch, not a home of our own. That won't look good to a judge. It won't appear we're any better off than when we were living in a travel trailer." She heard footsteps outside the door. "Listen, I have to go. I'll call in a few days. Pray for me, Yo, that I'll know what to do."

"You got it, girlfriend. Love you."

"Love you too." Allie clicked off the phone and put it down as Elijah stepped back into the office.

"Do you have any questions before I go outside?"

"No, I was on the phone. I'll start work now."

He tipped his head to one side and listened. "We have visitors."

Allie heard it then too, the distant growl of an engine.

"Set that aside for now. You shall find out what the ranch is all about. The group I mentioned is coming. We go meet them, *sí?*" He held out his hand for her.

She put her fingers on his forearm and rose, allowing him to escort her to the door. The rough-and-ready rodeo riders she knew never acted so courtly. She could get used to this treatment.

There was something about Elijah that comforted her. What would her life have been like if she'd had a relationship with him growing up? She'd always wanted grandparents. Rattling around the rodeo all her life, she never experienced the stability of deep family roots. Her parents loved her, but they were often busy.

The ranch was a world apart, a place where she longed to scrape away the hard surface soil and peer underneath to the reality. She was certain she would discover something beautiful. She longed to ask Elijah a million questions. Like did she have any other living relatives? An aunt or uncle?

Elijah opened the front door for her and followed her to the porch.

A van appeared on the road between the rocky outcroppings on each side. Dust billowed from its tires, and its engine revved up for the final approach to the house. The vehicle stopped, and the back door opened. Several teenagers emerged, blinking in the bright sunlight.

Allie counted four—two boys and two girls. A man exited the front of the van and corralled the teens. She could hear him directing the kids to get their luggage. The group moved en masse toward the porch.

"Hello, are you the lady of the house?" the man asked, his dark eyes sizing her up.

"I'm the housekeeper," she said. "Allie Siders."

In his forties, the man's eyes peered through metal-rimmed glasses. His black hair lay in a sleek cap on his head, and he wore a gray suit and black shoes that were already picking up traces of red dust.

He shook her hand. "Emilio Valdez. You must be Elijah," he said, glancing at the old man.

"*Sí*. You are new."

Emilio nodded. "Yeah, they sent me since this bunch is a little hard to handle. I'll ride shotgun over them and do schoolwork with them as well. Where do you want them?"

"Take the boys to the bunkhouse, out behind the barn. The girls have rooms inside the house on the second floor. If you'll show the boys to their bunks, Allie will take the girls inside."

"*Gracias*." Emilio turned to the huddled teens who were trying to look bored. "You heard the boss man. Boys, come with me."

"Why do the Betties get to stay in the house?" The boy who objected looked like he'd seen one too many tattoo parlors. Skulls and crossbones covered both arms, and he had rings in his ears, eyebrows, and lower lip.

The bright red hair matched his eyebrows, so Allie decided it must be natural.

The other boy shoved him. "To save them from dudes like you." Thin to the point of emaciation, the second boy picked up his backpack and turned to go.

"Are you going to introduce us?" Allie asked.

Emilio took a tighter grip on his briefcase. "Tattoo boy is Devin." He pointed to the skinny boy. "Leon. The girls are Latoya and Fern." He nodded toward Allie. "Go with the lady, girls. We'll be back as soon as we get things stowed, and you can see the ranch."

"Peachy," Devin said in a mocking voice. His untied shoelaces dragged in the red dirt as he slumped after Emilio and Leon.

Elijah went down the steps. "I will check on Cupcake. You can handle this, Allie."

Allie forced a smile. She wasn't used to being around teenagers much. "You both share a room beside mine." The girls followed her into the house.

Were these kids part of the foster care system? She'd heard Elijah had great success with troubled kids and had headed here without knowing more than that.

"Wow," Latoya breathed. "Cool digs."

Shapely with perfect dark skin, Latoya held her head high and surveyed her new domain. Allie could see she'd have her hands full with the young woman. Fern kept her head down, and only the pink of her scalp showed in the part between two yellow braids.

Why were they here? Drugs? Prostitution? For the first time, Allie realized she might have brought Betsy into contact with characters who might not be the best influences. She'd assumed the kids would all be younger, with problems similar to Betsy's. When she thought about it, though, she realized internal scars were the most profound.

She showed the girls their room and pointed to the dresser. "You can put your things away there."

The girls began to unload their backpacks. Latoya brought out a delicious color of hot-pink nail polish.

"Ooh, that's pretty." Allie picked it up. "Sparkles." She glanced at her bare nails. It had been all she could do not to bite them with no polish on them.

"Try it." Latoya put her hand over her mouth and exhaled. "Girl, I've got the dragon. My teeth feel like slime. Where's the bathroom?"

"At the end of the hall." Allie picked up the bottle of polish when Latoya went out. Why not? She sat on the edge of the bed and uncapped it, then slicked a thin coat over her nails. Holding out her left hand, she showed Fern. "What do you think?"

Fern barely glanced at her hand, but her head bobbed. "Pretty."

Latoya came back in with gloss on her lips. She pooched her lip out at Allie. "Minty fresh." She peeked at Allie's nails. "That's so you, girl."

"It's fresh," Allie said. "I like it."

"It's yours." Latoya leaned over and pressed the bottle into Allie's hands.

"Oh no, I can't take it." Was the girl trying to bribe her? Allie stared hard at Latoya, but the teenager just smiled back. "I'll borrow it sometime." She put the bottle back on the dresser. "Let's go find the guys." They all trooped back downstairs. She was careful with her wet nails when she peeked out the back door to check on Betsy. Her daughter lay in a hammock on the back porch with three kittens snuggled around her. They were all sleeping.

She and the girls tiptoed past the little girl into the backyard and headed toward the barn. Rick's familiar battered cowboy hat moved into her line of vision. He stood by the paddock with one boot on the bottom rail and his hands gripping the top. Funny how the same pose she'd seen Charlie take looked so much better on Rick.

Emilio and the boys clustered around the paddock with him.

"Who's that?" Latoya asked, her voice vibrating with awe.

"Rick Bailey, the foreman."

"He's gorgeous. Puts me in mind of a young Arnold Schwarzenegger with all those muscles." Latoya's hips took on an exaggerated sway as she made a beeline to join the guys.

Allie grinned, imagining the way Rick would put the girl in her place. Latoya didn't realize she was up against Prince Charmless, as Allie had dubbed him in her mind.

About to become her rescuer Prince Charming.

The thought shocked her.

"Want to see the horses?" she asked Fern. Her eyes still downcast, the girl nodded. "Do you have any brothers or sisters?" Allie asked.

"A brother," Fern said, her words so soft Allie had to strain to hear them.

It was going to take time to get through the wall Fern had built around her. Maybe the horses would be a good start. "Come with me," Allie said.

Cupcake's winter coat was a little rough and ragged, but she was still a beautiful mare. With little Frost following at her heels, she pranced around the paddock with her tail out and her head up.

Fern peeked at the horses, a smile starting across her pinched face. "A colt," she breathed.

"He's only two days old," Allie said. They had reached the rest of the group, and she saw Rick stiffen at the sound of her voice.

What a way to start a marriage.

Her assumptions had altered. His offer was a way out. Maybe the only way.

She focused on the needy teenager beside her. "Cupcake is a good mother. See how she keeps her body between us and her colt?"

Fern nodded. "She's beautiful."

The boys were hanging on the fence, watching the mare gallop past. "Hey, check out the rides," Devin said. "I wanna try."

"Nope, can't ride Cupcake," Rick said. "And Frost is way too young. He'll need to be at least two or three. But there are other horses you can ride." He glanced at Allie. "Would you help me saddle up enough horses for all of them?"

She went past him into the barn. The tack room door to her right stood ajar, and she pushed it open to glance around. The scent of the new stacks of hay in the corner made her sneeze.

She felt rather than saw Rick enter the room. His presence made her feel claustrophobic, which made no sense. She was used to being around overwhelmingly masculine men. But then, she'd never thought about *marrying* one of them. Grabbing a saddle, she turned to push past him and found his broad shoulders blocking the doorway.

"Stand aside, please," she said. He didn't move, and the way he stared made her cheeks grow hot. "I thought you wanted to saddle the horses."

"Have you thought about what I said? Jon's parents will find you soon."

"I know, I know," she muttered. "Let's not talk about it now." She moved to go around him, but he still blocked the doorway. "What?"

"Be careful with Elijah. Don't hurt him."

"What are you talking about?"

"Just back off, okay? Don't be so helpless and appealing. His family is all gone now. The daughter ran off when she was seventeen and abandoned a granddaughter she never saw again. Now Elijah doesn't even have her."

Allie opened her mouth, then closed it again. Could he be talking about her mother? She never left behind a grandchild. She set the saddle down a minute. "I thought the daughter left when she was pregnant. Did he have more than one?"

He gave her a curious look but didn't ask where she'd heard the story. "Just the one girl. Selena. She left when she was about eight months pregnant, but Elijah tracked down the baby and brought her here to live."

Her mother had abandoned Allie's sister?

Allie wanted to sit down. Her mother had told her the baby died.

Rick didn't seem to notice her shock. "He poured all his love into his granddaughter, but she died when she was twenty-five. She looked a lot like you, and I think that's why he's taken to you so much. But you're not his Maria."

Allie scrambled to recover her senses. "I saw her picture today."

"So you understand the resemblance. You could twist him around your finger, but if you try, I'll break it off."

She managed a smile, trying not to show her shock. "I'm attached to my fingers, so don't worry. I'm not here to get anything out of Elijah."

"No, just out of me. You made a decision yet?"

Was that dismay in his voice? She studied his features but couldn't penetrate his impassive expression. "It would save Betsy."

"It's the only way to be sure." Resignation settled over his mouth.

"I want to get one thing clear right up front. You are not Betsy's father." Her voice trembled just a little. "I will have the say over what's best for her."

His blue eyes narrowed. "Nope. Won't work, lady. This is a partnership. I'm doing this for Jon and for Betsy, not for you. She'll never talk with the way you're smothering her."

Allie gasped and took a step back. Her knees trembled, and she curled her fingers into her palms so she wouldn't hit him. "A mother protects her child."

"A mother's job is to teach her child to stand on her own."

"She's only five!"

"Old enough to be tying her own shoes, to make her bed. I saw you making it for her this morning while she colored on the floor. You have to teach her some responsibility."

Allie didn't trust herself to speak. Luckily, he took a saddle and went back outside. Maybe all men didn't get how important it was to protect children from the bumps of life. Jon thought she coddled Betsy too. She whisked a tear from her lashes. Rick wasn't a father and didn't understand.

She wasn't going to let him bully her or Betsy. Talk about a throwback to pioneer days! Here she was about to enter into a marriage of convenience. And really, it would have been impossible if he actually *wanted* to marry her. If he touched her . . . She suppressed a shudder. He didn't attract her *that way* at all.

This way they could both keep their distance.

She picked up the saddle and bridle and went out to the corral. Rick was on his cell phone, and she almost expected him to snarl like the cougar over whatever he'd been told. He snapped his phone shut and beckoned to her. Dropping the saddle over the fence post, she joined him at the gate.

"We need to rescue a horse, and I may need help catching it. Charlie is gone, and the other two hands need to stay here and take care of these kids. You'll have to do."

"What about Betsy?"

"She can hang out with the kids."

"Not a chance."

"Then bring her. But be quick about it."

The prospect of letting her daughter see how some people treated horses called her hasty decision into question. Still, she couldn't let a horse die because she was squeamish. "I'll get her."

Allie found her daughter still asleep in the hammock with the kittens lying on top of her.

"Betsy," she called in a soft voice.

Her daughter's eyes popped open. She sat up and rubbed her eyes, then rolled out of the hammock with a kitten in her arms.

"Rick needs us to go help a horse." Allie held out her hand, and Betsy ran to grasp it. She put down the kitten before taking her mother's hand. "Can you be big and brave? Some people aren't nice to their horses."

Betsy nodded, and the two of them went around the front of the house to where Rick sat waiting in his truck. Betsy climbed in next to Rick, and Allie fastened her daughter's seat belt and her own.

"How far?" she asked Rick.

"About ten miles."

"Who called you?"

"A neighbor saw the horse staggering across the desert."

"Owner?"

His mouth took on a grim slant. "I think I know. I've been keeping an eye on them for a few weeks. The owner is a city dude who thinks it's fun to fly out here three or four times a year."

"Can we do anything if he refuses to let us take the horse?"

"The sheriff will cite him for neglect. But it won't come to that. I'm taking him home with us, and we'll deal with what we have to later. He's not a bad guy, just stupid."

From the way he clamped his lips shut, Allie knew he didn't want to talk. Good thing, because she didn't want to either. She stared out the window.

The golden stipa grass mingled with the cactus and sage from horizon to horizon. It was a harsh land but beautiful. The purple haze of the mountains climbed to the sky in the distance, and the blue bowl overhead added to the isolation. The air smelled hot and dusty even though it was only March.

The thought of staying in this sanctuary comforted her. She and Betsy were safe here. They'd see anyone dangerous coming from miles away. A stranger would stick out like water in the desert.

Rick braked hard, and the truck slewed in the road before coming to rest near the ditch. "There she is!" He opened the door and grabbed a saddlebag from behind his seat. "Come on."

Allie unlatched her seat belt and got Betsy free as well. "Stay close to me," she told her daughter.

She nearly stepped on a tarantula lumbering across the road.

Withdrawing her foot, she let the arachnid have the road until it disappeared on the other side. Creepy things. With Betsy in her arms, she hopped a yucca plant and headed after Rick, who was disappearing behind thick brush.

If she saw another tarantula, she might scream.

At least she wore boots. She put Betsy down and took her hand. "Let's run to catch up."

The hot, dusty wind blew in her face, and her feet slipped so much on the thin soil that it took much longer to catch up with Rick than she'd imagined. She thought about calling for him to wait, but he was too far ahead. Besides, he was a man on a mission, and she doubted he'd listen.

Betsy tugged at her hand and pointed to their right. Allie stopped and stared at the pitiful sight. A blue roan mare stood outlined against a rocky hillside. Her bones stood out in stark relief through her ragged coat. She tried to move away from them, but she staggered as she walked.

When was the last time the mare had food or water? Allie feared they were too late to save her. "Let's see if we can get close, Betsy."

Betsy tugged her hand out of Allie's and ran toward the horse. Allie tried to grab her and grasped only air. "No, Betsy, you'll scare her." When Allie leaped after her daughter, her foot slipped, and she sprawled onto the ground. Her hand dove into a cactus. She scrambled up again, but Betsy was out of reach by then.

Rick's head turned at her shout, and he put out his hand as though to catch the little girl, but Betsy veered around him and continued on her course to the animal. When she got about ten feet away, she stopped.

Allie ran to catch up with her daughter. "Don't get any closer,

Bets," she called, still several feet from her daughter. "She might be dangerous." Though the poor horse looked like she didn't have the energy to walk, much less kick.

Betsy put her hand out and walked closer to the mare. "No, Betsy!" Allie put on an extra burst of speed, but she felt she was moving through air as thick as quicksand. Betsy would reach the horse before Allie could stop her.

But the mare put her head down, and her nose touched Betsy's outstretched hand. The shudders wracking the horse's body stopped, and she stood quietly as the little girl rubbed the white blaze on her head.

"Well, I'll be," Rick said softly as Allie fell into step beside him. "Keep her here. I'll go get the truck."

"It's not safe." Allie scooped her daughter into her arms.

Rick rolled his eyes. "She's fine. There's an affinity between them."

The horse stepped closer to where Allie stood with Betsy. The little girl put her hand out, and the horse nuzzled it. Hope shimmered in Allie's heart. Maybe he was right. Maybe this horse was the key to unlocking Betsy's heart.

7

Rick wasn't sure the horse would even survive the trip. Trying to avoid the bumps in the road, he drove slowly back to the ranch, but the trip took its toll on the mare. Her legs trembled as he opened the tailgate and prepared to lead her into the holding pen by the smaller of the two barns.

"What do you want me to do?" Allie asked him.

"Just stand out of the way while I get her out."

The mare kicked at him when he stepped up into the truck, and he darted away from her wicked hooves. He hadn't thought she had that much fight in her. "Come on, girl, you need some food and water."

Betsy climbed onto the wheel well of the trailer and put her hand out.

"No, Betsy!" Allie sprang toward her daughter.

Rick grabbed her arm. "The mare can't hurt her from there." The mare nuzzled the small hand, and the little girl smiled. It was the first smile Rick had seen on her.

He scooped her up and deposited her by the gate. "Betsy, call to her. See if she'll come to you."

"She won't talk," Allie whispered.

Rick glowered at her. "Give her a chance, woman. You're smothering her."

Sparks that could have electrocuted him flashed from her blue eyes. She opened her mouth to speak, but he turned his back on her. "Call to her, Bets."

Betsy looked down and shook her head. She started back toward the truck, but he stopped her. "Wait a minute. Let me get some sweet feed. She might come to you if you have food."

He ran to the small barn and scooped up a bucket of sweet feed. He stopped to grab some electrolytes and the stainless hand pump. The mare needed fluid fast. When he went back to the yard, he found Allie leading the horse out of the truck.

"I think she's afraid of men," Allie said.

Rick's elation faded. "You just spoiled the perfect opportunity for Betsy to bond with the mare," he said under his breath. "Cut me some slack here."

"She's my daughter. I know what's best for her." Allie's chin grew more determined. She led the horse toward the corral.

Too late to cry over spilt milk. "Looks like she's been beaten." Rick pointed to the stripes on the mare's flank.

"I noticed." Allie neared her daughter. "Stand back, Betsy. I don't want her to kick you." Betsy stood out of the way, and her mother led the mare through the gate.

"I want to tube her first. She needs water the most."

"She won't let you. I'll do it," Allie said.

"You know how?"

"I've done it before." She held out her hand for the tube.

Rick handed it over and watched her approach the mare. Allie stuck her fingers on each side of the animal's mouth, forcing her to open. Then she massaged the mare's esophagus, and the mare swallowed. As the horse swallowed, the tube advanced down her throat.

"Slick," he said. "I couldn't do it that well. Make sure it's in her stomach. If you get it in the lungs, she'll drown."

Allie shot him a look, and he shut up. She said she'd done it before, and he couldn't fault her technique.

She stepped back and nodded to him. "The lady is ready for a drink."

He dumped the powdered electrolytes into a bucket and turned the hose on. "Ready when you are."

Allie took the bucket he handed over, dropped the pump into the bucket, and began to pump the fluid into the mare's stomach.

"Take it slow," he warned, ignoring the way she rolled her eyes. He didn't want to lose this animal.

Allie pumped slowly, pausing often. Finally, the bucket emptied. The mare seemed to be stronger already.

"Try some feed," he said, handing her the feed bucket after she'd pulled the tube out. "See if she'll eat, Bets. I'd better stay away for now until she knows she can trust me."

He'd like to get his hands on the man who mistreated this animal. She'd been badly beaten, and maggots infested the cuts on her legs. He'd have to spend some time getting them out as soon as possible.

He seldom saw true meanness. Generally, neglect was the killer, but this wounding was deliberate.

Betsy climbed over the fence with the bucket and approached the mare. The old girl snorted and stepped closer to the child. Then the mare thrust her lips into Betsy's outstretched palm and delicately ate the nuggets of feed.

"Good girl," Rick said. "I'll be back in a minute to take care of her wounds."

"She won't let you," Allie said. "I'll do it."

"It's nasty," he warned.

"I see the maggots," she said in a soft voice. "I've handled things like this before."

So far all he'd felt toward her was guilt and obligation, and the admiration that welled at her competence with the horses surprised him. "I'll get the tweezers and antiseptic."

Once he brought her what she needed, he went to find Elijah. Last time he'd seen the old man, he was heading to the big barn. On the way, Rick's cell phone rang, and he saw Brendan's name flash on his caller ID. "That was fast," he said when he answered it.

"You're not going to like this."

Rick's earlier admiration spiraled down like a dust devil. "What is it?"

Brendan's sigh came loud through the phone. "You think this woman is capable of trafficking in Mexican illegals?"

"No way," he said with more conviction than he felt. Rick didn't want to believe Jon's widow would be involved in anything like that.

"The Border Patrol had some pretty strong evidence, and they have questions for her."

"That's not what I wanted to hear, Brendan. She said nothing about any trouble with the law."

"Of course not. I'd think she'd be afraid to tell you the whole truth for fear of you turning her in."

"If she goes to jail, Betsy will go to Jon's parents for sure. I can't let that happen." Had Jon known what his wife was up to? Was that why he made Rick promise not to let his parents get Betsy?

Brendan cleared his throat. "There's more. Jon's parents have charged her with kidnapping."

"What?"

"They'd filed for custody. She can't just up and disappear."

"So the FBI is looking for her?"

"Yep. I should tell them, but I'm not going to."

"Thanks, buddy." Rick ran his hand through his hair. Time was running out.

"What are you going to do?"

"I'm going to marry her," Rick said, his voice wobbling a little. He'd hoped to find a way out.

"You kidding me, man? Even Jon wouldn't expect you to go that far."

"He's tapping my shoulder even now," Rick said. "Thanks for checking it out, Brendan. If you find out any more, let me know."

"I will. But think before you leap, buddy."

"I already have." Rick shut his phone. Man, he wanted a shot of whiskey. Everything in him recoiled at the thought of marrying a woman he didn't know, but he'd promised Jon. Maybe if he followed through, the monkey of guilt on his back would go away.

Rick opened the barn door and stepped inside. Elijah sat on a bale of straw, watching Cupcake and her foal in the stall. The curry brush and comb lay abandoned on the floor beside him.

Rick could have sworn there were tears on Elijah's cheeks, but the old man bent his head and swiped at his face.

When Elijah turned to face him, the brown wrinkles were dry. "The new campers are settled?"

"Yeah, and I found that old mare of Allbright's half-dead and wandering the desert. I brought her home."

"Ah, that is what the commotion was about, *sí*? She will live?"

"I think so."

"Allbright may come by to get her."

"Over my dead body." Rick propped his boot on the lowest rail of the stall. "You okay?"

Elijah stared at the mare and colt. "Did you request Allie's references yet?"

"I talked to the rodeo boss, and he told me she was a great worker, and he hated to lose her."

Elijah nodded, his face without expression.

"Are you having second thoughts about hiring her?"

"Not at all. I was going to tell you not to bother with the references." Elijah seemed to snap back from whatever place he'd gone. "You've called your contacts about her, haven't you?"

"Yep."

The old man took a stogie out of his pocket and chewed on it before taking out a match. "Any word?"

"Some." Rick told Elijah what he'd found out. The boss would have to know. The Bluebird Ranch was prime land for carting Mexicans across the border. They'd have to watch Allie.

"I do not hear you calling for me to throw her off the ranch."

Rick settled onto a hay bale. "I'm going to marry her, Elijah."

Through the swirl of smoke, Elijah's dark eyes studied him. "Why would you do this?"

Staring into Elijah's dark eyes, Rick could smell the sharp, stinging odor of gunpowder, the underlying stench of raw sewage in the streets, and the stink of fear. Taking a deep breath, he began to recount to Elijah the promise he'd made to Jon.

RICK SAT ON A FOLDING CHAIR WITH A MAKESHIFT TABLE MADE FROM A cardboard box between him and his bunkmate Jon Siders. Rick glanced at the cards in his hand. A full house. Jon was toast.

He shoved an empty Tabasco bottle to join an assortment of Q-Tips and candy wrappers. "I'll see your dime and raise you a quarter." They'd had to improvise to play poker, but it helped the time pass.

Jon frowned at his hand, but his gaze wandered back to the letter in his lap. All he'd done since he got it was brood.

"Are you going to play?" Rick said, not bothering to hide his impatience.

"I need to get home."

"Don't we all."

Jon frowned and threw his cards to the table. "My parents are badgering Allie again."

"Man, just call them and tell them to lay off." It was a familiar discussion. While Rick had suffered from lack of parental care, Jon's parents had been the interfering type.

"I've done that. You don't know my parents." Jon pushed back from the table. "I'm afraid of what they might do if I don't come back."

If Rick had been a religious man, he would have crossed himself. "Don't give fate any ideas," he said. He wished he had a drink. A little Jack Daniels might help him bear this discussion.

"God's got my fate in his hands." Jon smiled. "Thanks for that reminder."

Rick shifted uncomfortably. Jon's only failing as a friend was how often he brought God into the conversation. Sometimes Rick almost expected to see the Big Guy sitting across from Jon, talking with him.

"What are they doing now?" he asked, more to change the subject than because he was interested. He'd never met the wife and kid. He was stationed in Europe by the time Jon married her.

"Telling her if she respects them, she'll change churches and start coming with them." Jon's eyes took on an uncharacteristically hard glint. "Over my dead body."

"What's so wrong with that? I thought you were all about family."

"Their church is practically a cult. At the very least it's a toxic environment. They won't even talk to people who leave it. It's all about the letter of the law and nothing about love. My parents believed mightily in the old adage 'spare the rod and spoil the child.' At church they were always smiling and sweet, but at home I rarely got more than a nod of recognition. I'm not having my family exposed to that."

The type of church Jon described was how Rick thought they all were, but he decided to keep this appraisal to himself. "Allie can just say no."

"And she has." Jon's gaze fixed on Rick's face. "We've gone to the wall together, buddy. You're the only one I'd trust to take care of things if I don't get home."

Death was not on Rick's agenda. Not his and not his best friend's. "Don't change the subject just because you're losing." He tapped his cards against the box. "You folding?"

Jon grinned, but his eyes held a trace of sadness. "And let you win? Not on your life." He shoved a handful of gum wrappers into the center. "I call. Show me what you've got."

Rick laid out his cards with a flourish. "Read 'em and weep, my friend." Even as he raked in his winnings, his thoughts danced away from Jon's words.

RICK SHUDDERED AND CAME BACK TO THE PRESENT. "JON TOOK A BULLET meant for me. I have to take care of his family," he told Elijah.

"He has been gone two years, *sí*? Why only now are you looking to help them?"

Rick winced at the blunt words. "I could make an excuse and tell you I couldn't find her, but the truth is, I didn't look very hard. I was wallowing under a mountain of guilt and just wanted peace. So I came here." He still couldn't tell Elijah the full truth of why he would carry that guilt all his life.

"And how did the child's death fit in with this?" Elijah asked.

Heat swept up Rick's neck. "That was a separate incident." But interconnected more than he wanted to face. He could still see the eight-year-old's face in his mind, the wide dark eyes, the fear. Until the gun barked in his hand and obliterated the boy.

The fact that it was an accident failed to expunge his guilt.

Elijah nodded, his dark eyes still studying Rick's face. "I have kept quiet to let you heal, but the time for silence is past. Sweeping your guilt under the straw will only make it stink. Better to bring it to the sunshine. Is this your penance, Rick? Coming here to *El Despoblado*?"

"I believe in this place just as much as you. Have you forgotten I was a throwaway kid myself once? If not for the Bluebird Ranch, I'd be in prison somewhere. The woman may not have been worthy of Jon, but she's still his wife. And I have to help her and the kid."

"You seem to have forgotten what it means to be desperate," Elijah said softly. "Could desperation be Allie's sin? I am content that you are to help her. But do not assume too much about her guilt and shut yourself off from a true marriage with her."

A true marriage? That was not the plan.

THE AROMA OF ENCHILADAS FILLED THE KITCHEN WITH WARMTH. ALLIE had the teenage girls help her prepare supper. They grumbled about it, but she held firm, and they'd fallen into line. The boys went out with the ranch hands to feed and water the stock. They were all too tired to talk much during supper.

The girls kept stealing glances at the black night devoid of streetlights. The barns' security lights provided the only illumination, and the darkness swallowed their beams only a few feet out.

"What do you do all evening?" Latoya asked after the dishes were done. "Let's hop in the whip and see some action."

"The whip?" Allie dried her hands.

"Some wheels," Devin said. "I'm with the Betty. This place is whacked."

"We've got board games," Allie said. She tried to hide her smile, but it came breaking through. "Monopoly, chess. Check out the game cabinet."

"Video games?" Devon asked, fingering the ring on his lip.

"They belong to Rick. You'll have to ask his permission," she said.

Leon fixed a stare on Rick. "What games you got?"

"Video games are a privilege. Once you earn the right to play, we'll scrounge up a game on Saturday night," Rick said.

"Earn 'em? Oh man, you talkin' smack!"

"You'll get points for grooming horses, feeding them, cleaning the pens. When you get enough points, you can take me on in Pac-Man."

"Pac-Man," Leon said. "Man, don't you got no Tomb Raider or Madden football?"

Rick shrugged. "Take it or leave it."

"Like we got a choice," Leon grumbled.

"Grow up," Rick said. "There are always choices in life. People are going to pull you in all directions. Where you end up is a direct result of how wise your decisions are."

Allie wondered if he really believed that. Did he own every wrong decision he'd made? It wasn't through any decision of hers that her parents were dead and that Jon had left her to raise Betsy alone.

Betsy rubbed her eyes, and Allie read the fatigue on her face. "Let's get you to bed, Bets. You've had a long day."

Betsy tugged on her hand and pointed to the door.

"You want to go tell the horse good night?" Rick asked.

"I'll take her," Allie said when he moved toward the door. She should have guessed what Betsy wanted before Rick had.

"I'll go with you. That cougar might still be prowling around."

Allie wanted to object, but maybe he wouldn't insist on talking in front of Betsy. She took Betsy's hand, and they stepped out into the moonlight.

"I can't get over how black it is here when night falls," Allie said, giving Betsy's hand a comforting squeeze. The new dew on the ground smelled fresh.

They reached the barn, and he shoved open the sliding door. Allie and Betsy went through first. Allie watched as her daughter ran to the stall holding the newest addition to the ranch. The sores on the mare's withers were crusty, and the harsh glare from the bare bulb overhead showed every bone through her rough coat. Rick scooped some sweet feed into a bucket and offered it to the mare. She nosed the bucket and began to eat.

"Do they always make it?" Allie asked. The guy had some good qualities, even if she hated to admit it.

"Not all." His gaze met hers. "We try our best, just like we do with the kids."

"How'd you end up here, Rick?" Allie wanted to know, but she wasn't sure he'd talk about it. He seemed different tonight. More wary, and she wasn't sure why.

He leaned on the rail and watched the mare eat. "Like most of the others. I'd been in trouble—shoplifting, a stolen-car spree, fights at school. A teacher who took an interest in me heard about Elijah's ranch and talked Child Protective Services into sending me and a few other kids here. I wanted nothing to do with Elijah, but I couldn't resist a horse that he'd rescued two months before." He smiled. "Whiskers was his name, and he was five. His owner had raised him to buck in the rodeo, but he beat Whiskers to get him to do it."

Allie winced. "The rodeo where I worked was always careful not to mistreat the animals. No rodeo boss would stand for that."

He nodded. "The chute boss saw lacerations on Whiskers and disqualified him. The owner was going to sell him to the pet-food factory, but Elijah got wind of it and bought him instead. But Whiskers wouldn't let anyone near him. The day I arrived, he looked in my eyes, and I looked in his, and we each saw a soul mate. He wouldn't let me ride him that day, but by the time my time here was over, I was riding him all over the ranch. I came back every summer until I joined the army."

"And then when you got out?"

He nodded. "Elijah wrote me all ten years I was in, then offered me a job when I told him I was resigning. He needed help, and I needed a sanctuary."

Sanctuary. The word made a warm sensation well up inside Allie. That's what she and Betsy needed—a safe haven where they could grow and put down roots. Elijah seemed all about helping other kids. Why had he never sought out Allie's mom? He'd been content to take his granddaughter and let his own daughter disappear into the underbelly of the city.

She'd come here expecting some kind of ogre and discovered a man who cared about kids. The dichotomy between what he professed and how he'd acted with his own child left her shaking her head and wondering who was the real Elijah.

Maybe when he found out who she really was, he'd throw her out the way he'd tossed her mother onto the street.

8

THE OFFICE HAD THE APPEAL OF A BEAUTIFUL SNAKE. LOVELY COLORS AND form, but inspiring the same dread in Allie as coming face-to-face with a rattlesnake. She looked forward to her time in the big, comfortable room with the tin ceiling until she looked down at the way the black marks jittered their way across the ledger page.

The last two days had been placid, and she began to relax—until she realized the work she had to do. Leaving Betsy napping on her bed, she entered the office prepared to do battle but was already mentally waving a white flag.

She dropped into the cracked leather chair and squinted at the new stack of receipts in the tray. These files wouldn't be easy to whip into shape. The sun was too bright in here. She closed the blinds, but her eyes weren't ready to deal with this yet.

She pulled open the lap drawer and glanced through it. Paper clips, rubber bands, a couple of erasers and mechanical pencils, a pack of gum, and a few keys. Nothing really interesting.

Allie tried the drawer on her right and found it full of file folders. The soft gold of the manila folders made it easier to read the tabs. Glancing through them, she found them labeled with different categories of bills like electricity, food, and maintenance. The next drawer held blank envelopes and postage stamps. The top drawer on her left contained cleared check stubs and blank checks.

She moved to the last drawer and tugged on it. It refused to budge. Maybe it was stuck. Yanking on it, she could feel the lock that held it in place. Why would Elijah have a locked drawer?

The keys in the lap drawer. She pulled it open again and glanced at the keys. They all looked like door keys until she moved them around and found a smaller key hiding under a large one. It might fit. Fingering it, she thought about whether she had the right to invade a place Elijah obviously wanted to keep hidden.

Maybe she didn't have the right, but she was going to take it anyway. She wanted to get at the truth behind all her mother had told her. Selena had told at least some lies. Fitting the key into the lock, she twisted it and heard it click. The drawer slid open with a gentle tug.

Several picture albums lay in the drawer. Cracks radiated across the leather cover of the top one, and the texture was worn smooth along the opening edges. Allie lifted it out and ran her hand across it. Maybe it was a record of the kids who had passed through this place over the years.

But if it was, why lock it up?

She lifted the top cover and peeked at the first page. Old black-and-white pictures with labels under them crowded the black paper. The first picture of a little girl looked a lot like Betsy. It had to be Allie's mother.

She flipped the pages and peered into a world fifty years in the past. Her mother looked so happy and carefree sitting on the fence rail with the horses in the pasture behind her. By her late teens, the smile changed to a deadpan scowl.

The last few pages were empty and appeared to have had pictures removed. Allie started to go to the next album when she heard the front door slam and boot heels clatter along the wooden floor. She dropped the album back into the drawer. Noiselessly sliding the drawer shut, she locked it and returned the key to its place just as Rick came through the door.

Her face felt hot and moist, and when he stared at her for an extra beat, she wondered if guilt stamped her features. "Everything okay?" she asked.

He had a rope in his hand, and dust streaked his face. "Peachy. The bull got out and is chasing the horses. Any chance you could help me get him? You've got a good arm."

Pleasure surged through her at his words. Better to do something she was good at than to sit here staring at words and numbers jumping across the page. She rose and grabbed her cowboy hat. "Where is he?"

"Back pasture." He led the way out the back door.

The sunlight pierced her eyes, and she lowered her hat on her forehead. Squinting against the dust and glare, she saw the big bull on the other side of the fence. Tossing his head with its sharp horns, he pranced around the field, looking as mean as any she'd seen in the ring.

"Whooee, what a brute. You ever take him to the rodeo?" she asked.

"Nope. I wouldn't want to be responsible for him killing someone.

I told Elijah we needed to get rid of him, but he won't hear of it. The old man loves Roscoe for some reason."

"Roscoe. He seems too big and mean for a Roscoe," she said, approaching the fence.

The bull quit his posturing and erupted into action. Dirt clods flew from under his sharp hooves as he chased the mares from corner to corner. Good thing Betsy wasn't out here to see him cornering her little mare. The poor thing barely had the strength to outrun the beast. How'd he get out anyway?

She took the rope from Rick and started to climb over the fence.

"No, stay on this side of the fence," he said, reaching for her arm.

She dodged his hand and vaulted. The bull hadn't seen her yet. Looping the rope, she waited for the bovine to get closer.

"Allie, he's dangerous!" Rick climbed the fence and came to stand beside her. "Let me get us some horses, and we'll rope him from horseback."

She shook her head. "He's about to catch up with Betsy's mare." She twirled the loop through the air as she waited for the right moment. The bull moved a few steps closer, and she waited. Missing at this close range would be dangerous.

"Let me get another rope then. We need to grab him from two directions so he doesn't trample you." Rick ran off toward the barn.

Allie wasn't worried. Animals usually tried to pull away from the rope, not run toward it. The bull's head jerked toward Rick as he jogged toward the barn. He snorted and pawed the ground, then charged toward Rick. Allie shouted a warning. Rick put on a spurt of speed and dived through the barn door, and the bull followed.

"Oh no," Allie whispered. She darted toward the barn as the beast erupted from the door. Skidding to a halt, she began to back away from the snorting animal. At least the bull hadn't been inside long enough to do much damage to Rick.

The bull's head swung away from her, and she spared a glance to her right to see what had attracted its attention.

Betsy.

Betsy was in the paddock, walking toward the animal with flowers in her hands. She seemed oblivious to the danger.

Allie's muscles felt rusty and slow as she tried to run toward her daughter. Time slowed as Allie saw Betsy's dark curls bounce with each step. The sunlight gleamed on the little girl's hair, and she wore a serene smile.

"Betsy, run!" Allie had lost the loop on her rope. Coiling it again, she screamed and shouted at the bull, but the animal fixated on her daughter. Her best chance was to rope the creature before it got any closer. She'd never be able to get to Betsy before the bull did.

The beast snorted and pawed the ground, but Betsy stood still with her eyes wide. The fear cleared from her face.

Allie became aware of a faint humming sound and realized it was coming from her child. Whipping the rope around her head, Allie tossed it through the air toward the bull. In her agitation, her aim was off, and the loop fell to the ground.

The animal ignored the rope and began to trot toward Betsy.

"No!" Allie jerked the rope back toward her and began to run toward her daughter. She was too far. Her mind noticed every detail of the way Roscoe was moving, the way he tossed his horns, the way his tail switched along his back.

Betsy looked so small and defenseless. The bull would get to her first. Allie had to try the rope again.

She stopped and twirled the rope over her head. *Please Lord, make my aim true.* She barely breathed as the rope sang through the air. It didn't even touch the animal's ears as it settled over his head. She dug her boot heels into the dirt and prepared for the animal to charge away.

Then another rope dropped over the bull's neck from the other direction, and Allie saw Rick winding the rope around his palms. The animal stopped but didn't try to get away. It did nothing but stand and breathe heavily.

Still humming, Betsy put her hand out toward the beast.

"Betsy, stay away!" Allie's gaze locked with Rick's. "Help," she mouthed.

He glanced behind him at the barn door, then stepped to it and looped the rope through the door handle. "Betsy, turn and walk toward me," he said in a deep, authoritative voice.

Betsy seemed lost in her own world. Her blue eyes stayed locked on the bull's. Rick was running toward her, and her steps quickened toward the animal.

Before Rick could grab her, Betsy was directly in front of Roscoe. The animal snuffled into her small, outstretched hand. She rubbed her fingers along its head.

Then Rick had her little girl in his arms. The rope burned into Allie's palms with the force of her grip. She was afraid to relax her hold on the big bull, though it seemed to have no inclination to attack the two, who were still within reach of the sharp horns.

Holding Betsy against his chest, Rick turned and raced away. Only when they were far enough away that Roscoe couldn't reach them did Allie relax her death grip on the rope. She let it fall into the red dirt and ran toward her daughter. All she wanted was to bury her face in Betsy's hair and assure herself that the little girl was all right.

"Allie, look out!" Rick was on the other side of the fence by now with Betsy. He was gesturing at something behind her.

Allie didn't have to turn around and look to know that Roscoe had managed to free himself from Rick's rope. She ran for the fence, but she didn't think she was going to make it. Even as her hand slapped the top rail and a splinter stabbed her palm, she felt the animal's hot breath on her neck. Any minute now, she would feel his sharp horns striking her back.

Praying for speed and strength, she gripped the railing and began to scramble over. Rick shouted again. She heard her jeans tear and felt a stab against her skin, then the hot spurt of blood on her thigh, but there was no pain yet.

Then she was falling on the ground with the smell of manure in her nose and the hard taste of dirt in her mouth. Rolling onto her back, she looked up into blue sky. Her hat was gone, and the pain started, first in her thigh and then in her shoulder.

Still trying to get to her, the bull was battering at the fence and snorting. She rose up on her elbows, then sat up. "Calm down," she said. She got up and dusted off her jeans. Blood had soaked her thigh, and standing made her feel dizzy.

"Are you okay?" Rick was still carrying Betsy as he came toward her. A red stain darkened his jeans below his right knee.

Allie tried to move toward them as her knees buckled and she sank to the ground.

RICK WAS STILL SHAKING BY THE TIME ALLIE CAME AROUND. WORRY wrinkling her brow, Betsy hovered over her mother's bed, and he kept watching the little girl. She'd calmed the bull with a song.

Any other person approaching the animal like that would have been trampled.

Betsy had a touch with the beasts. Had she always been that way? He'd have to ask Allie.

Elijah came to the bedroom door. "She will be all right, *sí?*"

"I think she'll be fine," the doctor said, moving away from the bed. "She's lost a little blood, but I think it was probably more shock that made her lose consciousness. She's coming around now." He left the room, and Rick and Elijah moved to stand beside the bed.

Allie moaned and moved her head. Her eyes opened, and Rick stared down into their blue depths. Her hand went to her head, and she tried to sit up.

"Don't move," Elijah said, putting a brown, wrinkled hand on her shoulder.

"Betsy," Allie whispered.

"She's right here," Rick said, putting Betsy closer to the bed.

Allie touched Betsy's face, and the little girl climbed into the bed with her mother. Allie snuggled her close, and Betsy's eyes closed.

"The bull?" Allie asked.

"Safe in the paddock," Elijah said in a clipped voice.

Rick had carried Allie in, then went out with the stock hands to capture the bull before coming back to check on Allie. He motioned to Elijah when Allie's eyes closed again. The two men stepped into the hall. "The door to Roscoe's stall was standing open. I think someone let him out. Any idea who would do that?" he asked Elijah.

The old man hesitated. "I have not wanted to worry you, but I have had an offer for the ranch—a good offer that I turned down."

"Who would want to buy clear out here in the middle of nowhere?"

"You have heard of Stuart Ifera, *sí*? He wants to put up a fancy resort much like Lajitos."

"How would releasing the bull force you to sell?"

Elijah shrugged. "He thought the animal worth more than it is, *sí*? But perhaps it was not this man." He nodded toward Allie. "Could it be something to do with Allie?"

"I don't see how."

Elijah shrugged. "If you will keep watch over her, I will get us some coffee and return."

Rick needed to talk to her anyway. Right now might not be the best time, but it would have to do. Maybe she'd be truthful in a weakened state. He stepped back into the room. Allie was studying a picture on the wall, with a sleeping Betsy curled beside her.

"You doing okay?"

"Fine." She shifted in the bed. "I should get up."

"I wanted to ask you about something." He let his gaze bore into her like an interrogator. "Are you moving illegal Mexicans around with the rodeo, Allie?"

Her eyes widened, and her lips parted. She started to sit up but Betsy stirred, and Allie subsided against the pillow. "That's ridiculous," she said. The blue of her eyes was as cold as an ice storm. "Why would you even ask me that?"

"So you didn't know the border patrol is looking for you with questions?"

"Border patrol? Are you serious?"

Unless he was a bad judge of character, he'd swear she had no idea about this. But he'd never been able to read women. His mother could look like an angel, then grab up a razor strap and lay his back open. "So you know nothing about it?"

"No," She shook her head violently, dark curls whipping against her cheeks. "I can't believe they would suspect me."

"They're going to come looking for you. If they take you away, Betsy will have no choice but to go to your in-laws. We need to get moving on protecting her." He needed to tell her all of it. "There's more bad news, Allie."

She swallowed hard. "Okay, give it to me."

"Jon's parents have charged you with kidnapping."

Her cheeks reddened. "They can't do that!"

"Evidently because they'd sued for custody, they were able to make a case for it. We have to get married right away."

She opened her mouth, then closed it again. Swallowing, she tried again. "Thank you, Rick." The words seemed pulled out of her.

Her obvious struggle to take it all in touched him. He shrugged. "You might not thank me after you've had to live with me for a few months."

"How—how long will this marriage need to last?"

"Probably at least a year. It will take time for the adoption to go through."

Her teeth bit into her colorless lower lip. "I'm worried about Betsy. First she has a new stepdad and then she doesn't? What will that do to her?"

"What will Jon's parents do to her?" he said bluntly.

She nodded. "It's the lesser of two evils, I guess."

She looked like she'd been handed a life sentence, and Rick had to admit he felt like he was facing a stint in a Mexican prison.

9

ALLIE WAS TIRED OF LYING IN BED. THE NIGHT HAD BEEN LONG, THOUGH she'd slept fitfully. Judging by the sun, it was nine or so. She eased her arm out from under Betsy's head and sat up. She had to think.

The border patrol was looking for her. The FBI too, if she'd been charged with kidnapping.

It made no sense. How could they think she would be involved in something like trafficking in illegals? Her testimony had sent Jimmy Hernandez to jail, and that should have shown how much she hated that kind of thing. If he hadn't died there, she'd think maybe he had implicated her to take his revenge.

And Jon's parents. She felt even more betrayed. They were family. How could they do this to her?

In an instant, Rick's marriage proposal had become more pressing. Marriage really was her most promising choice. She would make it very clear to him that she would be his wife in *name only*.

She swung her feet to the floor, and her vision began to blank out. She put her head onto her knees. When the fuzziness cleared, she grabbed the bedside table for support and managed to stand. She hurt all over, and her thigh especially pained her with a burning, throbbing persistence. The bull's horns had been sharp.

"You shouldn't be out of bed, *mujercita*." Elijah spoke from the rocking chair in the corner.

Allie hadn't seen him. "Have you been here all night?" She hoped not.

"*Sí*. I wanted to be here if you needed anything."

There was something different about him that Allie couldn't put her finger on. His expression toward her seemed soft and gentle. Maybe it was because she'd been injured.

"I wouldn't turn down a new leg." She smiled then to show she was joking. "I'm fine, really. You've been so kind."

"How could I do less for my own flesh and blood?"

He knew!

The lightheadedness swept over her again, and she sank back onto the bed. "When did you know?" she whispered.

"You think I would not keep track of my daughter? I knew her rodeo name, of course, and her children. I watched her career with pride, even though she excluded me from her life."

"You threw her out!"

The compassion in his eyes didn't change. "She told you this?"

"How could you?" She swept her hand toward the window. "You

have all this and help so many other kids. But you threw your own daughter out like road litter just because she was pregnant." Her conscience smote her. Apparently he'd taken in the baby. She didn't know the whole story, and who was she to judge it?

He rose. "If this is what you believe of me, why did you come?"

"Rick was here," she said. "And I was . . . curious." More than curious, she was driven to find some piece of her family left alive. Some blood connection.

His eyes filled with moisture. "Things are never as simple as they look to the young," he said.

"Rick told me you found the baby and brought her here. M-my mother said the baby died."

"*Sí*, my Maria died. But twenty-five years later." Elijah turned to stare out the window. "My daughter could have come home anytime. I would never turn her away."

"Why did you throw her out in the first place?"

He turned then. "You must discover the truth for yourself about that."

"My mother is dead. If you don't tell me, how can I find out?"

"Listen to your heart," he said softly.

Rick knocked, and they both glanced at the door. He stepped inside. "Your lawyer called. He said he has papers ready for you to sign."

Elijah nodded. "I must go to town." His gaze locked with Allie's. "We will discuss this later, *sí*?" Without waiting for an answer, he went to the door.

Allie watched his stooped shoulders and wanted to call him back. Tell him she forgave him. But she kept her mouth shut. There was so little she knew or understood.

AFTER HE'D TENDED TO ALL THE SICK AND MISTREATED HORSES, RICK made some calls and found out what he and Allie needed to do to get a marriage license. Marriage license. Mention of it was enough to strike fear in his heart. He pocketed his list and went out to feed the livestock. The familiar scent of corn and oats calmed his agitation as the sun sank lower in the sky.

Charlie entered the barn with the other two hands, Buzz and Guinn. The older men had been with Elijah since the days when Rick first came here, and they were both wrinkled as raisins.

"You heard from Elijah? He's still not back from town." Charlie's forehead creased, and he turned to look down the dirt track to the road.

Rick glanced at his watch. "It's nearly five. He's not usually gone this long. He said he'd be back by one."

"He hasn't called either," Guinn said. "I hope the old man is okay."

"Let me call Wally. Elijah went to see him. Did he say anything about another errand?" Rick asked.

"Nope." Guinn's dark eyes held worry.

Rick looked up the lawyer's number in his phone's address book. He talked to the receptionist, then closed his phone. "He left there before lunch. She said he talked about having to get home to tend to the new kids. I'd better go out looking for him. Maybe his Jeep broke down."

"Want me to come too?" Charlie asked.

"You'd better stay with the kids. You have your cell phone on you?"

Charlie nodded. "For all the good it does in the barn. What should I do with the kids?"

"Where are they now?"

"On a hike."

"Get them to curry the horses tonight. Keep them away from the two new mares though. They're fragile, and I'm not sure they're going to make it."

"Sundown will be here in an hour or so," Charlie observed. "You think Elijah is all right?"

"He's probably fine. He should have called though." He tried Elijah's cell number but got voice mail. Not an unusual occurrence with the spotty coverage out here. Even so, Rick had a bad feeling about this. It wasn't like Elijah to be out of touch, and he was rarely gone from the ranch longer than a morning or afternoon. He'd been gone nearly seven hours.

Rick unhitched the trailer, got in his truck, called for Jem, then drove out via the dirt lane. When he turned onto the road, the two-lane highway snaked out ahead and behind him with no other vehicles in sight. Town was only a few miles away. There would be no reason for Elijah to be gone this long.

He drove all the way to town without spotting Elijah's old SUV. There was no familiar Jeep in front of the café. The lot beside the grocery store held only a dirty brown pickup and the faint scent of exhaust. Turning around, he drove back the way he'd come.

About two miles from the ranch, something glinted in the dying sun to his right. Squinting against the glare on the glass, Rick pulled to the side of the road and stuck his head out the window. Was that the tail end of a vehicle? He drove as close as he could to a stand of honey mesquite bushes, then got out with Jem. He jogged the remaining distance. Fighting his way through the thorns, he arrived at the vehicle. The battered white Jeep was Elijah's.

Why would the old man pull his Jeep this far off the road, almost hiding it? The vehicle was empty. Rick cupped his hands around his mouth and shouted Elijah's name, but only a hawk answered him. Poking his head inside the vehicle, he discovered the keys still in the ignition.

Jem whined at his feet. "Find Elijah, boy." The dog barked and trotted off into the scrub. Rick kept shouting for Elijah as he walked farther from the road and followed the dog. There was no telling which direction the old man had gone. His gut told him to walk to the mountain. Elijah loved the high spots. Maybe he'd taken a yen to commune with God out here. It wasn't unheard-of.

Small rocks scattered from under the soles of Rick's boots. Jem trotted ahead like he knew where he was going. Rick walked steadily toward the soaring peaks. Cracks carved by rainwater made the rocks look like soldiers standing at attention. He was so intent on examining the mountaintop that he almost missed the splash of red at the base.

Jem began to bark. He leaped over a mesquite bush and began to sniff and whine at the red object.

Rick leaped forward. Elijah had been wearing a red shirt. As he neared, he saw the old man curled up on his side with his back to the road as if he were sleeping. Rick reached the crumpled form and touched the old man's shoulder.

He was cold, colder than seemed possible. And very dead.

WITH HER CHIN ON BETSY'S HAIR, ALLIE ROCKED ON THE PORCH. HER daughter slept peacefully, unaware of the trauma unfolding. Tears ran down Allie's cheeks, and her nose was stuffed from crying. She'd barely known the old man, but he was her grandfather.

She and Betsy were the only ones left in her family. They were all gone—parents, sister, husband, now grandfather. Clutching Betsy tighter, she struggled to get past the profound isolation. They were still a family, though there were only two.

"You okay?" Rick dropped onto the top step of the porch and leaned against a post. Weary lines radiated from his eyes. He sat still as if surrounded by a close wall that kept everyone out.

Allie wiped her eyes with a tissue. "It's my fault, Rick." She balled up the tissue in her hand. "I shouldn't have come here. I knew someone was after me, but I thought he couldn't find me here. I put Elijah in harm's way."

Rick straightened. "It was an accident," he said gently.

Allie shook her head. "No, no, it wasn't. The man doesn't want me to find sanctuary here. He's cutting off any help."

As soon as she'd heard Elijah had died, she knew his death was about her. How could it not be?

Rick stood and walked to where she sat in the rocker. "What man? You're not making any sense."

Betsy's breathing was still deep. She wouldn't hear. Allie leaned her head against the chair back. She should have been honest right up front. Rick deserved to know why she was really running.

Allie ran her fingers through Betsy's soft hair and inhaled her little girl scent. "Someone killed my parents, sabotaged their plane. That was a year ago. I had no idea it had anything to do with me. Not at first. Then the calls started coming." She stared into the blackness outside the circle of yellow cast by the porch light.

She could still feel the horror of the moment when she realized her parents had died because of her. "The man said he would strip me of everything I loved in life. That I should count each moment a gift, because I wouldn't have many of them."

Rick's stillness shattered when he walked restlessly across the porch. "Why didn't you tell me all this right from the beginning? You're saying the plane crash wasn't accidental?"

She nodded. "That's what the police thought, but it wasn't."

"The guy sounds like a nut case."

"I was afraid you wouldn't help me, that the danger was too great."

"Maybe it was a prank." Rick's voice was gentle.

Allie shook her head. "The calls stopped for six months. I began to relax, to believe they were a bad joke. My sister was murdered a month ago. It seemed a burglary gone bad." She shuddered and hugged herself. "Then he came to my trailer and trapped me in the bathroom, stuck a knife between the door and the jamb. He taunted me, saying he'd killed my sister. I knew he'd hurt Betsy. I'd planned to bring her here anyway, so I packed my suitcase and lit out."

His glance lingered on Betsy's head. "What about Betsy? You've never said why she doesn't talk."

She kissed the top of her sleeping daughter's head. "We were watching the plane take off at the airport. Betsy saw the crash, the fire. She's not talked since. It was a horrific scene." Her voice thickened. "Neither of us will ever forget it."

"I'm sorry."

He actually sounded like he was. For a Neanderthal, he was surprisingly sweet. "Thanks."

"How do you know the plane was sabotaged?"

"He claimed responsibility for it. I told the police, and they investigated."

"Did they find any evidence?"

"They don't tell me anything."

"And your sister? He claimed to have killed her too?"

"Yes."

Rick shook his head. "I don't buy it. How do you know you're not being stalked by some jerk who gets off on trying to scare you? Maybe both events were just tragic accidents. And who is this guy anyway? What's he got against you?"

"I don't *know* who it is! And he's not just trying to scare me. He was sticking a knife through the door when he told me he'd killed Tammy."

He sighed and took out a knife and a small block of wood. "Okay. But I don't see how this relates to Elijah. The guy can't know where you are." Sitting on the porch railing, he began to whittle. "I don't know what's going to happen to the ranch. Elijah didn't have any family." Putting the knife on his knee, he stared at her. "Elijah mentioned that guy who wanted to buy the ranch. I wonder . . ."

"What?"

He looked down at his block of wood and began to work it again. "Maybe it wasn't an accident. Elijah would have had no reason to be climbing that mountain. And the truck was kind of hidden, now that I think about it."

"You just tried to tell me it was an accident." She grabbed hold of the thought though. If only his death had nothing to do with her. If only it really was caused by something else.

"Maybe I was wrong. With no family to inherit, the killer might have assumed the ranch would go to someone more willing to sell."

She should tell him the truth, but she didn't want the ranch anyway. "Betsy loves that new mare," she said. "I had hopes that she'd . . ." She looked off into the darkness where the stars were beginning to wink on.

Rick looked up at her, then back down to the wood in his hand. "That's usually how the healing starts."

"What will happen to the horses here if the ranch is sold?"

"They'd probably go to the glue factory. Or be slaughtered for cat food." His mouth twisted as if he'd bitten into something bitter.

All the horses that had already been mistreated. A sick knot formed and grew. She couldn't bear to think about it. Maybe she could buy the one they rescued. Losing the mare now would crush Betsy.

"Maybe Elijah left the ranch to you."

"I don't know what he'd planned."

Allie squinted through the darkness at his face. "I think you do. He left it to you, didn't he?"

"He'd talked about it." Rick's voice was grudging.

"You'll keep the ranch going, won't you?"

"If it's my choice." He cleared his throat. "I found out about the marriage license today," Rick said. "There's a three-day waiting period."

"Do I have to wait for state residency?" She couldn't keep the hope out of her voice.

"Nope."

There went that idea. She wet her lips. "When do you want to do it?"

"I thought we'd just go get the license tomorrow. The sooner the better, if the Siders are after you. They could come riding up here anytime. We can at least get temporary custody papers drawn up in case the adoption isn't final when they track you down."

She couldn't believe this. Her life was scattering in all directions like sand in a dust storm. The tornado was sweeping her up and plunking her down in a life she didn't recognize.

"What about Elijah? It seems heartless to make these plans before he's even buried," she said finally.

"He'd want you and Betsy taken care of," he said.

Rick was right. If there was one thing she'd recognized in Elijah, it was his great heart. Tears welled in her eyes again. "Okay," she said.

CROSSING THE STREET TO THE COURTROOM, A COLD WIND SNAKED DOWN Rick's back, but he wasn't sure if it was real or the product of his desire to turn tail and run. He'd planned never to stand before a judge like this and tie himself to a woman, not with the way his mother caused him to distrust the gender. He reminded himself that Allie wasn't anything like the woman who put the scars on his back.

He spared a sideways glance at her. She wouldn't do anything to hurt Betsy. At least she had that much going for her.

The events of the past three days had left him numb. They'd had a quiet funeral for Elijah, attended only by a few friends in the area, the ranch hands, and the kids. Tomorrow, the day after the wedding—if you could call this sterile affair a wedding—Elijah's attorney, Wally Tatum, wanted to talk about Elijah's will.

Another issue Rick wasn't looking forward to dealing with. Had Elijah left him the ranch? While he hoped the good they'd done wasn't about to end, he didn't relish the thought of shouldering the burden by himself. But what if Elijah hadn't left him the ranch? He might have willed it to the feds to be part of the national park.

Maybe he could buy it. Rick examined the thought. He'd set by a little money in his savings account. Not enough for a down payment, but the bank manager knew him and trusted him. It might work.

But what about counseling for the kids? Elijah had done most of that, and while Rick had a degree in welfare, he didn't have the experience these kids would need. Devon's face flashed in his mind. The kid was so much like Rick when at that age, it was scary. Rick wanted to do everything possible to save him.

He glanced toward the woman and child beside him. Betsy clung to Allie's hand. She'd explained to the kid that they were getting married, but did Betsy understand how weird it all was?

Rick held open the door to the courthouse, and the Siderses entered ahead of him. They wouldn't have that name much longer. The shock of realizing he would be giving his name and protection to two people he barely knew made him freeze at the door. The wind whipped past him into the building.

He pulled the door shut behind him. His boots clicked along the tile floor, echoing against the high ceiling. The sound belonged to a condemned prisoner going to the gallows. Allie still hadn't said a word. She was probably as appalled by their choice as he was.

Still, Betsy would be safe, and he could dampen some of the guilt he felt about Jon's death.

Thrusting his hand into the pocket of his jeans, he fingered the simple wedding band he'd picked up for Allie after the funeral. Since the marriage wasn't going to last long, he'd hesitated to spend the money, but it didn't seem right not to have her wear a ring.

The registrar greeted them and ushered them into the judge's chambers. The place smelled ancient and musty, though the desk and chairs looked new.

He'd known Judge Julia Thompson for years, and her eyes were bright and curious when she greeted them. "Rick, congratulations." Her gaze turned to Allie. "And this is the lucky woman. Half the gals in town are mad at you, and the rest want to know how you managed to lasso this wily character."

Allie's smile was weak. "I'm very lucky."

"You certainly are," the judge agreed. She pulled a pair of glasses from atop her head and perched them on her nose to read the documents in front of her. "Just a civil ceremony? I must say I'm surprised, Rick. I would have thought you'd be married in the church."

Rick hadn't even told his pastor what he was doing. Grady would try to talk him out of it. "We were in a hurry," he said, ignoring the speculation in her smile. Let her think what she wanted. He didn't owe anyone an explanation.

Her expression sobered. "I'm sorry about Elijah." She riffled through some papers and pulled out a small book. "Let's get on with this, shall we?"

"Fine," Allie said. Her voice trembled, and she swayed on her feet. Her complexion was pasty.

"Are you both entering this agreement of your own free will?"

"Yes," Rick and Allie said in unison.

"Good." The judge turned to Rick first. "Rick, will you have this woman to be your wedded wife, to love her, comfort her, honor and keep her, and forsaking all others, keep you only unto her, for so long as you both shall live?"

He hadn't realized that forever promise would be in a civil ceremony. It felt wrong as a Christian to deliberately lie. If he made this promise, he'd have to keep it. He realized his silence had to look bad, but he needed to think, to decide. Glancing at Allie, he saw her go even paler.

Jon's face came to mind, so earnest and good. The man had believed in Rick even when he had no reason to. How could Rick not give his life for him?

"I will," he said, realizing, with a sick feeling in the pit of his stomach, what he'd just promised.

"Allie, will you have this man to be your wedded husband, to love him, comfort him, honor and keep him, and forsaking all others, keep you only unto him, so long as you both shall live?"

Rick could see the convulsive movement of Allie's throat as she swallowed hard. For just a moment he hoped she'd say she couldn't go through with it. Then he would be relieved of his responsibility.

"I will," she said in a firm voice.

"Rick, take your bride's hand."

When his fingers closed around Allie's hand, his eyebrows went up at how cold it was. He saw the fear in her eyes and gave her hand a reassuring squeeze.

The judge's no-nonsense tone droned on. "Take hands and repeat after me: I, Rick, take you, Allie, to be my wedded wife, to have and to hold, for better for worse, for richer for poorer, to love and to cherish, from this day forward."

To cherish. An old-fashioned word. Rick tried to remember if he'd ever cherished anything. He'd once loved whiskey, and he loved God—but cherish? What did it really mean?

"Rick?" the judge prodded.

"Sorry." Rick repeated the vows. He listened while Allie did the same.

"Do you have a ring for the bride?"

Rick nodded and dug the ring out of his pocket. Allie smiled for the first time since they'd entered the judge's chambers. She held out her hand to Betsy, and the little girl handed her a ring too. When had she gotten it? And how did she get the money?

Her hand had warmed up some, and he slipped the ring past her knuckles. When she tried to do the same to him, the ring got stuck after the first knuckle.

"Sorry," she whispered. "Jon wasn't as big as you."

This had been the ring Jon wore? The magnitude of what Rick was doing nearly made his knees buckle. This was *Jon's* wife he was promising to care for. And his daughter. Rick curled his fingers around the ring to keep it safe. Jon had been like a brother, and Rick remembered something in the Bible about a man's brothers being responsible for his wife.

"I'll get it sized," he said.

She nodded, and tears glimmered in her eyes. Did she remember the ceremony with Jon? She had to feel the lack of this one in comparison. He should have thought about what a woman needed in a wedding. He was an idiot.

"Inasmuch as Rick and Allie have consented together in wedlock and have witnessed the same before this company, and pledged their vows to each other, by the authority vested in me by the State of Texas, I now pronounce you husband and wife." The judge smiled. "You may now kiss your bride."

Rick put his hands on her shoulders and deposited a quick peck on her lips. They felt as soft as they looked. Her breath smelled minty and fresh, and it was with reluctance that he let his hands fall back to his sides.

His wife. He was a married man with all the responsibilities and trials of partnership. Not just for a year or two, but forever.

10

ALLIE FINGERED THE RING ON HER HAND. JON HAD BEEN GONE NEARLY TWO years, and the metal felt strange on a hand she usually kept bare. It had been all she could do to choke out her responses in the ceremony. Memories of her wedding to Jon nearly brought her to tears. For Betsy's sake, she managed to hold it together.

She sat on the porch, watching the glimmer of stars and breathing in the scent of creosote bushes, a pungent fragrance she loved. Betsy sat on her lap. Allie had tried to call Yolanda, but she'd been dumped into her voice mail. Not that Yo would be happy to hear the news, but Allie felt a need to share this event in her life with her best friend.

The kids were playing Yahtzee inside, and the sound of their voices and the rattle of dice on the table comforted her. Life would get back to normal, eventually.

Car lights winked and grew as a vehicle approached the ranch house. The engine cut off, and the interior lights of the car flickered on as a man got out. The bright yard light revealed a young man who looked like a throwback to the days of Jesse James. His thick mustache appeared waxed, and it curled up on the ends. His jeans were pressed, and his boots glinted in the light.

The screen door banged, and Allie jumped. Strangers always made her uneasy, and this guy looked dangerous.

Rick stepped onto the porch. "Wally. I didn't expect you tonight."

"Howdy, Rick," the man said. "I know you were coming in tomorrow, but I'm going to have to leave town for a few days, and I thought maybe we could handle this tonight."

"We can go to the office."

Wally came up the steps and nodded to Allie. "Is this little lady Allie Siders?"

"I'm Allie," she said. Let Rick announce the marriage if he wanted. Who was this guy? Rick was treating him with respect, and he seemed to know something about the ranch.

"Since Rick hasn't introduced us, I'd best do it myself. I'm Wally Tatum, Elijah's attorney. I'm sorry I missed Elijah's funeral. My wife was sick, and I had child-care duty." His smile became fixed. "You'll need to sit in on this meeting too, ma'am."

Allie saw Rick stiffen. "It has nothing to do with me," she said.

"Yes, ma'am, it does. Elijah changed some things in his will the day he died."

"What?" Allie and Rick spoke at the same time.

Wally's white teeth flashed beneath his mustache. "There was no holding Elijah back when he made up his mind about something." He nodded to the swing. "Mind if I sit a spell?"

Rick folded his arms across his chest. "What are you talking about?"

Allie didn't want to know. A vortex yawned above her, like a great Texas twister about to suck her into something deadly. She kept her mouth shut. Get this over with and get to her room. Elijah couldn't have left her much. He didn't even know her.

The swing creaked as Wally settled into it. He opened his briefcase and withdrew a sheaf of papers. "As you know, this ranch and the kids who have come through here have been Elijah's life for the past forty years."

"I know that better than anyone," Rick said. "I was a throwaway kid myself and came here when I was fifteen."

"Elijah could have bust his buttons over you," Wally said. "Until this recent change, he'd left the ranch to you. I'm only mentioning that because he wanted you to know how much he loved you. But he realized he couldn't do that—not when he has family who should rightly inherit."

"Family?" Rick asked slowly. "What family?"

Allie hadn't meant for Rick to find out the truth this way. Not blindsided. He'd poured so much of his life into this place, it didn't seem right to strip it away at the last minute. She'd refuse the bequest, let Rick have it.

Wally's gaze darted between them. "Elijah has left everything he owns to Betsy, his great-granddaughter."

Rick inhaled sharply, but she held her breath. It couldn't be. Why would he do that? Betsy was too young, and the responsibility would fall on Allie, who knew nothing about running a ranch for kids. Horses, she knew, but that was where her work began and ended.

"You're his granddaughter?" Rick turned to look at Allie.

She nodded, but she couldn't push any words past the constriction in her chest. The betrayal on Rick's face wounded her. Did he think she'd done this deliberately?

"I don't want it."

"Yes, ma'am, but he left it to Betsy," Wally pointed out.

"She's too young. I'm refusing it for her."

Rick finally seemed to rouse from his stupor. "You don't have that right."

"I know this is a shock, ma'am. Let it settle a spell. Elijah did the right thing." Wally rose, and his spurs jingled as he walked toward the steps. "I have some documents for you to sign in my office. Stop by at your convenience and my secretary can handle everything. The adoption papers are ready too."

Rick followed him to the edge of the porch. "Thanks for coming out," he said, his voice distant.

Wally touched his hat. "I didn't want there to be any misunderstandings about the future of the ranch. I'll be in touch."

Neither of them spoke as the sound of the car's tires on the dirt and gravel faded away. Allie peeked at Rick's face and gulped when she saw his thunderous expression.

"You liar. You came here knowing Elijah was your grandfather. Why bother with marrying me? You'd have a stable home here for Betsy, and he would have helped you keep custody."

Did he think she would have tied herself to him if she'd had any other choice? "I didn't plan to tell him."

He laughed, a short bark of derision. "Yeah, right. One look at you and he had to know. He kept track of his daughter. Did you really think he wouldn't realize?"

"He guessed," she admitted. "I was surprised at his welcome. I thought he would throw me out." She clutched her cold hands together. Dredging up some anger from the depths, she fired back at him. "Is that why you really married me? Because you knew he'd leave us the ranch? If you knew he kept track of her, you surely knew her name and that I was her daughter."

"I didn't know what he'd planned—or that you were his grand-daughter."

"Really? Then why were you in such a hurry to do this before you talked to the lawyer? Did you think if I had any other way out, I wouldn't do it? And besides, *you* pointed out my resemblance to Maria."

"I was trying to help you—and Elijah."

They were glaring at one another like two kids quarreling over the last piece of candy in the dish. Allie leaned her head against the back of the rocker. The day had sapped every bit of her ability to cope. "I'm sorry I said that," she said. "If there's one thing I know, it's that you loved Elijah like a father. Betsy having the ranch doesn't change much of anything as far as Jon's parents are concerned. They'd want her even more if they knew the ranch came with her."

He pulled out his knife and a piece of wood. The shavings flew as he applied himself to the whittling with a vengeance. "You've kept too many secrets from me, Allie. If we're going to stay married, we have to keep communication open."

Stay married? She eyed him. "It's only for a year or so. We can stand it for that long."

He opened his mouth, then closed it again. She wasn't quite sure what the expression on his face meant, and she was afraid to ask him.

Betsy's dead weight made Allie struggle to stand. "I think I'll put her to bed."

"Let me get the door." He strode to the door and opened it. "She's pretty big for you to carry all the way upstairs. Let me take her." He scooped Betsy out of her arms and went ahead of Allie.

She climbed the steps behind them. Betsy stirred but didn't awaken. It had been a busy day for her too. At the top of the stairs, Allie darted around Rick into the bedroom and pulled back the covers on Betsy's bed. He laid her gently on the mattress and pulled the covers around her. They both stood looking down at the little girl as the moon gilded her hair and illuminated the sweet curve of her round cheeks.

"She's worth anything we have to do to protect her," Rick said.

He almost sounded like he was trying to convince himself. Allie nodded without saying anything. His masculine presence over-whelmed the room. Her mouth went dry when he turned to her and put his big hands on her shoulders. Surely he didn't expect them to have a normal marriage.

The heat of his hands soaked through her blouse, and she couldn't look away from the intensity of his gaze. The howl of a coyote echoed from the hills, and the sound broke the magnetic pull of his eyes.

She stepped away, and his hands fell to his sides. "Thanks for bring-ing her up to bed."

He cleared his throat but didn't move away. "I just wanted to tell you I meant what I promised in the judge's chambers."

Which part? Allie's thoughts flew back to what Rick had said on the porch. That whole thing about staying married. "Thank you," she managed lamely. She didn't want to explore that subject, especially not here in her bedroom. His gaze still mesmerized her, and she forced herself to look away. "Good night."

"'Night." He moved to the door and pulled it shut behind him.

The strength ran out of her legs, and she sat heavily on her bed.

Did he mean their plan to divorce in a year was off? He couldn't just make that determination without her agreement. She didn't want to live her life with a man who despised her. Good thing she could divorce him even if he didn't want it.

Her hands shook.

Why did he unnerve her? He was just a stranger. But he didn't feel like it. She believed his eyes could see right inside her soul. And the way he cared for her and Betsy was like coming home. How could her life have spiraled so far out of control? Her identity as Jon's wife seemed to be slipping away right now. She was living someone else's life.

She stood and went to the door. Peeking out, she listened to the sounds of the kids downstairs playing card games. She could probably slip down the stairs and get to the library without being seen. She needed to hear Yo's voice.

She was so alone here. No one else knew everything she'd gone through. Rick still looked at her with suspicious eyes, and she felt like an outsider. Scrubbing the moisture from her cheeks, she lifted her head. Whining wasn't allowed in her life. She could handle this, especially if she could talk to Yo.

Easing through the door, she tiptoed to the stairs and moved noiselessly down to the first floor. Darting toward the library, she caught a glimpse of Rick's back, where he stood watching the kids. Emilio slapped his hand on the table and crowed his delight about winning. In the bedlam, she hoped no one heard the squeak of the door opening.

She just couldn't face Rick right now.

The lock snicked home, and she went to the phone. Listening to the dial tone, she wondered how upset Yolanda would be to hear she'd married a stranger. The phone seemed to ring forever. It was Yo's cell number, so maybe she was in a mall or something. Glancing at the clock on the desk, Allie realized it was too late for shopping. Maybe she'd left it at home.

Then a click came finally. "Hello." It wasn't Yolanda's voice.

"Oh, I'm sorry. I must have the wrong number."

"Allie, that you?"

Allie realized the voice was that of Yolanda's mother. "Mrs. Fleming? Yes, it's me. Is Yo around?"

A long pause hissed back at her. "You don't know?"

"Know what?" Something in the woman's voice made Allie clutch the phone and sink into the chair.

"My Yo, he killed her. She's dead, Allie." The woman's voice rose in a sob.

Allie's hand spasmed around the phone. "What are you saying?" she whispered. Dead? Yo couldn't be dead.

"Stabbed, she was stabbed." The woman's cries grew louder, near hysteria.

Not Yo, oh please God, not Yo.

Allie closed her eyes. She couldn't force any words past her frozen lips. Yo's laughing face flashed through her memory. She was going to win the barrel race this year. It wasn't fair.

"She called me, said the man said she was next. He say that you love her too much for him to let her live. I send her father to her house, but it is too late. The man, he get there first." Mrs. Fleming was wailing, her sobs piercing Allie's heart as well as her ears.

Allie's tears felt hot with guilt. "I'm so sorry," she whispered. "When did this happen?"

Mrs. Fleming's sobs tapered off. "Last night. Wait, wait, my husband, he want to talk to you."

Mr. Fleming was a big African-American truck driver who had met the pretty Mexican waitress and married her thirty-eight years ago. He'd always made Allie feel like part of the family. He probably hated her now.

"Allie? Stay there, girl. Don't come home."

"Mr. Fleming," she choked. "I'm so sorry. I loved Yo so much."

"I know, Allie, I know. And she loved you. This is not your fault, you hear? Don't try making it about you. Whoever he is, it was his evil that killed my baby, not you." His voice thickened and broke. "You stay put. Don't make Yo die in vain."

"I—I can't talk. I'll call you tomorrow." Allie clicked off the phone and buried her face in her hands. No matter what Mr. Fleming said, Yo wouldn't have died if it wasn't for Allie. He had taken everyone she loved.

Everyone but Betsy.

Allie shuddered, then jumped when someone rattled at the door. Rick's voice came from the other side. "Allie, are you in there?"

She scrubbed at her face and rushed to unlock the door. It opened as soon as she clicked the lock, and she hurtled into Rick's arms, not stopping to question why she needed his comfort, his strength.

"She's dead," she sobbed against his denim shirt.

His arms came around her, and a big hand smoothed the back of her head. "Who's dead?"

His shirt muffled her words. "My friend Yolanda. He's taking everyone I love." She clutched his shirt in both fists. "She can't be gone."

The scent of creosote clung to his clothing. He must have been clearing some of the bush out of the yard this afternoon. She hadn't been close enough to him to smell it before this. The aroma always made her think of summer rides across the desert with Jon, and the spring rains in El Paso that brought the pungent scent to life. It reminded her of sage and cactus, roasted marshmallows around the campfire.

And love later in the tent. But now there was only death all around her.

The thought made her cheeks burn, and she pulled away, swiping the back of her hand across her cheeks. "Sorry," she gulped.

Rick's hands moved to her shoulders, and he didn't let go. "So he doesn't know where you are. That should set your mind at ease that Elijah wasn't killed by him."

Allie hadn't thought of Elijah. "Then who killed him?"

"I'm going to check out this developer guy, the one who wanted to buy the ranch." He finally dropped his hands. "But we might be barking up the wrong tree. It might have been an accident."

"Maybe." Allie had found that most things in her life were interconnected. This probably was too, once they figured it out. "I should call the police in El Paso, tell them what Yo's dad said."

"I'm sure he's already talked to them. They'll be looking for you and might make you go back as a material witness. We can't risk that. You and Betsy are safe here." His eyes narrowed, and his mouth took on a determined pinch.

Allie was suddenly very glad he was on her side. Rick wouldn't let anything happen to her or Betsy.

Fatigue and grief weighed her down. This day seemed like it would never end. She told Rick good night and headed to her room. Walking back upstairs, she twisted the ring on her finger. She was a married woman.

One in name only. Was there anything more pathetic?

11

THE HOUSE WAS QUIET EXCEPT FOR THE TICKING OF THE GRANDFATHER clock in the hall. Rick sat in the leather desk chair with his feet propped on the desk. He still hadn't been able to take in the reality that Allie was Elijah's granddaughter. Elijah hadn't trusted him with the information, and the betrayal left some cuts that would take time to heal.

And Allie. Rick should have put two and two together when he saw the resemblance between her and Maria. Had she always planned to come in here and worm her way into Elijah's graces?

He decided to call Brendan again. His friend might have found some new information. The stakes had just escalated. If someone was coming after Allie and Betsy, he couldn't wait for the guy to show up.

It was after midnight on the East Coast, but he knew Brendan would be up working anyway. He listened to the ringing with one ear and to the noises outside with the other. Nothing stirred, a good sign.

There was a click on the line, then Brendan's voice. "Rick, you know how late it is? What if I were all toasty in bed?"

"You never get to bed before two," Rick said. He was in no mood for small talk. "Anything new about Allie?"

"Oh yeah, I meant to call you. We had a crisis pop up that we've been scrambling to fix."

The old familiar tug of interest waylaid Rick, but he squelched it. "Spill it."

"The crisis or the information about your woman?"

"She's not my woman. She's my . . . wife."

Brendan whistled. "Talk about a whirlwind courtship."

If Brendan only knew. Rick could hardly believe it himself. "Look, things are happening here. Elijah is dead, and someone is out to get Allie and Betsy."

"The FBI is looking at her now, buddy, and not just for kidnapping. They suspect her of being the ringleader of the immigrant smuggling ring."

The ringleader? Rick pinched the bridge of his nose. "It's a crock, buddy. No way." He told Brendan about the man who had killed Yolanda Fleming, and the calls Allie had gotten. "Could this guy have planted evidence?"

"Maybe. According to my sources, immigration was tipped off about the ring using the rodeo for a front. And here's the funny thing. Your woman testified against someone doing this about a year and a half ago. Because of her testimony, he got sent to jail. Then here we find she was involved all along. I gotta say, I wonder if they were lovers or something. Maybe he dumped her and she turned him in."

"She's not the type," Rick said. He hoped that was true, but what did he really know of her? "How'd they become suspicious of Allie now?"

"Someone faxed pictures of a bunch of Mexicans climbing out of the back of a pickup. The license plates were Allie's. Does she have an old Ford truck—green?"

"Yeah. Could the pictures be doctored? Don't you think this sounds suspicious, Brendan? Maybe it's revenge for sending the king-pin to jail."

"I thought that too. But the guy who went to prison—Jimmy Hernandez—is dead. He got caught up in a prison riot about a year ago and was stabbed."

"So it couldn't be him. Anything else?"

"The other thing they have on her is that bank account records show deposits of money in and out of her account. Like a quarter of a million dollars."

Rick leaned back and rubbed his eyes, his stomach taking a nose-dive. He should have known not to trust her. He was such a patsy. "She showed up here penniless."

"I'm just saying. You check out her purse to see if she really had no money? Women can lie while they're seducing you, buddy. I gotta say I'm shocked you fell for her line."

"She's Jon's widow."

"Look, when are you going to let go of that guilt?"

Rick's jaw clenched down in a painful spasm. "I killed him, Brendan. If I hadn't been drunk . . . I rushed in when I should have known better, and he came in after me. I think he knew how unlikely it was that he'd walk out again." Brendan was the only one who knew, and only because he'd been there.

"When was the last time you took a drink?" Brendan's voice was soft.

"Two years." Rick clipped his words. What difference did it make? All the sobriety in the world couldn't restore Jon to life.

"So live your life in the present. It's easier that way."

Rick knew better than to try to argue with Brendan. "Thanks for the help. You'd better get to bed."

"I've got hours of paperwork ahead of me yet."

Rick closed his phone. The most damning evidence would be money in her account. How did he check that out? If she hadn't just been through such a trauma, he'd march upstairs and drag her from her bed to question her.

Had he been completely duped?

A sound caught his ear, and he stood to look out the window. A pinprick of light danced and bobbed through the trees. Someone was out there. As far as he knew, everyone who belonged on the ranch was tucked inside.

Rick rushed to the door, grabbing a flashlight on his way. Jem met him on the porch and whined. "Quiet, boy," he whispered. "Come with me." He went across the yard and stepped into the coolness of the trees.

A twig snapped somewhere to his right, and he followed the faint noise. Creeping through the dark, he didn't dare flip on the light. That would only alert whoever it was to being spotted. He knew this ranch like the back of his hand, though, and didn't really need the light.

He skirted a big boulder and looked around to see a line of dark shapes moving low and fast toward the top of the hill. Now was the time to flip on his light. He aimed the flashlight at the nearest figure and pressed the soft button. The beam of light zeroed in on the face of a Hispanic man. He shouted in Spanish, and the rest of the people turned to run. He saw three men and two women carrying children. They streamed up the hill and disappeared.

Illegal immigrants, he was sure of it. And the first he'd seen since coming to work here. He didn't want to believe Allie had anything to do with this, but it sure fit.

It was too late and too dark to catch those poor souls tonight. He'd put in a call to the border patrol, but that was the best he could do.

And tomorrow he and Allie would have a talk.

ALLIE'S EYES WERE BLURRY, AND HER HEAD ACHED. SHE STOOD ON THE first rung of the corral fence and watched Emilio direct the teenagers on how to groom the horses. A dust storm was supposed to hit late today, but right now only a light breeze lifted her hair away from her face and filled her nose with the good fragrances of horse and hay.

Rick had been acting weird all morning, and she was tired of dancing around his strange glances. What was bothering him? At first she thought he'd been wondering how she was reacting to the news of Yolanda's death, but it wasn't that. There was no sympathy in his eyes, only speculation, and maybe even a pointed suspicion.

She'd been careful not to be alone with him. Finding out what was biting him was less urgent than avoiding any discussion of a real marriage. Surely he couldn't think she was keeping anything from him. Everything was out in the open now.

Emilio approached the fence, pushed his hat back off his forehead, then leaned against a post. "The kids are doing a pretty good job," he said. "I'm amazed at how well they've taken to ranch life."

Allie nodded. "Even Latoya is acting like a normal kid. She hasn't even been wearing makeup, let alone unbuttoning her blouse to the navel."

Emilio's eyes sobered. "She had a pretty rough go of it. Her mother sold her to the first man when she was ten."

Allie put her hand over her mouth. "I had no idea. That poor kid." Her gaze traveled to the other girl. "What about Fern?"

"Her parents and younger brother were killed in a boating accident in the Gulf. She's been in foster care for three years. She and her mother were really close, and the trauma of her whole family being wiped out about destroyed her." He gestured to the horses and kids. "She's really taken to that colt. I've seen a few smiles."

Fern and Allie shared the same heartache. If Allie had been that young, maybe she'd be as downtrodden as the girl. Allie vowed to do whatever she could to help the teenager regain goals and focus.

Allie was sure the boys' stories were equally horrific, but she couldn't face hearing them right now. Not with her own life weighing her down. "How'd you get into working with these kids?" she asked. "Have you done it long?"

His dark eyes flickered, then danced away, but not before she saw a shutter come down. "Just happened to fall into it," he said. "I'm big enough to scare some sense into them. No big story." He nodded toward the Rio Grande. "I thought I saw some guys on top of the hill. You ever get illegal aliens coming across?"

"Not while I've been here. I imagine it could be a problem though. I haven't even seen any border patrol around. Immigrants from Mexico could get on a boat and float down the river until they found a good landing spot."

"There aren't that many good places to land. A lot of the way is blocked by sheer cliffs that are impossible to climb. The patrol probably chooses to focus on the easiest spots."

His tone was full of assurance, and she gave him a curious stare. "You seem to know a lot about it."

Taking a tin from his pocket, he took out a pinch of snuff and stuffed it in his cheek. "Makes sense."

He must not want to talk about his past at all. Maybe it was too painful. The sun glared down from the sky, and she adjusted her cowboy hat to shade her eyes. "Betsy loves that new horse. We haven't named her. I keep hoping she'll start talking and name the mare herself."

"Don't give up on that idea. She just might. I saw her come out first thing this morning to feed her. She's hardly left the mare's side."

Allie nodded, her gaze on her daughter. Betsy was blooming here. Even though she still wasn't talking, she was smiling more as she ran and played in the barnyard. The animals flocked around her, from the kittens to Jem and the horses. Even the cattle watched her when she climbed up to sit on the fence.

A shadow blocked the sun from her eyes, and she squinted up into Rick's face.

"I thought we might run to town and file those adoption papers," he said.

She straightened. "Let me get Betsy." Without waiting for his answer, she climbed the fence and went to where her daughter stood currying the mangy mare. Fern was helping.

Poor thing. The mare's cuts were starting to heal, but all the bones still stuck out under the rough coat. "Betsy, let's go to town for a while."

Betsy thrust out her lower lip, and she fingered the buttons on her blue blouse.

"I'll watch her, Mrs. Bailey." Fern's voice was almost inaudible, and she ducked her head without looking Allie in the eye. "I like Betsy. She's the age of my little brother . . ."

"I'd rather she come with me." Panic dried into a bad taste in her mouth. Someone had killed Yolanda. That same someone might find them here.

Betsy tugged on her mother's arm and shook her head, tears filling her eyes. She pointed to the horse and then to Fern.

Allie was such a sucker for Betsy's entreaties. Rick assured her they were safe here. How could anyone find them clear out here? She'd left no trail. Still, someone had killed Elijah, even though the sheriff seemed to think it was an accident. "She'd better come with me. Why don't you come too, Fern?"

The girl's face lit with pleasure. "To town with you?"

"Sure. We'll stop and get an ice cream soda at the drugstore. We won't be gone long."

Fern took Betsy's hand, and the girls followed Allie. Sorrow welled in her throat, choking her. If only she'd let Yolanda come with her.

She rejoined Rick and Emilio. "Betsy wants to stay with Fern, but I don't think it's safe to leave her. I thought she could come with us."

"Sure," Emilio said. "Fern is good with kids."

His gaze toward Allie was intense and probing. Surely he wasn't interested in her, was he? She was a married woman now. Reaching up to tuck a strand of hair behind her ear, she made sure to turn toward him so he would see her new ring.

Rick still hadn't spoken. He headed toward the truck, and Allie followed with the girls. At the cab's door, she stopped and spoke too softly for the girls to hear. "Marriage must not agree with you. You're a bear this morning." She flashed her most winning smile, hoping to coax him out of whatever had brought this on.

He gave her a cold glare. "Let's not talk about it now. I want to get this adoption paperwork done first. We can sign the papers for the ranch, too."

Allie tried to think of anything she'd done to warrant this gruff treatment, but came up blank. He'd been so solicitous and caring last night when he heard the news about Yolanda. Let him stew. She'd done nothing to incur his wrath. And even if she had, what right did he have to act like an enraged rattlesnake?

She let the girls sit between them. They made the trip to town in a silence that seemed to thicken with every passing mile. Allie tried to distract herself with praying for Yolanda's family, but she found it hard to focus when every time she glanced Rick's way he was still glowering.

It was going to be a long year.

The attorney's secretary had the papers ready for them to sign. Allie's signature looked a little shaky, but Rick scrawled his name in bold, confident strokes. His determination to help her daughter made her more willing to overlook his bad mood.

The wind had picked up by the time they stepped back out into the sunshine. A few tumbleweeds lay nestled against the truck tires, and tiny bits of sand stung Allie's cheeks as the two of them hurried to the shelter of the drugstore. Rick had her by the arm to steady her. He opened the door, then shut it behind her.

The aroma of cheeseburgers and French fries, of sock hops and high school dates, washed over her. Black-and-white tiles on the floor and red vinyl booths made the place look like a set from the movie *Grease*. Rick led the way to the booth at the back.

"A jukebox," Fern breathed in a reverent tone.

"Here. Pick out some music." Rick dug a handful of coins from his pocket and dropped them into her cupped palms.

Fern and Betsy went to pick out the music. Allie folded her hands together to keep them from shaking. "Okay, let's have it. I'm tired of tiptoeing around your mood. If you've got a complaint, spill it."

Rick's icy and appraising eyes belonged to a stranger. Where was the warmth that he showed last night? For a few moments she thought he might refuse to speak.

Then he leaned against the seat. "I talked to my friend yesterday, the one who's in intelligence."

"So? I have nothing to hide."

"He had more details about your part in the moving of illegal aliens."

"I didn't have any part in that other than testifying."

"Then where did you get all the money?"

"What money?" Allie's gaze went to her bag containing exactly ten dollars and fifteen cents.

"A quarter of a million dollars has moved through your account in the last six months."

Allie gasped and put her hand over her mouth. "That's impossible." But was it? She never looked at her bank statements. They were too hard to make out. The only way she knew what she had in the bank at any given time was to run through the ATM and check her balance.

"I see you're suddenly remembering," Rick said. "Your face says it all."

"No, you don't understand," she protested. "I never know what's in my account. I—I can't read the statements."

He frowned then. "What are you talking about?"

She looked away from his intense gaze. "I have Scotopic Sensitivity

Syndrome. Some people call it Irlen Syndrome. It's really hard for me to read things on white paper. The letters jump and move around. So I don't read my statement."

"I've never heard of it."

From his tone, she guessed he thought she was lying. "Look it up," she snapped. "That's why I have to make sure I wear sunglasses in the glare, or a hat. My eyes can't handle glare."

The ice in his eyes thawed slightly. "I still find it hard to believe you don't know what's in your account."

She kept her gaze focused on her hands, tightly clenched in her lap. "Jon always handled the banking. Since his death, everything like that has been . . . difficult."

"Why didn't you ask Yolanda for help?"

She bristled at his persistent skepticism. "I wanted to stand on my own two feet. If Yo knew how tight things were, she'd insist on helping me. I couldn't accept that."

"Can you explain how so much money could be in your account? Did anyone else have access to it?"

She grabbed her purse and upended it. A bottle of nail polish rolled out, a comb, a lipstick clattered to the table, then her wallet plopped on the surface. Picking it up, she threw it at him. "Take a look. Ten dollars and some change."

He recoiled, but she dug in her purse again and brought out her checkbook. "Here, you want to see how incompetent I am? Make sure I'm a loser?" Her voice rose, and she saw the girls look toward her, so she gathered her self-control. "Here, take a look."

She knew what he would see. Chicken scratches scrawling their way across the page, strikeouts, messy entries that made no sense. Falling silent, sadness replaced the anger. "I'm not a criminal, Rick."

His hand closed around the checkbook. "I'm sorry, Allie. I believe you. If someone's messing with your account, we need to find out who."

Her gaze came up at the softening of his voice. Maybe he recognized the ring of truth. "I've never given anyone the number. Unless it's the guy who killed Yo and my family. Maybe he's trying to make me look guilty of something. That smuggling thing, maybe."

"He's doing a pretty good job of it." Rick laid the checkbook next to her other things. "The FBI will track you down in short order."

"I didn't leave a trail," she said. "No credit cards, nothing."

"Did you know you were under suspicion when you left El Paso?"

"I had no idea." She began to return the items to her purse.

"What about this Jimmy Hernandez that you testified against? How did that happen?"

Allie sighed. It was an old story, and she was sick of it. Everyone seemed to think it had some bearing on her present circumstances, and she knew it didn't. "He worked with me. He was in charge of getting stock handlers. I noticed he seemed to have a lot of men milling around who couldn't speak English, but I didn't think much about it at first. It's not unusual, you know? I was on my way to the grocery store one night and noticed him pull off onto a deserted road in front of me. He had a load of workers in his truck. It was long after hours, so I decided to circle back and see what he was doing. I parked my pickup along the road and walked back. The workers were all transferring to a van. The next day I started paying attention and noticed none of the workers Jimmy used were the same day to day. I got suspicious and told the police. A couple of months later he was arrested, and I was called to testify when the trial came up."

Rick's scowl turned thoughtful. "So he could be behind it if you sent him to prison."

"They had a lot more on him than my testimony."

"But you turned him in."

She held out her hands, palms up. "They were already suspicious."

"He might not know that."

This was getting them nowhere. Allie shook her head. "Look, he died in prison during a riot. It's not him."

"If you had nothing to do with any illegal alien traffic, then some-one is out to get you."

Allie wanted to slap her forehead. "That's what I've been trying to tell you. You're not listening."

"I'm listening now," he said. "Who hates you?"

Allie sighed. "Everyone asks that, and I just don't know." She could see he didn't believe she didn't know who was after her. But she could feel a noose tightening around her neck.

12

THE WIND HOWLED AND RAGED OUTSIDE THE WINDOW LIKE A PACK OF wolves baying for entrance. Allie stirred the pot of chili and watched the eddies of sand dance in the glow of sunset.

"Smells good." Charlie stood with his thumbs hooked in his pockets. The expression in his eyes said he was talking about her and not the chili. He looked washed-out.

Allie hid her smile. Rick seemed to barely notice how she looked, let alone how she smelled. "It'll be ready in a few minutes. You okay? You look a little pale."

He rubbed his forehead. "Just a headache." He smiled and held out a small, velvet box.

"What's this?" Allie took the box and opened it. A diamond eternity necklace lay nestled on the satin. The diamonds circling the pendant made her blink. "Charlie, it's beautiful. Who's it for?"

"You." His smile was shy.

Allie caught her breath. "Oh no, Charlie, I can't accept something so expensive." In her hand, the little box closed with a snap. She pressed it back into his hand. "I'm sorry."

"It's true, isn't it?"

"What is?"

He stuffed the box into the pocket of his jeans. "Someone in town said you and Rick got hitched."

"It's true."

He blinked rapidly, and his eyes looked moist. "You married Rick? You just got here."

"He knew my first husband." She knew it sounded lame.

"That's no reason to get married." Charlie's lips trembled like he wanted to cry. He pressed them together like he suddenly remembered he was a grown-up.

"Well, we did." She clamped her teeth against any explanation. It wasn't like Charlie was a good friend or anything. He was just disappointed not to make his conquest. He was on his way to growing up, and she'd just given him a valuable lesson in not counting chickens.

"Probably for Betsy," he mumbled, then turned and shuffled away.

If only she had someone she could really talk to here. Or anywhere, for that matter. There was no one left to her now, no one to help her see the path through the trees. Had she even done the right thing? But Jon had trusted Rick. Surely she could do the same.

Rick just seemed so sure of himself. She was anything but. Part of her insecurity came from the trouble she had with light, and part of it was the life she'd led—that of a nomad. The rodeo was her family, but the personnel often changed with every event. She'd learned to hide behind a smile and her work.

The thump of Rick's boots on the floor had become familiar, and she glanced up as he came into the kitchen. The expression on his face told her he had more questions.

"I've been thinking about who could be targeting you," he said, pulling out a chair from the table and sitting down. "I wonder if it could be someone who has something against Jon."

"Against Jon?" Allie shook her head. "Everyone liked him."

"Not everyone," Rick said.

Allie joined him at the table. "What do you mean? He was like a pied piper. At the sound of his voice, people flocked to him. He had that certain something that made people instantly warm to him."

"I know. But some people resented that. We had a colonel who couldn't stand him. He thought Jon was a fake who used his charisma to advance himself."

Allie stared at him. "Jon was genuine."

"I know. I'm just saying not everyone liked him."

"He's dead," she pointed out. "This stalker keeps saying he's going to strip me of everything I love. So it's personal and targeted at me."

"Yeah, that's true. Shoot, I thought maybe I was on to something." He stared at her. "Tell me about your life with Jon. About the rodeo. Maybe we'll see something you've missed."

"It was a fairy tale," she said softly.

"How'd you meet him?"

"He was on leave, and his buddy talked him into going to the rodeo. He hated it, you know. The dust, the smells. I was moving horses from one corral to the other, and he stepped into some horse dung. He was so mad. I laughed, and he looked up. Our eyes met and it was . . . magic. He asked me out, we saw each other every night for a week, and he asked me to marry him. I said yes."

"He moved fast."

"You moved faster." They locked gazes, and Allie laughed. No magic there, though Rick's steadiness drew her.

It was just as well. Loving Rick would be like trying to ride a horse that had never been broken. The flight into the air might be high, but the jarring when she came back down could crush her bones.

"We married right away, against the advice of his parents. They never really accepted me. He found a house off base, and we settled in. Betsy was born about ten months later. Life was perfect for three years." The few years she'd spent with Jon had been the best of her life—a home, a neighborhood, a church. Bliss.

"Then he was sent to Iraq."

"Yes." She looked down at her hands. "A few months later I got the news. I had no choice but to go back to the rodeo. I had to support Betsy, and it was the only way I knew how."

"Jon's insurance?"

"Only a little left over after the burial costs. He meant to get more," she added when she saw his frown.

"Anyone at the base you might have had a run-in with?"

She thought back. In her memory, the days spent with Jon at Fort Irwin, California were filled with sunshine and laughter. No darkness marred the halcyon days. She shook her head. "There was nothing."

"And the rodeo?"

She shrugged. "You get a lot of transients. People who think the rodeo is glamorous until they are faced with the reality of dust, sweat, and cow patties. Some hate being told what to do and walk off. I've had the usual rounds of misunderstandings, minor arguments. Nothing that stands out."

"What about competitors? Any sore losers?"

A face leaped to mind. "I just thought of someone," she said slowly. "There was a stock contractor we used for about five years. Ted Rediger. I found him injecting some bulls with something to make them buck harder. That's a big no-no. I turned him in, and he lost the contract with the rodeo."

"Did he know you were the reason he lost the contract?"

"I don't know. Maybe." She hadn't even thought about the incident until now. It had seemed so minor.

"He never confronted you?"

"No, I never saw him after that."

"I'll have Brendan check it out." Rick leaned back, and his unblinking eyes focused on her. "Are you afraid?"

Allie shuddered. "Wouldn't you be? Some faceless person wants to hurt me, and I don't even know why. It would help if I knew the reason."

"Did you date anyone before Jon? With looks like yours, you could break someone's heart."

Was that a flicker of awareness in his eyes? Allie wanted to look away and couldn't. His gaze bore into her, and she realized she liked Rick. And was drawn to him as well. He was steady and strong, and those broad shoulders could weather any storm. She felt so battered by life. The thought of a port in her storm was attractive. But maybe only because he was a link to Jon, and she was so lonely.

She'd have to be careful or she'd find herself in love with him, and that would be disastrous. Their goal was to help Betsy. Nothing more. She wanted to smile at her rationalizations.

The chili. Glad to tear her gaze away, she rose and went to stir the pot. "Jon was the only man I ever loved."

"But not the only man who ever loved you?" he persisted.

"There was a rodeo clown who asked me out a few times, and I went. He was . . . strange." She heard his chair scrape, and she tensed when he came up behind her. His proximity set her nerves tingling.

"Strange how?"

"Intense. A little too attentive. It was more than I was interested in, and I kept turning down his invitations. He didn't give up for six months or so."

"What happened to him?"

She turned and found Rick standing inside her personal space. With the stove behind her, there was nowhere to back up. "I don't know. He quit, and I never heard from him again."

"What was his name?" He took out his phone and starting inputting letters.

"Mark Haskell." She watched his focused, efficient movements. "You must be used to interrogating people. I've wracked my brain trying to remember anyone who might be behind this and came up blank. Not that I think either of these men is guilty, but at least we have a place to start. Somewhere to look."

Even though she believed her memories would only lead to dead ends, it felt good to be doing something. To hang a possible name on the faceless enemy. In a few days they'd be back to square one with no idea who her enemy could be, but right this minute, she felt hope— a foreign emotion that had vanished when the soldier showed up on her doorstep to tell her the love of her life had given his.

"Why didn't you come?" she said abruptly. "When Jon died. Why didn't you come to tell me instead of letting a stranger do it?"

He took a step back, and his gaze iced over. "I was a stranger too."

"Not really. You were Jon's friend, so I considered you one too. If you'd come to tell me—" She tore her gaze away and turned her back to him. Stirring the pot, she waited to see if he'd lie to her, deny the way he looked at her.

"I—I couldn't," he said.

Her hand with the wooden spoon in it paused above the steaming pot. "Were you injured?"

"No, I didn't have a scratch." His tone sharpened with an edge of bitterness. "Jon died, and I didn't have a bruise."

She put the spoon down on the stove and turned to face him again. "I'd like to know about that day. How Jon died. If he said anything."

"Now's not the time." He backed away. "I'll call the rest for dinner."

Watching him retreat—he was running away for sure—Allie began to wonder if there was more to Jon's death than she'd realized.

She would swear she saw guilt on Rick's face.

THE WHISKEY GLOWED GOLDEN IN THE GLASS. RICK COULD SEE IT IN HIS mind, taste the hot, smoky taste on his tongue. He hadn't wanted a drink this bad in two years. Seeing Allie's trusting blue eyes on him, knowing she thought he could fix everything, made him feel like a scorpion hiding under a rock.

She had no idea he'd cost her the perfect life she'd loved.

The story would come out sooner or later. He hadn't lived thirty-four years without seeing how wrongs never stayed hidden. What kind of friend was he that he'd kill his best friend and then take his wife? When he'd been doing it for Betsy and Jon's memory, Rick felt less confused. But standing in the kitchen, he realized he wanted Allie. Wanted her for his own, not to make amends.

He couldn't betray Jon like that. It would be as bad as King David killing Uriah so he could have Bathsheba. Somehow he had to find the courage to keep the wall up between them, to keep her from creeping into his heart.

Betsy and Fern were playing with the kittens on the back porch. He stepped through the screen door, and the two girls were so engrossed with the antics of the cats that they didn't look up.

"Supper, girls," he said. Betsy got up and ran to hug his leg. He lifted her in his arms. "You hungry?"

She nodded.

"How about after dinner we go check on your horse? She was moving around better today."

Betsy's brilliant smile was her answer. Watching her expressive face, Rick wondered if there was more to the story behind her silence. Could she have seen or heard something besides the plane crash that caused her to retreat?

He lifted Betsy to his shoulders and opened the door for Fern. "You liking it here, Fern?"

"Yes sir," she said in her soft, nearly inaudible voice.

"You're doing a good job with the horses. And with Betsy."

She peeked up at him through her lank bangs. A tremulous smile flashed across her face before it disappeared. "Thanks," she whispered. She went through the doorway ahead of him.

He bent his knees so he didn't bang Betsy's head on the doorframe and followed the others to the kitchen. Food covered the table, and the aroma of chili mingled with the scent of the apple dumplings she'd put on the windowsill to cool.

"Hey, man, I ain't eatin' no chili." Leon dropped into a chair and stretched out his long legs.

"You chicken, Leon?" Rick asked, lifting Betsy and depositing her in the chair beside Fern. "Can't handle the spice?"

Leon glowered at him. "Get off my grill. I can handle anything, man."

"Bet I can eat it hotter than you." Rick grinned and sat beside the boy. "Let's have a chili face-off. You game, Devon?"

The boy shook his head. "Dude, that's seriously messed up. Chili makes you fart. I want to be able to breathe tonight."

The girls snickered. Latoya ruffled Devon's red hair as she passed. "You don't need no help. You smelled yourself lately?"

The rest of the kids hooted with laughter. Rick grabbed the ladle. "Want some chili, Betsy?"

The little girl nodded, her smile breaking out.

"Then tell me. Say yes." He waited, but the little girl ducked her head. "Come on, Betsy, you can do it. You're a big girl."

Allie grabbed the ladle from his hand. "She already said she wanted the chili." Moments later a big spoonful of chili was steaming in Betsy's bowl. Allie crumpled crackers into it and blew on it before lifting a spoonful to Betsy's lips.

"Oh for Pete's sake! She's not a baby, Allie. She can talk, and she can feed herself if you'll let her."

Allie flushed and glanced around at the others listening to their conversation. She sat down, but Rick knew she would let him have it in private. Their minor spat squashed any banter, and the staff and the kids vanished as soon as they gulped down their supper.

Fern took Betsy up for her bath, and Rick leaned back in his chair. "I shouldn't have said anything in front of the others," he said, when she opened her mouth. "But Allie, you've got to quit babying her. It's not helping Betsy grow up."

Allie banged a pot down into the sink. "She is *my* daughter, Rick. Mine and Jon's, not yours."

"She's going to be mine shortly," he pointed out. "Legally and in every way."

"I think I know what's best for my daughter. You don't understand how fragile she is, Rick."

"I know what it's like to grow up too fast. I don't want that for her, but I *do* want her to grow up eventually. Yes, she's got a problem, but the way you coddle her, she's never going to talk. Quit answering for her, and start putting her in positions where she has to speak."

"I don't want to hurt her."

"She's already been hurt. Your job is to help her get past it, not wallow in it."

Allie's face reddened. "You're such a—a male!"

"I don't know how to be anything else."

"I love her. She's just a little girl."

"But growing up fast. We've got to get her past this no-talking thing before she goes to school. I've got a lot of experience here with kids. Trust me a little."

The expression in her eyes left no doubt that he was asking the impossible. She began to put the leftover chili away with jerky movements. She wasn't done with this argument, not judging by the tense set of her shoulders. When she finally whirled to face him, he was ready.

"Let's get something straight right now. I'm not going to have my parenting questioned at every turn. Betsy will always be my little girl. A piece of paper doesn't make her yours. You're only going to be in her life a year, and I don't want her confused about who her father really is. Jon is her daddy, and he'll always be her daddy. I don't want you mucking up her memories."

Like he'd do anything to hurt Jon's memory. "Where'd you learn to grip the people you love in such a stranglehold?" he asked softly.

She flushed nearly the color of the chili, but she didn't answer. It might take more patience than he had to get past her defenses.

13

THAT COUGAR'S LONELY CRY SENT GOOSE BUMPS UP HER BACK. ALLIE LAY ON the sagging mattress and listened to the animal's wail. Even though she knew what it was, the moan made her shudder. Betsy slept peacefully.

Allie rubbed her burning eyes. Yo's death still weighed heavily on her. The reality was impossible to wrap her mind around. She peered at the clock on the bed stand. It was after midnight, and the moon cast a soft wash of light through the curtains. She sat up and untangled her legs from the sheet before swinging them to the floor. On nights like this, she wished she didn't struggle so much to read.

She stood and walked to the window. Nothing moved tonight but the wind. The dust storm had descended with a vengeance after dinner, and drifts of dust piled against the porch, the barn, and the pump house. The howl of the wind had become more muted in the past hour, and she thought the storm had about blown itself out.

Her argument with Rick was another reason for her sleeplessness. Did she really have a stranglehold on Betsy? Her gaze touched her sleeping daughter. She wanted only the best for her baby girl. Rick didn't understand how important it was to keep Jon's memory alive. Maybe the most important thing in her life, other than Betsy herself.

A whisper of sound came from behind her, and she turned to see a white square of paper on the floor, highlighted in the glow of moonlight. Someone had slipped it under her door. Rick maybe? Allie stepped to the door and picked up the note, then carried it back to the window to look at it in the moonlight.

She laughed softly at the way her pulse raced. A midnight tryst with her husband. *Husband*. She'd never thought to experience marriage again. But why hadn't he knocked and asked her to talk?

Maybe it was an apology.

She unfolded the note. Holding it up to the light, she tried to make out the words, but her eyes refused to cooperate. Glare bothered her, but this small bit of light wasn't enough either.

Glancing at Betsy, she saw her daughter was still sound asleep. Allie grabbed her robe, stuffed her feet into slippers and tiptoed out of the room. She could use some company. Jem was outside, and the porch light might be enough to read by.

Padding noiselessly through the quiet house, she slipped out onto the front porch. The dog wasn't around, so she whistled for him, a light sound that seemed unduly loud in the night.

After a few minutes, she saw him coming over the hillside. The porch light illuminated the yard enough that she could see him do his little excited dance in the air before he joined her, but he didn't make any noise.

She patted his head, and he settled at her feet. "I could use some company," she told the dog in a soft voice. He wagged his tail and licked her hand. She slipped to the porch floor and wrapped her arms around him, relishing his warm fur and his happy tongue.

Yo was dead. The realization kept surprising her, then grief would well afresh. Tears slipped down her face, and she buried her face in Jem's fur.

He whined and nuzzled her neck. She let him comfort her until the pain eased, then pushed him away and got up. The forgotten note fell to the ground. She grabbed it from the floor, settled on the swing, then held the note under the wash of light, which was soft enough not to cast a glare on the page. Still, the black typewritten letters jumped around on the white paper. If only she had the money to replace her pink glasses.

Maybe someday.

She blinked and squinted and managed to make out the letters.

I've found you. Tag, I'm it. Your worst nightmare.

The blood congealed in her head, and she felt faint. "No," she whispered.

Jem whined, and she rubbed his ears, clinging to the contact with another living thing.

He couldn't have found her. It was impossible. She was misreading this. Squinting, she reread the note, but the words remained the same. Ominous words full of menace.

She gasped, her hand going to her throat. How had the guy gotten in? He was out there somewhere, maybe standing in the shadows.

Betsy!

Allie sprang to her feet and threw open the door. Rushing pell-mell up the steps, she bolted into the bedroom and ran to Betsy's bed. Her daughter was still sleeping, but a lingering scent of some kind of men's cologne made Allie whirl and flip on the light. She blinked at the bright light and stared hard into the shadows.

She and Betsy were alone.

Could it be one of the teenagers' idea of a joke? Maybe one of them had overheard her telling Rick about the stalker. They'd been up the night she found out about Yolanda's murder. She didn't want to believe they'd be so cruel, but they might not realize how hurtful it was.

Allie hugged herself. She had to tell Rick about this, but she didn't want to leave Betsy alone. Better to wake her daughter up than to have some madman take her. Allie scooped Betsy up in her arms, grunting softly with the little girl's weight as she headed down the hall to Rick's room.

Leaning against the doorframe, she supported Betsy with one arm and rapped on the door with her other hand. "Rick?" she called softly.

The silence of the house set Allie on edge. She wanted to turn her head and look behind her, but she was almost afraid to find out if *he* was watching her. "Rick," she called louder. A muffled click came through the door, then a light shone out from under the crack. Relief flooded her.

Rick could handle anything.

The door swung open, and she nearly fell into the room. Rick's hair stood on end. Dressed in pajama shorts and no shirt, he leaned on the doorframe and blinked the sleep from his eyes. "Allie? What's wrong?"

Allie's fears left her as soon as she saw him. She wanted to walk into his arms, let him wrap her in safety. How did he do it? She could be a bundle of terror, but one moment in his presence and she felt safe.

He lifted Betsy from her arms. "Is she sick?" His voice, roughed with sleep, held concern.

"No, no, she's fine." Allie walked past him into the bedroom. She'd been in here to clean, but it looked different at night with Rick's presence filling the room. His jeans lay atop his boots at the foot of the bed, and the rumpled covers lay in a heap.

Rick stepped past her to the bed and laid Betsy on it, then drew the covers around her before turning back to Allie. "You look scared. Did someone call?"

"Worse." She handed him the note.

He frowned and held it out to read it. His expression changed from bewilderment to anger. "Where was this?"

"Under my door." Allie cinched the belt on her robe tighter. "I was awake and heard him slip it into the room."

"Did you try to see who it was?"

She shook her head. "I—I thought it might be a note from you, so I wasn't concerned at first. I tried to read it in my room and couldn't, so I went to the porch. I didn't see anyone."

"The house wasn't locked. We never lock it in case one of the hands or the kids need something in the night. Anyone could have gotten in."

"How did he find me so fast?" Had it really been less than two weeks since she drove the long, lonely stretch of I-10 from El Paso? Life here at the ranch seemed so normal, so right.

"I don't know." Rick put the paper down on the bed and came to her. His hands dropped onto her shoulders. "I'll protect you, Allie. Don't look so afraid."

"I'm afraid for Betsy," she admitted.

He pulled her against his chest, and she inhaled the musky male scent of him. It had been so long since she'd relaxed in a man's arms.

His arms and chest were hard with muscle, and the hairs on his chest tickled her cheek. For the muscle-bound type, he was pretty nice.

She wasn't attracted to him, but to the safety he offered.

No!

She drew away and stepped back. Rick wasn't Jon. She was just lonely. It would be easy to forget herself in his arms, and she couldn't let that happen. The year would be up before she knew it, and her heart couldn't stand being broken again.

Besides, falling in love with anyone would be a betrayal of Jon. Jon had been an easygoing guy, content to let her do what she liked. She sensed controlling Rick would be like lassoing the wind. There were few things she still controlled in her life—Betsy and her heart—and Allie planned to keep a tight grip on both.

Rick's hands dropped away. "I'll find him, Allie. I promise." His gaze held hers. "I'm going to go search the house. Prop a chair against the door. I'll call to you when I come back. Don't go outside of this room until I tell you it's safe, okay?"

"Okay." He bent over his shirt and jeans, and Allie gasped. "Your back."

Thick scars crisscrossed his back. Someone had beat him badly, or cut him with something. Allie reached out and touched the worst one, and Rick flinched away.

"Old story," he said shortly. He jerked a T-shirt on over his bare chest and yanked on his jeans over his shorts. She followed him to the door and clicked it shut behind him. Dragging the ladder-back chair from the corner, she propped it under the doorknob and crawled into bed with Betsy.

The pillow smelled of Rick. She told herself not to be a fool, but she buried her face in the pillow anyway and pulled the covers around her neck as if she were enveloped in Rick's arms.

Stupid, stupid. She wasn't so naive that she didn't recognize how she was beginning to fall for her new husband. She kicked off the sheets. Betsy shuffled and rolled away from her. Maybe someday he'd tell her who had made those scars. And why.

THE HOUSE BLAZED WITH LIGHT. RICK HAD LOOKED IN EVERY CLOSET, behind every curtain in the empty bedrooms and in the downstairs. He hadn't wanted to awaken the teenage girls, but when he didn't find an intruder, he rapped on their door and had them come out while he searched their room.

Their hair a mess and dragging their sheets, they'd congregated in the hall while he poked around their room. It stank of cheap perfume and nail polish.

"If you want to hook up, just say so," Latoya said, batting her lashes. "You don't have to make no excuses to visit my bedroom."

Rick was in no mood for her antics. "You've got sleep in the corners of your eyes," he told her.

Her coy smile faded, and she cleaned the gunk out of her eyes. "Thanks," she said sullenly.

"Is there an intruder?" Fern asked, her voice barely audible but shaking.

"Yep. But he seems to be gone. Did either of you hear anything?"

Latoya tossed her rumpled head. "You mean other than you hollering at us to drag our booties out of bed? Not a thing."

"How about you?" he asked Fern.

She hesitated. "I thought I heard someone in the hall a while ago. But I was half-asleep."

It could have been him or Allie. "What did it sound like?"

"It sounded like someone opened the door, then closed it again. But like I said, I was half-asleep and didn't look up."

"Wishful thinking," Latoya scoffed. "She's got a crush on Charlie."

Fern flushed and looked down at her bare feet.

Rick stepped back into the hallway. "Go back to bed. There's no one in the house, and I locked the doors."

The girls shuffled back into their bedroom and shut the door. He could hear Latoya haranguing Fern about her ridiculous crush on Charlie. Poor kid. After running back downstairs to double-check the doors, he went back up the stairs and started toward his room. As he passed Allie's room, he decided to take one more look at the hall outside her door. The guy had slipped the paper under the door. If his aim was to hurt Allie, he could have just as easily gone into the bedroom.

Why hadn't he?

Rick didn't know what the guy's game was, but the thought that he'd waltzed in here and back out without detection really steamed him. He'd have to ask Brendan for help. Running his hand over Allie's doorjamb, he felt every nick and scratch. The guy wouldn't have had to pick a lock because there were none in this old house other than the outside door locks and the office.

He knelt on the rug and lifted the edge of it. Nothing there. Rising, he stepped into the room and glanced around again. Everything was neat and in its place. A few cosmetics lined the dresser. Before he realized it, he'd picked up the gaudy nail polish and turned it in his hand. She was such a contradiction—all cowgirl and competent—then very feminine with bright nail polish and sleek hair.

He put the bottle back, then picked up her cologne and brought it to his nose. It smelled sweet and dainty, just like Allie. He put the bottle back hastily.

Don't go there. She'd chew his heart up for breakfast and spit it out. Backing away as if a rattlesnake lay coiled on the dresser, he turned to the closet. He'd checked it once, but he wasn't ready to give up finding whoever was behind this. Opening the door, he swept his hand through the hanging clothes, and the sweet scent drifted out again. Her shoes, two pair, were lined up evenly in the bottom of the closet. Betsy's shoes were just as precisely placed.

She didn't seem the type to want everything so ordered. Maybe it was a way of controlling the things she *could* control when there was so much she couldn't. What was that eye problem she'd mentioned? Something about Irlen. He'd have to look it up. Maybe there was something he could do to help her.

Shutting the closet door, he went down the hall to his bedroom. He tapped on the door. "Allie? It's me."

He heard the bed springs squeak, then a few moments later, the scrape of the chair being removed from the doorknob. The door opened, and she looked up at him, her blue eyes wide with trust. Something shattered in the region of his heart when he saw how completely she believed in him.

Had anyone ever looked at him like that before—like he could conquer the world? Maybe Jon. At the reminder of his friend, he pulled his mental shield back into place. Allie and Betsy were Jon's, not his. He couldn't ever let himself forget he was just a stand-in.

"Everything's okay," he told her. "I'll carry Betsy back to bed for you."

She sighed at his perfunctory tone. "Thanks." She stepped aside to allow him space to enter.

He went to the bed and lifted the little girl. Betsy didn't stir as he carried her back to her bed. "You'll be okay?"

She nodded. "Fine. Thanks for checking." She hesitated. "Maybe we should leave, pack up and run."

"He found you here," Rick pointed out. "Running is never the answer. This guy is tenacious. At least here we can see someone coming from miles away."

"Just like tonight?" Her smile did little to take the sting from her words.

"We know he's found you now. I'll get some friends on it tomorrow. We'll find him."

Her eyes looked sad, but she nodded. "Thank you, Rick. I don't know what we'd have done without your help."

Her words sounded stilted and formal, and he wished she'd look at him with that trust again. He gave a curt nod and backed out of the room. "Put a chair under your door," he said.

She shut the door, and he waited until he heard a chair scrape across the floor and lodge under the knob. Retreating to his bedroom, he listened to the wind howl through the eaves. He used to howl like that when his back was laid bare.

He shut the door, shucked his jeans and shirt, and crawled between the sheets. The sweet scent of her in his sheets filled him with an emotion he couldn't bring himself to name.

14

Everything seemed different by the light of day. Betsy clung to Allie's side all morning. Even though she'd slept through the whole upheaval in the night, she seemed to understand that something had changed.

Her little girl sat by the refrigerator with her doll clutched in her hand and watched Allie slice roast beef and homemade bread for lunch. Allie hadn't seen her daughter have the doll out since they'd come.

"How about if we go out looking for bluebirds after lunch?" she asked Betsy. "We'll see if Rick will go with us."

She needed a distraction as badly as Betsy did. The realization that Yo was gone kept ambushing her.

Betsy looked up and nodded, her smile breaking out of the gloom. Allie's eyes burned as she watched her daughter bend her head until her dark curls touched the golden head of her doll. She wanted so much for her daughter, but it seemed Betsy was living the life of the cinder maid.

The haven they'd found here hadn't lasted nearly long enough. How could Rick protect them from a phantom who slipped in and out of sight like the fog?

The screen door banged, and Latoya strolled into the kitchen, followed by Fern. The two girls were so different. Latoya came in like she owned the world, while Fern slunk in with her head down and her shoulders slumped. Allie wanted to take Fern by the shoulders and tell her to stand up straight, look the world in the eye, and chart her course.

But had Allie done any better with her own life? She'd had big handicaps to overcome, and once upon a time, she thought she had done a pretty good job of scaling the mountains that had once seemed so daunting. But life had a way of dethroning you when you least expected it.

Allie wanted to be more like Latoya, certain of herself and her power over other people. But maybe the teenager was just better at hiding her fears. Maybe people were all the same inside.

"Girl, my stomach is growling like that lion I heard last night," Latoya complained.

"Lunch will be ready in a few minutes," Allie said, snapping out of her reverie and turning back to her task. "Did you get all your chores done?"

"That mare of Betsy's about chewed the bag up and spit it back out. She's one hungry mama. Did you go see her this morning, Bets?" Latoya squatted beside Betsy, who just nodded without looking at her.

Latoya stood and went to the cabinet, where she began to pull down plates and glasses.

Allie wanted to smile but hid it by turning away to get the mayo out of the refrigerator. A week ago, the teen would have sullenly agreed to set the table only after being asked numerous times.

The pottery clattered on the wood table as Latoya carelessly tossed the dishes into place. "That little colt loves me like his mama," she said in a conversational tone. "He followed me all over that corral." She giggled like a five-year-old. "He kept nibbling on my shirt." She sank onto the chair and crossed her legs at the ankles. "I like it here."

"Me too," Fern said, laying out the tableware. "I wish I never had to leave."

Allie felt a pang at the wistful tones of both girls. She might have thought her life was hard, but these girls had even more strikes against them. At least she'd had loving parents. She could see the attraction in helping kids like these.

"We're going to go look for bluebirds after lunch. You girls want to come?" she asked them.

"Bluebirds? What's up with that?" Latoya demanded.

"Betsy loves them. Haven't you ever heard of the bluebird of happiness? Betsy loves the old Shirley Temple movie called *The Blue Bird*. We could watch it tonight after supper if you've never seen it."

"I used to watch Shirley Temple at my grandma's," Fern said in a soft voice. "My brother had a crush on her. He never knew she was old enough now to be his grandma."

"Shirley Temple? She that curly-headed Betty in the old black-and-white movies?" Latoya demanded. "That's kid stuff."

"Aw, come on, Latoya," Fern said with more animation than Allie had ever seen. "It's a really good movie."

Latoya sniffed. "I'll watch it for a while, but if it gets too hokey, I'm outta there."

Allie wanted to gather the girl up in her arms and tell her it wasn't too late to regain her childhood, but she knew the words would seem empty. And maybe they were. Once innocence was lost, she wasn't sure it could ever be regained.

THE SKY HAD CLEARED OF THE SAND THAT YELLOWED THE AIR AND PILED around the foundations of the buildings. Rick and Charlie spent the morning tramping the ranch, looking for any sign of the man who had broken into the house last night.

Rick called the sheriff, and he came out too, but there was nothing to see, no one to interrogate. The two older hands had been here over twenty years, and Rick couldn't see Buzz or Guinn trying to frighten Allie. Charlie was just a kid. None of the help had any reason to terrorize her.

He ruled out Emilio and the kids too. Her stalker must be lurking nearby after tracking her here.

"You want me to stand guard tonight?" Charlie asked, a worried frown settling on his forehead when the men failed to turn up any clues. "Me and the hands could take turns."

"Maybe. I asked the sheriff if he'd give her some police protection."

Charlie snorted. "Good luck with that. I don't think he's got an officer smart enough to find his butt with both hands."

Charlie had a point. The sheriff's good ol' boys weren't capable of anything beyond arresting drunk and disorderly residents. There wasn't much crime here beyond the occasional theft from a tourist's car and the fights that broke out in Long Branch Saloon.

Maybe he should talk to Brendan, but he didn't see what his friend could do about the situation. He likely had his plate full saving the world. Still, maybe Brendan could at least put some feelers out and give him some indication of how the guy might have found Allie.

His wife. The thought still made his stomach plunge. The realization that he was married kept playing hide-and-seek in his mind. Rick couldn't quite grasp the reality of it, even yet.

Charlie was staring at him.

"What?" he asked.

"Allie told me."

"Told you what?"

"That you married her. You could have called dibs on her when she got here, but you kept mum." His glance was full of curiosity.

"She's too old for you anyway."

"I'm only ten years younger," Charlie said, his voice indignant. "Why didn't you say anything about knowing her?"

Rick shrugged. "I didn't know her, Charlie. She was my best friend's wife, and she came to me for help. I told her husband I'd take care of her."

Charlie pulled an aspirin bottle from his jeans and shook out three pills.

"Migraine again?"

"Yeah, my counselor says it's stress." Charlie pulled his canteen from his belt and uncapped it. Throwing back his head, he swallowed the pills and wiped his lips before resealing it and putting it away. "That's a rare brand of loyalty."

"Jon's parents are trying to get custody of Betsy. It seemed the best thing to do to keep Betsy with Allie."

Charlie grinned then. "Anything to get a woman like that in your bed, huh?"

"It wasn't like that." Rick clamped his teeth against any more explanation. "It's about lunchtime. We'd better get back."

Charlie's face took on its hurt expression again, and Rick wondered how the kid could have fallen for Allie so fast.

Who's talking? The voice whispered in his head. *You're just like Charlie.* He shook the thought away. He was just doing his duty. Charlie might succumb to her charms, but he wouldn't.

"I'm heading in," Charlie said.

"Be right there." Rick sat on the back porch step and listened to the cattle low in the back field. He pulled out his cell phone and called Brendan.

"Me again, buddy," he said when his friend answered. "Trouble came calling last night." He told Brendan about the intruder and the note. "How could he have tracked her here?"

"She talk to anyone back in El Paso?"

"No. Oh wait, yeah, she talked to her friend one day, then her friend's parents. The one who was killed."

"Maybe the guy had their phone tapped. You know how easy it is to get hold of a listening device."

"But she didn't tell them where she was."

"She call on the house phone?"

"Yeah," he said, his heart sinking. "Caller ID."

"Yep. Nothing's secret these days. Anything else I can do?"

"Nope, not unless you've got some personnel with nothing to do that you'd like to send me for protection."

"Wish I did, Rick. Sounds like you need some backup."

"I'll manage."

"She couldn't be in better hands." Brendan gave a knowing chuckle. "Pun intended, Mr. Newlywed."

"It's not like that," he said for the second time in five minutes.

"Whatever." Brendan's voice became brusque again. "Listen, I've gotta go. Keep me posted, and call if there's anything I can do."

Rick put his phone away and got up. Protecting Allie and Betsy lay squarely on his shoulders, and he wasn't sure he was up to the task anymore. He'd gotten soft living here on the ranch, where the only danger was from animals and the weather. Humans could be more treacherous and more deadly than any of their counterparts in the animal kingdom.

THEY FOUND TOO MANY BLUEBIRDS TO COUNT. ALLIE'S MUSCLES ACHED IN a pleasant way from the hike as she rested at the bottom of a rock formation Rick called Eye of the Needle. A thin plume of dust billowed up from the car that pitched and rocked its way along the potholes in the lane to the house. She watched it travel toward the buildings. The vehicle looked vaguely familiar, but she couldn't quite determine the make from this far away. Betsy and the girls sat among the bluebonnets, and she turned back to them to take their picture.

Betsy's smile radiated up at her, and Allie smiled back. All seemed right with the world this afternoon, and she wondered how she could feel so happy when she knew her enemy had found her. But he wasn't here today. Today she could lift her face to the hot sun and breathe in the aroma of sage and creosote.

She snapped the picture and put her camera back into her shirt pocket. When she turned to look back at the house, she saw a man step out of the car. The lawyer. Wally Tatum. Maybe he brought news about the adoption.

"I'm ready for some iced tea. How about you?" she called to the girls.

"Ice cream sounds better," Latoya said, getting up and dusting the dirt from her shorts. "With hot fudge."

"I think there's some in the freezer. How about you and Fern go fix it, and I'll be in shortly. I need to talk to the man down there."

"We'll take Betsy," Fern said, clasping the little girl's hand.

"I'll walk you to the house." Allie wasn't about to let Betsy out of her sight until they were safely inside.

As they neared the buildings, she saw Rick step off the front porch to greet Wally, and she quickened her steps. The girls ran ahead of her, and once they were inside, she stopped at Rick's side.

"Mrs. Bailey." Wally tipped his hat.

Mrs. Bailey. She saw the start Rick gave and knew the words had shocked him as much as they did her. She wasn't a Siders anymore, wasn't part of Jon's family. She hadn't even thought about that. Something squeezed in her chest, a sharp pang at just how much her life had changed. She'd thought she would die a Siders, would lay beside Jon in the little cemetery in El Paso.

Her fingers curled into her palms. "Mr. Tatum. Any news?"

"Please, ma'am, if you call me Wally, I'll call you Allie. We don't like formality here." Wally gestured to the rockers on the porch. "How about we set a spell, and I'll bring you up to speed."

Rick took Allie's arm, and they stepped onto the porch. She settled onto the swing while the men took the rockers. "Is it good news?"

Wally smiled broadly. "About as good as you can get. With most adoptions the child needs to reside with the adoptive parent for six months. The judge is waiving that requirement in your case since she knows Rick here. The home study will be done the first of the week if you're agreeable, and we can set the finalization of the adoption at the end of the month."

"You're kidding," Rick said. "I had no idea it would move that fast."

Wally grinned and put his boots on the porch railing. "The judge thinks you're a saint, and she was mighty fond of Elijah. Betsy's his great-granddaughter. Stands to reason the judge would do everything in her power to help out."

Allie could hardly believe it. All the dominoes were falling into place. She was so used to things going wrong that it didn't seem possible the adoption would be this easy. "No problems at all?"

"Nope. The road is clear before us." Wally stretched his arms over his head. "I could go for some iced tea right about now."

"With news like that, you deserve a hot-fudge sundae," Allie said, getting to her feet.

"I wouldn't turn it down," Wally said.

"How about you?" she asked Rick.

"A celebration sounds good," he said.

His eyes were smiling, and he looked as relieved as she felt. Had he thought it wouldn't go through? She knew so little about Rick. Was she doing the right thing? When he adopted Betsy, he would always be in their lives, even after the divorce. What if she found out things about him later when it was too late?

Staring into his face, she searched his gaze until he lifted a brow in question. "Anything wrong?" he asked.

"No, no, nothing," she said hastily.

But how did one ever know what was in the heart of another person? She had to trust that Jon had known him well and said she could rely on Rick. Sometimes you just had to trust.

Trust came hard to Allie anymore. When had that happened? She remembered her younger years, when she believed the best about everyone. Maybe she'd seen too much, lived through too much heartache to think there might not be secrets behind Rick's smile.

Today she would choose to trust though. Trust that God had led her to the right place for help, even when she didn't quite understand the method.

15

THE LANDSCAPE CHANGED FROM EMPTY DESERT TO SIGNS OF HABITATION as the truck neared the city limits of El Paso. Mr. Fleming had said not to come to the funeral, but Allie couldn't sit at the ranch while her best friend was laid to rest. Her beater truck would never make the six-hour trip each way to El Paso, and Rick wanted to take her anyway, so she'd agreed to let him.

She'd passed the drive dozing with her head against the window until about an hour ago. It was better than trying to make conversation when her heart felt as barren as the landscape at the ordeal ahead of her. She'd attended too many funerals the past two years.

Yo was Allie's last link with her old life. Everyone she loved except Betsy was gone now. It wasn't fair. If she'd done something wrong, why did her family have to suffer? She wished she knew what caused the man to fixate on her.

She dug her nail polish out and carefully applied a fresh coat of hot pink.

"Whew, that stuff stinks," Rick said, wrinkling his nose. "Why do you wear it anyway? It doesn't stay on long."

Allie held out a finished hand. "You don't think it looks pretty?"

"It looks fake."

Allie capped the polish and blew on her nails. "Nice nails are the difference between a lady and a woman."

"Who told you that? You're a lady no matter what."

"My mother."

Rick grunted, then shuffled some papers on his lap. "You awake enough to help me navigate?"

"Yes." Allie stretched and looked down at Betsy. "She's still asleep though."

"Can you help me look for the street? You're more familiar with El Paso than me."

Allie nodded and turned to look out the window. "The funeral home is about five lights or so in. You'll turn right, so get in the right-hand lane."

The familiar streets looked alien and dangerous. She'd gotten used to open land and blue skies. It would be hard to ever move back to the city again.

"You doing okay?"

She turned her head to glance at him. "It's going to be a hard day. Yo was the only Fleming kid."

"I still wish you wouldn't go. It's not safe."

She hunched her shoulders and ran her hand over the soft velour of the seat. "It's not safe at the ranch. Nowhere is really safe."

His eyes narrowed. "I won't leave your side. And I'll keep hold of Betsy every minute."

She nodded and turned to look back out the window. They passed Cowtown Boots, and nostalgia swept over her. Yo had bought Allie's boots there just three months ago. They'd mugged it up as they tried on every outlandish pair they saw before settling on something practical.

How could that bright spirit be dead?

Allie reminded herself that Yo wasn't really dead. She'd gone on to a better place. They would be together again someday.

But right now she felt like someone had ripped her heart out.

"Turn here," she said.

Rick slowed the truck and turned at the light. A few intersections later, she pointed out the funeral home, and he parked in the lot.

"I'll carry Betsy," he said. Rick unbuckled the little girl's seat belt and lifted her in his arms.

Allie's hand stayed on the door lever. All she'd done for the past year was stand by the caskets of those she loved.

"You coming?"

"Yes." She pushed open the door and got out, but she might as well have been slogging through knee-high mud. Yo's parents waited inside that building, and she would be expected to offer comfort when she had none.

Rick took her elbow and guided her toward the door. The strength of his fingers was a support she badly needed. He held open the door, and she walked into the crowd milling around the reception hall. A young woman pointed her in the right direction when she asked for the Fleming funeral.

Mr. Fleming spotted her first. His girth strained the buttons of his blue suit. The big lapels looked out-of-date, and Allie wondered if it was the suit he'd worn to his wedding thirty years ago. His kinky black hair was shorter than she'd ever seen it, and the dark face under it had developed new lines.

He enveloped her in a hug. "Told you not to come, girl."

Tears welled at the sorrow in his voice. "I had to say good-bye."

His beefy hands patted her shoulder. "Who's the Paul Bunyan type with Betsy?"

"Oh, I need to introduce you." Allie glanced around and gestured to Rick, who stood a few feet off as if to give her some time alone with the family.

He joined her with Betsy still in his arms. The little girl was awake now, but she clung to Rick like he was her port in the storm. Allie knew the feeling.

"Mr. Fleming, this is m-my husband, Rick Bailey."

The older man's smile seemed to freeze in place. He looked Rick over carefully. "My Yo, did she know of this?" Suspicion coated his words.

"I told her the last time we talked what I planned."

Mr. Fleming and Rick locked gazes, then Yolanda's father nodded. "You take good care of these girls, Mr. Bailey."

Rick shifted Betsy to his other arm. "I intend to."

THE WEEKEND HAD FILLED RICK WITH A STRANGE SENSE OF CONTENTMENT. Attending church with Allie and the kids beside him just like a real family, going bird-watching, watching Allie paint her nails and Betsy's tiny half moons with color. Rick could get used to this.

There had been no more incidents, though Rick watched over the ranch and every person there with a sharp gaze.

The home study on Monday had been a breeze. A form to fill out, a few perfunctory questions, and the woman had smiled and left. Rick didn't anticipate any problems. Everyone in town knew him and his commitment to working with kids.

He and Emilio talked out how to handle the kids with Elijah gone. Rick took over the group talk sessions and found them just like his studies had told him—sometimes frustrating and sometimes rewarding.

Tuesday morning he and Charlie stood at the corral fence and evaluated the condition of the horses. Three of them had been rescued within the last three months, and the latest one, which they'd all come to call Betsy's mare, was showing signs of lethargy—not a good thing when she'd been so perky.

"We can't lose her," he told Charlie. "Betsy would be devastated. Did you call Grady?"

"He's out of town. His assistant is going to come take a look at her this afternoon." Charlie popped a Hershey's kiss in his mouth from a bag he'd nearly emptied in the last fifteen minutes. "We got company."

Rick turned to see a Ford sedan approaching the house. The sedate blue color and tinted windows made his muscles tense, and somehow he knew before the two men stepped out in their navy suits and neat ties that the FBI had found Allie.

"I'll handle this," he told Charlie. "Don't say anything." He strode over to intercept the men who were approaching the porch. "I'm Rick Bailey, the ranch foreman," he said, sticking out his hand.

The closest man shook his hand, then pulled out a badge and flashed it. "FBI. We're looking for Allie Siders."

"No one here by that name." It wasn't exactly a lie. Her name was Allie Bailey now. Rick wanted to head them off long enough for the adoption to take place. "Just me and my wife live here, along with some kids in the foster system who are here temporarily."

The expressionless men didn't move away. "We know she's here," the leader said. "You might have married her, but we still need to talk to her."

He should have known they would know about the marriage. The feds always had their ducks in a row. "Look, she had nothing to do with the illegal aliens. She reported what she saw, that's all."

"Actually, we already know that," the guy said. "We're not here to arrest her. And her in-laws have dropped the kidnapping charge now that they know where she is. They'll be along to sort that issue out shortly."

Rick winced. Trouble was coming. "Then what do you want?"

The man nodded toward the door. "To talk to your wife."

The screen door opened behind him, and Allie stepped out. "I heard my name. Are you looking for me?"

"You're Allie Siders?"

"Yes—I mean no. It's Allie Bailey now." The door closed behind her, and she moved to stand beside Rick. She leaned against him slightly to steady herself. "You're cops?"

"FBI, ma'am. I'm Agent Marshall." He pointed to a blond guy with a crew cut. "Agent Baker. We'd like to talk to you."

Allie took a step back, her shoulders wilting and her head coming up in a defensive posture. "I didn't do anything."

"We know, ma'am. The investigation has turned away from you since Yolanda Fleming's murder in light of this." He handed her a paper. "This was in Ms. Fleming's car, under the seat."

She took it, her pink polish garish against the envelope. It had her name scrawled across it in bold letters.

"You want me to read it first?" he asked when her gaze touched his face.

She shook her head. "What is it?" she asked.

"A letter from the killer."

The envelope wasn't sealed. Allie lifted the flap and pulled out the single sheet of paper.

Rick craned his neck over her shoulder and read the words on the paper.

Doesn't Yolanda look lovely in her casket? But you'll look better.

Allie crumpled the letter in her hand. "He's not going to get away with this," she said. "I'm going to make sure he pays for what he did to Yo." Her voice shook with passion.

"So who hates you?" Agent Marshall asked. "What we want to know is who would want to make you look guilty of trafficking? If we can get some direction on that, we might be able to find the mastermind. Whoever it was tried to make you look like you were involved, but we followed the money trail and your spending habits, and it's clear it was a frame-up."

"But what about Yolanda?" Rick put in. "Was she involved in some way?"

"She seems to have been killed purely to hurt Allie."

Allie clasped her arms around herself. "They accomplished that." She told them about the man who claimed to have killed her family.

"You didn't recognize his voice? Nothing was familiar?" Agent Marshall asked.

"Everyone has asked her that, including me," Rick put in. "And the guy has found her here." He told the agents about the break-in the other night.

"Do you still have the letter?"

"Yes, it's in the office." Rick motioned for them to follow him, and he took them past the living room where Fern and Betsy were playing school. He unlocked the office door and stepped to the desk. He opened the drawer. "That's odd. I left it here." He rummaged through the stacks of papers and bills. "It's gone," he said.

Someone had stolen it. Rick distinctly remembered putting it in the desk drawer. He'd locked the room behind him, and only he and Allie had a key. His gaze tangled with hers, and she looked away. Had she taken it?

"Allie, you have any idea what happened to the letter?" he asked. He didn't want to believe she might have taken it, that she might not want a closer inspection of the letter.

She looked up and shook her head. "I haven't seen it since I gave it to you."

"Can you write down what it said?" Agent Baker asked.

"There wasn't much to it," Rick said, grabbing a blank sheet of paper. "It was typewritten and read, 'I've found you. Tag, I'm it. Your worst nightmare.'"

"Could it have been someone other than the man who killed Ms. Fleming? Maybe someone who knew you were running and thought to tease you?" Agent Baker asked.

"I don't think so," Allie said, shaking her head. "I'd even wondered if one of the teens did it as a joke, but I don't think that's it. I can't explain, but the feel of the words, the way he put them together, sounds like him. I don't believe it's a copycat."

The man handed Rick a card. "If you find it, give us a call." Agent Marshall smiled and went toward the door. The men exited the room.

Rick rummaged around the desk again. "I can't believe this. No one has a key to the office but you and me."

"You suspected me at first, didn't you?" Allie's gaze held steady.

"For a second," he admitted.

"Where's the trust, Rick?" She lifted her hand and flashed the gold ring his way. "Before you put this on my finger, don't you think you should have made sure you believed what I was telling you?"

"The marriage wasn't about you. It was about Jon."

She flinched. "Jon's not here, and I'm the one who has to see the suspicion in your face."

"Fair enough." He'd hurt her, and the thought pained him. More than he wanted to admit. He should tell her that the Siderses had tracked her down too, but he didn't want to see more discouragement in those blue eyes.

THE NEXT FEW DAYS ALLIE FOUND HERSELF CLEANING AN ALREADY SPOTless bathroom and dusting shining furniture with a lemony wax so she didn't have to think about Yo's death. If the guy thought he'd make her run again, he was wrong. She'd see him brought to justice no matter what it took.

Today she wasn't going to think about it. Rick was taking her and Betsy out to see his bluebird trail. The grassy meadow stretched out under the big sky, brushing the Rio Grande on one side and an escarpment that rose sharply on the other. They rode side by side, Rick and Betsy on Gunner and Allie on Jackson, a six-year-old Appaloosa that she'd been riding since her arrival.

A small cabin sat on the other end of the meadow. "Who lives there?" Allie asked.

"Our former housekeeper, Rosa Garcia. She'd be the one to ask about your mom, but she's visiting her sister right now. She should be back in another few days."

Allie followed Rick as he led the way toward the first birdhouse. Another was planted a few feet away.

"This is called a bluebird trail," Rick told Betsy. They dismounted and tied off the horses at a bar, then Rick lifted Betsy onto his shoulders. "Bluebirds like open, grassy areas. We can't put their houses by the feedlot because there are so many sparrows there eating the grain, and they'd steal the houses from the bluebirds." He hefted her higher and approached the nest. "Look inside, Bets. Are there any eggs?"

Allie stepped between them and the pole. "There might be lice."

"Get a grip," Rick said under his breath. "She's fine."

"She's going to get dirty poking around up there. And one of the birds might attack if she's messing with the nest." Allie shuddered at the thought.

An exasperated huff escaped Rick's mouth. "Look, just be quiet and let me try this, okay? Just let me handle this."

Why didn't he get a mother's concern? "I don't understand. She can watch the birds from down here."

He stared at her without saying another word until she shrugged, and against her better judgment, moved out of the way. She'd about had it with his interference.

He moved closer to the birdhouse. "See any eggs, Bets?"

Betsy peered into the birdhouse. A tiny squeak of excitement came from her throat. Allie's eyes widened, and she and Rick locked gazes. She gave him a tiny nod. Maybe the bluebirds would be a way of getting Betsy to talk.

"How many do you see?" he asked.

Allie forgot to breathe when Betsy opened her mouth. Then her daughter's lips clamped shut again, and she held up three fingers.

"Three, huh? It's called a clutch of eggs. What color are they?" Rick persisted.

Betsy exhaled through parted lips. Allie could almost hear the words wanting to escape, but Betsy ducked her head and didn't reply.

"Are they blue?" Rick asked gently. Betsy nodded. "We have to watch them until they hatch and make sure they're doing okay. When the babies get to be about twelve days old, we'll quit bothering them. We don't want them to get scared and try to fly away too soon."

The meadow stretched out over the hills in all directions. It felt peaceful here, and Allie wished she could let her guard down. It wasn't safe though, not with that man lurking about. He might even now be watching her.

Rick had brought a nightstick with him, and she had no doubt he knew how to use it. She would need every bit of his protection.

"Check this box, Betsy," Rick said, walking to the nearby birdhouse. "Any blue eggs in there?"

An iridescent green bird flew from the box. Betsy peered inside and shook her head.

"It's a tree swallow. They like the same type of home as the bluebird, so we put a house up for them. That way they don't take it away from the bluebird. The tree swallow is a protected species too." Rick lifted Betsy from his shoulders and put her on the grass. "Let's sit and rest awhile. I think your mom brought lunch for us."

Allie went to her horse and got the sandwiches and blanket out of her saddlebag. She spread out the red-and-white checked blanket, and Rick helped her put out the food and bottles of water. They ate in silence as they watched the bluebirds flutter around the pasture. The sun beat down, and she adjusted her hat to block out the glare. She felt relaxed for the first time in days.

Rick lay back with his hands behind his head. "Bets, did you know your daddy could make the most piercing whistle through his teeth? It was enough to break your eardrums."

Betsy giggled, and Allie could have kissed Rick for trying to help keep Jon's memory alive. "Pick me some flowers, Betsy," she said, glancing around at the bright display of bluebonnets and some yellow wildflowers. A roadrunner darted from one rock to another, then ran to the blue ribbon of water. Fragrance filled the air—wildflowers, sage, creosote, and river. She could live here forever.

Betsy smiled and got up from the blanket. She began to pick the three-foot stalks of bluebonnet, but before she got very far, the bluebirds grabbed her attention, and she sat down to watch them.

Allie turned her attention back to Rick. "The adoption hearing is in a couple of days. Are you sure you want to go through with this?"

"You trying to back out?"

"No, just giving you a final window of opportunity." She smiled and plucked a wildflower of her own to keep from touching his face with her fingertips.

"I've already come to care about Betsy," Rick said. "And not just for Jon anymore." He plucked a flower and twirled it in his fingers. "Betsy almost said something at the birdhouse. You've got to back off and let her fly, Allie."

Allie's contentment disappeared like the cottonwood fluff dancing around the meadow. "You're not her father," she said. "You can be her friend, but that's as far as it goes."

"What if I say that's not enough?"

"It has to be. That's all there is. I'm not letting you—or any man—take Jon's place with her."

"Even if it's not what's best for Betsy? Where's your trust, Allie? In me, in God for bringing us together? You going to toss that gift back in his face?" Rick turned his gaze on her. "There's something else I've been meaning to talk to you about," he said.

The solemnity in his face made her want to run. He was going to say he wanted a divorce sooner than a year. She didn't blame him. For a man like him who could have his pick of women, the thought of being saddled to a widow and her kid must be daunting.

"I don't want a divorce," he said. "Did you notice I hesitated before I said my vows?"

She nodded. "I'd wondered if you were about to back out."

"It wasn't that. As a Christian, the thought that we were planning on breaking the vows we took bothered me. Before I said them, I decided I would say them and mean the promise. I'd like us to think about working on making our marriage real. I don't want a divorce in a year."

"Real?" she echoed. Something inside, some last dying bloom of hope, lifted its head.

"I know it's a shock, and maybe I shouldn't have sprung it on you so fast." He took her small hand in his big, warm one. "I'm not saying we move fast, just that we inch along in the right direction."

Allie wasn't sure what to say, how to react. She'd dismissed his strange comment the night of the wedding when he hadn't said any more. And how exactly would they work on it? Wasn't love supposed to bloom by itself without being coaxed? Still, she thought she could learn to love Rick.

And she wanted Rick to love Betsy, to nurture and care for her, but a tiny twinge of longing for the same thing rattled her. If she plucked his other hand from his lap and held it to her lips, what would he do? For a moment she was tempted to find out, but then the cold light of reality washed over her. She wasn't in the market for more pain.

"What do you say?" he prodded, his thumb running in circles against her palm.

She found it hard to think with the way he was looking at her, the plea in his blue eyes. "I—I don't know," she faltered.

The light in his eyes dimmed. "Fair enough. But let's try it out."

Before she could react, he leaned over and took her shoulders in his hands. His head bent down, and he claimed her lips in a gentle kiss. His mouth coaxed her own to respond, and her fingers wrapped themselves in his shirt. She clung to him, and a passion she didn't expect flared between them.

His arm came around her back, and he pulled her closer. She didn't resist. The smell of him, the hard muscles under her fingers, the tenderness of his kiss broke through the defenses she thought she'd reinforced with grief and heartache. Her fingers trailed up to run along his roughened jaw. She cupped his face in her palm and kissed him back with all the loneliness of the past two years.

Dimly, she realized someone was tugging on her shirtsleeve. Betsy. Grasping for some shred of control, Allie pulled away and smoothed her hair. Her hand trembled.

"I think that might be a yes," Rick whispered.

She couldn't look at him. Was he laughing at how easily he'd battered down her walls? Her lips tingled and felt warm. She wanted to touch them but didn't want him to see. Swallowing hard, she gathered Betsy onto her lap.

The thought of sharing a life with this man was an oasis in the desert to her soul thirsting to belong.

16

THE SKY SHONE BLUER AND THE GRASS GLOWED BRIGHTER AS RICK RODE along the trail back to the ranch, with Betsy on the saddle in front of him and Allie riding her mare beside them. He hadn't planned on saying anything yet, but her response gave him hope.

And scared him to death.

He'd loved his mother, and she hurt him worse than any enemy. His back itched with the memories. For two cents, he'd call Brendan back and tell him he'd changed his mind and would be glad to help solve the world's problems.

They'd be a lot easier than solving his own.

When they reached the barn, he dismounted, then unsaddled the horses while Allie went inside with Betsy. She hadn't spoken a word on the trail. Maybe she was as taken aback by what happened between them as he was. They had a long road to navigate if they were going to stay together.

He poked his head in the house long enough to tell Allie he was going to town for a while. She was sitting at the desk with the bills spread out in front of her. Everything smelled of lemon polish. Betsy was in the big chair by the window and was already asleep. Squinting at the papers, Allie didn't look up when he spoke.

"You okay?" he asked.

"It's just hard to read these things," she said, tucking a lock of hair behind her ear. "I used to have tinted glasses that helped, but they broke."

"So get some more."

She looked up then, and a smile chased away her ferocious expression. "They're expensive. I get by okay. It just takes a little longer."

He heard the forced optimism in her voice. Maybe he could find out something about those glasses while he was in town. "I'll be back in a couple of hours. I've got some errands to run. Anything I can get for you while I'm there?"

"No, we're fine. You'll be back in time for supper?"

"Sure." He grabbed a paper and jotted down his cell number. "You can call me if you need anything."

She took the paper and tucked it into her jeans pocket. "Thanks."

An awkward silence fell between them. The dance of relationship was one Rick had never learned, and the crash course was beginning to wear him out. "Okay then," he said, backing out of the room.

On the way to town, he called Grady. If he wanted this marriage to work, they had to start out right. "Hey, buddy, got a favor," he said when Grady picked up the phone.

"Hey, Cowboy. How did you know I just walked in the door?"

Rick didn't want to even tell his friend he'd entered into a mockery of a marriage. "You got time to do some marriage counseling this week?" he asked, plunging right in.

Grady was an odd combination, a vet who pastored, but the tiny church couldn't support a full-time man, and Grady had stepped into the position with all the accompanying duties.

"But sure, and who is it?"

"Me."

There was silence on the other end of the line. "I'd heard something about this. You really married the woman, Rick?"

"Yep. If we want it to last, we're going to have to figure some things out about each other. I thought the best place to start would be with you. I'm going to adopt Betsy, and we have the hearing a week from tomorrow at nine. Would you have time later in the morning?"

"How about eleven?"

Rick wanted to thank Grady for not launching into a lecture, but he just agreed and marked it down. Time enough later to hear all the reasons he shouldn't have done what he did. It was too late to regret it now. "We'll be there. Oh, did your assistant get a chance to take a look at that new mare?"

"He did. He wormed her and gave her a shot of antibiotic. He thinks she'll be fine, said she looked like she's gaining weight." He cleared his throat. "Rick, you sure you know what you're doing?"

"Nope, but I'm winging it."

Grady sighed. "I'll be praying for you, bucko. Will you be in church this week?"

"We'll be there. And thanks for the prayers. I need them." Rick closed his phone and went to see the sheriff. He slowed and gawked at an accident along Dead Gulch Curve, but the pickup involved wasn't familiar, and an ambulance was already on the scene.

He found Barry Borland in his office. The big man was kneeling in front of a filing cabinet that overflowed with papers. He lumbered to his feet when Rick rapped on the doorjamb.

"Have a seat, Rick." He gestured to the green chair in front of his desk.

Rick dropped into the chair and fished out his notebook. "I need your help, Sheriff."

"You know we don't have the manpower to station someone out there," Borland said.

"No problem, I've got that covered. But could you tell me if there have been any other break-ins in the area? Any reports of illegals being moved through here? Any strangers hanging around town? I reported some suspected illegals to border patrol last week."

The sheriff scratched his huge belly. "Well, now that you mention it, we did get a report of a vanload of Mexicans being detained by the border patrol. Seems a coyote had told them they could slip right through here without a problem. There was another truck seen speeding away when the van broke down. No one got a good make or description, though. And the folks aren't talking about who the coyote is. They were deported pronto."

"Someone recommended this area?"

"Yep."

"Robberies, transients?" Rick asked.

Borland shook his head. "Nothing unusual. Mary Beth Lucas had a window broken by a baseball. A few tourists wandered in and out of town without incident."

"Thanks, I just thought it was worth a shot." Rick hesitated and let his pencil rest against the notebook. "Anything new on Elijah's death?"

The sheriff's expression grew sober. "Sorry, I can't talk about that."

"It was murder?"

"Quit fishing, Rick." The sheriff shot him a long, hard look. "The autopsy report isn't back."

"Have you checked out Stuart Ifera? He was trying to strong-arm Elijah into selling the ranch."

"I've got it covered." Borland shuffled his papers. "Beat it, kid. I've got stuff to do."

"Ifera a friend or something?" Rick shot back.

Borland scowled. "Look, he's my brother-in-law, okay? He had nothing to do with Elijah's death. Now get out of my face."

Rick leaned forward. "Just do your job, Sheriff. Check it out."

"I did! You want me to arrest you, Bailey? I said get out of here." The sheriff looked like he was about to have a stroke.

Rick bolted to his feet and stormed from the room. What a joke the law enforcement was here. The breeze did little to cool his mood. Sitting on a stone wall, he called Brendan. "Hey buddy, did you find out anything on Hernandez's family?"

"Cowboy, you never let up, do you?" Brendan laughed with a trace of annoyance. "That's what made you such a good operative though. And, yeah, I ran a check. It's pretty interesting. You might be onto something with him. He had a brother, Luis. A small-town bully who's been arrested a few times for drunk and disorderly and assault. After Hernandez died in prison, Luis went on a drinking binge. He threatened to get 'the bopper' who killed his brother."

Rick stood and paced along the sidewalk. "So he could be our man. Any idea where he is now?"

"We lost him in Albuquerque. I've got the police keeping a look-out for him there."

"So he's close. He could be in the area. Could you fax me a picture?"

"Sure, no problem."

"I've got two other guys for you to check out. Mark Haskell and Ted Rediger, both from El Paso." Rick gave him the details Allie had given him. "Haskell stalked her once, maybe he's back."

"I'll see what I can find out."

Rick put his phone away. The library was across the street. He dodged the cars and bounded up the steps of the stone building. There were several computers free, so he stopped at the first one and began to look for information on Allie's vision problem. The information astounded him. No wonder she hated doing paperwork. An hour later he'd ordered pinkish lenses and colored overlays for reading.

The thought of her delighted smile when she got them made him grin as he strode back to his truck.

ALLIE SWATTED THE DUST FROM HER JEANS AND SHIRT AS SHE WATCHED the kids ride. Rick should be back from town soon, and she couldn't help glancing toward the lane every few seconds. The realization of how important he was becoming to her scared her.

"Good form, Bets," she called. Her daughter sat with her back straight and her knees hugging the mare's body. Her dark curls flew around her laughing face.

The child could ride anything with four legs. Allie had never seen anything like her daughter's ability with animals.

Allie hadn't been able to think about anything but Rick all afternoon. His desire to stay together had rattled her to the core. Watching her daughter's carefree face, she knew she couldn't take the security Betsy felt here away from her.

And she didn't want to leave either.

The promise of the future was as joy-filled as a glimpse of Betsy's bluebirds. No place had ever been permanent though, and Allie couldn't wrap her mind around the fact that maybe this time could be forever.

What if she fell in love with Rick and he left her too? Jon hadn't wanted to leave, but God had taken him just the same. There were no guarantees in life.

"They're doing good," Charlie said, putting a boot on the fence beside hers.

"I can't believe how well. Look at Fern. She's got her head up and is smiling from ear to ear. And even Latoya doesn't seem to care about getting dirty."

"They go home in another couple of weeks. We'll see if they keep what they've learned."

Allie glanced at him curiously. "You sound a little jaded, Charlie. Don't you think the ranch helps kids?"

"Sure it does. Just not all of them. They have to plant their boots and refuse to be moved."

"Like you did?" She wondered why he never talked about his past.

"Sure, like I did. I figured out my course and stuck to it."

"Were you a foster kid?"

He shook his head. "I had both parents and a brother."

"So you weren't one of Elijah's pet projects." Allie smiled. "He was an interesting guy."

"I was at the rodeo looking for a job, and someone told me about him. The ranch is in the boonies, and not many cowboys want to work out here when it's hot. You wait until summer comes and you may run screaming for the city too."

"I'm from El Paso," she reminded him.

"Another desert jackrabbit," he said, grinning.

Stuck clear out here, he probably had little opportunity to meet young women, but at least he'd taken the hint after her marriage became open knowledge. The campers here were off-limits to staff, and she was too old. And married, to boot. Poor kid couldn't win.

"You still see your parents, your brother?"

"Sure. My brother especially. He's a congressman in northern Texas. He'll be president one day." His voice vibrated with pride.

Allie hid her smile. She guessed he had something to be proud of.

Leon cantered up to them and reined in his horse. "Dude! I wish I could take my horse back with me. The brothers would freak to see this big guy." He patted the black gelding on the neck.

"Scout out the riding stables in San Antonio," Charlie told him. "See if you can get a job there and stay around the horses."

Leon's dark eyes reflected interest. "They probably wouldn't hire me. Too chicken."

"I'll write you a reference," Allie said.

"Way!" Leon urged the horse forward and took off in a canter around the lot.

The sound of an engine made Allie turn, and she saw Rick's truck coming down the driveway.

The way her pulse rattled should have scared the horses.

17

THE MONDAY MORNING ALBUQUERQUE TRAFFIC WAS SNARLED WORSE THAN a mess of baby rattlers. Rick negotiated the rental car through the streets thick with the slush of a late-spring snow. It would take longer to get to his destination than it had taken him to fly the small plane from the ranch. He'd left before daylight this morning, and he hoped to be back by midafternoon, but not if this traffic had its way.

He found a small hole in the line of cars and zipped off the freeway. Glancing at the piece of paper on the passenger seat, he watched for the Raynolds housing addition. Five minutes later he parked at the address.

Trash littered the lawn of the small, southwestern-style apartment building. Gouges marked the front door, and a broken window upstairs blared the details of a knockdown, drag-out fight between a shouting man and a screaming woman.

Rick took another look at the picture Brendan had faxed him, then got out of the car and went to the door. He stepped inside and found the apartment number he was looking for. Doubling his fist, he pounded on the door.

The smell of onions and hamburger hung in the hallway. Behind the door, he could hear a baby crying. He knocked again, his knuckles scraping across the gouged wood. The door finally opened to reveal a young Hispanic woman with a baby on her hip. About twenty, she had the kind of beauty that made any man take a second look. Long black hair swung to her hips, and her skirt barely covered the tops of her thighs.

"I'm looking for Luis Hernandez," he said.

"Luis, a five-o is here for you," she shouted over her shoulder, her gaze never leaving his.

"I'm not a cop," he said quickly.

"No? You look like one." She stepped aside, and he entered the small living room. Everything was in perfect order, and the furniture gleamed.

A young man entered the room. Dressed in jeans and a clean T-shirt, his frown grew more worried when he saw Rick. "You looking for me?"

"If you're Luis Hernandez."

"*Sí*. That's me," he said in a heavy Hispanic accent.

Rick introduced himself. "Do you know Allie Siders?"

"*Sí*. She's the *muchacha* who wasted my brother. Sent him to prison, and he never come out."

"I heard you threatened to get even."

Luis shrugged. "*Sí*, so what? Someone kill her?"

"No, she's fine. I want to make sure she stays that way."

"I don't care about the *muchacha*. My brother, he dead now anyway. I have my own *bebé* to raise. I stay out of trouble."

Looking into the young man's dark, earnest eyes, Rick decided he believed him. He'd come all this way for a dead end. He thanked them both and hurried back to his car.

Once Brendan found out where Mark Haskell was, he'd talk to him too, but Rick was beginning to wonder if he was looking in the wrong direction. Maybe it was just some random nut who'd fixated on Allie.

He drove back to the airport, dropped the rental car, and walked out to the small plane. An hour later, he was back at the ranch with a day wasted and not one iota wiser. He couldn't stand to waste the day. Maybe he'd go to the library and look around on the Internet.

Before he went to his truck, he stopped by the corral and found Allie. She was teaching the kids about horse etiquette.

She joined him at the fence. "How'd it go?"

He shrugged. "It was a washout. I don't think he had anything to do with it." He saw the cloud pass over her face and quickly added, "but I'm going to go into town and try to locate that stock supplier guy, Ted Rediger. You need me for anything?"

"No, we're fine." She put her hand over his. "Thanks for trying, Rick. It means a lot."

"I'll be back in time for dinner." In the car, he realized he hadn't told her what the FBI said about Jon's parents knowing where she was. He made a mental note to talk to her about it once the adoption hearing was over tomorrow. No reason to worry her before then.

He went to his truck and drove to town. As he passed town hall, he saw a man in a suit exit the sheriff's office. Could it be Stuart Ifera?

Taking a chance, Rick pulled his truck to the curb and jumped out. "Mr. Ifera," he called.

The man turned and shaded his eyes from the sun with his hand. "Yes?"

Bingo.

Rick stopped two feet away from the man. Natty dresser. Tie perfectly aligned, pinstriped suit, shoes buffed to a high shine. He could have stepped out of one of those fancy men's magazines.

His high-powered cologne made Rick sneeze. He stuck his hand out. "Rick Bailey."

Ifera shook it. "What can I do for you?"

"I'm foreman out at the Bluebird." Rick watched the man's face change from curiosity to a guarded wariness.

"Terrible about Elijah," Ifera said. "Just terrible."

"You saw him the week before he died. He told me you made an offer on the ranch that he refused."

"What of it?" The man's shrug was delicate. "I make offers on land all the time."

"Were you angry he turned you down?"

Ifera laughed. "Not angry enough to kill him, if that's what you're implying." He swept his hand over the landscape. "Look around you, Mr. Bailey. Land isn't hard to come by out here."

"We're by the river with lush vegetation. I can see where it would be a nice place to set a resort. The park borders us on one side, which would be convenient. Not much available with those amenities."

"Perhaps not," Ifera conceded. "But really, I didn't want it bad enough to kill him. After all, the new owner wouldn't necessarily be ready to sell either."

"She's not. She's my daughter, and I'll make sure it's here for her when she's ready." It was a slightly premature statement since the adoption wouldn't be final until Friday.

"Of course." Ifera's head bobbed in agreement. "If that's all you have, I'm late for an appointment." He turned and scurried away, a rat back to his hole.

Rick's intense dislike of the man didn't keep him from recognizing that everything Ifera had said was true. There was plenty of land to be had in the area. Ifera didn't need the Bluebird.

THE DENIM SKIRT TOUCHED THE TOP OF HER BOOTS, BUT IT WAS LOOSE AT the waist. Allie hadn't realized she'd lost weight since she'd been here. Nearly a month. It was hard to believe how much her life had changed.

She fluffed up her hair in the mirror. Her ruffled white blouse looked pretty and demure, but dark circles marred the pale skin under her eyes.

The judge had to grant the adoption today. Once it was final, Betsy would be safe from Jon's parents.

Her hair refused to be tamed, and she swiped at the tendrils that sprang from her head, trying and failing to tuck them behind her ears. For a dollar, she'd cut it all off.

Her nails shone glossy and perfect. She was ready. Her knees shook as she grabbed her bag and went downstairs to join Rick in the entry. He'd been gone all day yesterday and had returned with a defeated air.

Standing by the front door with Betsy in his arms, he looked uncomfortable in his khakis and starched shirt. They'd explained everything to her last night, and she'd looked at Rick with shining eyes when he told her he would be her new daddy.

He'd wormed his way into Betsy's heart even faster than he got into Allie's.

"Ready?" he asked.

She put her hand on her stomach. "We'd better go."

He held open the door for her to step through, then followed her onto the porch. The sun stabbed knives into Allie's eyes, and she winced. "I should have brought my hat."

"I'll get it." Rick set Betsy on the porch and went back inside.

Allie shaded her eyes with her hand and looked out to the purple cast of hills. A glint of sun on glass made her close her eyes. She slitted them open again and saw a familiar car come careening up the lane.

Everything in her tensed. "Not now," she whispered as the car came to a stop and her in-laws erupted from the vehicle.

"My baby!" Erika Siders ran toward the porch with her arms outstretched.

Allie couldn't remember ever seeing Erika wear anything other than a sensible gray or black dress that came to the bottom curve of her calf, and today was no exception. The thin blond hair was pulled back in a severe bun, and not a stitch of makeup brightened her pale face. Somehow dust found the nerve to settle on the sensible pumps on her mother-in-law's feet.

The controlled appearance was an effort to deny the squalor Erika had grown up in, but Allie knew the effects of that upbringing festered under the pristine surface.

Hugh Siders followed his wife more slowly. A black suit encased his tall, lanky frame. Gold-frame glasses perched on his nose, and he walked with determination toward Allie and Betsy. He could have passed for the most austere of undertakers.

Betsy pressed back against Allie's legs, then attempted to climb her skirt. Allie scooped her up. "Shh, it's okay," she whispered.

"You had no right," Erika said, her initial loud voice modulating to a cultured purr. "How could you disappear without telling us where you'd gone?" She held out her hands. "Come see Grandma, Betsy," she said.

Betsy buried her face in Allie's neck. "You should have called first," Allie said. "We've got an appointment in town."

"Oh, I know all about the appointment." Hugh arrived at the bottom of the porch and shook his finger at her. "It can't be allowed, you know."

"You have no say in it. I'm married now." Exquisite relief flooded her when she heard Rick's boots on the floor behind her.

"What's going on here?" he asked.

"These are Jon's parents," Allie said, hiking Betsy a little higher.

Rick nodded. "Rick Bailey. Your son was like a brother to me," he said. "But we've got an appointment in town. Feel free to wander around the ranch. We'll be back in a couple of hours."

His fingers touched Allie's elbow and helped break her paralysis. They moved to the steps, but Hugh and Erika still blocked the path.

"The appointment will have to be canceled. We dropped the kidnapping charge, but we won't let you adopt our granddaughter."

Rick's jaw flexed. He stepped out a foot ahead of Allie and shouldered through the couple. Hugh reeled back, his face going red. He made a grab for Betsy, who seized Allie's neck in a death grip.

Rick stepped between them. "I don't want to have to get rough, but you're scaring Betsy."

While Rick blocked the Siders couple, Allie ran with Betsy to the truck. She got inside and clicked the lock. The muted sounds of Hugh's raised voice and Rick's quick, commanding tones filtered through the window. What would she have done if Rick wasn't there? The Siderses always made her feel useless and damaged. It was hard to stand up against that kind of mental pressure, though she always managed to survive their insinuations.

Erika went flying back to their car, and Hugh stalked back as well with his fists clenched. Rick slid into the truck and jammed the key into the dash. Allie's hands shook as she fastened Betsy's seat belt.

"Where are they going?" Allie asked as the car peeled away in front of them with dust spuming from under the tires.

"To the courthouse," he said grimly. He tromped on the accelerator, and the truck fishtailed before the tires found purchase.

Out on the open road, he followed close behind the Siderses car, then made a sharp right turn onto a dirt road. "Shortcut," he said, his lips lifting in a grim smile.

"Can they stop us?" she asked.

"I don't think so."

From the way his hands gripped the wheel and the tightness of his jaw, she knew he was worried, in spite of his reassuring words.

She should have known things would go south at the last minute. This time, she'd fight with every ounce of strength she had to protect Betsy.

"They're really something, aren't they?" Rick said after a long pause.

The truck bucked like a wild mustang along the potholes. Allie grabbed the armrest to steady herself. "They've always interfered a lot. It drove Jon crazy."

"He told me about his childhood."

Allie nodded, glancing down to see that Betsy had put her earphones on. Even though he'd probably heard it, she needed to talk it out. "They had eight to ten foster kids at any one time, mostly for the money, Jon always thought. He was pretty much neglected and left to run wild. He never thought they cared about him except as an extension of themselves. He warned me that if anything happened to him, they'd try to get Betsy."

"But why? Sounds like they have plenty of other kids around."

She shrugged. "I think they want to make sure she's raised 'right' by their standards. Their brand of Christianity allows for picking and choosing what they want, like a smorgasbord. Their favorite saying is, 'Spare the rod, spoil the child.' Jon got his share of the razor strap." She looked at him sideways. "You might know something about that." When he didn't answer, she said, "They put on a great show at church and for the court, but at home there was always shouting and fighting."

A quick glance from under his brows at her, then he turned his attention back to the road. "Don't let them shake your confidence, Allie. You're doing a great job with Betsy."

"She still doesn't talk. Maybe it's my fault." She reached out and smoothed Betsy's dark curls.

"We're getting through. She's going to talk a blue streak one of these days. She's so much more animated than she was when she first came. Excitement is going to cause some words to come bubbling out eventually."

"I keep praying that happens."

Another quick glance from Rick. "Speaking of praying, I made an appointment with my pastor for us to have some marriage counseling. We go for our first session after the hearing."

She gulped. "Marriage counseling?"

He nodded without adding anything more.

"The pastor looked familiar, like I'd met him before. He's a nice guy."

"You did meet him, early in the week you came here. He's our vet too."

"Pastor O'Sullivan is a vet?"

"The church is too small to support a full-time pastor. Grady is a real man of God and was called to do both. Counseling with him should be easy."

"I didn't realize we were fighting," she said, sending a teasing smile his way.

He shot an answering grin back. "We want to keep it that way. I thought some counseling might help us learn to know each other a little faster."

Her voice softened. "I—I'm a little scared, Rick."

"Me too," he admitted. "I don't know how to be a husband or a dad. I've got a lot to learn. Getting a solid foundation can't do anything but help us."

Warmth flooded Allie. It took a lot of guts for him to admit his feelings of inadequacy. He felt as unprepared as she did. Maybe together they could bungle along and find their way.

THE COURTROOM FELT COLD AND DRAFTY. RICK HELD ALLIE'S HAND AND stood as the judge entered. So far he'd seen no sign of the Siderses, and he prayed they'd lost their way.

"Good morning," the judge said, adjusting her glasses on the end of her nose. Judge Thompson peered at them over the top of her spectacles. "Rick, you're a good man to be willing to take on this burden."

"It's not a burden, Your Honor. I'm eager to be a permanent part of Betsy's life." Rick felt Allie squeeze his fingers, and he returned the pressure.

"I've reviewed the documents and see no reason not to grant this request." The judge looked down at Betsy standing beside Allie. "Do you want a new daddy, young lady?"

Betsy nodded, and her smile blossomed out. She looked up at Rick with an adoring expression.

The judge laughed. "You always were someone the ladies liked, Rick."

"Stop!" The sound came from the door, and a fresh breeze blew in with the words.

Allie turned to see Hugh and Erika hurry into the courtroom and rush toward the judge's bench. *Oh no.* She wanted to grab her daughter and run from the room.

"What's the meaning of this interruption?" The judge frowned and glared over the top of her glasses at the intruders.

"We're Betsy's grandparents," Hugh said, his voice loud and strident. He pointed a finger at Allie. "She sneaked away when she heard we were suing for custody of Betsy. She's unfit to raise her, Your Honor." He raised a file of papers. "All the evidence is in here."

Allie gripped Rick's hand in a convulsive clutch.

Rick returned the pressure. "Judge Thompson is too smart to fall for this," he whispered to her.

She took courage from his words and tipped her face up to the judge. "That's not true, Your Honor. I'm a good mother."

"Did you know they were filing for custody?"

Allie wanted to look away from the judge's penetrating stare, but she forced herself to look the woman in the eye. "Yes, but I came here for Betsy. I'd heard about the ranch and thought it might be able to help her."

"And she came to be with me, Your Honor," Rick put in.

A smile flitted across the judge's face, then disappeared. "Be that as it may, I'll need time to review the custody suit. If I deem they have a case, I'll order it argued in court."

"But, Your Honor," Rick protested. "We're a family. The uncertainty isn't good for Betsy."

The judge waved her hand. "I'm sure you have nothing to worry about, but I have to review the case. Betsy's future depends on my making the right decision. The court will reconvene in a week, and I'll give you my opinion then." She smacked the gavel down. "Court adjourned."

The triumph on Hugh's face made Rick want to put his fist through it. Silent tears coursed down Betsy's face, and she pressed her cheek against his leg. He swept her into his arms. "It doesn't matter," he whispered into her hair. "The judge will fix things next week. You're not to worry, okay?"

She nodded, her wet cheek brushing his face. His gaze locked with Allie's, and he silently promised her everything would be all right.

18

A FEW CARS ROLLED THROUGH TOWN, THEIR WINDOWS DOWN AND MUSIC blaring from CD players. There was no radio reception out here. Allie stood beside Rick and Betsy on the sidewalk as the few pedestrians walked around them. The Siderses were smiling with triumph.

Allie wanted to hurt them.

All the plans, the excitement of the last few days, blew away like tumbleweeds. She'd tried so hard not to let this happen. The last thing Betsy needed was to be in the middle of this turmoil. She'd made such progress the last month, and Allie couldn't bear to see it slip away.

"We'd like to take Betsy to dinner," Erika said. "Is there any place to eat in this one-horse town?"

"The drugstore has milk shakes and hamburgers," Rick said. "And there's a small café. But we can't let you take Betsy. To tell you the truth, I'm not convinced you wouldn't just get her in the car and keep driving."

Erika's fair skin lit with pink. "Please. What do you think we are?" She held up her hand. "Don't answer that. It's obvious." She turned her gaze on Allie. "Surely you won't deny us the opportunity to spend some time with Betsy."

Allie had never wanted to deny them the right to see their grand-daughter. Betsy was all they had left of Jon, but their actions had altered the situation. "I can't let you take her. But you can join us for supper at the ranch."

Erika's brown eyes, so like Jon's, softened as they studied Allie's face. "That will do. Can I bring anything? And what hotel should we stay in?"

"There isn't a hotel in the area," Rick said.

Erika's face clouded. "Where is the nearest?"

"Twenty miles." Rick jabbed his finger to the north. "That way."

Allie's conscience was beginning to bother her. They'd come all this way to fight for Betsy. No child could get too much love. She'd do the best she could to be friendly and encouraging. Maybe they could resolve this out of court.

"You don't need to bring anything," she told Erika.

Hugh took his wife's arm. "We'll go see about that hotel."

His tone had softened too. Now that the urgency of the moment had passed, everyone seemed to be taking a step back and thinking about their reactions. Allie took heart. Maybe they could find their way through this amicably.

Once Jon's parents got in their car and drove away, Rick said, "Our first counseling meeting is in a few minutes. You up for it?"

Not really. Allie just nodded. She felt too upset to deal with anything else, but Rick had gone to all the trouble to set this up, and he was trying so hard.

"Grady lives just down the street by the church. We can walk." Rick hefted Betsy to his shoulders.

Allie followed him down the street. The day had turned warm, at least ninety even though it was late March. Rick turned up the walk of a two-story stone house that had vines growing up the sides. A welcome wreath decorated the cheery red door, and a scarecrow made out of the same vines stood beside the entrance.

The scent of honeysuckle wafted their way from somewhere. Rick pressed the doorbell, and a pretty blond with uncontrollable curls opened the door.

"Rick! I've missed you." She patted him on the arm and looked up at Betsy on Rick's shoulders. "You must be Betsy. I've got a little girl about your age. Her name is Courtney. She's been looking forward to playing with you."

"Allie, this is Dolly O'Sullivan," Rick said.

Dolly turned her bright smile on Allie, then hugged her. "Don't stand on the doorstep. I've been dying to meet the woman who managed to snatch Rick from the open market. I'm usually in the church nursery and don't always get to meet the visitors." She stood aside to allow them to enter.

A little girl with fiery red hair and big hazel eyes stood in the hallway. Her gaze went to Betsy, and she smiled. Betsy smiled back as Rick set her on the floor.

"Say hello, Courtney," Dolly said.

"Hi," Courtney said. "I made a fort in my room. You want to see it?" Betsy nodded, and Courtney took her hand. The two girls went down the hall. Allie stared after them. Betsy hadn't had a friend her own age to play with in ages. Could that make a difference?

She realized with a start that Dolly had been speaking to her. "I'm sorry?"

"I wondered if you'd like some coffee or tea?"

"Tea would be great."

"Iced or hot?"

"Iced today. Can I help you fix it?"

"No, no, come on into the living room." Dolly led the way to a large living room with overstuffed furniture.

Watercolors decorated the walls, and baskets of flowers were on every table, along with small wooden handcrafts. Some held eucalyptus, and the entrancing scent filled the room. The tables were all distressed wood, washed in white. A very country-looking place, warm and inviting.

Allie sank onto a sofa that threatened to swallow her. "This is lovely. I love the pictures."

"She painted them," a man said, stepping into the room through a swinging door that had small handprints painted on the white surface. "She's always dabbling in something." He beamed proudly at his wife, then approached Allie with his hand out. "Hello, Allie. It's good to see you again."

Allie shook his hand. "You did a good job with the mare. I think she's going to make it." The guy exuded confidence. With his help, maybe their marriage would make it too. "And I enjoyed the message last week."

"Thanks. It's good to have you in church." He shook Rick's hand and slapped him on the shoulder. "Cowboy, how could you get married behind my back? You surprised me, bucko." He settled into a recliner. "We can talk in here as easy as my office. It's probably more comfortable."

Rick's bulk sank onto the sofa beside Allie, and the depression rolled her toward him. He put his arm around her shoulders. The warmth of his body soaked into her like sunshine. It felt good to be cared for. She could get used to it.

Grady folded his arms. "We've got a lot to discuss. You two are basically strangers, isn't that right?"

Allie nodded, though Rick felt anything but a stranger now. His presence had quickly grown to be a comfort and a thrill at the same time.

"There are all sorts of potential landmines ahead," Grady said. "You need to work out how you'll handle things like conflicts over money, childrearing, housekeeping, even watching TV." He grinned and nodded at Rick. "In case you haven't realized it yet, Cowboy here is a sports nut. He'd watch any sport on TV until he turned into a turnip."

"I've noticed," she said.

Rick grinned. "Hey, she's got her quirks too. I just have to figure out what they are."

"I've got a form for you to fill out. We'll start with that. I want you to list your likes and dislikes, your pet peeves, your faults. There are also some questions for you to answer about how you were raised. We'll identify the trouble spots and talk them out over the next few weeks."

Allie thought she might actually enjoy it until she saw Rick exchange a long look with Grady. She knew so little about her new husband, but it looked like there might be something in his past he didn't want her to know. If it had to do with the scars on his back, she felt only sympathy.

IT WAS ALL GOING TO COME OUT. RICK KNEW HE DIDN'T HAVE A SNOW-ball's chance of keeping it from her. And even if he could, he knew he shouldn't if he wanted the marriage to work. Still, anticipating having to tell her, he wanted to stop at the Long Branch and get a tall cold one.

Some days he got tired of fighting the desire to drink. He could give in, let the liquor numb the pain and guilt that gnawed at him every day of his life. God had forgiven him, but he couldn't forgive himself, and the whiskey helped him forget it.

He shoved the thoughts away, refusing to entertain them. Staying sober meant keeping his thoughts positive.

Allie didn't have much to say as they started for home. He pointed the truck to the hills between town and the ranch. The truck felt a little sluggish, and he made a mental note to give it a tune-up. It was overdue.

Spring this year had been lush so far. Cactus and wildflowers bloomed along the roadside as far as he could see. The tension eased from his shoulders. He took his right hand off the wheel and stretched it across the seat, his arm brushing the top of Betsy's head, letting his fingers tangle in Allie's hair.

She turned and smiled at him. Then it happened.

The truck lurched to the right, and he saw the front right wheel go rolling off into the ditch. The screech of metal on pavement nearly deafened him. The vehicle careened toward the embankment, and as he fought the wheel, jamming on the brakes to no avail, he heard Allie scream.

The truck tilted to the right, and he prayed that it wouldn't roll. Allie's door would be crushed in. The wheel bucked and jerked in his hands like a wild bull. The scenery rushed past, but he managed to keep the truck on the road as he sent a shout up to God for help.

Dead Gulch Curve was just up ahead. The road tilted to the right, and the vehicle with it. Rick wrenched the truck to the left, then saw an SUV coming toward him in the opposite lane. He veered back to the right, and the vehicle roared toward the ditch.

A large boulder jutted out from the rock face into the drop-off. He wasn't going to be able to miss it.

"Hang on!" With his foot buried in the brake pedal, he aimed for a glancing blow. From the corner of his eye, he saw sparks fly up from the right front end.

The truck slammed into the boulder in what seemed like slow motion. Allie flung out her arm to protect Betsy, and Rick's right arm did the same. Their hands locked across the little girl as the cab crumpled like a candy wrapper and folded in accordion style.

The three of them rocked forward, and he heard Allie's head strike the glass, a sickening sound that made him tighten his fingers on hers.

The silence after the wild ride was eerie. The only sound was the engine ticking as it cooled. Then the horn began to blare in a nightmarish, never-ending alarm.

"Allie? You okay?" Rick's gaze touched Betsy, who was sobbing and touching her mother's arm, trying to shake her. His attention moved on to his wife. His gut clenched when he saw the bright splash of blood on the window, and the way it had shattered to a star.

Her eyes were closed, and blood ran down her face from a cut on her forehead. "Allie?" He reached over Betsy and touched her face. Her eyes still didn't open.

Digging out his cell phone, he dialed 9-1-1, but even as he reported the accident, he knew he'd have to help her now. It would take an ambulance forever to get here.

The SUV in the opposite lane had stopped as well, and a man leaped out and jogged over to Rick's truck. "You okay?"

"My wife is hurt," Rick said through his shattered window. He was trying not to panic and wasn't doing a very good job of it.

"I'm a physician's assistant. Let me take a look at her." The man went around to the other side of the truck and tugged on the door. "It's stuck. I'll have to come in from your side." The man moved back to Rick's door and opened it with Rick's help.

Rick unfastened Betsy's seat belt and pulled her out with him. The other driver crawled inside the truck, and Rick began to pray.

19

Every bone ached like she'd been thrown from a bucking bronco. Allie tried to open her eyes, but they felt glued shut. Her face felt swollen. Had she fallen from a horse?

She tried to move and groaned when the pain intensified. Even the softness of the sheets scraped her wounded face.

"Lie still," Rick's voice spoke in her ear. His hand smoothed her hair.

"Wha-what happened?" She managed to get her eyes open.

"We had an accident."

Her memory flooded back. The wheel coming off, the crash. "Betsy!" She tried to rise up.

"She's fine." His hands pressed her back against the pillow.

She squinted through slitted eyes. The sunlight filtered through blinds in an unfamiliar room. "Where am I?"

"The hospital in Alpine. You've got a concussion."

She managed to focus on Rick's face. Drawn and wearing a worried frown, he sat in a chair pulled up to the side of her bed. "Where's Betsy?"

"Grady and Dolly took her. I told them to be careful to watch her," he said when she frowned.

"I need to get out of here. She needs me." Panic raced across her face again. "Jon's parents. Where are they?"

"I don't know. They probably went to the house for dinner, but we never made it home."

"Make sure Grady knows not to let them have Betsy." She struggled against his hands again. "I've got to get out of here."

"The doctors haven't released you yet," he said.

"I don't care. I want to go home." Strange that she thought of the ranch as home already. She knew she couldn't resist the pressure of his hands. "Could I have some water?"

When he turned to get her water glass, she rose from the pillow and swung her feet to the side of the bed. Her head swam, but she began pulling the needles out of her arms. The blackness receded, and the nausea began to subside. Her head still ached, but it wasn't enough to stop her from getting to her daughter.

"Stop! What are you doing?" Rick sprang toward her, spilling the water in the cup onto her lap.

With all the needles out, she stood, though shaky. "I'm going home. Where are my clothes?" Blood trickled down her arm from the holes left by the IVs.

"Mrs. Bailey, what are you doing?" A nurse's rubber soles squeaked on the floor as she rushed into the room. She grabbed at Allie's arm.

Allie shook her off, practically falling into Rick. She looked up at him, letting him see all her hope and desperation. "I can't stay here. Betsy needs me."

"She's fine, Allie." Rick took her by the shoulders. "I wouldn't let anything happen to her."

"You're here," she pointed out. "Two hours away from her." She pulled away from his grip and nearly fell. "Where are my clothes? I'm checking myself out."

The nurse bit her lip and glanced at Rick. "We don't have the right to keep her," she said, her tone apologetic. "You'll have to sign a paper stating you are leaving against the advice of your doctor," she told Allie. She dug white tape out of the pocket on her smock. "Let me stop the bleeding."

Allie held out her arm. "Hurry, please. My clothes?"

The nurse put a cotton ball and tape over her wrist and pressed it down. "They were cut off you. I'm afraid there's not much left of them." She went to the small closet and drew out a plastic bag full of material. She unzipped it and pulled out the remains of Allie's denim skirt and blouse. "They're not wearable."

"I can't go home naked." For such a small problem, it felt over-whelming, and Allie wanted to sit on the edge of the bed and burst into tears. She gritted her teeth and forced back her emotion.

"I can give you another gown to put on backward," the nurse said. "Just a minute." She disappeared through the door.

"Have a little trust," Rick said. "Grady and Dolly will take care of Betsy."

"She's going to be beside herself, Rick. I'm sure she saw the ambulance cart me off all bloody and unconscious."

"I called and had Grady put her on the phone. I told her you were going to be okay."

"That's not the same as seeing me. I'm fine, it's just a concussion." In truth, her head was hurting more and more, and she felt dizzy and disoriented. But she'd be all right when she got home in her own bed.

"Here, you can talk to her." He pulled out his phone and punched in the number. "Grady? Put Bets on again." He waited a moment, then passed the phone over to her.

"Betsy? It's Mommy. I just wanted you to know I'm okay. I'm coming to get you, okay?" She could hear breathing on the other end and the sound of a sob. "Mommy's okay, sweetie. Don't you worry. You have fun with Courtney."

A moment later Grady came on the line. "She's smiling, Allie. You sure you're okay?"

"Just sore. We're coming after her now."

"You're sure the doctors say you can?"

"The doctors don't know everything. Listen, Grady, if Jon's parents try to take Betsy with them, don't let them have her."

"I won't. She's safe with us, Allie. Rest easy."

"Thanks." She closed the phone and handed it to Rick.

He slipped it into his pocket. "I wish you'd stay. She knows you're okay now."

"I'll be better in my own bed."

And when she held Betsy.

She gave him a curious stare. "How'd you get here with the truck disabled?"

"Charlie came and got me in your pickup. I dropped him at the ranch and came on here."

Allie winced at the thought of a ride back in the old rattletrap truck littered with grain and smelling of horse manure. "What happened? It's all a little fuzzy."

He narrowed his eyes, and his mouth took on a grim slant. "It's pretty strange. The lug nuts didn't break off, which is what I thought at first. But I took a look at the bolts, and they're perfectly fine. I couldn't find any of the lugs laying around in the ditch or the road either."

"A-are you saying someone took the lugs off?"

"I'm suspicious," he said. "That truck's only a year old. I rotated the tires a month ago. Everything was fine. The truck was parked in town for hours. I guess someone could have tampered with it."

All the blood rushed to her feet, and she swayed where she stood. Rick grabbed her arm. "I have to get to Betsy," she said. "She's in danger."

"Grady will take care of her." Though he protested, a worried frown formed between his eyes.

The nurse returned with another gown. "You're making a mistake," she said, holding it out for Allie to slip into.

By the time Allie signed the papers and Rick helped her to the truck, she was shaking with fatigue, and her head felt like it was as big as the boulder they'd hit. It was hard to think past the pain, and she had to keep swallowing down the bile that burned the back of her throat.

She could do this. Betsy had to be protected.

"You can put your head on my lap," Rick said, shooting her a concerned glance.

"Maybe I will." She put on the lap belt, then loosened it enough to crumple onto the seat, her head on the hard muscles of his leg. "Not exactly the softest pillow I've ever laid on," she said, turning her head and smiling up at him.

"Sorry." He drove with one hand on the wheel, and his right hand came down to settle on her shoulder as if to keep her safe.

Even Jon wasn't this protective. Allie had never felt so treasured and cared for. Why did he do it? He couldn't love her, not yet. She didn't quite get it, and though she wanted to ask, the words hid in the back of her throat.

He must have sensed her emotion, because he looked down with his eyebrows winging up. "Something wrong?"

"How can you act this way toward me?" She blurted the words out before she could lose her nerve.

"What way?"

"So sweet—and loving. You don't love me." She watched his face to see if it would give away his emotions. Rick was so hard for her to read. She'd never met anyone like him.

He was silent for so long, she began to think he wasn't going to answer her. Warmth radiated down through his arm and fingers and transferred to her shoulder.

"I haven't had a lot of unconditional love in my life," he said. "Only from God. Grady said something from the pulpit once I've never forgotten. He said, 'Love isn't an emotion, it's an action.' I figure if I *act* with love toward you, I might start feeling it."

Allie had never heard such a thing before. "Not an emotion? What did he mean?"

Rick shrugged. "You should have him tell you. He's better at explaining stuff like that. But I took it to mean that the giddy feelings can come and go. I think he called that infatuation. Real love means I go to work when I'd rather stay home in bed. Real love puts up with burned dinner and no clean underwear." He grinned when she grimaced. "He said love is an action verb. So I decided if we were going to stay married, I'd work out the love and wait for the giddy emotion."

He was basically saying she didn't give him the butterflies she felt even now flying around her insides, and she wasn't sure whether to be offended or to hug him. The thought of steadfast care and support felt like a safety net she'd never had. Her mother had always preferred Allie's sister, who was as good a barrel racer as she'd ever seen. Though she was loved, Allie always felt she came up lacking.

Rick didn't seem to be comparing her against anyone, and she'd been comparing him to Jon constantly. Jon was two years in his grave, and she was still alive. Could it be all right to accept what Rick offered? For the first time, she didn't shudder at the thought of letting down Jon's memory.

"So you're not attracted to me?" She couldn't help but remember the kiss they'd shared in the meadow, a kiss that nearly ignited a prairie fire.

"I didn't say that." His grin widened. "I'm a red-blooded male, you know. And you're a beautiful woman. But real love isn't about chemistry. Or at least not *only* about chemistry. If it were, when I've got a pot belly and you've got a turkey neck, we'll want to go look for someone younger. I want more than that from a marriage."

So did she.

And she was only beginning to realize how much.

RICK SAT IN THE OFFICE WITH HIS FEET ON THE DESK LATE INTO THE night. He hadn't wanted to tell Allie how worried he was about the accident two days ago. It was all he could handle to keep the Siderses from hauling off Betsy, and to get Allie to stay in bed. At least the pain meds had kept her worry at bay.

But not his.

Someone had made a deliberate attempt to harm them and almost succeeded. The doctor told him that if she'd hit her head just a little harder, she would have fractured her skull. He couldn't wait for Brendan or the sheriff to figure out who was behind this. First thing tomorrow he'd go see the border patrol. Maybe they had some new information.

He heard the soft movement of bare feet on the wood floor. Removing his feet from the desk, he stepped to the door and peered through the dark house. A shadowy movement came on the stairs, and he saw Latoya tiptoeing to the landing.

She was fully dressed in jeans and carried her shoes in one hand. She reeked of perfume, some flowery scent that made his eyes water when he got closer.

"What are you doing?" he asked.

She jumped, and her shoes clattered on the floor. Retrieving them, she turned and shook her finger at him. "You scared me out of an inch of nail growth."

"I repeat, what are you doing? If I didn't know better, I'd think you were sneaking out to meet someone."

She tossed her head, and her black cornrows bobbed. "What if I am? Whatcha going to do about it, boss man? Turn me in?"

Rick stepped closer to her. "Nothing," he said. "You're nearly an adult, Latoya. If you're going to make something of your life, you're the only one who can choose your actions. I could make you march back upstairs, but that would just make you resentful. Instead, I want you to think before you walk out that door. The direction of your life hinges on the choices you make."

Her dark eyes never left his face, and he saw the defiance slip out of her tense shoulders and tightly clenched fists.

"You don't know what it's like," she said, plopping down on the bottom step. "To want to *be* someone, to have someone love you."

"Sex isn't love, girl. I think you know that by now. And I *do* know what it's like." He moved to join her. "Move over." She scooted over, and he sat down beside her. "I was where you are once. Only instead of sex, my drug of choice was whiskey. It cost me my best friend and my self-respect. You're young enough to stop that downward spiral. You've got a lot on the ball—you're smart, pretty, enthusiastic. If you want to make people respect you, you've got to respect yourself first."

"Easy for you to say," she said. "My mama brings home her boy-friends. They . . . do things to me."

"You don't live there now. Take back your life, Latoya. Don't let the nightmares of the past destroy it."

She lowered her head, and he caught the glint of a tear on her cheek. Anything he said now would be too much. All he could do is let her think it through.

"You got a way with words," she said grudgingly. "Do you really think I'm smart?"

"I do. And you've got a way with the animals. That shows a lot of heart."

She fell silent again for a few long moments, then she slowly rose with her shoes in hand and turned to go back up the stairs. "Mornin' will be here too soon. I'm going back to bed."

"Good girl. I'm proud of you."

"Whatever. It's just one day."

"It only takes one day at a time. Believe me, I know." He watched her sashay back upstairs. It was so easy to dispense advice and so hard to live by it.

When was he going to let go of his past? All it took was a choice like Latoya had made tonight. God had forgiven him—he had no doubt about that. It was time he forgave himself.

He bowed his head and vowed to make a choice this one day to let go of the guilt.

20

SHE WOULDN'T EVEN NEED MAKEUP TO BE A RODEO CLOWN. ALLIE PEERED through swollen lids at her reflection in the mirror. Purple discoloration bloomed around her eyes and forehead. Her lips looked swollen too. A large goose egg jutted from her forehead.

It was enough to frighten little children.

She pulled on her jeans, wincing at the pain the movements caused. Betsy watched her with big, scared eyes. "It's okay," she told her daughter. "It looks worse than it is. I'm fine. My muscles are just sore like when I work hard all day."

After two days, this soreness should have been gone. She should be moving around by now instead of letting everyone force her to stay in bed.

She held out her hand to Betsy, and the little girl climbed off the bed and came to her. "Let's go fix breakfast," she told her. "Everyone will be starved, and I need to get everything back to normal. I can't stay in this room another minute. I might scream. Want to hear me scream, Bets?"

Betsy giggled, putting her hand over her mouth. She nodded. Allie smiled back. "Ah!" she screamed.

Betsy giggled again. A giggle was a sound. It was the promise of hope.

When Allie opened her bedroom door, she could smell the aroma of bacon. "Guess they thought they were going to make me stay up here another day," she said. Her head felt clear for the first time in three days, but she took her time getting down the steps to the kitchen.

Rick stood at the stove with a fork in his hand. When the frying bacon popped, he winced and put the back of his hand to his mouth. The bacon was beginning to smell a little burned. Jem sat at his feet with his tongue hanging out.

"You practicing for the fire department?" she asked.

He whipped around and pointed the fork at her. "You're supposed to be resting. I can handle this."

"Uh-huh, I think your bacon is burning."

He turned back around with an exclamation and began to fork up the bacon onto a plate. A few pieces fell to the floor, and Jem gobbled them up.

Allie chuckled to herself and moved to the stove. She bumped him out of the way. "Scoot before you have to break out the big hoses." Plucking the fork from his hand, she turned off the heat and moved the skillet away so she could get the bacon to the plate. Half-cooked scrambled eggs were mounded in a bowl on the counter. The congealed mess looked hardly edible.

Allie got out a fresh skillet, transferred a little bacon drippings from the old skillet and dumped the eggs back in to finish cooking. The bacon was a little overdone but salvageable. "You can fix some toast," she said.

He gave her a shamefaced grin and took the bread out of the breadbox. "I'm a lousy cook."

"I noticed." Smiling made her face hurt, but in a good way.

God had protected all of them, and she was alive. There was much to be thankful for.

"Did things go well with Jon's parents and Betsy?" she asked. She vaguely remembered their brief visit in her room.

"They only stayed an hour. Betsy seemed afraid of them. Has she not been around them much?"

"We used to visit every week, but they're so loud and bossy that they scare her. And me," she admitted. "Sunday dinners were just painful. Betsy could never sit quietly enough or eat nicely enough. I quit going about three months ago except for an occasional visit. They might be her grandparents, but they weren't helping her get well. She'd wet the bed for two nights after every visit."

Rick put his big hand on her shoulder. "They won't get her away from us," he said.

Smiling up at him, she thought about how she'd misjudged him the night they met. For all his size, his gentleness and caring were rare.

And very appealing.

Rick called the rest of the bunch for breakfast. Latoya seemed unusually quiet, and even the boys were morose. Fern didn't say anything, but that wasn't unusual.

"What's with everyone?" Allie asked. "You'd think someone died."

The kids just looked at one another, then their gazes went back to their plates. Allie met Rick's gaze across the table. He shrugged and raised his brows as if to say he didn't know what was up.

"One week, and we're checkin' out," Devon said finally. "Gotta go back to the city."

Latoya put out her lip. "I wanted to learn to barrel race first."

"How about if I teach you before you leave?" Allie stood and began to clear the table.

"You're not well enough to do much with that," Rick said, taking the plates from her hands. "Go rest."

"I'm not an invalid." She tried to snatch the plates back, but he held them up out of her reach.

"Then go do your book work."

Her hands fell to her sides. She was so far behind on that book work. Did he know? She examined his face. There was something in his eyes that made her wonder if he realized how out of her element she was with paperwork.

"I'll do that," she said evenly. She turned to the teenagers. "You guys go curry the horses and get them saddled. We'll practice some barrel racing."

"Can I take Betsy with me?" Fern asked in her soft voice.

Allie grappled with the thought of Betsy being out of her sight. "She'd better stay with me."

"I'll be out there," Rick said. "It's okay."

Allie opened her mouth to protest, then closed it again. Rick had been on her to quit coddling Bets, and he was right. Nothing would happen to her daughter with Rick there.

"I'll guard her with my life. You know that."

Allie nodded. "I'll be out in a little while." She headed to the office, and her head began to ache with every step toward the torture chamber. The bright sunlight cast spears of pain into her eyes, and she crossed the room to close the blinds. When she turned back to the desk, she saw a box on it.

It was addressed to her. Dread seized her throat. Could it be another message from the killer?

Taking a step back, she stared at it. She wasn't going to let him terrorize her. She grabbed a letter opener and held it like a knife. Flipping it around, she slit the tape and opened the box. She didn't want to look inside.

He might have put a dead snake or something in it.

She should probably call Rick, but she told herself not to be a ninny. It was only a package. Snapping open the top, she peered inside. Wads of bubble wrap obscured the contents. Unable to help herself, she popped a bubble before lifting it out. Under it was an eyeglass case. Under that was a folder.

A movement by the door caught her eye, and she looked up to see Rick leaning against the doorjamb with Betsy in his arms. They were both smiling.

"Open the case," he said, crossing the room to join her at the desk. He set Betsy on the floor.

"This is from you?"

He nodded. "It's to celebrate our new beginning." His smile widened.

Then she realized what this was. "Overlays for reading, and pink glasses?" She didn't wait for him to answer but picked up the case and opened it. The glasses were as precious as gold. She perched them on her nose, and the soft color washed the hard glare out of her vision.

"Rick, they're wonderful." She whirled and leaped at him. He caught her, and she wrapped her arms around his neck. "Thank you, thank you!" Before she could have second thoughts, she kissed him.

His lips were firm and gentle. She pulled away and looked into his eyes. "It's the nicest present anyone ever got me."

"I'm glad," he whispered.

"You can put me down now." Her feet dangled at least eight inches off the floor.

"What if I don't want to?" He grinned, but his eyes told her he was serious. He brushed her lips with a soft kiss, then set her on the floor.

Allie stepped away and looked around the room. Her eyes widened as she took in details of the room she'd missed before. The soft patina of oak bookshelves, the detail in the oriental rug on the floor. "Everything is so much clearer!"

"Glad they help you." He shoved his hands into the pockets of his jeans.

"How'd you get them?"

"Ordered them online at the library. I want to give you what you need," he said.

Her exuberance gave way to self-consciousness. Did he expect something from her for them? She wasn't ready to do anything more than share a quick kiss.

His gaze searched hers as if he were looking for something. A heavy sigh eased out. She wasn't quite sure what he'd hoped to see, but it hurt that she'd disappointed him.

The light in his eyes dimmed. He took Betsy's hand and disappeared from the room. Allie sighed and got to work. She found the book work a breeze with her new eyeglasses and the overlays. The numbers and letters didn't jump around, and she quickly input the data in the account book and wrote the checks for the bills.

It only took an hour, then she shut the book and locked it in the desk. The kids would be ready for their first barrel-racing lesson. She stepped to the door. The phone rang, and she backtracked.

"Bluebird Ranch," she said into the receiver. There was only silence on the line. "Hello, is anyone there?"

A song began to play. Eddy Arnold's rich voice came to her ear, singing, "Gonna Find Me a Bluebird." The phone dropped from her fingers.

How did he know she loved that song?

She backed away from the phone, then bolted from the room. In her haste, she banged her shoulder against the doorjamb, but the pain barely slowed her down. Her boots slid on the polished wood floor of the hallway, but she managed to stay on her feet and ran to the front door. Throwing it open, she stepped out into the sunlight and stood blinking on the porch.

The hills had a watching quality, as if he stood hidden among the rocks with binoculars trained on her. Maybe he did. How could he know so much about her unless he was nearby?

RICK LENGTHENED THE STIRRUPS ON THE SADDLE HE HAD PUT ON BETSY'S mare. "We're going to see how she likes being ridden, Betsy."

The little girl had an uneasy frown between her eyes, but she nodded. Her gaze cleared, and she looked up at him with such trust that he felt ten feet tall and bulletproof.

"Don't you think she needs a name?" he asked. "It would make her feel more at home."

Betsy hesitated, then nodded. The tip of her tongue came out, and she wetted her lips. Rick held his breath.

Say something, honey. He didn't dare say the words for fear of breaking the spell.

"Bluebird," Betsy said in a voice so soft and hoarse it barely carried above the sound of the wind.

Rick wanted to sweep her into his arms and lift her high, but he tempered his excitement. He glanced toward the house, wanting to run and tell Allie, but if Betsy thought it was a huge deal, she might clam up again. "Okay, Bluebird is what we'll call her. She's a blue roan, so it fits." He ran his hand over the horse's neck. "How do you like your new name, Bluebird?"

The horse turned and looked at him, and he could have almost sworn the mare recognized how important it was that Betsy had named her. He rubbed the mare's face and ears. "I'm going to get on your back, girl. I'll try not to hurt you."

He fitted his boot into the stirrup. Bluebird didn't move away but stood still and quiet. Testing his weight, he stepped onto the stirrup, then back off, but again she didn't move. Though she'd been abused, she was going to let him mount.

With a smooth, easy movement, he swung onto her back. Mistake. The mare began to buck and snort, arching her back into the air like a rodeo bronco. She tossed Rick so high he could have snatched at the clouds. Seconds later, he was flat on his back with his mouth full of dust and staring up at the mare's underbelly. She was still bucking, and he rolled away before she could trample him.

Betsy ran to him and patted his face with her small hands. "Okay?" she asked in her rusty voice.

"I'm fine, Bets. We should go find your mother though."

Betsy must have thought he meant he needed Allie's help, because she took off like a roadrunner, running so fast she kicked dust back into his face. He spit it out and sat up as Betsy returned with her mother in tow. Allie must have already been outside and on her way. At least she hadn't seen his humiliating fall.

He bolted to his feet before she could help him. "Betsy, tell your mom what you named your mare."

Allie's eyes went wide, and her lips parted. "You gave your horse a name, Betsy?"

The little girl nodded. "Bluebird," she said again in her rough voice.

Allie dropped to her knees and pulled Betsy into her arms. "That's a wonderful name, Bets," she said in a choked voice. "It suits her."

"Bluebirds can be vicious if you've ever seen them shaking a worm. Bluebird isn't as sweet as she looks." Rick said, dusting off his jeans.

"She threw you?" Allie stood but kept Betsy's hand in hers.

"Like a roadrunner shaking a snake." He grinned and took Betsy's other hand, but the little girl pulled away from both of them and ran to climb onto the fence to watch her horse.

"Are you okay?" Allie asked.

"The only thing hurt is my pride. The old girl fooled me. Stood so quiet I thought she was used to being ridden." He looked at Allie then and realized she was on the verge of tears. Her hands were clasped tightly together in front of her. Her agitation wasn't the joyous kind Betsy's talking would bring about.

He took her hand, unhooking it from the other one. "You're shaking. What's wrong?"

"I don't know whether to laugh or cry." She rubbed her eyes. "Betsy's talking," she said. "But for how long? He called me while I was working."

"Who?"

She clung to his hand. "The guy who's after me."

His fingers tightened, and he drew her close to his chest. She fit so well in his arms, like she was made to be there. His hands stroked her soft hair, so fine and silky. The trembling eased. "Now tell me what he said."

"Nothing," she mumbled. "He played a song."

"What song?"

"'Gonna Find Me a Bluebird.' It's my favorite."

"How'd he know that?"

She pulled away and glanced up at him. "That's what scares me. He knows things about me, whoever he is."

He pulled her tight again. "You're safe here."

But was she? He looked out over her head and saw the glint of binoculars on the hillside.

He grabbed Gunner from the corral and rode up the hill. Jem ran along beside the horse. No weapons, he realized. His nightstick was in the umbrella stand by the front door.

Pebbles scattered and slid down the slope as the horse's hooves dislodged them. The wind nearly blew his hat off when he reached the top of the incline. Turning in his saddle, he looked down toward the ranch. It was about here he'd seen the glint of something.

He dismounted and led Gunner along the narrow trail. His gaze scanned the thin, rocky soil for tracks.

Jem growled, then took off toward a big rock that looked like a jackrabbit. Rick leaped after the dog. He heard a man's voice shout, then a figure shot up from behind the rock and backed away from the snarling dog. Jem never barked or snarled, so Rick grabbed a rock in each hand and rushed forward to see who would rile the dog like that.

A Hispanic man who looked like he was in his fifties was kicking at the dog and screaming in Spanish. He seemed oblivious to Rick's approach.

"Diablo!" the man shouted. *"Perro diablo."*

Devil dog. Jem was anything but that. Rick grinned when he realized the guy wasn't armed. He called the dog, and Jem trotted over to sit at Rick's feet.

"Who are you?" he asked the man.

The guy spread his hands out. "No Engless," he said in a heavily accented voice.

Rick switched to Spanish and asked the question again. The man told him he was heading to Mexico to take money to his mother. He was quick to pull out his card to prove he was legal.

It was only after Rick let him go and returned to the ranch that he realized the guy didn't have anything shiny on his person. So where had the glint come from?

21

WHILE RICK WAS CHECKING OUT THE HILLS, ALLIE PULLED BETSY ONTO her lap and smoothed her curls. "I'm so glad to hear your voice, sweetheart. I've missed it so much." Her own voice was choked, and she swallowed to regain control. She didn't want Betsy to feel bad. "Now when you play with Courtney, you can talk to her too."

Her eyes bright, Betsy smiled. Pride shone out all over her.

Rick had performed a miracle here. Allie still couldn't believe it, but the big guy had gotten through Betsy's defenses. And the horse helped too, of course. The ranch had worked its magic.

Betsy looked over Allie's shoulder. "Grammy and Grandpa." She pointed.

Allie turned to see the familiar car rumbling along the bumps toward them. Careful to hide her displeasure, she let Betsy stand, then groaned as she got to her feet to greet the Siderses.

Erika got out, smoothed her skirt, then started toward the corral. Hugh followed. Her gaze traveled from Allie's head to her jeans, and she grimaced. Then a pleasant smile dropped into view as if she changed masks. "Allie, my dear, should you be out of bed?"

Allie wanted to brush any dust from her clothing and hair, but she wasn't going to give Erika the satisfaction of knowing she felt self-conscious. "I'm fine. I'm about to teach the kids how to barrel race."

"I hope you're not letting Betsy participate in something so dangerous."

"Not yet," Allie said. "But she'll learn when she's ready."

A disagreeable expression twisted Erika's mouth, and she started to answer, then snapped her lips shut. When her smile returned, it looked forced. "We thought we might take you to lunch."

"It's only ten o'clock," Allie said.

"We can visit until then," Hugh said. "You need us to help out with anything?"

Like they were dressed for ranch work. Hugh's black suit was already picking up dust.

"No, we're fine," Allie said. What was she going to do with them for two hours? Her gaze settled on Betsy's head. "I've got good news—Betsy is talking again!"

She expected them to be overjoyed, but instead suspicion narrowed their eyes. They glanced from her to Betsy.

"Is this a scam?" Hugh demanded.

Allie rolled her eyes. "Betsy, say hello to Grammy and Grandpa."

Betsy didn't look up, but she shook her head.

"You're just trying to bolster your position with the court," Erika said. "You think if you can say Betsy is talking again, you won't look so incompetent. What do you take us for, Allie? The judge won't be taken in either."

"No, she won't. She'll see right through the two of you," Allie shot back before she could bite her tongue.

Hugh's face reddened. "I should have known you wouldn't accept an olive branch. Erika, get in the car." He stomped back toward the car.

Erika opened her mouth, then closed it again and followed her husband.

Allie ran her hand over her daughter's curls. "Why wouldn't you talk to Grammy?"

"She doesn't like me," Betsy said.

"Of course she does, sweetheart. She loves you."

Betsy shook her head, her chin taking on a stubborn jut. "She yells."

"That's just her way. Everyone loves you, Bets."

Betsy smiled up at her, and Allie felt a fresh burst of joy. Her soul had been so hungry for communion with her child. It was one thing to talk to Betsy and know she heard, but another thing for her to listen to her daughter's sweet voice answering back. She wasn't sure how she'd survived the silence this past year.

Rick came back down from the hills. "Just someone walking," he said. "Nothing to worry about."

But Allie saw how Rick kept glancing back toward the hills. She sensed his worry. Setting her focus on the kids, she decided she wasn't going to think about it. The kids were depending on her to have a fun day, and she was not going to let anything mess it up, not Jon's parents, and not some wanderer.

She went to the corral and joined the kids. "The most important thing about barrel racing is the connection between you and your horse. You've all been here long enough to figure out which horse is your favorite," she told the kids. "A good horse can go for fifty thousand dollars or more, so the horse means everything. None of these horses have been trained yet, but that doesn't mean they can't learn what you want and expect. All of you go get the horse of your choice."

She and Rick watched as the teenagers glanced at one another, then trotted off to take charge of a horse. Latoya grabbed Moonbeam's reins, and Fern gave a longing glance at Cupcake.

"You can ride her, Fern. It's been nearly a month, and she's doing good," Rick said.

The girl's smile beamed out, and she went to the mare. The boys chose Winston and Rebel. They all looked half-scared as Rick rolled barrels from the garage into the corral.

"Okay, the object is to go around the barrels in a cloverleaf pattern and to do it without knocking over any of the barrels. The winner is the one who takes the least time. Let me show you." Her muscles complaining, Allie mounted Jackson.

This was going to be hard with the way her body ached, but the exercise would be good for that. The gelding's hard muscles moved under her legs. She patted his sleek neck. "It's hard for the horse if you come at the barrel straight on," she said, urging her horse to a trot. "I'm going to go slow at first and show you the angles."

Jackson responded to the pressure of her knees on his sides and the reins on his neck. The gelding went around the barrel completely, then turned to cross to the other barrel. With his body tipping to the right, Allie felt the saddle give a little. She tried to adjust her position when she felt it give a little more.

What was wrong with the thing? Shifting her weight, she felt it give again.

Then it was sliding down the horse's belly.

She kicked her left foot free of the stirrup and tried to do the same with the right as she vaulted away from the horse, but her boot caught. Tugging on it, she slid down the horse's belly with the saddle. Dangling by her right foot, her back slammed into the dirt.

Allie tasted dust.

She tried to reach up and grab the reins, but Jackson went wild, racing over the hard ground with his hooves hitting dangerously near her head. Those wicked hooves flung pebbles and rocks up into her face, and one narrowly missed her left eye.

She flinched and twisted her foot in the stirrup, but it still refused to budge. Everything moved so fast, she barely felt the rocks and twigs dig into her back. She flailed again, trying to reach up to disentangle her boot, but it was impossible.

She became aware of Rick shouting. His voice sounded close, but all she could see was the ground quickly racing past her gaze. Then the landscape's passage began to slow, and finally she was lying stunned beneath Jackson's hooves while the sweat dripped from his neck onto her face.

She felt gentle hands release her foot, then Rick touched her face. "Are you all right?"

She blinked and tried to rise up, then groaned as her already sore muscles protested at the new indignities. "I think I'm alive."

"Thank God." He ran his hands over her limbs. "I don't think anything is broken. Can you stand?"

"Let me try." She really just wanted to lie there until she caught her breath, but Betsy would be worried.

He slipped his arm under her shoulders and helped her sit up. Her head spun, and pain stabbed at her neck, but with his help, she managed to get up.

"What happened?" he murmured in her ear as he helped her toward the house.

"I don't know. The saddle just slid. Who saddled him?"

"I did. The cinch was tight." He got her to the fence. "Here, sit down while I take a look at the saddle."

Hanging on to his arm, she bit back a groan as she lowered herself to a rock. The teenagers flocked around her with big, worried eyes. "I'm fine," she assured them. "Come here, Bets," she told her daughter. Betsy huddled at her feet and laid her head against Allie's leg.

"Dude, barrel racing ain't for sissies," Devon said. "That was awesome to watch."

"I thought you were toast," Leon said.

"Me too," Latoya said. She knelt beside Allie. "You need some water or something?"

"That would be good," Allie said. "I've got dust in my mouth. How about you all go inside while I wait for Rick? You could fix me some tea. There are cookies in the tin on top of the fridge."

"You're sure you're okay?" Latoya asked.

"Fine." Allie managed a smile. It was all she could do to tear her gaze away from Rick. From his clenched fists and tight jaw, she figured he'd found something ominous. "Go with Fern, Bets."

Betsy got up with a show of reluctance but took Fern's hand, and the kids all went toward the house.

Rick came toward her with the saddle in his hands. He tossed it at her feet. "Someone cut the cinch ring with snips," he said. He showed her the sharp, cut edges.

Allie didn't often cry. Tears were a weakness she didn't like to show, but her eyes burned with the need for release. "I'm so tired of this," she choked out. "If he would just show himself, or tell me why he hates me. I don't understand."

Rick went to his knees beside her and caressed her cheek with the back of his hand. "We'll find him. Somehow we'll stop him. I'll go see the border patrol. I meant to go before now."

The border patrol. Big deal. They weren't going to help her. "But what does that have to do with me?"

"I don't know, but it's the only place I have to look. I still wonder about the illegal alien thing. There was a lot of money run through your account. Whoever this guy is, he's got money to burn, and he had to earn it somehow. You want to go with me?"

She shook her head. "Maybe Betsy and I will go see Dolly." She wanted to forget the problems, to laugh and pretend everything was normal for just a little while.

"Okay." He rose and held out his hand. "Can you walk to the house?"

"I think so." She accepted his hand and struggled to her feet. Her legs felt shaky, and she leaned against his chest.

The thump of his heart's steady rhythm under her ear was as comforting as a hot water bottle to a puppy. His arms came around her, and without thinking, she wrapped her arms around his waist. The way his pulse accelerated made her look up to find him staring down at her.

She told herself to move, but she didn't want to. Lost in the vast blueness of his gaze, she clung to him.

Then his head came down, and his lips brushed hers. She inhaled his breath, the scent of his skin, and the response it brought in her caught her off guard. When he would have pulled away, she kissed him back and tightened her hold on him. She could sense his start of surprise, but then he pulled her tighter and kissed her until she was breathless.

Allie wanted to lose herself in his kiss, to forget the danger that threatened, to find a new path to walk with this husband she barely knew. *To live* when it seemed as though her life might soon be over.

Her knees trembled, and she would have sagged to the ground except for his strong arms supporting her. When his lips left hers, she felt abandoned, bereft. With reluctance, she opened her eyes again and gazed up into his face. His eyes blazed with a passion she hadn't seen in a man's face in too long.

Did they dare have a real marriage? Staring into her husband's face, Allie thought she might risk it.

SOME PROTECTOR HE WAS. RICK TUCKED BETSY INTO BED, THEN CAME downstairs and watched his wife's face in the glow of lamplight as the group played Yahtzee after dinner. Someone had tried to hurt her twice now, and he'd had to stand back and watch it happen.

It was hard to fight a phantom. He'd called Brendan several times, but his friend hadn't turned up anything yet on Mark Haskell or Ted Rediger. Too busy, he said. Tomorrow, when Rick went to Alpine, he'd stop at the library and use the computer to see what he could find out on his own.

Remembering the way she'd kissed him today heated his blood. He was falling for her in a big way, and it was enough to make him want to run. What if he failed her? He hadn't done good by her so far. The responsibility made him lick his lips and look toward the wine cabinet.

Elijah had always refused to get rid of the liquor. He said Rick would never conquer the need if he wasn't faced with making the right choice every day, but Rick wasn't sure he agreed with that. It would be so much easier to have temptation out of the way.

Elijah was gone now. There was no reason to leave the stuff there.

He could clean out that cabinet once and for all. Pour the liquor down the sink and smash the bottles. Tonight, after everyone was in bed, he'd do just that.

His gaze went back to Allie's face. Battered and bruised though she looked, she was a temptation he didn't think he could resist much longer.

The thought of it was driving him crazy. He stood and stretched. "I think I'll go to town for an ice-cream sundae. Want to come, Allie?"

"Sure. I'm getting stiff sitting here," Allie said. "I need to walk some of the pain out of my muscles." She held her hand up for him to haul her up. She winced as she maneuvered out of the chair. "I can't sit here much longer or I won't be able to move tomorrow." She put her hand on his arm and stared up at him with an appeal in her eyes.

When had his willingness to love begun to turn into the real thing? He'd tried Grady's advice, and by golly, the guy had been right. Love was about the action of loving. What a weird truth to discover.

He hadn't even been attracted to her when she'd first come here, and now his pulse soared like a bald eagle when he caught a whiff of her shampoo.

"Keep an ear out for Betsy," Allie told Fern, who nodded.

They went toward the door, Allie limping a little. He tucked her hand in the crook of his elbow, then grabbed a sweater from a hook by the door as they went past and slipped it around her. The soft glance of gratitude in her eyes made his palms grow sweaty.

They stepped out into the dark night, illuminated only by the stars. Only a sliver of moon showed. The night air was rich with the scents of the ranch: sage, creosote, hay, and a hint of horse on the wind blowing past the barn.

He helped Allie down the steps. "I'll bring the truck around. Wait here by the porch." He jogged to the vehicle and drove to the base of the steps. She slipped into the cab before he had a chance to get out and help her.

"I finished my paperwork for our next counseling session," she said once they'd started to town. "How are you coming?"

"Haven't had a chance." He knew his voice was a little sharp when he saw her flinch.

There was no answer from her at first. "Is—is there something you're not wanting to tell me?" she asked finally. "I hope you know whatever it is, it can't be any worse than the mess I've made of my life."

Tell her. The prompting dried his mouth. No way could he spill it. Not when they were just starting to get into a comfortable relationship.

"Nothing important," he said. "We'll get to know one another better every day."

Allie nodded. "I still can't believe Bets is talking. I guess you were right after all." She turned and looked out into the dark night. "Maybe I was babying her too much."

The tension drained from his neck and shoulders at the passing of the dangerous topic. "No maybe about it."

She stiffened. "I want you to quit tucking her into bed at night. It's . . . dangerous. She is beginning to get too attached to you."

His fingers tightened on the steering wheel. "Kids can never have too much love, Allie. You're trying to deprive Betsy of the most important thing in life. Jon's gone. He'll never be able to pull her up on his lap or read her a story." He knew his words were harsh, but she had to understand. "Look, I loved Jon too. And I admit it took me a while to get past the thought that I was taking his place. But he's not here to fill it. I am. And I'm going to."

"She can't forget Jon," she fired back. "I don't want anyone to take his place."

His inclination was to let go of his temper, but he took a tighter grip on it instead. "I know you don't want her to be hurt. Neither do I. You should know that. She needs me, and so do you."

"I think she's already forgetting," she whispered, her voice desolate.

"Allie, she's five years old. How much do you remember from when you were five? But at least both of us loved Jon. We'll talk about him, about what a great man he was. That's better than if I were jealous of him and didn't hold him up in her eyes."

She finally nodded, and her shoulder slumped against the door. "I guess it's inevitable."

They reached the drugstore and stepped inside to a nearly deserted space filled with the sweet smells of chocolate, whipped cream, and butterscotch. Nothing much was said over their ice cream. Rick knew she was mulling over what he'd said. Maybe she'd finally quit challenging him on every action.

After licking the last of his hot-fudge sundae from the spoon, he paid the bill and held the door open for her. A warm breeze blew across his face, and he inhaled the scent of the roses blooming along the tree lawn.

A sharp report echoed against the buildings, followed by a zip past his ear. "Look out!" Something stung the side of his face. He bore her to the ground and covered her with his own body. "Someone's shooting at us."

The night sounds of tree frogs and crickets went silent, then resumed. Rick strained to hear anything else: the footfall of someone walking their way, the harsh breath of someone running. There was nothing but the sound of the wind and the rumble of a truck passing them on the street.

Glancing behind him, he saw the lights go out in the drugstore. The door was probably locked. The rest of the businesses had closed down when the streets were rolled up at five. "We've got to make a run for the truck," he whispered in her ear.

She nodded. He rolled off her, bounded to his feet, then yanked her up and ran toward the vehicle. No rifle crack sounded, no more bullets zinged past his ears. He flung open the door and shoved her inside before running around to the driver's side.

"Lock your door!" He slammed the door and locked it, then started the truck. He tossed her the cell phone. "Call the sheriff." He rattled off the number to her.

She nodded and punched in the number. Listening to her tell the sheriff's office what happened, he began to shake at the close call.

The sheriff was waiting at the curb when Rick pulled the truck up and stopped.

By the time he and Allie recounted what had happened, it was nearly eleven. A deputy followed them home. He waved his thanks to the deputy and ran with Allie to the house.

Locking the door behind them, he left Allie in the living room to explain what happened while he made a beeline for the office. He went to the gun cabinet and stared at the weapons. He'd sworn never to take one in his hand again. The dark, frightened eyes of the boy he'd shot accidentally in Baghdad swam in his memory. Guilt made him slam the door again.

The boys congregated in the doorway. "Cool, dude, can I have some heat?" Leon asked.

"Not on your life." Rick peered out the window into the darkness. Who was in his neighborhood? And what was his game?

22

AFTER CHANGING INTO HER PAJAMAS, ALLIE SAT IN HER BEDROOM ROCKER and watched her daughter sleep.

The thought of going to sleep after someone shot at them made Allie shudder. He'd been in the house once, at least long enough to slip a note under her door. What if he got in again?

She should have brought a gun up here with her. The madman wasn't going to hurt her daughter. Allie pondered this. Maybe the stalker wouldn't stoop so low as to hurt a child. He'd had several opportunities to harm Betsy but didn't. The realization only vaguely comforted her.

The man's attacks seemed relentless. If she only knew why he hated her. All Rick's efforts to identify him led only to dead ends. Maybe that's the way it was supposed to be though. Maybe God had put her in this position so she had to face this danger herself and deal with it. Nothing could happen to her that didn't first pass through God's hands. She had to remember that.

He'd protected them so far.

Her gaze lingered on Betsy. Rick wanted to be her daddy. Did she dare allow it? Her eyes burned, and she rubbed the moisture from her lashes. Rick was right—Jon was gone. It wasn't fair to Betsy to deprive her of love. But it was so hard to give up on Jon's memory.

A peck came at the door, and she got up from the chair. It had to be Rick, and the way her blood pressure rose made her shake her head at her silly self. She was thirty-two, not seventeen.

When she flung open the door and looked into his eyes, she *felt* seventeen and giddy though. How did he manage to do that to her? She felt anything but a sedate widow when she was around him.

"Everything's buttoned down," he whispered, stepping into the room. "But I don't want the two of you to stay here alone. I've moved a cot into my room, and we'll all stay there." Without waiting for her to agree, he stepped past her and lifted Betsy from the bed. She stirred but didn't awaken.

Allie's pulse hammered in her throat. There was only one bed in his room, and he'd brought in one cot. Did he mean to sleep on it?

She trailed down the hall behind him to his bedroom. Her gaze fastened on the big bed that dwarfed the room. She'd made up the bed that morning when she changed all the sheets in the house and washed them, but she'd never expected to sleep there tonight.

Rick laid Betsy on the cot and pulled the covers around her. After pressing a kiss to her forehead, he backed away and turned to face Allie. "I'll sleep on the floor. There was only room for one cot."

It was *his* bed. It didn't seem fair he should sleep on the hard floor. "I'll sleep there," she said. "Where are the blankets?"

His chin came out. "No way I'm letting my wife sleep on the floor."

His wife. The words started a warm feeling in the pit of her being. She glanced at the bed. "The bed is big. If you stay on your side, I'll promise to stay on mine."

His lips twitched. "What if I don't want you to stay on your side?"

Her laugh felt a little hollow. "We could put a board between us."

The glint of laughter in his eyes dimmed. "Not necessary. I'll be good."

"Okay," she said, not yet ready to explore what he meant by his comments.

Avoiding his gaze, she went around to the left side and pulled back the quilt and top sheet. A picture of a young boy sat on the stand beside the bed. "Who's this? He looks a little like you."

"My brother, Chad." His clipped tone told her he didn't want to talk about it.

Allie let it drop. "I hope I'm not taking your favorite side."

"Nope. I always sleep on the other edge." He went to the dresser and took out pajama bottoms, then disappeared through the door. A moment later, the bathroom door down the hall closed.

Allie slipped between the sheets. She rolled onto her side with her back to the center of the mattress. It was going to be impossible to make herself breathe like she was asleep when all she wanted to do was gulp in air through her tight throat.

Her eyes slammed shut when she heard him come back into the room. The bed springs groaned when his bulk settled onto the mattress. The covers tugged, and he settled into the bed. The musky scent of his presence filled her senses, and soon the warmth of his body drifted toward her as well.

Her tension began to ease when he made no attempt to roll toward her and embrace her. The day's events had worn on her. Every muscle in her body ached.

"Allie?" Rick's whisper came near her ear.

Her eyes flew open, and she rolled to the center to find herself nose to nose with Rick, though in the darkness, she could barely make out his features. "What's wrong?"

"I wondered if you'd like me to rub your back. Are you sore?"

"Yes, but you're tired too. Rest is the best thing." She didn't dare let him touch her. Her responses to him were too unpredictable.

Or maybe totally predictable.

"I like having you here," he whispered. His lips brushed hers.

Before she could respond, he rolled over, presenting his back to her. She touched her fingers to her lips and closed her eyes.

Though she'd been determined not to trust her heart again, he was battering down her defenses.

It was after three the last time she looked at the clock, then the sun was streaming in her eyes. Allie blinked against the brightness. She tried to move and found something heavy lying across her waist.

It was Rick's arm.

She stared in fascination at the thick black hair growing on his skin. Her gaze traveled up his arm to his strong shoulders, bare above his pajama bottoms. The dark stubble on his face made him all the more appealing.

His eyes were closed, and she let herself look to her heart's content. Always before she'd been afraid he'd notice her studying him. His hair curled a little where it touched his neck. He needed a trim, but the extra length combined with the morning beard made him look a bit like an outlaw. And only inches away. He'd rolled onto his side with his arm flung over her. If she leaned forward a few inches, she could kiss him.

She'd always been attracted to the bad boys.

Even Jon had had a wild streak, one that caused him to leave her and Betsy and go off to save the world. Allie wondered how many of those impulses Rick had. He seemed so upright, so steady. Someone to depend on. Jon certainly had trusted him.

His eyes opened, and she found herself staring into the depths of those blue pools of light. He stared at her with a steady gaze she couldn't look away from.

"Good morning," he said. He made no move to pull his arm away.

She wet her lips. "Good morning." She barely breathed, let alone moved. One part of her wanted to bolt from the bed, and the other wanted to move closer.

His arm shifted, and she felt a stab of disappointment until she realized he was moving his hand up to cup her face.

"You're beautiful even in the morning," he said. His thumb rubbed her bottom lip.

Warning bells screamed in her head, but she ignored them and shifted closer ever so slightly. His eyes darkened at her response, and he pulled her closer, his lips seeking hers. She fit so perfectly in his arms.

"Mommy?" Betsy's voice was still rusty and hoarse.

Allie jerked from Rick's arms and rolled over to stare at her daughter, whose face was by the pillow. "Hi, baby. Did you sleep well?" Her cheeks burned, and she was sure her face had to be red.

Betsy nodded. She tugged on Allie's hand. "Can I have pancakes?"

"Okay, I'm coming." With a rueful glance at Rick, she threw back the covers and climbed out of bed.

She wasn't sure if the reprieve was good or not.

THE TEENAGERS TALKED EXCITEDLY OVER BREAKFAST, AND RICK DIDN'T get a word in edgewise—a good thing since he wasn't sure what to say to Allie.

He'd totally fallen for her. Five foot two and maybe a hundred pounds soaking wet, she had a heart as big as Texas. She'd take down a tiger in defense of her daughter too. He liked that kind of courage in a woman. Okay, loved that kind of courage.

He grabbed the keys to Elijah's Jeep. "Charlie, I'm going to town today. I'll be gone most of the day, so you're in charge," he told the young man. Eyeing the boy's plate, he grinned. "That has to be your tenth pancake. You can sure put them away."

Charlie grinned and shrugged. "The kids want to practice barrel racing. That okay with you?"

"Fine. Just be careful."

"Always." The kid gave him a cheeky grin.

"You ready?" Rick asked Allie. She nodded but still hadn't looked him fully in the face since she'd scrambled from the bed.

He couldn't blame her. Everything was so weird and off kilter right now. She'd slept in his bed, and they hadn't really acknowledged the depth of their relationship yet. Between the guy terrorizing her and Rick himself trying to win her heart, she must be confused.

But he wasn't going to let this continue. He would find that man and get him out of Allie's life. Then they could plan for the future.

Future. The very word set his teeth on edge. All his plans had been set spinning by her arrival. He hadn't had a single peaceful moment since she arrived. Maybe that was a good thing. He'd been getting complacent, settled on a course that might have taken him right into a life of more isolation.

He hadn't felt this alive since he'd been a kid.

Neither of them talked on the way to town. Instead of just dropping her off to spend the day with Dolly, he went inside with her to say hello to Grady. Betsy and Courtney ran off together, and Dolly and Allie went to the kitchen for tea.

He found Grady in his office. "Got a minute?"

Grady looked up from his Bible with a smile. "Sure, I was ready for a break." His grin faded. "Did God die or something, bucko?"

Rick managed a weak grin. "Do I look that bad?" He should have known Grady would call him to task.

"Worse." Grady pointed at the chair. "Sit."

Rick shut the door and dropped onto the armchair. "Someone shot at Allie last night."

Grady studied Rick's face. "What else?"

"Isn't that enough?" Rick was in no mood to be analyzed.

"You're all still alive, so no, me bucko. You look like someone died."

Rick gave a short laugh. "I can't seem to keep my wife safe."

"She's dead?"

"No, she's in the kitchen with Dolly." In spite of himself, a grin started to lift the corners of his mouth. Grady always did that to him.

"Then you've managed to keep her safe." Grady grinned. "You've fallen for her, haven't you? That's the real problem. The mighty Rick Bailey has finally fallen hard."

"Don't joke about it."

"Why not? You've gone through your life keeping everyone at arm's length because you think you might fail them. That's being only half-alive, bucko, and you're finally finding it out."

Rick pressed his lips together. "I'm scared," he admitted. "Why would she want to stay with someone like me? I've got no family, no real assets other than a strong back. I told her I wanted to work on making the marriage a real one, and she hasn't really given me a clear answer."

"Maybe she's scared too. Have you thought about that?"

He hadn't. "Why would she be scared? She's been married before. She knows more about it than I do."

"Exactly. She knows how bad it can hurt when things go wrong. Maybe she's afraid of being hurt again, of loving again."

"She's probably smart to be afraid I couldn't do it," Rick muttered.

"Have you told her about your problem?"

"Nope, and I'm not going to." Rick set his jaw. "It's behind me."

Grady pointed a pencil at him. "But it's shaped you. She needs to know the demons you deal with, just like you need to know hers. You need to tell her before the next counseling session. It will come out sooner or later."

"Then make it later. I'm just not ready to show her what a loser she married," Rick muttered, standing. "I'm going down to talk to the border patrol today. Maybe they've heard of something going on through here."

"I thought her troubles started before she came here."

"They did." Rick shrugged. "I've got nowhere else to look." And keeping busy was the only way to avoid running scared. On the outside, he was this strong, take-charge guy, and on the inside, he knew his shortcomings. The trick was to make sure no one else did.

23

THE TEA WAS AS STRONG AS HER HUSBAND. ALLIE CHUCKLED TO HERSELF and sipped from her mug before setting it on the coffee table. The girls were in Courtney's room, and she and Dolly sat in the living room. Allie was hungry for some girl talk, and maybe she'd even find out more about her fascinating husband.

"How long have you known Rick?" she asked, curling her legs under herself on the comfortable sofa.

"Seems like forever." Dolly stopped knitting and wrinkled her nose. "I guess it was about two years ago that he came to help Elijah." She shook her head. "Man, he was such a case when he walked into the church the first time."

"What do you mean?"

"He had this tortured expression, like he'd just come through the desert and survived. I think it was a month before he even spoke to me or anyone else. He'd slip into the back pew at the last minute, then rush out at the final amen."

"Was it the war?"

"I think it was more than that." Dolly's glance held curiosity. "You don't really know him very well, do you?"

"I'd never met him before we came here."

Dolly put her hand to her mouth. "I didn't know. Grady never tells me anything told to him in confidence." Her tone was injured. "I don't get it, Allie. How did you marry so fast?"

"Rick was my husband's best friend. Jon, my husband, told me if I was ever in trouble to go to Rick. My in-laws were trying to take Bets from me, so I ran to Rick."

"And that guy was after you."

Allie nodded. "Still is. I was most afraid for Betsy. When I told Rick about the custody issue, he told me he'd promised Jon he'd take care of us. The marriage was all Rick's idea."

Dolly sighed. "So romantic."

Allie's lips twitched with the need to laugh. If Dolly only knew how the marriage really was.

"He's quite a hunk." Dolly waggled her eyebrows.

Allie burst out laughing. "You're terrible."

"I tease Rick like that all the time. He knows I love my Grady." Dolly's smile was impish. "I just like to embarrass Rick. He is so clueless around women and doesn't know what to say. It's quite endearing."

Endearing was an understatement. Appealing, infuriating, compelling.

Allie couldn't stop thinking about Rick and what life was like for him while growing up. The little snippets Dolly had told her indicated his childhood wasn't pleasant. What about the scars on his back? How did he get them?

There was so much about her husband she didn't know. "I—I noticed scars on his back. Has he ever said anything about them?"

Dolly winced. "I've seen them. He always passes them off as nothing. If he's told Grady, I wouldn't know. I know he was removed from the care of his parents. He'd been in trouble—some breaking and entering, taking a car on a joyride. Elijah turned him around."

"I saw a picture of his brother on his nightstand. Where is he?"

"They were separated in the foster-care system. Rick used to look for him, but all the records were lost in a fire a few years back, and he ran up against a dead end. Chad was five when he was removed from the home, I think. Rick never forgave himself for it. He always felt if he'd taken better care of Chad, welfare wouldn't have moved him to foster care. Rick never saw him again."

"And he's searched for him all these years?" Allie's heart swelled at the thought of such devotion and dedication. There was so much more to him than brawn.

"He gave up about a year ago. Grady told him the kid could have changed his name. Maybe he was even adopted."

"I wish I could find him for Rick," Allie said. "What a gift that would be. A way to say thank you for all he's done to protect Betsy and me."

"You never know," Dolly said slowly. "Even though Rick has given up, Grady and I try now and again to find out something. Grady tracked down Chad's sixth-grade teacher."

A surge of excitement rolled through Allie. "Where is she?"

"She's retired now and is in an assisted-living facility in Alpine."

An hour and a half away. Still Allie had to try. "Maybe I could call."

Dolly shook her head. "Grady tried that. The woman has Alzheimer's, and she didn't make much sense on the phone."

So much for that idea. "It probably would be a worthless trip to try to go talk to her then."

"Maybe not. She probably has lucid times like most Alzheimer's patients. It's worth a try. We could leave the girls with Grady and run up there."

"You think he'd mind?"

"Nope. They won't be any trouble, and he's off today anyway."

"Then let's do it!" Allie found the more she dug under Rick's brawny surface, the more tenderness she found.

ONE OF RICK'S FRIENDS FROM CHURCH WAS A BORDER PATROL AGENT. RICK knew Walker Rivera would be his only hope of getting some insider information. After stopping at the checkpoint, he was directed out to one of the landings along the Rio Grande.

Cactus tore at his tires and bumper, and he nearly bottomed out in the potholes along the narrow dirt road down to the river. The area was a desolate desert until he got close to the water where trees grew and vegetation sprouted, grabbing onto the moisture the river gave up. The fresh scent of water made the day brighter.

Walker's SUV sat on hardpan clay. A large patch of prickly pear cactus sprouted from under it. Rick parked behind his friend's vehicle, then followed the voices he heard echoing off the red canyon walls that lined the river. The walk down to the river was a little steep and treacherous, with small pebbles sliding away from his boots.

Walker and his partner were interrogating two handcuffed men.

About five ten with stocky features and a handlebar mustache, Walker had been with the border patrol nearly twenty years. The other agent was younger, blond, and scared.

Walker fired questions at the prisoners in Spanish, then turned to march them to the SUV. The Baggies of brown weed in his hands told the story.

When he saw Rick, he motioned for his partner to take the prisoners on to the vehicle. "Hey buddy, what are you doing out here?"

"Looking for information. Drugs?" he asked, nodding toward the men who were nearly to the top of the slope.

"Marijuana."

"Seen any evidence of coyotes running illegals through the area?" When Walker raised his eyebrows, amused, Rick added, "More so than usual."

Walker's gaze sharpened. "How'd you know? There have been nearly three times what we usually see."

Rick told him about the group he'd seen on the ranch and about Allie's situation. "I even checked out the brother of the guy she sent to prison, and he seems clean. He was up in Albuquerque."

The men had started walking up the hillside. Walker stopped and grabbed his arm. "Albuquerque. What's his name?"

"Luis Hernandez."

Walker began to smile. "He's been on our radar, and I've got a search warrant to deliver. That's my next stop."

Rick could have sworn the young man was clean. He was losing his touch. "I'd like to tag along."

Walker studied Rick's face. "You know, maybe you can get us in the door without him running. I've got a pilot ready to go. You free right now?"

"You bet. Let's hit it."

The men climbed back in their vehicles and headed to the post. Walker and his partner turned over the prisoners, filled out their forms, and came out to join Rick at his truck.

Two hours later they parked outside the same dilapidated apartment house that smelled of black beans and tacos.

"Let me go to the door first," Rick said. "Once they open the door, I'll motion to you." He still worried it might be a waste of time, but Walker obviously had something on the kid.

He got out, veered around four Hispanic children playing dodgeball in the street, then went to the door and pounded on it. "Luis? It's Rick Bailey again. I've got a couple of questions."

The baby wailed, and a woman's voice spoke soothingly. The door swung open, and Luis didn't look nearly as patient and understanding today. His glare stabbed at Rick, and his mouth was pinched.

"What now?"

Rick flicked his fingers at his side. Moments later, the two border patrol agents were showing the warrant. Walker had his foot stuck between the doorjamb and the door to keep Luis from slamming it in their faces.

Luis turned to run, and Walker grabbed his arm. "Not so fast, *amigo*. We've got some questions." The men shoved inside.

Rick shot an apologetic glance to the young woman, who stood off to one side, her dark eyes full of fear. The wails of the baby added to the chaos as Walker pushed Luis into a chair and stood over him.

"Keep an eye on him," Walker said. "I need to help Mike search."

Rick stood between Luis and the door. The young man sat on the edge of the chair like he might bolt. Waves of animosity rolled off the kid, and he kept glaring daggers of betrayal at Rick.

Rick stared down at the young man. "Did you try to implicate Allie Siders in running illegals through the rodeo?" he asked quietly.

Luis turned his head, but not before Rick saw a knowing smirk twist his lips. Rage simmered along Rick's nerves. If this guy had been terrorizing his wife all this time . . . He heard the border agents tapping along the walls, dragging drawers open, looking in cabinets.

Nervous energy jittered along Luis's body. His hands shook, and Rick could see he had something to hide. A boulder began to form in Rick's stomach at the thought he might have ended this nightmare days ago if he'd been able to see through the guy. Allie was suffering, and he'd had the power to stop it.

He was losing his touch. A few years ago he could read these degenerates like reading spoor in the forest. He'd let this guy bamboozle him. Some protector he was.

Walker came back holding a ledger book. "It's all in here." He flipped it open and showed Rick the money trail. Hundreds of thousands of dollars. When he handed the book back to Walker, something fell from between the pages. He picked it up and found a picture of Allie standing by a horse trailer at a rodeo.

"It was you," he said. "You were trying to frame her."

"She killed his brother, destroyed his business," the woman said, taking a step forward.

"*Cállete!*" Luis snarled.

The woman clamped her mouth closed at Luis's command to be quiet. She scuttled back to the couch with the baby.

Rick let his contempt show in his eyes as he stared at Luis. The young man looked down, but his mouth still held a line of defiance.

It was over. Rick's relief couldn't be described. He could go home, tell Allie to let the fear drift away like puffs of cottonwood seeds. They could begin to work on making a new life together. Once the adoption was final, he would have a real family.

The thought made him smile.

24

THE CARE FACILITY WAS ONE OF THE NEWER ONES THAT LOOKED LIKE A Victorian mansion rather than an institution. Allie could hardly wait to get inside. What if she was able to find Rick's brother? What a kick it would be to reunite them and see Rick's face.

She and Dolly stopped at the nurses' station and got directions to Rosanna Hilgers's room. They found her seated in a chair, her beefy arms propped on a side table and five cards in her hand. The green sweater she wore over her housedress had more pills than straight fibers.

"Mrs. Hilgers?" Allie said.

"I'll call you," she said in a shrill voice.

Allie glanced at Dolly and touched the woman's shoulder. "My name is Allie Bailey, and I'd like to ask you about a former student."

The woman's bleary eyes blinked, then she pulled her gaze from the cards in her hand and focused on Allie. "I taught you?"

"No, ma'am, not me. But you taught a boy named Chad Bailey. I was wondering if you knew how I might get in touch with him."

"Who wants to know?"

"I do. My name is Allie Bailey."

"You're his sister?"

"His sister-in-law. Do you know where he is?"

The woman shuffled her slippered feet. "Who wants to know?"

"Me, Allie Bailey."

"Want to play poker? I promise not to take too much of your money."

"I don't know how to play."

"Sit down and I'll show you."

Allie gave Dolly a helpless look and pulled over a chair from under the window. "About Chad," she said.

"Such a good boy," the woman said. "Terrible he had to go to Africa."

Dolly rolled her eyes, but Allie leaned forward. "He went to Africa?"

"With his parents. I was so upset. He came to see me on his giraffe when he got back though. So grown up and handsome."

"When was he here last?" Allie knew this was likely all false, but she might find a glimmer of reality in the stories somewhere.

"Just last week. He came on his elephant this time. He could name every part of that beast. I taught him well." Her eyes glazed over, then closed, and her mouth sagged. A snore ripped from her throat.

"She's not making any sense," Dolly whispered. "Let's go."

"I'm going to talk to the nurse." Allie rose and followed her friend from the room.

"Poor lady. She's delusional. All that talk about elephants and giraffes. I doubt you'll learn anything from the nurses."

"Just a quick question." Allie stopped at the hubbub of activity by the entrance and waited until one of the women was free. "Excuse me. I was wondering if you knew if Rosanna Hilgers gets many visitors?"

The young woman's tired smile brightened. "Oh, Mrs. Hilgers! Isn't she a sweetheart? We just love her. Some of her former students drop by from time to time, though since her mind has failed more, not so many."

Allie allowed herself a glimmer of hope. "I'm looking for a young man who would be in his early twenties now. Chad Bailey?"

The woman frowned. "Bailey. The name isn't familiar. There's another Chad that comes by though. He's about that age."

Allie exchanged a glance with Dolly. "Do you know how I might get hold of him?"

"No, I'm sorry. Visitors don't leave their information or anything."

Allie dug in her purse for a pen and paper. "Listen, could I leave a note for you to give him if he comes in again?"

"Sure. I'll put it in her file."

Allie scribbled out a note explaining who she was and what she wanted, then folded it and handed it over. "Thanks so much."

"No problem. I hope you find him." The woman tucked the note into a file folder.

It was the best Allie could do, but it felt like a pitiful attempt. Still, God was in control of this, and he could move mountains.

The women drove back to Dolly's house, but the conversation was much more subdued on the trip home. They stopped at the corner grocery and bought some milk, then went to the O'Sullivan home.

As they pulled into the driveway, she saw Rick's truck parked along the curb. "Don't tell him where we were," she told Dolly.

"I won't. I warned Grady to keep it mum too." Dolly held up the gallon of milk. "We'll tell him we went after this."

"I hope he hasn't been here long," Allie muttered. She got out and followed Dolly to the house. "Rick?" she called.

His voice came from her left. "In the living room."

Allie went to find him. "Did you find out anything?" She eyed him, noticing the triumphant grin he wore.

He stood from his seat on the couch and stepped to where she stood.

"It's over." Rick folded Allie in his arms.

She could hear his pulse thumping against her ear, sense the elation that filled him. "What do you mean?" she asked against his shirt.

His hands gripped her shoulders and pulled her out so he was staring into her face. "It was Luis Hernandez. They found the money trail and a picture of you at the rodeo. He put money in your account and tipped off the authorities, then pulled out the money and moved it around to some other accounts of his own offshore."

She felt giddy, and her knees threatened to buckle under her. She clung to Rick's strength. The nightmare was over. "How did he know I'd come here?"

Rick shrugged. "I suppose he tapped Yo's phone or something. The border patrol will figure it out. Let's celebrate. I'll take you to supper."

She wanted to smile, but it didn't seem real. "Are you sure? I never met him."

"He had a picture of you, and the money trail was clear."

For someone to hate her so passionately when she'd never even met him saddened her. "He must have loved his brother very much."

"You're feeling sorry for the guy? Get over it," Rick said. "He deserves what he's got coming to him. He murdered your family."

Allie shuddered. "It's hard to understand."

"I think the two of you need some time alone," Dolly said. "The girls would love to be together tonight. Why not let Betsy stay with us? There's no need to worry about her now."

It felt strange to let go of her anxiety, to let loose of her daughter. She felt light, airy, as the reality sank in that the danger was behind her. The future stretched ahead like a beautiful blue sky.

"Allie?" Rick said. "It's safe. You can leave Betsy with no worries."

"She's not used to being without me." Going off without Betsy would be like losing her arm.

Dolly laughed. "Listen to the girls chattering. She won't miss you."

Sure enough, Allie could hear the high, sweet sounds of the girls talking. *Talking.* Betsy was talking again, and life might actually return to normal, whatever that meant. "If you're sure." She couldn't look at Rick.

"I'm positive." Dolly made a shooing motion with her hands. "Get out of here, you two. Go celebrate."

Rick took her arm, and his warm fingers jump-started her pulse. "We'll get her first thing in the morning."

"No rush," Dolly said, smiling.

Rick led her from the living room and out the door. "What sounds good for supper? Let's walk. It's not far."

"Do we have a choice?" She turned to smile at him. The air suddenly smelled fresher, clean with the scent of citrus from the groves along the path. The sunset cast a subdued light over the tiny village, bathing it with a heavenly glow.

Free. She was free to love Rick and build a new life with him. And that's what this emotion she'd been unwilling to name was. Love. How did he feel? She glanced at him from the corners of her eyes.

He'd said if he acted love, maybe he'd feel it. Sure enough, the trans-formation had occurred in his heart as well. How was she to know about her own heart though?

The emotion swelled within her, lodging in her throat, choking off anything she might say. Not yet. She couldn't tell him yet. Maybe after supper.

He kept possession of her hand as they strolled along the sidewalk to the little café two blocks down. Allie glanced in the windows of the homes they passed, noticing the families living and loving. She wouldn't have to envy the other families any longer. She had a place of her own.

Carrying this much joy felt overwhelming.

Rick held open the door of the café for her, and she stepped onto the battered wooden floor. Red-and-white checked table-cloths covered the square tables, and the air was thick with the smell of chicken enchiladas, tonight's special according to the chalk-board. A few locals looked up and spoke to Rick, tipping their hats to her as well.

Rick led her to a corner table that looked out on the patio where pots of flowers bloomed. He sat across from her and smiled with so much contentment that she had to smile back.

His smile changed as he looked over her shoulder at someone. "Judge," he said.

Judge Thompson was smiling, and Allie let herself hope. The older woman stopped at the table. "You two look awfully happy."

"The border patrol just arrested the man who's been giving Allie so much trouble," Rick said. "And if that's not enough, Betsy is talking again, so we're celebrating."

The judge's smile widened. "Glad to hear it. Come see me

tomorrow, and I'll give you the ruling. I think you'll be pleased." She winked and walked away.

"Ah, the joys of small-town living," Rick murmured. "No tightly held secrets." He laughed, then stretched his hand across the table to take Allie's. "Enchiladas just doesn't sound like a celebratory meal. I think we should have steak."

"Me too." Though right now she felt she couldn't eat a thing. They placed their order, and the waitress left them alone.

"What are we going to do about Jon's parents?" Allie asked. "They are going to still want to see Betsy, even if the adoption goes through."

"How do you feel about it?"

"They're her grandparents. I'd like her to know and love them, but I hate for her to be forced to visit when she doesn't want to."

"Sometimes blood can't make family," he said. The sun dipped below the horizon as he spoke, and the shadows deepened on his face. His voice darkened as well. "Adoption can. Love is what counts."

"You never talk about your family," she said. Maybe he would open up now. She wanted to know more about this man who'd slipped into her heart when she wasn't looking.

The triumphant smile he'd worn since she first saw him tonight took a dip. He pulled his hand away and took a gulp of his water. "Not much to say. I haven't seen my parents in years. Last I heard, my dad was in prison for assault and battery over a dispute at work, and my mom was waiting tables in San Antonio and living with man number six."

"Dolly told me about your brother, Chad."

His brows drew together. "You could have asked me instead of gossiping behind my back."

Her cheeks heated. "You're right. I'm sorry. So tell me now." She held his gaze.

He took her hand again, rubbing his thumb over it. "I haven't seen him since he was five. I looked for him for a long time, ever since I threw over my career with the military and came back to Bluebird. Every door was shut though, and I finally had to accept it. Maybe he'll come looking for me someday."

Her trip today was on the tip of her tongue, but she so badly wanted to surprise him. She choked back the information, imagining his expression when Chad finally stood before him. No matter what it took, she would find his brother.

"Why so serious?" he asked.

She put as much of her love into her gaze as she dared. "What happened to your back? The scars, they're dreadful."

A slight smile tipped his lips. "My mother didn't take kindly to me burning the chili when I was ten. She took a whip to my back."

Tears burned Allie's eyes. "Oh, Rick." She squeezed his fingers. "I can't imagine a mother doing that."

"Most people can't," he said dryly. "It was one reason I swore I'd never marry. I didn't trust women. But watching you with Betsy has shown me how a real mother loves her child."

With his thumb rubbing her palm, she found it hard to think. "My parents were good to me," she said.

"Then why are you frowning?"

"My mom lied to me about Elijah," she said. "She said he kicked her out when he found out she was pregnant, and that she lost the baby. Instead, she gave my sister up for adoption, and Elijah brought Maria to the ranch. All these years I could have known her. I don't know why my mom broke ties with Elijah. It was only after she died that I realized he was even still alive."

"Maybe she didn't want your father to know about the baby."

"Maybe. But why did she refuse to have anything to do with Elijah? It doesn't make sense."

"Now that things have settled down, maybe we can try to find out."

The waitress brought their food, and the conversation lulled as they ate their tender steaks. It was the best meal Allie could remember. Maybe because she wasn't looking over her shoulder for danger every minute. Or maybe because of the loving glances Rick sent her way.

Replete with hot food, Allie leaned back in her chair. "The kids will be gone in a few days. When does our next batch come?"

"In a couple of weeks. The rest of the bunkhouse will be finished, and we'll have a group for the month of April. Summer is busy, even though it's hot. The kids like swimming in the river and riding the horses early morning before the sun heats everything up."

Allie's sigh was a happy one. Life was going to be good. "I'll be right back." She took her purse and walked to the bathroom.

The room smelled fresh from a pine detergent. Thankful it was empty, Allie found a chair and opened her purse. She pulled out a small photo of her and Jon together on their wedding day. They both looked so young and happy.

Rick wasn't Jon. Maybe it was best they were so different. Rick had his own place in her heart. "Good-bye, Jon," she whispered. "I hope you're looking down from heaven and are happy Rick and I are together. I think you are." Tears pricked her eyes as she put the picture away.

RICK HELD ALLIE'S HAND IN THE TRUCK. THE STARS AND THE MOON LIT THE vegetation on both sides of the road with a golden glow. With his window rolled down, the fragrance of creosote and sage filled his lungs.

He parked in front of the house. "Looks like the kids are watching TV." The blue glow of the television flickered through the window.

Rick's spirit deflated a bit. He'd hoped for the evening alone with Allie. Peeking at his watch, he saw it was only seven. It would be an hour before he could send the kids off to bed.

The security light illuminated the corral around the barn. They could be alone in the barn. He got out and went around to open her door.

Allie looked up at him with such trust it scared him. What if he failed her? She was bound to find out he had feet of clay soon.

"Let's make sure the kids took care of the horses," he said. Allie slid out, and he took her hand again. Jem ran to greet them, doing his little air dance of joy.

Allie stopped to pet the dog. "Hey, Jem, you keeping everyone safe for us?"

Rick led her toward the barn. "He'd only lick someone to death."

"Poor Jem, did you hear that? Rick has no faith in you."

"Oh, I have plenty of faith." Rick squeezed her fingers. "Faith that he's the friendliest dog on the planet."

The cougar screamed from a rocky hillside, and he saw Allie shiver. "It's probably two miles away," he told her.

"I know. I worry one of these days it will come after one of the horses. Or even worse, Betsy."

"Jem protects us pretty well from animal intruders. It's the human ones that were the problem." He rubbed the dog's head as he trotted beside them.

"That he does," she said, smiling.

They reached the barn, and he slid open the door. The scent of horse and hay greeted them like old friends. A mouse scurried away from their feet, then a dark shape swooped down.

Allie screamed and ducked behind him as the bat barely missed her hair, then cruised on out the door. "I hate bats," she said.

"They're interesting," he said. "There's a big colony in an old mine shaft about five miles from here. They're western pipistrelle bats, and they only eat insects, not pretty girls."

She shuddered. "Interesting to you maybe. Nasty things."

"They eat tons of mosquitoes," he said. "And scorpions and centipedes."

"They're still not my friends." She went past him to the stall that held Moonbeam. "Hey boy, you doing okay?" She rubbed the white blaze on his face.

Rick did a quick walk through, and all was quiet. He eyed the stack of hay in the corner. With a blanket over it, they could settle there and . . . talk. Suppressing a grin, he grabbed an old quilt they kept in the barn for sick horses. When he sniffed it, it smelled slightly horsy but not bad. He spread it over the hay and fell back onto it. He propped his head up with his arms folded under it.

Allie turned toward him and smiled when she saw his comfortable pose. "I take it you are in no hurry to go check on the kids?"

"Emilio is with them." He patted the spot beside him. Her smile widened, and she approached his little nest. "The kitchen is probably a mess."

"I'll help you with it later." Reaching up, he grabbed her hand and tugged her down onto the quilt with him. He put his arm around her, and she snuggled against him. Her hair, smelling like a yucca blossom, tickled his nose, but he didn't mind.

He settled his chin against the top of her head. The words he wanted to say hovered behind his teeth.

I love you.

He'd never told anyone that except his little brother. His parents weren't ones for soft words, and he'd learned that early. But Chad was different. And so was Allie. He'd never imagined he could be so happy, so content. But how did she feel? If she left him, he couldn't handle it.

She still didn't know the role he'd played in Jon's death. And he couldn't tell her. Not right now, with the hay so soft and sweet-smelling, and her trust in him so heady.

"Are you happy, Allie?"

"Very happy." Her voice had a little hitch in it. She pulled away and looked into his face. Her hand came up to cup his cheek. "I love you, Rick," she whispered.

Joy exploded in Rick's chest, radiating heat through his body. "You do? Really?" He sounded like a sixteen-year-old kid, and he nearly groaned. His lips found hers. So soft and yielding. He drank in the love she poured over him like the desert drank up rain.

Tell her. The words lodged behind his teeth. Three little words. I love you. Why couldn't he say them? He was afraid to let them loose in case they grew into something he couldn't manage.

Love made you vulnerable, tore your heart out when you weren't looking. If he said the words, they might bite him later. So instead he poured how he felt into the kiss. Surely she would understand.

They necked like two kids at the drive-in until he heard the kids laughing as they went past the barn to the bunkhouse.

"Let's go to the house," he whispered. "The bed is softer."

Her questioning gaze softened, and she nodded. Hand in hand, they slipped out of the barn and moved through the pools of moonlight to the house.

25

Contentment softened Rick's bones. He propped himself on one elbow and watched his wife's face in the morning light. Had he ever been this happy, even once? He didn't think so.

His conscience had torn at him all night in spite of it. Until she knew the truth, how could he trust her vows of love? Before he got in any deeper, he needed to know how she'd react to the truth.

And he still hadn't told her he loved her. Rick believed in showing how he felt with action. She rolled closer, tucking her head onto his shoulder. He pulled her closer.

"You okay?" Her voice was husky.

"Fine."

His hand rubbed against the flesh of her upper arm in a loving caress. He had to tell her. Tension tightened the muscles in his back and arms. It wasn't fair to keep it from her. If only he had some whiskey to bolster his courage.

"What's wrong?" she asked.

"There's something I have to tell you," he said. Her smile bloomed out, and he knew she thought he was going to say something sweet, like the three little words that hovered on his tongue.

He rushed on before he lost his courage. "It's about Jon's death. My part in it."

Rolling onto her back, she propped herself up on the pillow and stared at him. "What are you talking about?"

He sat up and ran his hand through his rumpled hair. His courage began to fail. How could she forgive him when he couldn't forgive himself? "Forget it."

"No. No, I'm not going to forget it. Something is between us, Rick, even after last night. If we are going to build a future, we have to knock down the wall."

He knew she was right. "It's my fault he's dead."

She folded her arms across her chest as though to ward off whatever he was trying to tell her. "How can it be your fault?"

"Allie, I'm an alcoholic. A recovering one, but it's something I struggle with every day." He couldn't look away from her stunned face, though he wanted to.

"An alcoholic." Her blue eyes cleared, and she touched his arm. "It's okay, Rick. We all have something we're ashamed of in our past. I'll be here for you."

She wouldn't be so glib once she knew the truth. Rick held her gaze. "You don't understand, Allie. I was drunk the day Jon died." He looked away, unable to watch the words he was about to say pierce her. In an instant he was back in Iraq with the raw sewage making his eyes water and the stink of gunpowder lingering on his clothes.

THE SOUND OF THE TROOPS' BOOTS CLOCKED ALONG THE PAVEMENT. RICK staggered when they stopped at the end of the street. The rest of the unit hunkered down behind some trash barrels. Rick fell clumsily beside his buddy. Some hair of the dog would clear his mind. He fumbled for the little flask he'd slipped into his pocket.

"You've had enough," Jon hissed. He grabbed the flask from Rick's hand and started to put it in his own pocket.

"No sermon," Rick slurred. "Give it back." He made an awkward swipe at Jon's arm.

A shadow loomed over them. Colonel Preston glared down at Jon. "I knew you weren't as pure as you tried to seem, Lieutenant Siders. Hand it over. You'll be brought up for courtmartial on this."

Rick tried to slide out of the way. He had enough presence of mind to know that if the colonel saw him like this, he'd be placed under arrest. Jon was too good of a buddy to squeal on him.

"Yes sir," Jon said, straightening. He passed the flask to his superior. "I'm sorry, sir."

"Sorry doesn't cut it," the colonel snapped. "Stand up. Walk a line for me."

"I didn't drink any of it, sir. I'm competent to fight." Jon leaped to his feet, walked a line, turned, and came back.

Shame clutched Rick's gut. He'd make it up to Jon though. His buddy had been eyeing a dress for his wife but didn't have the money to buy it. Jon sent every cent back to his little family in El Paso. Rick would buy it and send it, then tell Jon what he'd done.

"Enough. But this isn't over." The colonel grabbed the flask and moved away with a final contemptuous glare.

"Thanks, buddy," Rick muttered. "You saved my bacon there."

Jon's gaze held pity and love. "You've got to quit the drinking, Rick. It's going to kill you."

"I know, I know." Rick stood, still wavering. "Let's get this job done." He couldn't stand to look his buddy in the eye. Jon was the best friend he'd ever had.

"Stop!" Jon grabbed Rick's arm when he started toward the house that had pieces of plaster missing and no windows. "Wait for the order."

Rick shrugged off his friend's hand. "No glory in waiting," he said, his words slurred. Before Jon could grab him again, he leaped to the door and kicked it open.

His gaze collided with the five insurgents pointing guns at him. He brought his own weapon up, but slowly, too slowly. Expecting to feel bullets tearing through his skin, he closed his eyes. The next thing he knew, Jon's rebel call echoed into the small room. His buddy leaped into the house in front of the men.

The bullets meant for him entered Jon's chest, and his blood-spattered body fell across Rick as the other soldiers came through the door.

HE COULDN'T LOOK AT HER AS HE RECOUNTED THE STORY. WHEN IT WAS over, he lifted his gaze to her face. "Don't hate me, Allie. I hate myself enough for both of us."

A stunned expression dulled the brightness of her eyes. "No," she said. "You're lying. You're afraid to love me, so you're trying to drive me away."

"It's the truth, honey," he said, his voice barely above a whisper. "It's eaten me up all this time. It's the reason I had to help you. I owed it to Jon."

She clapped her hands over her ears. "No, I won't listen."

He grabbed her wrists and pulled her hands down. "If we're going to go on from here, it has to be with truth between us. I killed him, Allie. I need you to forgive me. Can you do that?"

"That's the only reason you married me?"

Her whimper cut him to bloody shreds inside. "The only reason. But it's not the reason I want to stay married now."

"Then why?" She held up her hand. "Wait, don't say anything. I have to think about this. It's too much to take in." She got out of bed and gathered her clothes from the floor. "I've got to get out of here for a while."

He watched her walk away. Saying the words "I love you" might have stopped her, but he still couldn't get them out past his tongue. Maybe it was a good thing. If she couldn't forgive him, he wasn't going to run the risk of rejection.

MOONBEAM MOVED SMOOTHLY UNDER HER. ALLIE BARELY NOTICED THE clouds overhead, the blackness deepening as the storm approached. Her second husband had killed her first.

Murderer.

She couldn't stop the tears. Why couldn't he have kept the truth to himself? Dealing with it was going to be impossible. She had loved Jon, and now she loved Rick.

Oh, how she loved him.

But he had kept this one vital piece of information to himself until she threw everything to the winds and gave herself to him. Had he thought if he told her last night, he wouldn't get her into his bed?

Her hard laugh turned to a sob as the wind picked up pieces of sand and flung them against her face. The stinging attack broke her from her thoughts, and she looked up to see the towering thunderheads still building.

She had some time before it hit. The cabin where Rosa Garcia lived was just over the hill. She could head there to escape the coming rain. It would be an excuse to ask Rosa the questions she needed answered.

The tiny cabin looked barely bigger than an outhouse, a mere fifteen-by-fifteen square. Flowers bloomed beside the porch, and the rocker looked worn and well used.

Glancing at her watch, Allie saw it was barely six thirty. The old woman might still be in bed. But before she could decide what to do, the front door opened, and a tiny, wizened figure stepped into view. An apron covered the dark dress that touched her boot tops, and the woman wore her white hair coiled in a knot at the back of her neck.

"Finally, you have come for a visit." Rosa's dark eyes examined her. "You have the look of Maria, *sí*, and of your mother. Coffee is brewing. Come." She hooked a finger toward Allie.

Allie dismounted, tied the reins to the porch railing, and followed the woman inside. The tiny cabin was as spotless inside as out. A bright rug covered the worn floorboards, and three candles burned on the fireplace mantel. Coffee boiled on a woodstove in the corner.

Rosa wrapped her hand in her apron, lifted the coffeepot from the heat, and poured two cups. "Cream and sugar, *sí*?"

"Yes, please." Allie accepted the coffee the woman handed her, then went to sit on the ladder-back chair. "You sounded like you were expecting me."

"*Sí.* I knew you would come in your own time. You want to know of your mother." Rosa settled at the table with Allie. "I am the only one left who knows all the story. The rest—all dead."

Rain began to patter against the metal roof over their heads. "You were at the ranch when my mother was a child?"

Rosa nodded. "*Sí.* From the time your *madre* was crawling on the floor."

She might as well start at the beginning. "What happened to my grandmother?"

Rosa's dark eyes softened. "Ah, Francesca was a darling girl. Elijah, he loved her very much. I thought he would die himself when the pneumonia took her from him. But he had your *madre* to care for."

"I saw some pictures of my mother growing up. She looked so happy until she got to her teens. What happened? Who was Maria's father?"

Rosa winced. "It is an unhappy story. Elijah carried the hurt to his grave. He blamed himself."

Wrapping her fingers around her warm cup, Allie tried to prepare herself for whatever information was coming. Thunder rumbled overhead. She would be trapped here all morning unless Rosa hurried up.

"Elijah had a partner. Nolan Webster. Handsome as *el diablo* himself. His wife was Francesca's best friend. He took a special interest in Anna, showed her rodeo tricks, took her to her first rodeo. Elijah thought nothing of it until his daughter told him she was pregnant. And Nolan was the father."

Allie shuddered, suddenly cold. "How old was this Nolan?"

"Forty, he was. And Anna was fifteen."

A lech. "He should have been shot," Allie said fiercely. "He could have been prosecuted for statutory rape."

"*Sí*. Elijah did just that, dear girl."

Allie opened her mouth and shut it again. "Did what? You don't mean Elijah shot him?" That couldn't be what Rosa meant. Elijah was no murderer.

Rosa's lively dark eyes narrowed. "*Sí*. Elijah, he shot Nolan and buried him in an old well. Anna was the only one who knew. She left the ranch that night and never returned. It was the only way she could cope with knowing her father was a murderer."

Allie swallowed hard. "Elijah seemed to be such a good man."

Rosa grabbed her hand with tough, sinewy fingers. "*Sí*, he was a very good man. But even good men have their breaking points. He spent the rest of his life atoning for his sin. That is when he converted the ranch to a place for hurting young people."

"And Maria?"

"Elijah had many eyes and ears. When Anna left, he found her again a year later. By then she was beginning to make a name for herself in the rodeo. She refused to come home. When she had no *bebé* with her, Elijah found out what had happened to the little one. She was to be adopted, but he fought and won custody and brought her home."

"My mother never objected?"

"No." Rosa shrugged her wizened shoulders. "Perhaps she never knew. She abandoned the *bebé* at a church."

"How could she do that?" The action didn't compute. Her mother had always been so caring and supportive of Allie and her sister. It just went to show how so many people wore a mask. Like Rick. She pushed the memory of his face away.

She took a sip of her coffee. It wasn't as bitter as her heart.

Rosa stood and went to rinse out her cup at the old hand pump. "I do not know, *mujercita*. Perhaps by then, she had come to hate everything about Nolan and the ranch, all the past memories. I am glad she was a good *madre* to you. She learned from her past, as we all should."

Had Rick learned from his past? She hadn't seen him take a single drop of liquor. But he had hidden his alcoholism from her. It would be hard to get past that failure if she was even willing to try, and right now, she wasn't too sure about that.

ALLIE HAD BEEN GONE AN HOUR. RICK KNEW SHE NEEDED TIME, BUT HE couldn't hang around and watch for her or he'd go crazy. Maybe he could see what Walker had found out about Luis Hernandez since yesterday.

Hoping to catch him before he went to work, he drove to Walker's house. Splashes of rain peppered the windshield, and he flipped on his wipers. Looked like they could have a real gulley-washer. Rick parked behind his friend's truck and honked when he saw Walker exiting the house.

Walker waved and walked back to stand beside Rick's open window. "I was going to call you when I got to the office, Mr. Impatience." His easy smile came. "We did good work yesterday. The money trail checks out. The ring raked in over five hundred thousand dollars."

"And it definitely went through Allie's account?"

"Yep."

"And he killed Allie's family. Man, that took a lot of hate."

Walker's brow clouded. "Uh, actually Rick, we're not finding evidence of any murder. He was in Mexico when the plane crash happened, and then when the sister was killed, he was in Canada."

"Maybe he hired someone."

"Maybe. But if he did, there's no money trail pointing to a hit man."

"I'm sure you'll find the connection. He's good at covering his tracks."

"Maybe." Walker glanced at his watch. "Listen, I've got to run. I'll call you if I find out anything new."

"Thanks." Rick backed out of the driveway and turned his truck toward home. He should get Betsy, but considering the weather, she'd be safer with the O'Sullivans. They had a basement, and this storm just might have a twister in it.

He mulled over what he'd found out. Luis had to be the murderer. Rick might have to help pin this down himself. The last thing he wanted was for the man to get off on a lighter charge and come looking for Allie again.

The clouds drew his gaze again, thunderheads building in the southwest. As purple-black as a bruise, they towered over the landscape. They were in for a bad one. He needed to make sure Allie wasn't out in this weather. He tried to reach her on his cell phone, but she didn't answer. The best he could do was get home as soon as possible. If she was still out, he'd take Jem and go find her.

His cell phone rang and he flipped it open. "Bailey."

"Rick, Betsy is gone." Dolly was babbling, nearly hysterical. "The bedroom window is open, and she's just gone."

Time froze.

Rick jammed on the brakes and pulled to the side of the road. What should he do? Go look for Betsy or find Allie? He started to turn the truck around. Allie would want him to find Betsy.

But for some reason he couldn't name, he veered the wheel the other way and headed to the ranch. "Call the sheriff," he barked into the phone. "I'm going after Allie, and we'll be there as soon as we can."

Allie was roaming on her own, but Rick had a feeling the guy would take Betsy to flaunt his power over her. He could only take the impulse as direction from God and trust he was reading it right.

THE SPLATTERS OF RAIN CHILLED HER ARMS. ALLIE LOOKED UP INTO THE rolling underbelly of a monster. A doozy of a storm was going to hit any minute, more than just the rain that had eased off before she left Rosa's. She was exposed to the vicious lightning flickering in the clouds. A rumble followed that made Moonbeam startle. She could sense the horse's agitation as the storm grew nearer.

She probably should have stayed at Rosa's. Her gaze swept the landscape as she looked for a place to get her and the horse in from the storm. There was nothing in the rock face, and the ranch was an hour's ride behind her.

She saw something in the distance and realized it was Bluebird. She whistled to the horse, and the mare turned toward her. Allie trotted Moonbeam over to the other mare and grabbed her halter. "What are you doing here, girl?"

The horse snorted but didn't try to run away. Allie leaned her face against the mare's neck and inhaled the aroma of horse. Rosa's words came back to her.

Maybe she learned from her past.

Didn't everyone have regrets for things they'd done in the past? She sure did. Who was she to judge Rick? She hadn't lived his life and been faced with his hurts. Love was a choice, he'd said. He'd chosen love early on and proven it by his actions.

She could do the same. The anger seeped out of her heart. Rick deserved the best she could give.

"Allie!"

She turned in the saddle to see Charlie coming toward her on horseback. She waved and waited for him. He would help her.

"Are you crazy? Coming out here in the middle of a storm," he said, stopping his horse about five feet from her. "The lightning will get you if the wind doesn't."

"You're out here too," she said, smiling.

"I was looking for you. Rick was worried, and so was I. He went to town to get Betsy and asked me to try to find you. You two have a fight?" His smile suggested he'd be glad to hear the juicy details.

"Something like that," she said shortly, irritation wiping away her initial happiness at seeing him. "How'd Bluebird get out?"

He shrugged. "No clue."

"Any idea where we can hole up?"

"I've got the perfect spot. Follow me." Digging his heels into his horse's belly, he led the way up the hillside and disappeared around the curve in the trail.

Muttering under her breath that she wanted to go down, not up, Allie followed with Bluebird. As soon as she got past the creosote bush that stuck halfway into the path, she saw Charlie waving from the opening to an old mine shaft.

She rode up to join him. "I don't want to go in there. Bats." She shuddered.

"They're sleeping," he said.

A brilliant flash of light superimposed itself on her eyes. Her hair stood on end, and the lightning crackled a hundred feet away, where it split a piñon tree right down the center. The smell of ozone burned her throat.

Bluebird snorted and tried to jerk away, but she hung on. Moonbeam pranced along the wet ground too, his eyes rolling to the whites.

"Come on!" Charlie and his horse disappeared into the shaft.

The hot scent from the burning tree and the way the wind picked up made Allie dismount and follow, leading Moonbeam and Bluebird in with her. The cool muskiness of the mine made her instantly want to go back outside. She hated closed-in spaces. The rough walls and low ceiling made her chest feel tight.

"Over here, Allie," Charlie called.

He was brandishing a flashlight. The friendly beam pushed back the edges of the darkness. Allie dropped Moonbeam's reins and sat beside Charlie on a big rock near the ashes of an old campfire.

"Looks like someone uses this place." Kicking at the ashes with the toe of her boot, she glanced around the space.

Black things in the corners made her shudder. Bats, but they weren't moving. The storm would blow itself out soon, and she could get home to Betsy.

Once she figured out what to say to Rick. Tears welled in her eyes again, and she turned her head, but not fast enough to hide her emotion from Charlie.

"Hey, you okay?"

"Fine." She sniffed and gulped back her pain.

"Rick have a drinking binge or something?"

She looked up then. "You knew?"

"Well, sure. The whole ranch knows. Elijah was waiting for Rick to fall, but he hasn't so far. Maybe you weakened him. You have that effect on men."

She wasn't going there. Uh-uh. Charlie seemed to have words of confession hanging on his tongue, and she wasn't going to give him a chance to tell her he was crazy about her or something equally embarrassing.

Standing, she walked around the cavern, though she was careful not to look up at the bats. If she saw one move, she might scream. "What kind of mine is this?"

Charlie stood and joined her. "Mercury." He kicked an orange rock with his toe. "Cinnabar rock carries it."

"Why isn't it mined anymore?"

"I don't know, do I look like a park ranger?" He laughed, but there was an edge to it. "I've been wanting to talk to you. Sit down." He took her arm in a surprisingly hard grasp and marched her back to the rock.

There was no getting around it. She was going to have to hurt his feelings. Just what she needed on top of an upsetting day. "Look, Charlie, let's not go there. I'm happily married."

His laughter barked, echoing off the sides of the mine. "Get real. You're not as pretty as you think you are."

She drew back at the derisive edge to his voice. "My mistake," she said in a cool voice. "So what's on your mind?"

"Women like you can twist a guy until he doesn't know which way is up." Charlie swore and stomped at the ashes and charred wood, scattering them in all directions. Vile words spewed from his mouth as he waved his hands and roared around the space.

Allie wanted to grab Moonbeam and run, but the storm had descended in full fury. The wind howled outside the mine opening, and the thunder boomed in a continuous roll. Rain sluiced over the entrance like a waterfall.

"Calm down, Charlie. Tell me what this is all about." She tried to speak in a soft, calm voice, and it seemed to work. He quit kicking at the ground and turned to look at her.

Then she saw his hand come up with a gun.

"Put that away." She spoke in her strongest, most assertive voice.

"You killed my brother." His voice was calm and reasonable.

"Jimmy Hernandez is your brother? Bu—but you're not Hispanic."

His short laugh made Moonbeam prick his ears and step back. "This has nothing to do with *Hernandez*. You're so stupid. I gave you plenty of time to figure it out."

"Who's your brother? I thought you said he was a politician."

"He wanted to run for office, but you killed him. The name Mark Haskell ring a bell?" He watched until she flinched, then he smiled.

"Mark's dead? I didn't know."

He leaned over her, yelling at the top of his lungs, "Of course he's dead, you heartless witch! He hung himself when you broke his heart. You led him on, then tossed him aside like a piece of trash when you were done."

Allie winced as spittle sprayed from his mouth over her face. "Charlie, it wasn't like that. We weren't romantically involved. He never even kissed me."

"You're a liar! He'd come home at night and tell me what you said about loving him forever. Then some new cowboy walked in and whisked you away from him."

"He lied to you," she said, trying to edge away. Her back was up against the wall of the mine. "You have to believe me."

The storm was beginning to abate. She could hear the thunder moving off. They had to get down off this mountain and through the wash before a flash flood hit.

Charlie quit looming over her. He stepped back, and she took hope that maybe he was listening to the truth.

"Please, you have to believe me, Charlie. I only went out with him a couple of times." Did Charlie kill her family and Yo? Staring into his face, suffused with red, she could believe it.

And she was stuck here in a mine with him training a gun on her. Praying, she tried to think of what to do. She couldn't leave Betsy alone.

26

THE WIND RATTLED THE TRUCK LIKE A COUGAR SHAKING A RABBIT. RICK gripped the wheel and fought to keep it on the road. He kept shooting cautious glances at the sky. While tornadoes weren't common in the Big Bend area, they weren't unheard-of either.

Lightning snaked across the sky, and thunder chased it, a rumble that he felt clear through the vehicle. Allie and Betsy were out in this. He had to find them.

Squinting through the driving rain, he struggled to see the road. With the storm obscuring the landscape, he had no idea where he was. Then he saw a lane off to the right and recognized his neighbor's drive. The ranch was still ten miles away. He should pull off and wait this out a few minutes.

He wanted to press on, but if he ended up in a ditch, Allie and Betsy would be lost. He angled the truck into the lane, keeping it on the high part so runoff wouldn't flood him out. With the truck shut off and stationary, the storm battered the vehicle so much, he thought it might tip over. There could be a twister in this sucker.

His cell phone rang, and he fished it out of his shirt pocket. "Bailey," he said. He heard a voice on the other end, but the storm was so loud, he couldn't hear well. Then he realized it was Brendan.

"Got word about—"

"Say again, Brendan?" he shouted. "I'm in the middle of a spring thunderstorm."

"Mark Haskell," Brendan said, the connection suddenly clearing. "He hung himself, which is why Allie didn't hear from him again."

"Holy cow. Listen, Brendan, this is important." Rick had to shout over the sound of the wind. "Betsy's missing. I thought we found the guy who was after Allie, but I was wrong. Did this Haskell have any family?"

"Just a brother he was raising. Half-brother actually. The kid ended up in a mental hospital for a while. Charles—" The rest of the name disappeared in a crackle of static.

"What was that, Brendan? You cut out. What's Charles's last name?"

"Reyes," Brendan said. "Charles Reyes."

Charlie!

His friend Charlie, who was out looking for Allie. Could they have been wrong? Maybe Luis had nothing to do with the deaths. He claimed he didn't.

The static in his phone grew louder. The connection was about to die. "Brendan, I don't think my phone is going to hold. If you can hear me, call the sheriff in town. Tell him Charlie Reyes has Betsy and is going to kill her and Allie. I'm going to the ranch now."

Brendan's response was garbled, then the phone went dead. Rick could only hope and pray his friend got the last of the words. He started the engine, backed out onto the road he still couldn't see, then sped back toward the ranch as fast as the buffeting rain would allow.

He couldn't believe it. Not Charlie. He was just a kid. But then murder didn't seem to have an age requirement.

He reached the turnoff to the ranch. A new river had sprung into existence while he was gone. The wash across the road ran heavy and deep. He was going to have to try to make it through anyway. The truck shuddered as Rick gunned it. The tires found purchase in the mud under the water, then a wave slapped against the door. The truck bucked again. The tires lost their grip, and the water lifted the vehicle.

In seconds, the truck was riding the waves in the middle of the current. Hurtling toward the Eye of the Needle, as they called the hole between two huge boulders. No way would the truck fit through there.

Rick unfastened his seat belt and prepared to abandon the truck. With the force of the current, the vehicle would slam into those rocks, and he didn't want to be trapped in the cab when it happened. He might be unable to get out with the doors and windows jammed up.

The truck slewed sideways, and the passenger door became the leading edge. Rick tried to open his door, but the water pressure was too great. He jerked around to see the approaching rocks, then ran the window down to try to get out that way. Sitting on the top of the window opening, he grabbed the top of the truck and hauled himself up until his feet were on the armrest.

Then he was atop the truck, looking down at the red-brown, swirling water. The bank was fifteen feet away, and it would be a hard swim to make it, but he had no choice. The rocks loomed ahead, and the impact would knock him in the water anyway.

The rain continued to drench him. He shot up a prayer for help, then leaped. The water closed over his head, and then his feet touched the bottom. He kicked with his heels and shot up to the surface, where he gulped in air. He couldn't see which way was to safety, but he saw the truck barreling toward the rocks and struck out perpendicular to its trajectory.

Flotsam and debris battered him as he struggled to swim in the turbulent water. Pieces of sheet metal barreled by, and he ducked out of their way, but one raked a sharp edge across his arm. He grabbed a piece of wood and hung on to it for buoyancy. Fatigue was already beginning to slow him, and he wasn't sure he'd make it. Then his boot touched bottom, and he used the stability to propel himself forward. His arm struck a tree limb, this time not one floating in the water but anchored in the soil.

He grabbed the limb, hauled himself to shore, and lay in the mud with the rain pounding on his back. Half-unconscious, he coughed up the dirty water from his lungs.

Allie. Betsy.

They needed him. He managed to get onto his hands and knees, then finally to his feet. Patting his pocket, he realized his cell phone was still there, though it was probably useless.

The rain began to slow, and he blinked water out of his eyes. He needed a horse and Jem to try to find Allie. The barn was three hundred feet up the lane, but on the other side of the water. He'd have to climb the rocks and sidle across the Eye of the Needle.

Gathering his strength, he started for the rocks. With his boots wet and the rocks slick with water and mud, it would be a hard trail.

He reached the base of the hillside and started up. Cold mud and muck clung to his hands and caked his boots. Several times he fell on the slippery surface. Finally he was at the summit.

Below him, the truck rocked and scraped against the rocks as the roaring flood battered it. The door had crumpled in, and the rolling of the water had smashed it from all sides. He straddled the narrow rock and began to scoot along toward the other side. The water rose higher and higher on the face of the cliff until it touched the soles of his boots.

But by then, he was nearly across. With a last shove, he gained the boulder on the other side and began his descent. It was just as treacherous going down as it had been going up. One false step, and he'd hurtle to his death.

There weren't as many finger holds on this side. When he was about ten feet from the ground, his hand slipped from the rock, and he began to slide down. Scrabbling for a finger hold, he tore the nail from his thumb but continued to fall. His other hand flailed out but found nothing to grab hold of.

The next thing he knew, he was lying on his back in the mud, staring into roiling black clouds. On either side of him were more rocks, but he'd fallen into the only safe spot. *Thank you, God.* He struggled to his feet in spite of his screaming muscles. Hobbling toward the ranch, he finally managed to break into a run. The barn and house were just ahead.

First he should see if Allie was back. Maybe his fear was for nothing. He rushed up the steps, threw open the door, and stepped inside. The welcome respite from the storm made him pause, then he hurried to the living room.

Empty.

He turned and ran back outside. His boots smacked through the mud puddles as he ran to the barn. The doors to the barn hung open, and so did the gate. He heard voices around the back of the barn and veered to the back paddock.

The horses were gone. He could see several of them at the far edge of the field. Several of the hands and the teenagers were chasing them.

He caught sight of Fern coming from the barn with a halter in her hand. "Have you seen Allie?" he asked.

"What's wrong?"

He hesitated, unsure if he should alarm her. "She went out for a ride this morning, and I don't want her caught in this storm."

"I haven't seen her all day," Fern said.

"Me neither," Latoya echoed, exiting the barn behind Fern.

"Hang on. I only want to say this once." Rick waved over the rest of the group.

Devon and Emilio jogged toward him with Leon coming up a few paces behind. The ranch hands gathered around too.

"Look, Betsy and Allie are missing, probably out in this storm," he said.

"Dude, you need help?" Devon asked. "We can go out too."

"I can organize them into a search party," Emilio said.

Rick hesitated. While he could use the help, he didn't want the kids in danger from Charlie. "Just pray, guys. Emilio, call the sheriff. Tell him I found out Charlie might be a danger to Allie, and I'm looking for them now."

"Charlie? No way," Devon said.

"It looks like he's behind the attempts on Allie's life. And someone stole Betsy out of the bedroom early this morning. I've got to find them."

"Let me come," Emilio said.

"The kids need protection in case he comes back. You'd better stay here." Rick turned toward the house. "Get in the house. Lock the door, and don't let Charlie in if he comes back."

He jogged across the muddy yard to the house and rushed into the office. The glass in the gun cabinet gleamed. The key was in the desk. He fished it out and opened the cabinet. The black barrels looked deadly. Rick touched the gunstock, so smooth and slick.

He'd sworn never to point a gun at another human being after the accident that killed a child in Iraq. But this was his wife, his child. Didn't he have the right to protect his family?

His hand hovered over the gunstock, then dropped. He couldn't do it. God would have to provide another way. Grabbing up the nightstick, he wheeled and ran to save his family.

THE GUN'S BORE SEEMED TO GROW BIGGER WITH EVERY SECOND. NOW THAT the rain had stopped and moisture shimmered in the air, Allie felt the danger growing. He would do something now that they weren't trapped here.

"What do you want me to say, Charlie? I'm sorry Mark is dead. I never meant to hurt him. Or you. I thought we were friends."

"Friends?" He laughed. "I'm a better actor than I thought. I don't want you to say anything, Allie. I want you to die. But first you'll watch Betsy drown."

All the air left Allie's lungs. "What are you saying?"

He laughed. "Got your attention now, don't I?" He grabbed her arm and dragged her toward a small opening. The hallway was so tiny, she had to bend over to walk through it.

He forced her in front of him, the gun digging into her back. Then she stepped through into a smaller circular room about twelve feet in diameter.

Betsy leaped to her feet. "Mommy!" She ran to Allie, but Betsy's hands were tied behind her, and all she could do was lean against her mother's leg and cry.

Allie's fingers tore at the rope's knot, and even before Charlie emerged from the corridor, she had her daughter freed.

"Here, brat." Charlie grabbed at Betsy.

Allie pushed her daughter behind her and faced him down. "Leave her alone! What kind of monster does this to a child?"

"I didn't want to," he said, a sulky pout to his lips. "You forced me. Always around Rick, never coming out for a ride with me. I told you I was going to strip you of everything you loved. I would have settled for the adults if you hadn't been so smug." He sneered. "All joy and light. You had another fish on your hook, and I couldn't take it anymore."

"Let her go, Charlie. Please. I'll go with you, do anything you want, anything to make amends. Just don't hurt her. She's just a little girl, and you've hurt her enough."

"I haven't done a thing to her yet."

"Didn't you wonder why she didn't talk? It was seeing the—the accident." She lowered her voice, hoping Betsy wouldn't be able to make out her words. "For a year she didn't utter a word. Don't you think that's enough?"

For a minute she thought maybe her plea had gotten through to him. His gaze fell on Betsy, and his mouth softened.

"She's a cute kid," he said. His lips pressed together. "I'm sorry, but the sins of the mother fall on the child too." He reached around her.

Allie screamed and beat at him with her fists. She leaped onto his back and pummeled him. "Run, Bets! Run!"

Her daughter leaped past her, squeezed between Charlie's legs, and darted into the tunnel. Charlie whirled around and around in the chamber. He fell against the wall, slamming Allie's back against rock. The pain made her loosen her grip, and he managed to throw her down to the floor.

"You'll pay for that." He dragged her to her feet and forced her into the tunnel.

Praying for God to save her daughter, Allie moved slowly. Betsy needed as long as possible to run for help, to escape. Charlie shoved at her with the gun, and she stumbled to her knees, then took her time getting moving again.

All too soon, her head emerged into the high-ceilinged room. But there was no sign of Betsy, and Allie closed her eyes with thankfulness. All three horses were gone too.

"I'll find her," Charlie said, his teeth gritted together. "You can count on that." He shoved her out of the mine opening onto the ledge outside.

The storm had passed, and she could see a glimmer of blue in the clouds, smell the freshness in the air. Allie breathed in the life, knowing it would be only a few minutes until she lay broken and drowned at the bottom of this cliff where the flood raged. Her gaze swept the valley until she saw a small figure on horseback at the bottom of the path, still above the water's reach. A gulf separated Betsy and Bluebird from the safety of the other side.

Charlie had seen them too. He started toward them, but Allie grabbed his arm. "I admit it. I wanted to hurt your brother. He was such a nerd, and he deserved everything he got."

Charlie stopped and turned his gaze on her. It was odd, looking death in the face. Allie had never expected to see it so clearly. Cold and implacable, his eyes reflected no humanity that she could see.

Then he smiled. "You can't distract me that easily."

He turned toward her daughter again, but the mare and little girl melded into one blur as the combined figure leaped the gulf and gained the safety of the other side.

"Thank you, God," Allie whispered. With her daughter safe, she could handle what came next. She wasn't afraid to die, though she desperately wished she'd told Rick she forgave him.

He'd feel guilt over her death, and she regretted that.

She sagged to the ground, her legs like rubber. Charlie's fingers tightened on the trigger, and Allie squeezed her eyes shut, expecting a bullet to slam into her skull at any moment. When nothing happened, she opened her eyes and stared up at his smiling face. The smile made her shudder.

She could find no pity or remorse in Charlie's set face, but she wasn't dead yet. Maybe she was giving up too soon. He wasn't going to shoot her, so she had hope. Slim hope, but a tiny sliver at least. The only weapons at her disposal were rocks and her own hands.

"I want you to suffer like Mark did," Charlie said. "He climbed that chair, put the rope around his neck, knowing he was about to die. He kicked over the chair, but his neck didn't break and he slowly strangled to death. It wasn't clean and easy."

He grabbed her arm and yanked her to her feet. Grabbing her hands, he pulled them roughly behind her back. She felt rope chafe her wrists, and he tightened it down until she groaned.

"What are you going to do?" she asked when he shoved her closer to the edge of the cliff.

"Make the most of a storm like this." He propelled her to the very edge of the cliff.

Rivulets of water ran down the hillside to join an ocean of rushing, tumbling water. Churning brown waves tossed up pieces of wood and debris before sucking them under the deadly current again. The flash flood stretched from the base of the cliff across to the next rocky outcropping, a distance of three hundred feet.

Allie caught just a glimpse of her daughter's curls on top of the hill. Rick was standing beside her!

She turned to face Charlie. "You won't get away with my murder. You'll be caught and tried. You'll go to prison or the electric chair, Charlie. Stop this now before it's too late."

"It's already too late. I've killed five people. One more won't make a difference." He smiled, a brief gleam of teeth. "But they won't know I killed you. They'll think the flash flood caught you. It's perfectly understandable. I'll find Betsy and dispose of her before she can tell. All neat and tidy."

He meant to toss her into the raging water.

Lord, help me.

She struggled then, fighting his grip on her arm. "They'll know I was murdered," she gasped. "My hands will be tied."

She spared a glance toward her daughter and found Rick atop the horse with Betsy. They were turning this way. What was he thinking to bring her back into danger?

Charlie turned her around and untied her wrists. "You won't be able to fight the waves anyway." He flipped her around to face the water again.

His hand shoved her in the small of the back, and she was standing on the very edge of the rock. Looking down into the swirling water, she knew Rick wouldn't get here in time.

She wasn't a strong swimmer. The waves would overpower her in seconds. Her only chance was to not go there at all, but Charlie was prodding her. Only a few inches kept her from plummeting down the slope to the hungry waves.

Her gaze fastened on the roots of a tree jutting out from the rock above her head. The closest one looked strong enough to support her weight. She might be able to reach it.

Without waiting to consider the outcome, she leaped up. Her palms slapped onto the thick root, and her fingers closed around the support. Drawing her knees to her chest, she snatched her legs from Charlie's grasp as he lunged for them.

"Allie!"

She heard Rick's voice, and her head turned toward the sound. He was dismounting from Bluebird, who had leaped the gap again. Once he was on the ground, he smacked Bluebird's rump, and the horse carried Betsy back to safety.

Rick's voice made Charlie falter in his lunge. His leap brought him closer to the edge, and she kicked out, her left foot connecting with his head. His arms pinwheeled as he tried to catch himself, but his right boot slid out from under him.

Rick's nightstick sailed through the air. It struck Charlie on the head, and in that instant, he lost his battle for balance. His face turned up to her, and she saw terror in his eyes. Out of instinct, she let go of the roots with one hand and started to reach down for him. She couldn't let him die without at least trying.

"Allie, no!" Rick dove toward Charlie too, but it was too late. Without a sound, he pitched over the side and disappeared in the brown foam.

Allie dropped down and flung herself onto her stomach beside Rick to peer over the side. "Charlie!"

Charlie's head bobbed up, and one arm flung toward the skies before he disappeared again. He never came up.

THE FRESH SCENT OF RAIN WASHED AWAY THE DANK SMELL OF FEAR. IT was truly over now. Rick held Allie as she curled onto his lap and clutched at his shirt as if to assure herself—and him—that they were both really alive. He still wasn't sure if they were alive or just in heaven.

"You're safe," he murmured in her hair.

"You're wet," she said, pulling her head away.

"I had a little swim in the river to get here." He smiled down at her.

"You swam *that?*" Her gaze went to the raging floodwaters below their perch.

"I'd swim the ocean to get to you." His arms tightened around her. "I—I love you, Allie." He wanted to say the words before he lost his nerve. Even if she couldn't forgive him for keeping the truth from her, he had to tell her.

She didn't answer for so long, he thought she would pull away and tell him she was leaving. His muscles tightened for the blow.

Her fingers toyed with the buttons on his shirt, but her eyes stayed downcast. "I hated you for all of fifteen minutes," she said. Her gaze finally lifted to lock with his. "I wanted to dig the love up by the roots and fling it back in your face, but the tentacles went clear to bedrock. You're stuck with me."

"You forgive me?"

"Yes." She curled her fists into his shirt and gave him a slight shake. "Just don't ever hide anything from me again."

"You've got a lot of room to talk," he said, his grin breaking out. "I seem to remember all kinds of things you didn't tell me in the beginning."

Her smile was shamefaced. "That's different." She swatted his arm. "Okay, I was wrong too. Let's go home. I need to see Betsy. You're *sure* she was okay when you saw her?"

"Riding like the wind. She'll be proud she played a part in your rescue. I would never have been able to get across that water without a horse to jump it."

"Why did you bring Betsy with you?"

"Bluebird wouldn't let me on without her. You know how Bets calms animals. It was with Betsy or not at all. They're back to the ranch by now, and this place will be crawling with cops any minute."

"We need to go. I have to hold her."

"In a minute." He gathered her closer and bent his head. There was nothing between them now. Everything was out in the open. He loved and was loved in return. It was too much to hold in.

His lips brushed hers. She wound her arms around his neck and kissed him back. His. She was all his. Now and forever.

EPILOGUE

THE BIRDS FILLED THE MEADOW WITH SONG. THERE HAD BEEN NO NEED TO buy flowers for the ceremony because God provided them himself. The rains had brought the wildflowers into full bloom, and their fragrance and color flooded Allie's senses.

She glanced at her watch. Where was he? The ceremony was about to begin, and she wanted to give Rick his surprise first. It was supposed to be bad luck to see the groom before the wedding, but it hardly counted since they were already married.

"You're more jittery than me," the young man at her side said.

Allie smiled at her newly met brother-in-law. "Chad, don't be mad if he doesn't recognize you, okay? It's been fifteen years. You look a little different than you did at five."

Rick had shown her the last picture he had of his younger brother. Chad's hair was blond then, and he had mud on his face. This quiet young man with starched hair and clothes didn't even come close.

"I know." Chad's nervous smile chased away the picture he'd presented of a polished young yuppie. "I just barely remember him, but he was like Superman to me."

"There he is," Allie whispered when her husband's broad shoulders moved through the crowd. "Stand behind me and turn around so he only sees the back of your head."

She blocked the view to Chad as Rick spotted her. His face brightened, and he wagged a finger at her to indicate he wasn't supposed to see her yet. She waved him to her, and his smile beamed out.

He glanced around. "If Dolly sees us together, we're in trouble."

"I have a present for you," she said. She couldn't stand it much longer. Rick's face would be a picture.

"I have something for you too, but you can't have it until after the wedding." He waggled his brows at her.

She laughed and felt heat on her cheeks. "Shh, people will hear."

He laughed. "Girl, your mind is in the gutter. That's not what I meant, but it's not a bad idea. This is something more—um—substantial." He glanced at her hands. "So where's this big present?"

"Right here." She stepped aside. "I'd like you to meet someone."

Chad's face was pale, but he mustered a smile. "Hi, Rick."

Rick looked perplexed for a minute, then his gaze locked with Chad's before sweeping up and down the young man. "Wh-who are you?" A dawning hope filled his eyes.

Allie grabbed his arm. "If you could have one person here to witness our wedding, who would it be, Rick?"

"Chad?" he whispered.

Chad nodded jerkily. "It's me, Rick."

Rick stepped forward first, his arms coming up awkwardly. Chad embraced the bigger man, nearly swallowed up by Rick's muscular arms. Though the older man was bulkier, the resemblance was impossible to deny. Chad had Rick's nose and thick hair. The shape of the eyes was the same too.

Allie swiped at her wet cheeks. She wanted to sit down and just howl with indescribable joy. She couldn't help but think how she'd feel if the sister she knew was dead walked up to her. That was a little how she imagined Rick felt right now.

Then Rick was pounding his brother on the back, and saying over and over, "Chad, I can't believe it." His voice was choked with emotion.

Chad had wet eyes. His knuckles were white with the clutch he had on his older brother.

Rick finally stepped back and gripped him by the shoulders. "How did you find me?"

Chad wiped his face with the back of his hand. He nodded at Allie. "Your wife found me through an old teacher. She got a message to me through a nurse." He looked down at his perfectly shined shoes. "I thought you'd forgotten all about me."

"Never, Chad." Rick gave him a little shake. "Never for a minute."

"I know that now. My foster parents adopted me when I was twelve. They were missionaries, and we went to South Africa six months after the adoption. I was there for five years, then came back here for college. I'm in San Antonio."

"No wonder I couldn't find you," Rick said, his grin rueful. He swiped at his eyes. "Man, you're a sight for sore eyes."

Allie couldn't stop crying as she watched the reunion. Rick had known his brother with one look.

Betsy tugged on her hand. "Why is Daddy crying?" she whispered. "I'm scared."

Allie knelt beside her daughter. "Those are happy tears, Bets. Like when Mommy heard you talk again. Sometimes the happiness just bubbles out, and you can't help it." Her vision was blurry, but her daughter was still the most beautiful thing she'd ever seen.

Allie had come so close to losing everything, and she didn't think she'd ever take anything for granted again.

Betsy nodded, but she still looked wary as she watched the two men. Allie stood again, unable to get enough of the joy that filled the meadow.

Rick's gaze locked with hers over his brother's shoulder. "Allie, you did this? How did you know where to look?"

"Dolly had a lead on the teacher. I went to see her, and she rambled about missionaries and Africa. It made no sense, but I left a note at the nursing home in case he came by to see her again. He called me two days ago."

Rick left his brother then and grabbed her up so her toes dangled above the ground. He dropped a kiss onto her lips. "Thank you," he said. "That's all I can say. I have everything I've ever wanted right here, right now."

He set her back on the ground, and she let her love shine through her eyes as she stared up at him. She had another present for him later, a very special one, but that would have to come when they were alone. Her hand dropped to her tummy in a protective gesture. He was going to be buried with new family.

She saw Rosa standing apart from the crowd. Allie waved to her and went to join her. "Thanks for coming, Rosa. It means the world to me."

The woman smiled. "You must wear something old, so I bring you this, *sí*?" She held out a soft christening gown and bonnet. "It belonged to your *madre*. You can fold the bonnet and tuck it into your garter. Your *bebé* will wear it."

"How did you know?" Allie whispered.

"It is in your eyes," Rosa said, her smile soft.

Allie's throat closed. She took the bonnet. Turning her back to the guests, she lifted the edge of her dress and tucked the hat into her garter. The soft fabric felt like a touch from her mother. "Thank you, Rosa," she said. "If you'll keep the gown, I'll get it before we leave."

"Of course." Rosa pressed her lips to Allie's cheek. "I pray for you, just like I pray for your *madre*."

Dolly called for them to get started. Rick walked to Grady's side under the gazebo they'd moved into the clearing. From somewhere, the wedding processional began to play, the sound a perfect blend with the birds chirping and the song of the wind in the trees.

Jon's parents stood along the sidelines, their faces reflecting their unease. But at least they'd chosen to support her, and Betsy was gradually warming up to them. The teenagers they'd helped crowded around. They'd come so far in the few weeks they'd been here. Allie hated to let them go, but she knew they'd be all right. They'd learned important lessons here, ones they'd never forget.

Just like she had.

Fern's tremulous smile filled Allie with joy. She smiled back, and Fern's blush held joy.

"Go on, Bets," Allie whispered, giving her daughter a little shove.

Betsy moved out from her mother's side. She dropped flower petals along the path to join her new daddy. They were bright splashes of blue against the yellow sea of wildflowers.

Then it was Allie's turn. Her white slippers trod the petals underfoot. She was Cinderella, though her fairy godmother had been Dolly, who had made her dress with her magic sewing machine. Though the bluebirds hadn't come to help her make her dress, she caught flashes of their blue feathers from the corner of her eye and smiled.

For once in her life, Allie actually felt beautiful.

As she and Rick repeated their vows, this time with meaning and intention, she couldn't look away from the promise in his blue eyes. They might have troubles in the future, but together they could weather the storms.

"I now pronounce you husband and wife. Rick, have at it," Grady said.

Laughter rippled through the guests standing around the clearing. Rick's hands came down on her shoulders, and he drew her to him. His kiss was a gentle caress full of forever. Allie drank it in without fear of the future.

When she lifted her head, she saw her husband nod to Dolly. Cages snicked open around them, and Allie saw blue feathers everywhere. A sea of bluebirds filled the air, their wings fluttering past her ears, their bright flashes of color mimicking the blue in her husband's eyes.

She'd found her bluebird of happiness. Now and forever.

ACKNOWLEDGEMENTS

I ALWAYS KNEW I WAS A TEXAN AT HEART. IF YOU'VE NEVER VISITED THE Big Bend region in southwest Texas, you should make it a priority. My brothers, Rick, Dave, and Randy Rhoads, have always been Wild West nuts, and their love of all things western transferred itself to me long ago. I started out writing western romances, and my first book in that genre came out in 1998. Writing this book was almost like going back to the good old days for me. Though this book is set in contemporary times, a ranch is a ranch.

My thanks to Andrea Doering at Crossings for suggesting I set this book in the Lonestar state. I'm almost ready to move—well, if it weren't for the tarantulas!

They may get tired of me thanking them, but I've got the best possible publishing team at Thomas Nelson. Allen Arnold, Ami McConnell, Natalie Hanemann, Amanda Bostic, Jennifer Deshler,

Carrie Wagner, and Lisa Young are always cooking up new schemes to gain me new readers. My love and thanks to you all, especially Allen for this particular book. And my fabulous cover designers, Mark Ross and Belinda Bass, deserve a hand of applause as well. I'm always excited to get a new cover from Nelson because of all the work they put into it. And thanks to Erin Healy, my terrific freelance editor who is always pushing me to stretch and be better than I think I can. You all rock, and I thank God for you!

No author rises or falls on her own talent (I'd be in trouble if I were expected to!), and in my case I've got a great team that extends beyond my Nelson family. It all starts with my great agent, Karen Solem, who makes me dig deep in a story for the things that matter. My critique team is a constant source of encouragement and handholding, and you deserve a medal! Thanks to the girls (www.girlswriteout.blogspot.com): Kristin Billerbeck, Diann Hunt, and Denise Hunter. And thanks to Robin Miller, who holds me up to high standards on the suspense thread. If she figures out the killer early, I'm in trouble!

I wouldn't be writing today if it weren't for the support of my family. My great husband doesn't mind when the laundry isn't done or dinner isn't on the table because I'm off somewhere roping bulls. My love and appreciation go out to my great family and to my wonderful Jesus, who has kicked open so many doors.

And you, dear reader, are a constant source of light in my day with your e-mails and letters. You're the focus of much of what I do every day. Thank you for the joy you bring to my life. Stop by my Web site for a visit at www.colleencoble.com or e-mail me at colleen@colleencoble.com. If your book club of twenty members or more is reading one of my books, I'd be happy to call in if you contact me.

READING GROUP GUIDE

1. The perennial question is why bad things happen to good people. What gets you through times like Allie suffered?

2. We all have things that we struggle with. For a while Rick turned to the bottle to deal with his guilt over Jon's death. What other crutches do you see people use?

3. Have you ever given up a dream for someone you love? If so, what was it and how did it turn out?

4. Rick was passionate about the plight of abused horses and abused children. What are you passionate about? Does anything move you to action? If not, what is stopping you?

5. As parents we can tend to overprotect our children. Discuss Allie's relationship with her daughter, the good and the bad.

6. Rick believed love is an action word. Was he right?

7. Can secrets ever be good?

8. The villain allowed revenge to rule his life, and it's hard to forgive someone who has hurt a loved one. How do you manage it?

9. How do you feel about the fact that Elijah never went looking for his other granddaughters, Allie and Tammy?

10. Is there a dream for a better life that God has never let die in your heart? What are you going to do about it?

Can a secret
be kept forever?

"Colleen is a master storyteller."
KAREN KINGSBURY
Best-selling author of Take One

LONESTAR SECRETS
COLLEEN COBLE
Best-Selling Author of *Lonestar Sanctuary*

THOMAS NELSON
Since 1798

Enter a world of romance where wild beauty
soothes the soul and the wounded heart
finds love and sanctuary.

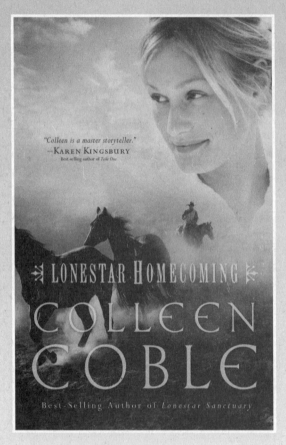

"Colleen is a master storyteller."
—KAREN KINGSBURY
Best-selling author of *Take One*

LONESTAR HOMECOMING

COLLEEN COBLE

Best-Selling Author of *Lonestar Sanctuary*

COMING APRIL 2010

THOMAS NELSON
Since 1798

THE ROCK HARBOR MYSTERY SERIES

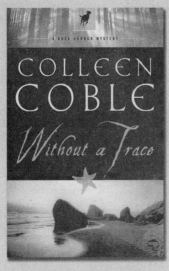

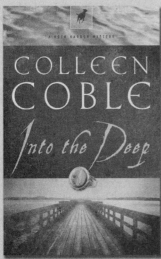

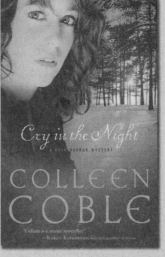

THOMAS NELSON
Since 1798

An Amish Romantic Mystery

"Heart-wrenching drama, heart-racing suspense, and a heart-changing underlying message of the power of forgiveness all combine to create a non-stop reading experience."

—KIM SAWYER, AWARD-WINNING AUTHOR OF *BYGONES*

THOMAS NELSON
Since 1798

ABOUT THE AUTHOR

COLLEEN COBLE IS THE BEST-SELLING AUTHOR OF SEVERAL NOVELS including *Cry in the Night*, *Lonestar Secrets*, and *Anathema*. She and her husband, Dave, live in Indiana.

SWEETWATER
gap

Other Novels by Denise Hunter Include

The Seaside Letters

The Convenient Groom

Surrender Bay

Finding Faith

Saving Grace

Mending Places

one

Josephine Mitchell was up to her wrists in dirt when she heard the whistle. She looked past the ornamental iron railing down to street level where Cody Something shut the door of his '79 Mustang.

He approached her veranda, shading his eyes from the sun with his hand. "Hey, Apartment 2B, my friend came through." Cody tugged two tickets from the back pocket of his khaki shorts. "Louisville versus UK."

Josie pulled her hands from under the wisteria's roots and patted the dirt down. "Answer's still no." She smiled to soften the rejection, then poured more of the sandy loam around the vine's woody roots.

"Forty-yard line. Biggest game of the year . . ." A shadow puddled in his dimple.

"Sorry."

He sighed. "When are you going to break down and say yes?"

Josie's cell phone pealed and vibrated simultaneously in her pocket. "Saved by the bell." She wiped her hands on her jeans and checked the screen.

A frown pulled her brows. Her sister hadn't called since she'd gotten the big news four months ago. Josie hoped she was okay.

"Sorry, gotta take this," she told Cody, then flipped open the phone. "Hey, Laurel."

There was a pause at the other end. "Josie? It's Nate. Your brother-in-law." As if Josie didn't know his name or voice. He'd only dated her sister four years before finally proposing.

But Nate had never called Josie, and the fact that he was now only reinforced her previous suspicion. "Is everything okay? Laurel and the baby?"

"They're fine."

Thank God. Laurel and Nate had wanted a baby for so long. They'd been ready to start trying, but then Laurel and Josie's dad had the stroke, and the newlyweds had to move in with him and take care of him and the family orchard. Laurel hadn't had the time or energy for a baby.

Josie sat back on her haunches and wiped her hair from her eyes with a semiclean finger.

"I'm calling about the orchard." Nate's tone was short and clipped. "I think it's high time you hauled your city-slicker fanny back here to help your sister."

She almost thought he was joking—Nate was as easygoing as they came, and she'd never heard him sound so adamant or abrupt. But there was no laughter on the other end of the line.

Words stuck in Josie's throat. She swallowed hard. "I don't understand."

"No, you don't. *Responsibility* is a foreign word to you. I get that. But there comes a time when a person has to step up to the plate and—"

"Wait a minute."

"—help when they're needed. And Laurel needs your help. We can't afford to hire anyone else, you know."

This didn't sound like Nate. True, she hadn't talked to him in ages, but he'd always been the picture of Southern hospitality.

Below the veranda, Cody caught her eye and waved the tickets temptingly. When she shook her head no, his lips turned down in an exaggerated pout, his chin fell dramatically to his chest, and he sulked toward the apartment's main door. But not before he turned and flashed his dimple one more time, just to let her know he wasn't too heartbroken. They both knew he was already mentally sorting through the other candidates in his little black book.

Nate's angry voice pulled her back to the conversation, which, she realized belatedly, had been silent on her end for too long.

"I don't know why I thought you'd care," he muttered. She could barely hear his words over the roar of a passing motorcycle. "You didn't bother coming after the stroke, or for the funeral, why would you care about this?"

"What *this*? Would you please tell me what's going on?"

His breaths were harsh, as if he expected a fight.

"Laurel is having twins. She just found out yesterday at the ultrasound."

Twins. The word brought back a cluster of memories, none of them good.

But Laurel was undoubtedly thrilled. Josie was surprised she hadn't called, but then again, they hadn't spoken much since the funeral almost a year ago. "Well, that's great news."

"The doctor wants her to take it easy. And you know Laurel."

With harvest just around the bend, there wasn't much that was easy about working an apple orchard this time of year. The phone call was making sense now. All except Nate's antagonism. But then he'd always been protective of Laurel.

"When I came home from work today, I found her painting the nursery, and yesterday she spent the afternoon packing apples in cold storage for a new vendor she got. Every time I turn around, she's sneaking off to work somewhere, usually the orchard because she's so worried about it."

Josie stood, stretching her legs, then leaned her elbows on the railing. "She's never been one to be idle."

"She really wants these babies, Josephine. We both do. And after what happened with your mom . . ." His voice wobbled as the sentence trailed off, pinching something inside her.

"Of course, I completely get that." It was all sinking in now. She knew why he'd called. And she knew she wouldn't say no, because, despite the distance between them, she loved her sister.

"She needs help, that's the bottom line. I don't need to tell you how much work is involved this time of year, and she can't do it. We can hardly afford to hire more help."

"No, she can't work the harvest," Josie agreed. His words from a moment ago replayed in her head like a delayed tape. "You said you can't hire someone." Laurel hadn't mentioned financial troubles. She talked about their manager, Grady, as if he were God's gift to apples.

"Not after last year's failure."

"Failure?" Her sister hadn't said anything of the kind. True, they didn't speak often, but when the topic of the orchard did come up, Laurel said everything was fine. At least, Josie thought she had.

"Laurel didn't tell you? There was an Easter frost. We lost the apples."

"Frost?" An orchard could lose a whole crop to frost, though this was the first time it had happened at Blue Ridge. Why hadn't Laurel said something?

Nate sighed. "I'm sorry. I thought she told you."

What else had her sister omitted? Laurel was always trying to protect her. Josie should've inquired more directly. "How bad is it?" The fragrance from her lavender plant wafted by on a breeze, and Josie closed her eyes, inhaled the calming scent, letting it fill her up, soothe her frayed nerves.

"The place is a money pit. We don't have anything else to put into it."

This changes everything, Josie. Do you realize that?

The selfish thought materialized before she could stop it. Her plans . . . How could she follow through now? When Laurel was overburdened with a failing orchard and pregnant with twins?

Nate was speaking again. "Grady insists he can turn the place around, but I'm wondering if we shouldn't sell it."

She and Laurel were the third generation to own the orchard, and as far as Josie knew, not one of the Mitchells had thought those words, much less said them. And she'd thought Laurel would be the last one to do so.

"Laurel's considering that?" Their father's death had left Josie with shares that tied her to the place. Even three hundred and fifty miles away, it dragged behind her wherever she went, weighing her down like an anchor. But if Laurel was considering a sale . . .

Now that she'd slipped the thought on for size, it was starting to feel more comfortable, like her favorite pair of Levi's.

"I haven't exactly broached the topic," Nate said.

That was precisely what needed to happen. It was something

her father should've done long ago, before he'd saddled Laurel with his own care and the care of the orchard.

"How does this year's crop look?"

"Promising. She was hoping this year would put us in the black. But a strong crop means extra work and plenty of hands on deck. And I can't afford time off."

Nate ran Shelbyville's one and only insurance agency. Good thing they'd had his income to fall back on.

"So can you come back and help us through the harvest?" he asked.

Josie's eyes flitted over the lacy white alyssum, past the potted strawberry plant toward the haven of her darkened apartment. She closed her eyes and was, in an instant, back at Blue Ridge Orchard. She could almost smell the apples ripening on the trees. Hear the snap of the branch as an apple twisted free. See the ripples of Sweetwater Creek running alongside the property.

And with that thought, the other memories came. The ones that had chased her from Shelbyville six years ago. The ones that still chased her every day. The ones that, at the mention of going home, caused a dread, deep and thick in her belly.

"Josie, you there?"

She opened her eyes, swallowing hard. "I'm here."

"I know you've got your photography job and your plans and your life."

She breathed a wry laugh. Ironically, none of that mattered. The one plan that did matter could still play out. Same tune, different venue.

What mattered most now was seeing that Laurel's life was settled. And Laurel's life wouldn't be settled until she was out from under the orchard. Josie saw that clearly now. And it wouldn't happen, she knew, without a lot of coaxing. She only hoped there was enough time.

"I wouldn't have called if we weren't desperate."

Josie took one last deep breath of the lavender, shoved down the dread, and forced the words.

"I'll come."

two

Josie pulled into the long winding drive that led to her child-hood home. Gravel popped under her tires, echoing the irregular rhythm of her heart. She passed the shingled storefront where Aunt Lola worked all summer and fall, then accelerated down the hill and into the valley. Out the left window was the dangerously steep slope that led toward Sweetwater Creek where it wound between the high hills like a slithering snake. It was there that everything had changed.

She gripped the sticky leather steering wheel and blinked the memory away. But just as quickly, it was replaced with another: the last time she'd driven this lane, heading the opposite direc-tion, tires spinning, thoughts tumbling, fears pushing her farther from the orchard.

Stop it, Josie. That was a long time ago. None of it mattered now. Not the rippling creek out her window, not the memories that chased her still, not even the family cemetery, high on the hill behind the house.

Think of the orchard. The apples. Getting through harvest. She rounded a bend and started up the hill where she and Laurel had once tried to build a tree house in the gnarly-branched oak beside the drive. It had collapsed before the summer ended, the splintered boards piled in a cockeyed heap at the tree's roots.

Just beyond the highest point of the ridge, she made a sharp turn, and the orchard opened up on both sides. Her breath caught at the rows of leafy trees lining the drive, their branches heavy with red and yellow striped Galas. It was past mid-August, and they would need to be picked soon; should've already begun, but she couldn't find evidence that they'd been touched. It would soon be time to start on the large Jonagold grove. The Ginger Golds, however, seemed to be picked clean, a rusty ladder still leaning against the side of a barren tree.

The drive progressed toward the old farmhouse, through the groves of Jonagold, Red Delicious, and Fuji still ripening on the branches. Nate was right, it was a good crop, and the sight of it made her heart quicken. But a good harvest meant a lot of work and a lot of help needed.

He'd told her they'd already hired the crew of migrant workers, but not enough if they hadn't yet finished the Galas. A part of her itched to hit the fields and start working. It had been so long, and even with her windows up, she could almost smell the tangy fruit and feel the smooth, glossy texture of the apples.

The orchard opened to the lawn, and as she drove under a canopy of oak and maple trees, it seemed evening had fallen instantly. The old tire swing in the back still hung from the branch Josie had once climbed to on a dare. She pulled her Celica up to the side of the house and parked it by an old, beat-up Ford pickup she didn't recognize.

She exited the car, leaving her suitcases for later. The house's white paint was peeling in spots, but otherwise the building looked the same with its green metal roof and wraparound porch. The pines that had once served as family Christmas trees now towered over the roof. Aunt Lola had lined the walk with clusters of orange marigolds and yellow pansies that her sister hadn't managed to kill off yet with her black thumb.

Josie passed the flowers, then took the porch steps, feeling the stretch of her muscles, tight from the long drive. Before she reached the front door, Laurel appeared at the screen.

Her sister stopped, her hand on the knob, her eyes widening. Laurel was wearing her coffee brown hair longer now, just grazing her shoulders. It suited her.

"Josie!" Laurel burst through the screen door, and it slapped against the frame as Laurel pulled Josie into a hug.

She could feel the rounded bump of Laurel's belly against her stomach. "Look at you," Josie said, feeling a full smile pull at her lips for the first time since she couldn't remember when. "You've got a tummy."

"I should hope so. I'm twenty-seven weeks, you know. And guess what?" She pulled back, her palms still on Josie's shoulders, her hazel eyes sparkling. "It's twins."

I know was on the tip of her tongue, but on instinct she changed her reply. "That's wonderful. I'm so happy for you."

Laurel rubbed Josie's arms as if she couldn't quite believe her sister was standing there. She'd inherited their mother's high cheekbones, and the pregnancy had put a blush in just the right places.

Laurel gave Josie's arm one last squeeze. "This is such a wonderful surprise!"

Surprise?

"Can you stay awhile? Your room's still just as it was, though we almost decided to use it as a nursery. We're using my old room instead since it's closer to ours."

Nate appeared behind the screen door, his image grayed by the wire mesh. "Hello, Josie." His hair was clipped short like he'd just returned from the barber, and he wore his church clothes. He still had a baseball player's build, though he'd filled out a little in the middle.

"Hi, Nate."

"We're just sitting down to supper," Laurel said. "Come in. Aunt Lola will be so tickled."

"I'll get your things," Nate said, giving her a stiff hug.

Inside the door, the smell of home greeted her, taking her back years. Under her Birkenstocks the wood floor creaked where it always had at the base of the stairs. She half expected her dad to lumber around the corner, cradling his coffee mug with both hands, his belly stretching his T-shirt. It didn't seem real that he was gone.

She blinked the image from her mind. "Where's Aunt Lola?"

"In the kitchen finishing supper. I swear, she won't let me do a thing since she found out about the twins. Come on, let's surprise her."

Laurel led her toward the dining room, through the butler's pantry, and into the kitchen where Aunt Lola's backside protruded into the room as she pulled a pan of biscuits from the oven. She slid them into the bread basket and turned, coming up short.

"Guess who's here?" Laurel asked.

"You startled the daylights out of me, missy." Aunt Lola glared at Laurel before settling her eyes on Josie. Her mouth slackened, then her eyes lifted at the corners. "Well, if you aren't a sight for sore eyes. What are you standing there for? Get over here and give an old woman a hug."

Laurel took the bread basket, and Aunt Lola enfolded Josie in one of her sturdy hugs.

"It's about time you came around." Aunt Lola squeezed her shoulders, then released her, looking Josie over.

Her aunt's small, round eyes, set too close, had always reminded Josie of a hawk, and she had the fortitude to match.

She narrowed those eyes now in a critical appraisal. "You're as frail as a starving sparrow," Aunt Lola said. "Don't they feed you up in the big city? Never mind. Go sit down and we'll get some food in you." Aunt Lola poured tea from the old yellow pitcher, her arthritic hand shaking. "I hope you can stay long enough to get some meat on your bones."

"Let me get that, Aunt Lola."

Josie expected a snarl, but her aunt let her finish pouring, then carried the glasses to the table while Josie turned off the oven and put the oven mitt in the drawer.

Laurel and Aunt Lola were already seated when she entered the dining room and Nate breezed in, setting her suitcases by the stairs. It was then she noticed another man in the room, seated in her dad's chair at the head of the table.

The first thing she noticed was his rugged good looks. She couldn't help it.

"Josie, this is Grady, our manager. I told you about him. Grady, this is my sister, Josie."

His chair grated as he stood. The act said Southern Gentleman, but his shadowed eyes and tensed jaw screamed Danger Ahead. She instantly felt like she was invading his turf, and the thought disturbed her. This was her home. Her orchard.

She flipped her hair out of her face and held out her hand. "Nice to meet you."

"Likewise." He shook her hand, his grip firm and confident.

When he released it, Josie took the only empty chair, which was right beside him, as luck would have it. She wondered what bee he had in his bonnet, and she wasn't too thrilled with the fact that he'd assumed her father's old seat like he was the head of the household.

On her other side, Laurel took her hand. "I'm so glad you're here. How long can you stay?"

"Let's say grace before the food gets cold," Nate said.

Hands came up to the table as they joined together. Beside her plate, Grady's large, calloused palm lay open. She placed her hand in it.

She didn't hear a word of Aunt Lola's prayer, only felt the heat of Grady's palm as her thoughts spun like a whirligig twirling down from a maple tree. Why was her arrival a surprise? She'd told Nate she was coming over a week ago. And why was their manager treating her like an intruder? You'd think he'd be grateful for the extra help.

". . . For it's in his precious name we pray, amen."

Josie pulled her hand from Grady's.

"Now, how long can you stay?" Laurel asked.

Josie looked at Nate, who was intent on dishing out a scoop of green beans.

"Well, I—I came to help out for a while." She looked at Nate again, expecting him to speak up.

Finally, he cleared his throat. "I asked her to come and help out through the harvest." He said it like an admission of guilt, and a current of something Josie didn't understand went through the room.

Beside her, she felt Grady go still.

"Are you serious?" Laurel asked. "Can you afford the time away? What about your job, your apartment?"

"Don't look a gift horse in the mouth, Laurel Jane," Aunt Lola said. "Lord knows we need as many hands as we can get to keep you still."

"My lease was about up anyway, so I put my things in storage. And I can find another job easily enough when I go back." If she needed to. She'd worry about that later, after they got the apples in and had the orchard on the market.

"You quit your job?" her sister asked. "Nate, you shouldn't have asked her to up and leave her life, for heaven's sake."

"I wanted to come."

"You should've told me you were coming," Laurel said. "I would've gotten your room ready for you."

"*I* would've gotten the room ready for you," Aunt Lola said.

Josie didn't know why Nate hadn't told them, but his silence on the subject wasn't sitting well with her. "I'm sorry, I thought you knew."

Beside her, Grady dished out a ladle of gravy.

"I didn't want to tell you," Nate said. "Just in case."

Just in case she didn't show. Josie knew the meaning wasn't lost on anyone at the table, probably not even Sunshine over there.

"Well, she's here now's what matters," Aunt Lola said. "Grady says there's plenty of work to be done."

All eyes were on Grady. Josie decided it was his longish dark hair and stubble-lined jaw that made him look all Marlboro Man. Though the brooding expression didn't help much either. His skin was weathered dark from working outdoors, and Josie put him at thirty, maybe thirty-two years old.

Nate spoke up instead. He winked at his wife. "Maybe you can finally relax and settle down. Now that Josie's here, everything's going to be all right."

Josie sneaked a peek at Grady from under her lashes. Seeing his tight grip on his fork and his lips pressed in a straight line, she had the feeling everything wasn't all right. Not by a long shot.

"Can I have a word before I go?" Grady asked Nate after Laurel took her sister upstairs to settle in.

"Sure." Nate scooted out from the table. "Why don't we go out on the porch?"

Grady followed Nate outside and leaned against the porch rail while Nate sank onto the swing. He gathered his thoughts, calming himself. He'd stuffed down his frustration throughout supper, but it would do no good to lose his temper with Nate.

"You're upset about Josie coming," Nate said.

He shoved his hands in his pockets. "Why did you ask her to come? I told you I could handle the orchard."

"We need more help, and you know as well as I do that we can't afford to hire more hands."

"We're doing fine—"

"We're behind schedule and you know it."

"We would've caught up if you would've given me a chance."

"You think Laurel doesn't notice you've only just now finished the Ginger Golds?"

Reality grated sometimes. "I'm working as hard as I can."

Nate held up a hand, palm out. "I'm not blaming you. You're working all the hours a man can work, but it's not enough. You can't do the impossible, and no one's asking you to."

"We could've made do with another migrant."

"It would've taken three of them to equal one Josie. She's done this most of her life, and she's used to managing things around here."

Could've fooled him. Wasn't she the sister who up and deserted the family right after she graduated? The one who hadn't come home to help Laurel nurse her daddy when he had the stroke, or even be there when he passed? The one who'd left her sister to take on the funeral and the orchard?

The last thing he needed was some scatterbrained woman out there confusing the workers. Not to mention distracting them with her sea green eyes and beguiling smile.

"How do I know she'll be dependable?" After all, Nate hadn't even mentioned she was coming for fear she'd flake out.

Nate crossed his arms. "Look, you need the extra hands and Josie knows what she's doing. She came, didn't she? Laurel will be able to relax now and know the work's getting done."

That was something, he supposed. It seemed he spent half the day assuring Laurel everything was fine, and even still, he was more likely to find her in cold storage than in the house.

"She's got the babies to be concerned about. I don't want her worrying over the orchard too."

Grady had been doing enough worrying for both of them. And now that he had the good crop he'd hoped for, he'd been worried about picking them on schedule so Laurel could get them sold.

"Josie will be good for Laurel. She's missed her sister, and it's important to me that she has what she needs right now."

Much as Grady didn't want the absentee sister around for the next three months, he understood Nate's concern for his wife. Still, he didn't have to like it.

three

Josie flopped on her old twin bed, the mattress springs creaking as she settled against the headboard. The ruffles of the frilly, white canopy wiggled and shimmied as if celebrating the room's inhabitance.

Laurel dragged her finger across the top of the white dresser. "It's been awhile, I guess."

"Never mind that. I'll clean it tomorrow." The old mirror, still tilting slightly toward the floor, bore the mascot sticker of the Shelbyville High School Beavers, half scratched off by her best friend, Ashley.

"Aunt Lola will see to it. I would, but heaven knows, she wouldn't let me."

"You have to think of the babies."

"The doctor said take it easy, not fall into a coma."

"You never were good at sitting still."

Laurel's hand went to her belly, a large bump beneath her navy polo. "I never knew it was so difficult."

Josie sat Indian-style and hugged her pillow. "Have you picked names yet?"

"We've tossed some around, but haven't settled on anything."

It was good to see Laurel. Good to see her smiling and content. She'd wanted a baby for so long. "You are going to be a great mom."

"I still can't believe it's happening."

"Well, it is, times two." Josie ran her hand along the quilted bedspread, its fabric soft, nearly threadbare. "Aunt Lola still minding the store?"

Laurel sank onto the desk chair and crossed her bare feet in front of her, lacing her hands over her stomach. "Yes, she's practically had me tethered to the cash register for the past week."

"You can hardly be climbing ladders and picking apples."

"There's so much work to be done. It's hard not being able to help."

"Well, now you don't have to worry about that, do you?"

"Smarty-pants."

Josie was already getting stir-crazy herself from sitting around all evening. As much as she liked catching up with the family, she yearned to get out into the fields. Here in the house, old memories were hovering in the corner of her mind, pressing in and taking hold of her.

"Everyone is going to be glad to see you," Laurel said.

"Any news I should know about? I heard Jackie and Ashley are sharing an apartment in Asheville now." Her best friends from high school had tried to keep in contact, but Josie wasn't very good at that kind of thing.

"You know how Shelbyville is. Nothing ever changes except the hair on Maggie Lou's head. It's red at the moment, just so you know."

"Good to know." Maggie Lou's hair notwithstanding, the town was as stagnant as a pond. It was something Josie used to love.

Now, with three long months ahead of her, she wondered if the stagnation wasn't going to smother her.

"Boone still asks about you."

"Good ol' Boone. How's he doing?"

"Still head over heels for you."

She'd known him since they were in diapers. Josie wished she were attracted to him, but love was never that simple, was it? The men she was attracted to weren't just playing hard to get, they actually were. For some reason, she seemed to prefer the dangerous ones, and she'd paid for it many times over.

"What's the scoop on your manager?" *Now where did that come from?*

"Grady?" Her sister smiled coquettishly and fluttered her lashes. "Now why are you asking about him, Josephine Mitchell? Could it be because he's so tall, dark, and handsome?"

Dark, most of all. "Shame, shame, you're a married woman, Laurel Evans."

"Married, not dead, and don't change the subject."

She shrugged. "I'm going to be working with him for the next three months. I figure I should know what I'm up against since he seems to have a chip on his shoulder."

"Don't let his demeanor fool you. He's a big teddy bear."

"Grizzly bear, more like."

"You always did like the dangerous ones."

Josie pressed her lips together and glared.

"All right, all right. What do you want to know?"

She knew her dad had hired him when Hank Leland retired. The thought of the old manager instantly conjured up thoughts of his son, Ian. She could see the boy climbing up a ladder, pressed against the wood, filling his sack with enviable speed.

Not Ian. Don't think about him. She pushed the image away, wishing she could keep it under lock and key.

"Josie?"

She shook her head. "How'd Grady end up here?" Shelbyville, North Carolina, wasn't exactly the go-to capital of the United States. Other than her friend Ashley's family, she couldn't think of a single person in town who wasn't born and raised here.

"I don't know much about his personal history. He was married once, but he's never really elaborated on that subject."

Josie rolled her eyes. "I meant information that actually relates to the orchard."

"How boring. Well, he came from Chicago and has a degree in agriculture. He worked for some kind of urban development company. I think he was tired of city life and wanted to slow down a bit."

"Can't get much slower than Shelbyville."

"Ain't that the truth."

She pictured Grady sitting in her father's old seat as if he were a member of the family. "He always eat here?"

Laurel shrugged. "Just supper. We don't pay the man much, we had to supplement his income somehow. Besides, Aunt Lola always cooks enough for an army, and we couldn't very well pass up a man with so much skill. Daddy was impressed with him from the start. After the stroke, Grady really took the reins around here. He's as dependable as the sunrise, the crew respects him, and he's got great ideas for this place."

If he was so wonderful, why was the orchard in such desperate straits? "Nate told me about the frost last year," Josie said.

Laurel gave a little frown. "I wondered if he had."

"Why didn't you tell me?"

She shrugged. "I didn't want you to worry."

She wondered how they'd afforded to keep going. There were costs involved in maintaining a crop. Bees for pollination, equipment upkeep, not to mention Grady's pay. There was no way they'd had that kind of money set back. "How'd you make it through and manage a bumper crop to boot?"

Her sister shifted, pulling in her legs as far as her stomach would allow. "I was going to talk to you about that."

Josie didn't like the look on her sister's face. She'd had the same look when she had spilled Josie's goldfish onto the floor and it had slid into the crevice between the floor and baseboard and died.

"What did you do?" Josie asked.

"Things were tight financially. We didn't have the money to keep the orchard going for another year—"

"Laurel . . ."

"I sold some of my shares."

Josie dropped her pillow. "You what?"

"I didn't want to take out a loan, you know how I feel about that."

"I can't believe you—" She shook her head and huffed. "Who did you sell them to?"

Her sister ducked her head and raised her eyes, wincing. "Grady?"

Josie sucked in a breath. "Grady!"

"He'd been wanting to buy in. Plus, he has a vested interest now. It made sense."

"Why didn't you offer them to me?"

Laurel cocked her head, smiling gently. "Honey, I knew you wouldn't have that kind of money."

The fact that Laurel was right only irked her more. She'd never been much of a saver. "Still, you could've asked. How much did you sell him?"

"Just fifteen percent. Enough to dig us out of the hole and fund this year's crop. And look how good it turned out."

This new discovery threw a kink in her plans. Josie's thoughts spun. How was she going to convince her sister to sell now? She went over the business arrangement in her mind. Josie owned fifty percent. If she could convince Laurel to sell, Grady wouldn't have a choice but to go along.

Maybe since Laurel had been willing to part with some of her shares, she wouldn't be opposed to selling the whole thing. Because even if this year turned out as well as she hoped, there was always the next year, and the one after that. And with Laurel having twins, how would they make ends meet, especially when she'd just given up fifteen percent of her profits?

four

~

"Thanks for breakfast, Aunt Lola." Josie wiped her mouth on the napkin and slid from her chair. "I don't suppose Duncan is still around?"

Aunt Lola covered the pancakes with foil to keep them warm for Nate and Laurel. Josie was more than relieved that Grady hadn't made an appearance.

"He's still snorting around in that fence back there."

"I can't believe he hasn't made it to the supper table yet."

"Don't think I haven't thought about it."

Josie slipped on her jacket. "Is Mr. Barrow still bringing him breakfast?"

"Yep. He should be arriving anytime now."

"Good. I think I'll pay him a visit before I head to the orchard."

"Mind that you don't leave the gate open or he'll trample my flowers."

Josie zipped her jacket as she made her way down the porch and around back. Dawn still clung to the horizon, coloring it with brushstrokes of deep purple and pink. The air smelled like marigolds and morning dew. It would be chilly for a couple of hours, then the sun would climb over the mountains and make her wish for the shade of a cloud or two.

Back at the base of the hill, the manager's cabin nestled under the protection of towering white pines. A lone light shone from the window, reminding her there was still life in there, and it wasn't Ian or his father. Her gaze flitted to the top of the hill before she forced herself to look away.

A loud snort caught her attention. Duncan stood at the gate, his fat snout sticking through the mesh of the fence.

"Hey there, big guy." The hinges creaked as she opened the gate. She slid inside, then shut it behind her. Duncan lumbered toward her, and the acrid odor got worse as he neared. "You remember me, Dunky boy?"

Dried dirt caked his snout, and his beady little eyes gazed at her. "You do, don't you?"

He snorted, tossing his huge head backward. "Yes, I know you're hungry." She looked him over. "You've gained weight, mister, you know that? Has Laurel been sneaking you table scraps?"

He'd just been a wee piglet when she'd caught him, all greased up and slick, inside the pen that had been fashioned for the Shelbyville Apple Festival. Her dad had let her keep him only because he'd seen tasty pork chops in his future, but Laurel had talked him out of that eventually.

Josie straightened at the sound of an approaching vehicle. "I think breakfast is here, big guy. Has Mr. Ted been feeding you well?"

She leaned on the gate, watching the car pull to a stop near the big red barn. It wasn't Ted Barrow exiting the vehicle, but his son, Boone.

He waved at her, then pulled three white boxes from his

backseat and joined her. His bowlegged walk and the curls peeking from under a green John Deere cap were as familiar as the sunrise.

"Hey, Josephine. Heard you's back."

Josie cocked her head. "Now, where'd you hear that? I just pulled into town last night."

"Nettie Albert passed you on your way in."

"Ah, by now all of Shelbyville knows I'm back." She had no doubt there'd been speculation about her sudden departure, probably everything from an unexpected pregnancy to a secret lover she'd met on the Internet.

Boone handed her the boxes. "You look good, Josephine." He ducked his head, suddenly shy.

Boone's thick hair hung just to his eyelashes, and his ruddy complexion bloomed pink under her gaze. "You do too, Boone. You still making donuts for your dad?"

"I took over the shop for him last July. He started going downhill, and, long story short, we found out he has Alzheimer's."

Josie touched his arm. "I'm sorry. I hadn't heard."

Boone looked down, shuffling his feet. "It's been an adjustment. It's been especially hard on Mom, but we're getting along best we can."

Duncan let out a snort and nudged her jean-clad leg.

"All right, all right, you big pig."

Boone helped her take the lids off the boxes, and they dumped the day-old donuts in the trough. Duncan scarfed down the treat, making quiet snorts in his greediness.

"What brings you back?" Boone settled his weight on the fence.

"The orchard. Laurel needs help with the harvest, what with the babies coming and all," she said.

"That's something else about the twins, huh?"

"Sure is."

"You've got a nice crop this year."

"Looks good so far. But only one thing is sure with an orchard. You can never count your apples until they're picked and sold. How're your mom and Jackie? I heard she moved to Asheville." Josie and Boone's older sister, Jackie, had been tight as the skin on a coon since grade school. Then Ashley had joined their friendship in seventh grade, and the girls had been the closest of friends.

"Mom's in good health. Jackie's the same ol' Jackie. Living it up in the city."

"I hear that tone, Boone Barrow. Jackie's never been a bad seed, she just craves excitement. It's one of the things that makes her fun company."

"Maybe. So, you're staying through harvest, huh? Folks around here thought you'd turned city slicker for good, but I knew it couldn't be true."

Josie let her eyes roam over the landscape, taking in the evergreens and rolling land, the hills, silhouetted against the sunrise. It used to be the place she'd loved most.

"Louisville is my home now. I'll be going back after harvest."

"Shame you can't stay around."

The thought tightened something deep inside her like a knot. If only things were different. If only she could be here without feeling . . . trapped and troubled by the memory of that night.

The truck and trailer were nearly beside the fence before Josie heard it. Grady's elbow poked through the open window of his pickup truck. "'Morning, Boone. Josie."

"'Morning," they called.

Grady's eyes swung to Josie. "Need a lift?"

The invitation was reluctant, but she couldn't think of a good reason to turn it down. Maybe on the short drive she could figure out what his problem was.

"Sure."

Boone relieved her of the empty boxes. "I'll get these."

She shut the gate, making sure it latched. "Thanks for the donuts."

"See you tomorrow, Josephine."

She was aware of Boone's eyes on her as she walked around the truck and got in the cab. She gave Boone a wave as Grady pulled onto the drive that led to the crew's dorms.

"How's the crew this year?"

"Good."

"Some years are better than others, don't you think? Repeaters help because they know what's expected."

"True."

True. *Okay, try again, Josie.* "So are we starting on the Galas today?"

"Finishing up the Golds."

Silence settled in the wake of his words. Maybe he wasn't a morning person. A towering thermos lay on the seat between them. Maybe he needed more coffee. Lots more.

The cab smelled of gasoline and man. Grady's nylon jacket swished as he pulled his hand from the stick shift and rested it on the steering wheel.

Outside, she heard a dove calling from the branches of a pine and the answering jeer of a bluebird. Even the birds were having better success at conversation.

When they arrived at the crew's housing, Josie hopped out of the truck and extended her hand to the men as they approached the truck. "*Hola, amigos. Me llamo Josie.*"

The men were friendly and greeted her in their native tongue, introducing themselves, then they hopped in the pickup bed.

"You speak fluently," Grady said.

She shrugged. Between three years of high school Spanish and the Hispanic crew every summer, she'd gotten plenty of practice. "Comes in handy around here."

Once they were in the field, it took about two seconds for Josie to orient herself. There were only a couple of rows of Golds left. Laurel had told her she'd gotten an order for Galas that needed to be filled immediately, so she sent two of the crew down to start on those, ignoring the tight-lipped look Grady sent her way.

What, did he think she was going to stand around waiting for orders? While she'd been communicating with the crew, he'd moved the empty bin forward with the forklift.

She climbed a ladder and began picking the Golds alongside the crew. The feel of the apples, smooth and hard against her palm, was as familiar as the sound of the doves calling from nearby trees.

The motion of picking was like second nature. *Grab, twist, pluck.* The smell of the apples, sweet and tangy, mixed with the musty smell of morning dew. This was her element, where she knew who she was and what she was doing. She thought of her plants back home, so carefully cultivated and tended, and hoped Mrs. Rebar from 3B would take good care of them in her absence.

While she worked, she conversed in Spanish with Hernando and Miguel as they picked the other side of the tree. Then when the crew started up a tune, Josie focused on her work. The branch snapped back in place as she plucked an apple. Behind her, Grady fired up the forklift and moved the full bin into the trailer. The smell of fuel and exhaust filled the air.

As the morning wore on, her energy waned, and by the second

coffee break, her arms ached. She'd be hurting tomorrow. And her speed had decreased as the hours passed. The crew was picking circles around her.

Josie poured a cup of coffee into her thermos lid, her hand shaking, then boosted herself onto the truck tailgate. The coffee was still hot and strong, and felt good sliding down her dry throat. How was she going to make it through the day? Then all the days after that?

After a few minutes, Grady approached, propping his hip on the tailgate. "Tired?"

Did he have to look so smug? "Not at all." She rested the shaking cup against her thigh. She could keep up with Grady.

Under a nearby tree, Miguel and Hernando conversed in rapid Spanish about their wives. Something about their cooking, though Josie could only hear snatches of the conversation. The silence between her and Grady stretched like a thin, taut wire.

"Where'd you send Juan and Emilio off to?"

He just couldn't stand that she'd come out here and taken the reins, could he? "Laurel got an order for some Galas and she needs them right away."

"She didn't mention it."

What, did he think she was lying? She wasn't going to dignify that with a response. She took a deep breath. They could get along. They'd have to if they were going to bear each other's company for three months.

Maybe a compliment would soothe his ruffled feathers. "You've got a good crew this year." She could tell they looked up to Grady in the way they responded to him. He spoke Spanish as fluently as she did, and she wondered how he'd come by it.

"They're good men and fast pickers. Can't ask for much more

than that." He drained the last of his coffee, then straightened, screwing the lid on his thermos. "I'll get the crew back to work. Take a few extra minutes if you need it," he said, his tone condescending. He tossed his thermos through the open cab window.

Josie dumped the remainder of her coffee and hopped off the tailgate, shooting a glare through the back of Grady's head. Yeah, she'd take a few extra minutes. In his dreams. She would keep up with him and the others as if her life depended on it.

five

$\mathcal{J}$osie let the hot water run over her head until it ran cold, then she stepped out of the shower and toweled off. Deciding on a comfy pair of shorts and a T-shirt, she slipped into them. She was tired, but it was too early to go to bed.

The house was quiet as she made her way downstairs and to the porch. The screen door slapped softly into place and the warm wind ruffled her damp hair. As she sank into the porch swing, it creaked under her. She'd hoped her muscles would loosen under the warm water, but they were already knotting up again. She wasn't sure she could get up from the swing if she tried, and she was too exhausted to try.

Her arms ached and her legs shook with fatigue, but there was no way she was going to quit with Grady standing there while they worked, probably expecting her to bail.

It was more than just being out of shape. The fatigue was getting worse; there was no denying it.

The door swung open, and Laurel appeared under the halo of the porch light, sporting a white gown with tiny pink rosebuds. Her dark hair tumbled around her shoulders.

Josie scooched over, making room on the swing. They swung

in silence, listening to the cadence of cicadas and the ripple of the creek just down the valley.

Laurel kicked a leaf aside as she shuffled her feet. "The porch is a mess."

A thin film of dirt coated the concrete, and grass clippings lay scattered around the edges. "It's a big place to keep up. Especially this time of year."

"You look tired, if you don't mind my saying so," Laurel said.

"I guess I'm not used to manual labor anymore. Clicking a camera takes considerably less effort, even when an event runs late into the night or when kids fail to cooperate in group shots. I guess I thought working the orchard would be like it was when I was younger."

"You didn't eat much at supper."

She'd been ravenous when she smelled the roasted chicken, but after a couple of bites, the nausea started. "Too tired to eat. I'll get used to it."

They talked about Laurel's plans for the nursery. Laurel fetched a brochure from a store in Asheville with the baby furniture she wanted. "It's too expensive, but Peggy Tackett has a niece who works there, and she told me they're having a twenty-five percent sale on it in October. That's cutting it close to my due date, but I fell in love with it."

The sleigh-style crib and matching bureau were oak and stained a golden honey finish. They'd look great with the house's woodwork. "It's exquisite."

As Laurel talked about the colors she'd selected for the nursery walls, Josie wondered if it was too soon to mention the idea of selling the orchard. But when a break came in the conversation, she broached the topic.

"Have you thought about how things are going to be after the babies are born?"

Laurel swept the dirt off the swing's arm. "What do you mean?"

"The orchard. Grady's used to having your help, and with you having the twins to care for . . ."

"I guess I haven't thought too much about it. I hope we'll have a good enough year that we can afford full-time help. At least through harvest."

"What about the pruning? It's a lot of orchard for one man." There was no way one person could handle it, no matter how hardworking Grady might be. Unbidden, an image formed of him lifting heavy sacks of apples. He'd had his jacket off by eight o'clock, and in his sleeveless white T-shirt, she saw he was more cut than she'd imagined. Not that she'd imagined.

She shook the thought and looked at Laurel, watching lines form between her brows.

"You're right. I guess I hadn't thought that far ahead what with the pregnancy and just trying to get through this harvest."

Josie fussed with the blue ribbon drawstring on her shorts. "I know this is something we've never talked about. But I can't help but think this place is going to be a strain on you after the babies arrive. Not that it hasn't been a strain already. And you never did care much for working the orchard anyway. You always preferred keeping to the house like Mom."

"We're managing, Josie."

"Barely. Last year's loss about put you under."

"But we turned it around, and look at this year's crop."

"You had to sell shares to make it happen. What are you going to do next time? Sell more shares?"

"There won't be a next time."

"You can't be sure of that. I know you love this place." She nearly said, *I do too* but stopped herself, realizing it was only partly true. "But you know the pressure it put on Mom and Dad, and that was with Dad working the orchard full-time. You won't have that option once the babies are here."

"No one said farming was easy, but it's our way of life. My way of life."

"It doesn't have to be. What about your dreams? You always wanted to sell your crafts, not work the orchard. Maybe Grady would be interested in buying us out."

"Grady doesn't have that kind of money. It took his life savings to buy the fifteen percent."

"How does Nate feel about it? Have you talked to him about the future?"

Laurel ducked her head and pushed the swing until it swayed gently. "He's concerned about me. He's concerned about our financial stability and doesn't want to keep funding the orchard. But he doesn't understand it's our heritage. We're third-generation owners. That means something to me."

How many times had their father told them the story of their grandfather coming from Germany and working at the mill, buying apple seedlings with every extra penny?

"Don't force yourself into a future you don't want out of obligation to our ancestors. It was our grandfather's dream, not ours."

Laurel sighed hard. "And Daddy's. It's mine now, and I thought it was yours too. Running this place always came as easily to you as breathing. What happened to that?" Her sister sounded more hurt than angry.

The fact was, Josie had thought she'd stay on the orchard all her life, get married, raise her children here. Despite her relationship with her dad, she'd always felt at home here on the orchard. In some ways, the orchard had nurtured her as much as she'd nurtured these trees.

But sometimes plans changed as quickly as the wind's direction.

"I love it here," Laurel continued. "Sure, it's a lot of work, but I want to raise my family here just like our parents did and their parents before that. Are you forgetting all the memories?"

Josie wished she could, at least some of them. But Laurel had always been good at blocking the bad ones, remembering only the good things.

"You've already sold fifteen percent to Grady. And when things get desperate again, you'll have no choice but to sell off a little more. We'll lose the place anyway, slowly."

"Not necessarily."

"Would you at least think about selling? Wouldn't it be better to do it now while the orchard is producing well than wait until things are desperate?"

Laurel's eyes went wide under the porch light. "I know I don't have that natural knack like you and Grady, but two other generations have hung on to Blue Ridge. Surely I can manage too."

"Things are different now," Josie said gently. "Back then men worked the orchard with their wives' help. It took Dad and Hank working full-time to run the place, not to mention us kids when we were old enough." She thought of Ian but couldn't bring herself to say his name aloud. "Nate has his own business to worry about. He doesn't have time to run the orchard too."

"I don't expect him to." Silence settled around them like an itchy wool blanket.

The swing swayed back and forth under their weight, the chains squawking with each pass, their bare feet shuffling quietly on the dirty cement floor.

Grady was watching *Farmer's Forecast* when he remembered an issue that had come up about Miguel's paycheck. He'd meant to discuss it with Laurel over supper, but somehow it had slipped his mind. Josie's image hovered in his mind like a pesky fly, and he swatted it away.

The clock read half past eight, and he hated to bother Laurel, but he wouldn't see her in the morning since he was in the orchard by dawn, and it needed to be resolved before she cut the checks.

He dialed the house and waited for the ring. A busy signal blared across the line. Probably Aunt Lola talking to Mr. Murphy. Within twelve minutes of their conversation in the cereal aisle at Ingles two weeks earlier, the Shelbyville grapevine had picked up that the two were a new item.

He slipped on his shoes and left the cabin. His eyes adjusted to the darkness as he made his way down the dirt path. The sky was clear, and a million stars twinkled back at him, giving the landscape a faint glow. Somewhere an owl hooted, its call sad and lonely, echoing through the valley.

All was quiet in Duncan's pen. He was a large, lumpy shadow in the corner by the barn. Grady thought of Josie and how he'd seen her that morning feeding the pig with Boone Barrow. The kid could hardly take his eyes off her. He had a lot to learn about women. Grady had pegged her for a spoiled city slicker before he met her, and working with her had only confirmed his opinion.

For all the hype about her work ethic, he'd been frustrated by her performance in the orchard. She'd started strong, but by mid-morning, his migrants were working circles around her. Although he had to admit, she knew her way around the orchard. And she knew how to connect with the crew. He'd thought they might have trouble taking orders from a woman, but one pretty smile and they were putty in her hands.

That's not fair. She did go out of her way to build a relationship with them and she knew what she was doing, he'd give her that much. He'd wondered when Laurel bragged about her. From what he knew of Josie, he'd surmised that she was flaky and unreliable, but he was unsure what to think of her now.

He heard voices as he approached the side of the house. Maybe Laurel was on the porch and he wouldn't have to disturb the family.

He heard his name and slowed his footsteps, coming to a halt at the corner of the house. He probably shouldn't interrupt the private conversation. Grady turned to go, figuring he'd have to leave a note for Laurel in the morning.

". . . things get desperate again, you'll have no choice but to sell off a little more. We'll lose the place anyway, slowly."

It was Josie's voice. He stopped, torn between going and staying.

"Would you at least think about selling?"

Sell the orchard? Is that what Josie was trying to convince Laurel to do? His jaw tightened.

She had some nerve. He and Laurel had been here working their tail ends off, trying to get this place back on its feet, and she wanted to sell the place out from under them.

Maybe that was the only reason she'd come to begin with.

She probably wanted the money so she could go out and waste it on fancy clothes or refurnishing her house. She was more like Danielle than he'd ever expected.

The women had gone quiet on the porch. Would her sister's suggestion persuade Laurel?

The squawk of the porch swing faltered, and he heard Josie bid Laurel good night and enter the house. Just as well. He needed to talk with Laurel, and he was too angry to face Josie.

He didn't have to read his contract to know how this worked. With only fifteen percent of the place, he'd have no say at all if Laurel agreed to sell. He'd lose it—all his hard work down the drain. He'd already lost one orchard, and he wouldn't lose another—not if he had any say in the matter.

six

The bad thing about manual labor was it left too much time to think. Josie's hands went through the mechanical motions. *Grab, twist, pluck, bag. Grab, twist, pluck, bag.* The crew worked on ladders around her, and she picked the Galas from ground level, grateful she didn't have to worry about losing her balance in her fatigue. Still, her neck and back ached from reaching up.

On the other side of the tree, Miguel stepped down from the ladder and emptied his canvas bag into the bin, filling it to the brim. He exchanged a few words with Grady, who answered in Spanish.

The crew worked hard and carefully for Grady. Josie had learned that most of their wives washed and packed the apples after Grady moved them to cold storage.

Miguel climbed the ladder again, and Josie continued working. *Grab, twist, pluck, bag.* When her right arm tired, she switched to her left until that one fatigued.

The lift tractor roared to life as Grady moved the bin to the trailer. She was glad it was full now and he would be taking the load to cold storage. She was in dire need of a break, but with Grady around, she'd felt compelled to push herself. He already thought she was a slacker. She could tell by the way he spoke to her, treating her like one of the crew instead of the majority owner.

Today he'd hardly spoken to her at all.

One of the crew started a Mexican song and several others joined in. The sun beat down hot and harsh, making her wish she were picking on the shady side of the tree. Sweat trickled down her back.

She was picking as fast as she could, but on the other side of the tree, she could hear the apples dropping into Miguel's bag twice as fast. She tried not to think about it. Miguel was used to this work, and her body wasn't up to speed.

The image of Ian floated into her mind, an unwelcome intrusion. How many hours had she spent picking with him and her dad?

"Step it up, Jo," her dad had said from the ground, waiting for another sackful that would finish off the bin.

"Here you go, Mr. Mitchell." Ian had descended the ladder and was emptying his canvas bag into the bin, turning his boyish face up to her father as if he lit the moon.

"Good work, son."

Josie grabbed for the next apple, trying to match Hank's pace on the next tree. The apple slipped from her small hand and thunked to the ground.

Her dad gave her a look that said more than words. Her face heated. She could pick just as fast, just as well, as Ian. Her dad made her nervous, was all. She tried so hard to be what he wanted, but it seemed she always was falling short.

Ian interrupted her thoughts. "Your dad said the trout are

biting. Wanna go fishing after supper? I got some new gang hooks, and I can't wait to try them out."

Still smarting from her dad's look, she was disinclined to do anything with Ian. "Not today."

Ian peered around the tree, smiling as he twisted off an apple lickety-split. His freckles were popping up faster than air bubbles in a can of 7UP.

"I already have the worms. I'll bait your hook . . ."

She didn't want to be reminded that she was still a girl under the scruffy jeans and baggy T-shirt. "I said no, Ian." Her tone came out sharper than she intended.

His smile slipped and she felt a little guilty. She tried to remind herself it wasn't his fault her dad liked him so much, but it didn't work. It never did.

"Well, I'll be down by the sunken log if you change your mind."

Why was he always so nice to her? Couldn't he see she didn't like him? He was always tagging along behind her as if he were her little brother or something.

Behind her, the truck started up, choking out a blue cloud of smoke that smelled of fuel. "Ian," her dad called from the open window. "Ride with me. I need your help unloading."

Ian scurried down from the ladder and set his canvas bag beside an empty bin, then hopped into the passenger side of the truck.

Josie let her arm fall to her side, a knot tightening in her throat as she watched them ride between the rows of trees, the trailer bumping along behind them.

Now, Grady's truck roared to life, startling her from her thoughts. The bad memory lingered as she watched Grady guide the trailer between the rows of trees, just as she'd watched her dad and Ian that afternoon so long ago. She wasn't good enough then, and it seemed she wasn't good enough now. Because long after Ian was gone, the memory of him clung to her like a heavy morning mist.

seven

Josie was walking up the porch steps when she heard Aunt Lola call that supper was ready. The concrete all but sparkled beneath her feet and a few potted plants had been set along the perimeter.

When they were seated at the supper table, Aunt Lola led a prayer, then they all dug into the ham and fried okra.

Josie sliced into her ham with the side of her fork. "Aunt Lola, the porch looks terrific. I can actually see some paint from when Dad painted it green." They'd all hated it, though no one had the nerve to tell him that. "Remember that, Laurel?"

"It wasn't me." Aunt Lola aimed a glare at Laurel, who shifted.

"It needed to be swept," Laurel said, then promptly stuffed her mouth with okra.

"Laurel, you didn't." The porch had been more than just swept. Someone had gotten down on her hands and knees with a scrub brush.

"You have got to relax, hon." The endearment softened Nate's firm tone. He shot Josie a look as if it was her fault.

What? her eyes tried to communicate.

"I'm sorry. I'll do better." Laurel squeezed Nate's hand, but he didn't look mollified.

"The ham is delicious, Aunt Lola," Laurel said, changing the subject.

"You just like how salty it is. Mind you don't eat too much of it or your feet'll swell up like helium balloons."

"Too late." Laurel gave a dry smile.

"That cleaning frenzy probably didn't help," Aunt Lola said. "But your mama was in house slippers her last three months with the both of you. And she swore her feet never did go back to normal."

Josie's mom had passed away when she was nine, and she remembered very little about her. She did recall sitting on her lap every Sunday while her mom read the comics. And she remembered her mom's obsession with root beer floats.

Her dad had seemed different then. More content. Or maybe Josie had been too young to notice.

"Remember that, Josie?" Laurel was asking.

Josie chewed a bite of ham. "What?"

"I was telling Grady about the time we caught Mr. Murphy's bushes on fire. Gracious, Mom about had a conniption."

"I should think so," Nate teased.

"I have trouble imagining you as a mischievous child," Grady said to Laurel.

Josie noted he had no such compunctions about her.

"We were only setting off firecrackers, weren't we, Josie? And Mr. Murphy's grandson was the instigator. Well, I guess Josie was too."

"Sure, blame it on me."

"Well, you were the one who wanted to see what would happen when we lit a whole package. Who threw them in the bushes?"

"They were going to catch me on fire otherwise. Besides, I was only a little kid."

"It was your idea to run. That's what really honked Mom off."

"Not to mention Mr. Murphy," Josie said. Poor Logan had to face his grandfather alone, but he'd squealed quick enough.

"I'll have to remind Mr. Murphy about that next time I talk to him," Aunt Lola said.

"Which will probably be tonight," Laurel teased. "You two tie up the phone lines like a couple of teenagers."

"I'm sure Mr. Murphy didn't forget our little mishap," Josie said. "We weren't allowed to play with Logan for three summers."

"But Dad hired Hank the next summer, so we had Ian to corrupt," Laurel said.

"That was Hank's son?" Grady asked. He took a deep sip of iced tea, his big hands shrinking the glass.

"Right," Laurel said. "He was a sweet kid, a few years behind Josie, though he was always very mature for his age."

Discomfort filled Josie at the mention of Ian. It was as if he were still here, haunting her. She couldn't get away from him in the orchard or the house. He'd made things hard while he was living, and had made them even more difficult in his death.

"Remember when we played hooky from our work and went creek stomping that time?" Laurel turned to Nate. "That was the hottest summer ever—it was above one hundred degrees for days. We were supposed to be picking apples, but soon as Dad left for the farmer's market, we sneaked off to the creek."

"He was so mad when he came back." Josie remembered that day as if it were yesterday. She'd thought he was cruel for making them work in the orchard when it was so hot. She'd talked Laurel and Ian into taking a dip with her. Their dad had forgotten something, and when he returned home, he caught them.

"I can still see the look on Ian's face," Laurel said. "He was all flushed and nearly in tears when Daddy showed up."

Josie remembered too. Ian had apologized sincerely, and her dad had nodded and told him he could ride into town with him. Laurel had been sent inside to help their mom with the apple pies for the store. Only Josie had been sent back to the field to pick apples.

Somehow she'd been blamed for everything that went wrong, and even when she'd managed to do something right, her dad didn't notice. But Ian, her dad noticed every little thing he did. It was almost like Ian was more his child than Josie was.

The memories stirred up the past the way tires stirred up dust. She could hardly breathe in this house, on this property, without choking on them. The thought of three months here made her throat swell and her insides hollow out. There was so much she hadn't faced, and she feared if she opened the past now, it would swallow her whole.

The ham she'd eaten churned uneasily in her stomach, and the rest of the food on her plate mocked her.

She set her fork down and took a sip of water. "Supper was great, Aunt Lola." She put her napkin on her plate and stood.

"I made Apple Delight for dessert," Laurel said.

"And left flour all over the counter," Aunt Lola added.

"Whoops. I'll clean it up."

"Already done."

"I'll have some later." Josie took her plate to the sink and took the back stairs to her room. The walls felt too tight, confining and suffocating.

Ian.

She shook her head as if to dislodge his name.

She had to get out of here, if only for one night, one day. Tomorrow was Sunday and she didn't have to work. She could just as easily spend those hours someplace else.

She thought of her friends in Asheville and knew they wouldn't mind a last-minute guest.

Once in her room, she pulled her address book from her purse and looked up the number she hadn't called in months, her hands shaking.

They probably had plans—it was a Saturday night after all— but it was early, only six thirty.

Jackie answered on the second ring. "Josie! It's great to hear from you. Boone said you were back in Shelbyville. When can you come see us?"

After feeling like an unwanted intruder in the orchard all week, Jackie's enthusiasm was a relief. "Uh, tonight?"

Jackie laughed. "Hey, Ash, Josie's coming over tonight." She addressed Josie. "When can you get here?"

She had to pack a few things and her car needed gas. "An hour and a half?"

The line clicked and Ashley was there. "Are you serious? Tonight? It'll be just like old times."

"You don't have plans?"

"Of course we do," Ashley said. "But we'll wait for you. One of my friends has a show at an art gallery, then we're going out after that."

Josie smiled, feeling better already. "That doesn't sound like your cup of tea." Ashley had been a jock in high school, leading the girls' basketball team in rebounds and setting school records.

"The gallery will be a drag for me, but you might enjoy it. Plus, we'll party afterward."

"There won't be time for any of it if you don't let her off the phone," Jackie said in the background.

"I need your address."

She wrote down the address and directions to her friends' apartment, then threw a change of clothing into her duffel bag. She needed to change too.

She put on a pair of black pants, heels, and a trendy red top that flattered her skin tone. There wasn't much time, so she made do with a coat of mascara and a little blush, then threw her cosmetics in the bag. She needed to find Laurel and Aunt Lola and tell them she was taking a quick trip.

Finding them was easy since they were still gathered around the supper table, finishing the apple dessert.

Laurel's fork stopped in midair when Josie entered the room with her overnight bag.

"Going somewhere?"

Her sudden trip would seem strange, no matter how she worded it. "I was just talking to Jackie on the phone. She and Ashley invited me down for the night."

"Oh, that's nice," Laurel said.

"I haven't seen them in several years." They'd visited her twice since she'd left Shelbyville, but the last visit was a long time ago.

"I was hoping you'd go to church with us tomorrow," Aunt Lola said. "Pastor Keeley was asking after you the other day."

"Pastor Keeley's still preaching? Maybe I'll go next week." Josie moved toward the door. The clock was ticking, and now that she'd made plans, she couldn't wait to follow through.

"Well, have fun and drive safely," Laurel called as the screen door slammed.

Grady heard the door shut behind Josie and breathed a sigh of relief at her departure. He didn't know why the woman made him so tense. It disturbed him that she had any effect on him at all.

"Well, that was sudden," Nate said.

"She can't seem to sit still these days," Laurel said, frowning.

"Wonder where she gets that." Aunt Lola rubbed her hands, probably aching with arthritis again. "She ought to go to church while she's here."

"Don't push her, Aunt Lola. Josie's always had a mind of her own."

Grady had seen that already. The other day he'd asked her to take part of the crew down by the creek to pick some Arlets for an order. Before he knew what hit him, she'd turned everything around, and he was the one filling bins down by the creek.

And after one week in the country, she was already taking off for the city like a bat out of hell. He watched Laurel smile gently at her husband and wondered how two sisters could be so different.

"Well, I think I'll head home." Grady said good night and made his way back to the cabin. The moon lit the trees and the rooftop of his cabin. He passed the smelly pigpen and continued up the stone walk to his door.

Warm, stuffy air greeted him, and he turned on the air conditioner before grabbing a coke and settling in his recliner. He'd already read the thin copy of the *Shelbyville Gazette* that lay on the end table. What would he do with the rest of the night? Normally he looked forward to the peace and quiet of his cabin, but tonight it just felt . . . lonely. He was thirty-one, with nothing but the company of a TV on a Saturday night.

Maybe it was time to start dating again. The image of Josie's pixie face and solemn green eyes filled his mind, startling him. He set his coke down hard on the table.

What is wrong with you? Can't you see she's just like Danielle? Trouble with a capital T.

He was just bored, needed something to do. He flipped on the radio where WFJT was hosting *House Call with Dr. Shay*. A caller was explaining her problem with bunions, and even if Grady hadn't recognized her voice, he would've known it was Peggy Tackett. Everyone in Shelbyville knew the history of her bunions.

He turned to WXKC, and a country ballad filled the room. The music broke the silence, but the house felt no less empty.

There had been things he'd liked about marriage, things he'd liked a lot. In the beginning, he'd thought he was the luckiest man alive, but how quickly that had changed.

Danielle seemed content at first in their suburban Chicago home. Her trips to the city became more and more frequent though, and when he talked of moving to the country and starting his own orchard, she looked at him as if he were crazy. As if he hadn't gone to school with that dream in mind, as if he hadn't spent hours talking about it when they'd dated. He should've seen the signs.

But he hadn't—not until it was too late. Until he'd already been made a fool of ten times over.

It had been the first Saturday evening after Thanksgiving, and Danielle had gone into the city to shop for Christmas. She thrived on the holiday, an excuse to spend more money than they earned. A light snow fell and began to coat their small, square lawn.

Notre Dame was playing at Stanford that night, and he intended to watch them finish their season. The thought of watching the game alone held no appeal though.

Mike, his best friend since college, was an even bigger Notre Dame fan than he. Grady decided to run over to his house, only several miles away in a new subdivision, and watch the game there. He dialed Mike's number and got a busy signal. His cell phone was off, so Grady grabbed his keys and left. The game would start in fifteen minutes. They'd have enough time to grab a coke and a snack before kickoff.

The streets looked like they'd been dusted with powdered sugar as he pulled onto the main road. When had he last gotten together with Mike? A couple of months ago at least. Mike's new position at Citibank came with too many hours. Whenever Grady had called, he'd been working overtime. But he had no wife, and his money was probably piling up in the bank because he had no time to spend it.

He turned on the heat, and a blast of cold air hit his face. He wondered if something was wrong with Danielle. She'd seemed distracted lately, and she hardly sat still long enough to talk. He supposed her mind was on her job. They'd recently hired another interior designer, and maybe Danielle felt threatened. She'd been putting in more hours, but with their credit card debt, he wasn't complaining.

The tires of his Jeep slid as he made the turn into Mike's driveway. Faint tire tracks, leading into the two-car garage, were barely visible through the fresh layer of snow. Hopefully those tracks were from him coming, not going. Seven minutes 'til game time.

He slid from the Jeep, pocketed his keys, and left his hands there for warmth. The wind was brutal tonight, whipping snow into his face, biting his skin. Danielle was probably freezing on her trek from store to store. She'd worn one of her trendy coats that was built more for fashion than warmth.

He stepped up on the stoop and pulled open the door, eager to escape the bitter cold. "Mike, it's me," he called. A lone lamp shone in the living room, and the noise that filled the house wasn't a TV but music blaring from a radio or CD. The TV wasn't even on yet.

He wiped the snow from his shoes and went into the kitchen, following the light. But when he got there, it was empty. On the counter, a half-empty bottle of wine and one empty wine glass sat on the counter.

Above the chorus, he heard Mike laugh in the next room—the bedroom.

Grady winced. He hadn't known Mike was dating anyone, much less dating someone seriously enough to have her in there. He suddenly felt foolish for stopping over as if his friend didn't have a life. But Grady was going to have a man-to-man with him about this. Mike had never been promiscuous, and Grady was disappointed in him.

For now, though, a quiet exit was in order.

He padded across the kitchen, eager to escape unnoticed, and nearly ran into someone coming around the corner.

He stopped short as the woman let out a squeal.

His eyes focused on her tousled blonde hair, her flushed face, her doe-brown eyes.

Danielle.

Confusion swirled his mind the way the wind swirled the snow outside. *Danielle?* He noticed her clothes. Or rather, lack of. She stood barefoot, a man's shirt skimming her slender thighs.

"Grady!" She clutched at the stiff collar. The music swelled in the background.

Danielle was here. Not in the city. She was here. With Mike.

In the bedroom with Mike, wearing this . . . this little scrap of nothing.

Mike came around the corner, oblivious, wearing a smile. He stopped in the hall, behind Danielle.

His eyes collided with Grady's, the smile sliding from his face. He swore.

"Grady," Danielle was saying.

But Grady heard no more. A thick fog of black welled up inside of him and he charged Mike, knocking him flat against the wall. A picture slid to the wood floor and cracked.

His fists pummeled blindly, a rage he'd never felt overpowering him. A moment later, Mike regained his composure and rallied, calling out his name.

Somewhere behind him Danielle was calling his name too. "Stop it, Grady!"

But her words meant nothing to him. Nothing, like all her words of affection. How long had this been going on? This affair between his wife and the person who'd been the best man at his wedding.

They fought until they were staggering to stand, both of them with bloody cuts. Mike had a trickle of blood streaming from his nose. His right eye had already begun to swell, and his lip bulged at the corner.

Grady felt no pain other than the deep ache in his heart.

"I'm sorry," Mike grated out when they were both breathless.

"I didn't mean for it to happen." He dragged his hand across his mouth, smearing the blood.

Grady glared. Then his eyes swept back to his wife. Danielle stared back from the corner, her scrawny arms hugging her chest, her eyes wide in her pale face. He wanted to yell at her. Curse her out.

He turned and left, slamming the door behind him. Left his wife, standing in his best friend's house, in his best friend's shirt. He drove until his tank was nearly empty, and when he got home, Danielle was there. They fought loud and hard that night.

Later he found out Mike was the second affair in their fifteen-month marriage. If he'd hoped to salvage the relationship, that fact had changed everything.

Now, the jingle from JD's Used Cars rang from the radio, snagging his attention. He hated divorce, still did, but it had been the best thing under the circumstances. Maybe he was a little lonely now and then, but that was better than living with an unfaithful wife.

He looked forward to sharing his life someday with a good woman, a Christian woman, whom he could trust and take care of.

One thing he was sure of—that woman was not Josie Mitchell.

eight

Josie followed Ashley and Jackie to a table in the darkened corner of The Bistro and took a seat. On the ceiling, someone had painted a Michelangelo-like painting that was filled with chubby cherubs and fluffy clouds.

"You'll like this place, Josie," Ashley said. "Especially the dessert. They have a cobbler that's to die for."

Josie wasn't hungry, but she was so glad to be out on the town, she didn't care. The Bistro was noisy with boisterous chatter and silverware scraping plates. In the background, jazz music played. After the quiet of Blue Ridge, the atmosphere was energizing.

Josie ordered a bowl of soup to sip while the other two ate supper. When the server left, Ashley leaned forward, planting her elbows on the table, her broad shoulders looking awkward in the spaghetti-strapped dress. "So what did you think of the show?"

The gallery had featured photographs of city life. "Your friend is good. She has a way with capturing light."

"You're just as good as her," Jackie said.

"I should rediscover my passion for artistic photography while I'm here. When I'm shooting events, my mind is always on pleasing the customer. I left my digital camera in Louisville, but I'm sure my old camera's still buried in my closet somewhere."

"You should dig it out," Ashley said.

There had been a stirring inside her to do just that as she'd browsed the exhibit's photographs. Josie had spent hours photographing the orchard and mountains when she was in high school. Then when she'd been chosen as the photographer for the school yearbook, she'd traipsed all over the school shooting pictures of her classmates. She'd attended more athletic events her senior year than in all the rest of her life combined.

"Remember that shot you took of me spiking the ball on Haley Hannigan? I still have that photo framed on my dresser."

"Right—that's one of my favorites." The look of intent concentration on Ashley's face and the play of her arm muscles as she slammed the ball, all of it frozen for eternity.

"I *should* dig out my camera," Josie mused aloud. She felt in control when she was snapping pictures. An observer, not a participant. There was something safe in that.

"Okay, enough small talk," Ashley said. "We've been dying to know what you think of him."

The server set their drinks down, then went to take the next table's order. "Did I miss something?" Josie asked.

"She means a certain Mr. Grady Mackenzie." Jackie made the most of her Southern drawl.

"Otherwise known as tall, dark, and dreamy." Ashley winked.

"He is a hunk," Jackie said. "Too bad he's such a stick-in-the-mud."

Ashley grinned. "You're just sore he didn't ask you for a second date."

"You went out with Grady?" Josie had trouble imagining dark, brooding Grady with her vibrant friend. She couldn't image two people less suited.

"I think he must've asked me on a dare," Jackie joked.

"He did not," Ashley said. "It was her mom's doing."

Jackie took it from there. "Grady walked into the donut shop one day, and Mom was certain he was just the right Christian man to turn me from my wild ways."

"And Jackie took one look at him and agreed."

"Can you blame me?"

"Where'd you go?" Josie asked.

Jackie shrugged. "We went up the Blue Ridge Parkway, had a picnic, and stopped at Grandfather Mountain. That long drive, and he never even made a move."

For some reason that set off a flare of relief in Josie. The fact that it did sent off an entirely different kind of flare.

"But enough of Jackie's sad tale. What do *you* think of Grady?" Ashley wiggled her blonde brows.

Josie took a sip of her tea and set it back on the Navajo-print cloth. "He's a reliable manager. He's produced a good harvest this year, and he manages the crew particularly—"

Jackie's head fell sideways as her eyes closed and she pretended to snore.

"What?" Josie asked, all innocence.

"Come on. Aren't you working with him in the hot, sweaty orchard all day?" Ashley asked. "Give us the dirt."

"There is no dirt. He took one look at me and decided he didn't want me there."

"Ooh, sexual chemistry!" Jackie said.

"Details . . . ," Ashley chimed in.

"Oh, for heaven's sake. There is no sexual chemistry. He doesn't even like me."

"That's the way it always starts in romance novels," Jackie said. "They meet, they don't like one another, they zing barbs back and forth, and next thing you know, they're locked in a passionate embrace."

"That's true," Ashley said.

Josie shook her head at the absurdity of it, the image of them together filling her mind. *Stop it, Josie.* Good grief, she was as bad as her friends were.

"Look, she's blushing," Jackie said.

"I am not. You guys are barking up the wrong tree."

"I thinketh the lady doth protest too much," Jackie said.

"Didn't you flunk senior lit?" Josie sipped her iced tea, cooling her hand on the glass.

Jackie wagged her head. "I paid attention when it counted."

Josie was relieved when the server brought the food, setting their plates in front of them. The steaming soup tempted her. "Y'all need anything else?" the server asked.

The girls said no and dug into their meals.

"So," Josie said after blowing on a spoonful of the creamy soup. "How are your jobs going?"

Ashley filled her in on her promotion at the bank, and Jackie told her about plans to expand her jewelry-making business. Several boutiques were already carrying her jewelry line, and one of the local jewelry stores wanted to stock a case and see how it sold.

After they finished their meal, Josie felt nauseated again and skipped the wildberry cobbler the girls were crazy about. As they returned to the apartment, dread swelled inside Josie. As much fun as tonight had been, and as much fun as tomorrow would be, she would soon have to turn her car toward Shelbyville, toward the place that deluged her with memories faster than a sudden summer storm.

nine

The girls talked Josie into staying Sunday night and leaving early Monday morning. It had seemed like a good plan the night before, but now, as she pulled into the drive, she knew it had been a mistake. It already felt like she'd been up half the day; she was groggy from staying up late two nights in a row, and she was going to be two hours late getting to the field. A fact that was sure to go over well with Grady.

Josie tried not to let it bother her. *What do you care what he thinks? Who's the majority owner here anyway?*

Still, as she walked out to the field where the crew was picking, she felt like a schoolgirl on her way to the principal's office. Grady turned just then, and his arms stuttered as he dumped a sack of apples into the wooden bin.

He probably wouldn't say a word. She should walk over, grab a sack, and get started. She didn't owe him an explanation. Laurel would have told him she was coming home this morning.

She grabbed a sack from the truck and slung it over her shoulder.

"Nice of you to join us," Grady called out.

She let the comment go and chose a tree far away from Grady, greeting the crew as she went.

She worked hard all day, breaking only when the crew did. Instead of focusing on her aching body, she breathed in the fresh air and listened to sounds distinct to the orchard: branches snapping, apples thunking to the ground, blue jays' jeers.

Grady ignored her, not even making eye contact when she dumped her sack into the bin.

Supper was much the same, and through it all, Josie felt indignation rising from deep inside her. What had she done to him? Who did he think he was, treating her like a fungus that had invaded his precious grove? Did she need to remind him it wasn't even his orchard? A measly fifteen percent didn't make him the king of the apples.

Josie shifted on the sofa. Beside her, Laurel snuggled up in a quilt, then flipped the TV channel to a news program. The *Shelbyville Gazette* crinkled as Nate flipped a page.

Josie stared at the TV, letting it go blurry as she reviewed the day. The crew members, who hardly even spoke English, were beginning to sense the tension between her and Grady. When she'd asked Antonio and Juan to pick some Arlets, they'd looked to Grady, waiting for his approval. Finally, he'd given a silent nod.

The more she thought about it, the more it annoyed her. He was undermining her authority with his attitude. It was affecting the crew and her work in the orchard, and she wasn't putting up with it.

She stood abruptly and Laurel looked at her.

"I'm going out to—I need to talk to Grady for a minute."

Laurel raised her eyebrows, the corners of her mouth tilting.

Let her sister think what she would. It seemed everyone wanted to think something was going on between her and Grady. They couldn't be further from the truth.

She slid on her Birkenstocks and took the porch steps quickly. The air was still warm and even the slight breeze felt like a hot breath on the back of her neck. The sky was clear and the moon cast a silvery glow, glazing the treetops with shimmering light.

She tried to collect her thoughts. What was she going to say? She needed to know what his problem was. Maybe if they got it out in the open, there would be no need for his passive-aggressive behavior.

She approached his porch with quick strides and stopped short when she saw him sitting there, his ankle propped on his knee. He'd been watching her advance in the dark. A light filtered through the front window, shedding a golden glow on his skin. It was then she noticed that more of his skin was showing than she'd seen before. The light streamed over his bare torso, shadows carving valleys between his stomach muscles.

Don't just stand here staring, for heaven's sake. She met his gaze.

He cocked a brow, waiting.

He wasn't going to offer her a seat or say good evening. She crossed her arms, glad she was standing in the dark, grateful it would hide the flush that was undoubtedly climbing her face.

Get on with it, Josie. "I think we need to talk."

Silence stared her in the face, and she shifted awkwardly. Finally, he gestured toward the wooden chair catty-corner from him.

She took the one porch step and sat. He had yet to speak. He was intentionally making this as uncomfortable as possible. It was what he'd done since she'd arrived a week ago.

Just get to the point and get it over with. "Since I've been here, I can't help but notice that you don't seem to like me. Have I done something wrong?"

She sounded needy. "Not that you have to like me, but you obviously resent my presence—I think it's important that the crew respects my authority, and right now, I'm not sure that's the case."

She hated when she rambled, but he was sitting there so stinking quiet. *You do not need to fill the silence.* She snapped her mouth closed.

He set something aside, a folded copy of the newspaper. He stretched his arm across the wide seat and shifted. "The crew will respect your authority when you prove you're a responsible member of the team."

Little prickles of heat bit at the skin under her arms, then spread to the base of her neck. "I called Laurel last night and asked her to tell you I'd be late."

He raised his chin a notch and stared at her. "Show up on time and work as hard as the crew, and you'll have their respect."

A fire burned in her gut. She was working as hard as she could under the circumstances. He was trying to change this all around to be about her, but it was really about him and his attitude.

"That's not the point," she said. "You've been rude to me since I arrived—"

"Rude?"

"Yes, rude." If not in what he said, then in what he didn't say. He had a chip on his shoulder, and she'd knock it off if she had to.

He looked away then, his jaw working.

"Just say it. Have I said something, done something? I came here to help, for heaven's sake."

"I don't need your help."

She gave a wry laugh. "Well, Nate felt otherwise. And apparently so did Laurel, because he could hardly keep her from working before I arrived."

It had to be more than that. Why should he care if Josie was here? He couldn't be that stubbornly independent.

His gaze fixed on her, his eyes hard, unyielding. "I might be a minority owner, but this orchard means a lot to me. I won't lose it."

She shifted under his gaze, an uneasy feeling swelling inside her. He knew she wanted to sell the orchard. Despite the dim light, she could see it written clearly on his face. She couldn't believe Laurel told him.

He must've read her thoughts. "I overheard you on the porch."

She was relieved Laurel hadn't told him. Still . . . "You were eavesdropping?"

"I came over to talk business with Laurel. It's not my fault you were spilling your guts in public."

"You could have said something."

"I'm saying it now."

Saying what? That he was going to fight her tooth and nail? She wondered why it meant so much to Grady. It was only fifteen percent. Sure, he'd worked hard on the orchard, but nothing like Josie's family. They had three generations invested.

On the other hand, Laurel listened to and trusted Grady. If he was bent on keeping the orchard, his opinion would carry a lot of weight with her sister.

Maybe if she knew why it meant so much to him, she could find a way to convince him selling it was for the best.

She did nothing but breathe for a moment. Getting angry wouldn't accomplish anything. It was unfortunate he knew she wanted to sell the orchard. It had certainly done nothing to help his opinion of her, which, she reminded herself, had been poor even before he'd set eyes on her. But she'd explore that another time.

She took a deep breath and swallowed her pride, feeling it go down in a tasteless lump. "I'm sorry I went off on you. I didn't get much sleep over the weekend, and I guess I'm a little irritable."

He studied her as if weighing her sincerity. Was he always so skeptical? Even when she was trying her darndest to be nice, he still treated her with all the warmth of an ice pack.

Grady listened to Josie's reluctant apology and tried to think beyond the fact that she'd had a wild weekend away with her friends. She'd probably been drinking at some bar in the city, picking up guys. Maybe she'd stayed the night because she was too drunk to drive home and was hungover this morning.

That would explain the dark circles under her eyes and her testiness, though, to her credit, she'd managed to hold her tongue all day.

Her thumbnail clicked as she picked at it with her middle finger. She seemed to be waiting for a reply.

Fine. Whatever. "Apology accepted," he muttered.

Her hair, still damp from her shower, hung in waves around her freshly washed face. The lamplight was complimentary to her skin tone, and with those long eyelashes and full lips, he thought she looked better without any makeup.

He looked away, disturbed by his thoughts. A cricket chirped from somewhere just off the porch.

"Why don't we start over?" she was saying. "Tell me about yourself. You've probably heard plenty about me."

She was trying, he'd give her that. The least he could do was meet her halfway. He shrugged. "I grew up on an orchard in Indiana near a little town called Middlebury. We lost the orchard to hard times when I was fourteen, and my parents divorced shortly after that. My mom and I moved to Chicago then."

"That must've been a big change." Her voice was soft now, and he noticed a lilt, the remnants of a Southern accent.

"I adjusted—made friends and all that. Never lost my love of the country though."

"And apple orchards in particular?"

Chicago had always felt like a place he was visiting. Even after he married and settled there, it was never home. "Mom always said I have apple juice flowing through my veins."

"Is that why you studied agriculture?"

"I dreamed of having my own orchard someday. There's just, I don't know, a sense of belonging when I'm working an orchard, a calling, you might say." He wondered if he'd said too much. It wasn't as if he was trying to take over Blue Ridge. But Josie had settled in her chair and didn't seem alarmed by his words.

"Did you accept the position here right out of college?"

If only he had. If only he'd skipped the whole ordeal with Danielle. "No, I—I lived in Chicago for a while. I was married." He didn't know why he added that last bit.

Josie didn't seem surprised. Maybe her sister had mentioned it.

"After the divorce I saw an ad online for the foreman position. Your dad posted it, I guess."

"Right." She stared into the darkened yard. "After Hank retired."

"In Chicago I worked at a company that transformed urban lots into agricultural centers. It was rewarding work, but I was eager to escape the city and try my hand at an orchard. This was only going to be a step toward getting back to my roots, so to speak. Being a family operation, I didn't hold out any hopes for ownership."

"Then the frost came."

It wasn't like he'd planned it. The loss had hit hard after all the work he'd done to prepare the trees.

"It was a difficult time for your sister. I had money set back and she offered to sell me some shares." He hoped he wasn't stepping on a minefield by bringing up the subject, but Josie needed to see how much this place meant to him. Surely she knew how much it meant to her sister.

He wanted to ask why she wanted to sell the place. Didn't three generations of family ownership mean anything? What he'd give for that kind of history. All he had was an absentee alcoholic father and a newly married mom who lived too far away.

"Enough about me. What do you do in Louisville? I don't think Laurel's ever said."

She shrugged. "I'm a photographer. I work—or worked, I should say—at Special Occasion Photography."

"They fired you?"

"Not exactly. I might have a job when I get back, just depends how busy they are."

He hadn't given too much thought to what she'd left behind.

"I can get another job if I have to."

"How did you get into photography?"

"I've always been snapping photos. When I left here, I moved to Pittsburgh and got a job at a restaurant, but I took some courses in photography. It eventually turned into an associate's degree." Her eyelids dropped, a shutter over her eyes, as she studied her feet. She laid her head against the back of the chair and sighed. She looked tired, ready for bed, but suddenly he didn't want her to go.

You really are lonely, pal.

He'd finished the newspaper, and there was nothing on TV tonight. At least she was someone to talk to. She was being amiable at least, and their conversation was easing some of the tension that had flowed between them.

"Ever married?" *Now, why'd you go and bring that up?* She didn't seem surprised by his tactless question.

"Nope." Her lips tilted, just at the corner, underlining her world-weary sigh. "Never found the right person."

She sounded like it was over, like she was seventy and it was too late. She couldn't be older than twenty-five, twenty-six.

"I heard you went out with my friend Jackie." The other side of her mouth rose until she was almost grinning.

"Does that amuse you?"

"Little bit." A full-fledged smile, the kind that could take a man's breath away.

"We didn't have much in common."

"No kidding."

She'd been talking about him with her friends over the week-end. He'd give his best ladder to know what they'd said.

"I can set you up with some of my old friends," she offered.

"I'm doing fine on my own, thanks just the same."

"That's not what Laurel seems to think." She was teasing him.

How long had it been since he'd been teased by a woman? "You seem to be spending an inordinate amount of time talking about me."

He was sure if the porch weren't so dim, he would've seen a

blush bloom on her cheeks. Finally, she lifted her little chin and crossed her arms as if she were chilly.

"Don't flatter yourself," she said. "It was nothing good."

He felt a smile work its way to his own lips. Sassy thing.

"So, who'd you set me up with?" he asked, not even sure he wanted to hear the answer.

She squinted, biting the corner of her lips. "Emaline Jacobs maybe?"

Their town clerk, Emaline Jacobs, talked in long run-on sentences and had hips so narrow, she could squeeze through a crack without turning sideways. "Not my type."

Her face brightened. "Oh, I know. Anna Tackett."

She was a server at the café. Cute, but loud and bossy. She was known for deliberately changing orders she felt were less than nutritious. She would've been fired by now if it wasn't for the fact that her mother owned the place.

"Nuh-uh," he said.

Josie laughed. "She'd keep you in line."

"I can do that on my own."

"That so?" She was flirting.

And he liked it. Too much. *What are you doing, Mackenzie? Making friends with the enemy? She wants to sell the place from under you.*

They did say keep your friends close and your enemies closer. Still, in this case, he didn't think it was wise. He was enjoying her attention, her company, but she was the last kind of woman he needed. Too much like Danielle, a danger to his heart.

Maybe he did need someone to keep him in line. He sure wasn't doing a good job of it. He picked up the newspaper and shifted forward on the chair, leaning his elbows on his knees. "Getting late. I think I'll turn in now."

Josie's eyes flickered. "Oh. Okay." She stood slowly, as if puzzled, maybe even hurt, by his sudden announcement.

For one awkward moment he felt frozen to his chair, frozen by her vulnerability. She'd been enjoying herself too. Maybe she was just as surprised by that as he was.

"Well," she said. "Good night."

"'Night." He watched her walk into the darkness, fading like a ghost as she distanced herself from the halo of light. He wished she would fade so easily from his own thoughts.

ten

*J*osie's cell phone rang as she pulled up to the front of the house. She took it out and looked at the screen, hoping for reception. Two bars, hopefully that was enough.

"Hi, Josephine, this is Allen Linkletter from Dunbarger and Associates."

Josie turned off the car and greeted the attorney.

"I sent those papers we finalized a couple weeks ago, but they were returned in the mail. I was wondering if you had a new address."

She'd forgotten to have her mail forwarded. She'd have to handle that.

She gave Allen the new address and hung up, relieved that was taken care of. If she could only convince Laurel to sell the orchard, everything would be in place.

The house smelled like lemons when she entered. Laurel stopped midswipe, a dusting rag in hand.

"What are you doing?" Josie snatched the rag from her sister.

"You're home early."

"Is this what you do when no one is around to keep an eye on you?"

"I feel fine." Laurel tried to grab the dust cloth, but Josie pulled it from her reach.

"Go sit down. I'll bring you a nice glass of tea."

"Why don't you just hook me up to an IV and be done with it?"

Josie pointed at her. "Don't tempt me."

When Josie returned from the kitchen, Laurel was sitting in the recliner, her feet propped on the ottoman.

"If I have to sit, so do you," Laurel said. "You're looking pretty tired yourself."

Josie didn't want to admit she'd been relieved when Grady asked her to take a bushel of Galas to the store for Aunt Lola. By the time she was done, it would've been a waste of time to return to the field.

Josie sank onto the sofa, glad for the reprieve.

"Are you feeling okay?" Laurel asked.

Her eyes popped open. "I'm fine." Had Laurel seen her symptoms? She'd tried so hard to hide them.

"You haven't seemed yourself since you've been home. And you haven't been eating much."

"Maybe I'm getting sympathy morning sickness," she joked.

"So you have been feeling sick."

"Can't a girl watch her weight without everyone getting paranoid?"

Laurel narrowed her eyes. "Don't even talk about weight." Laurel looked at her own belly, burgeoning beneath her maternity top.

"What do you expect? You're carrying two people in there."

"Am I carrying them in my thighs too?"

"You look great, Laurel. Besides, Nate doesn't seem to mind your new figure." Laurel's husband always seemed to have an arm around her sister, as if he couldn't keep from touching her.

Their closeness sometimes made the hollow spot inside Josie stretch open. Not that she wasn't happy for Laurel.

The back door shut and sounds emerged from the kitchen— the refrigerator door sucking open, a pot being pulled from its cupboard.

"Aunt Lola's fixing her famous spaghetti tonight."

"Sounds good." Josie's empty stomach complained, whether from hunger or in revolt, she wasn't sure.

"Who's been in my kitchen?" Aunt Lola called from the kitchen.

"Sorry!" Cringing, Laurel addressed Josie. "I baked cookies," she said. "Hey, did I tell you I have an ultrasound this week?"

Josie had seen the ultrasound she'd had weeks ago, but the fuzzy black-and-white photo looked more like bad TV reception than two babies. She imagined that would be different now. "How exciting. Is Nate going?"

Laurel sipped her tea. "He wouldn't miss it. I'll bring home a picture for you."

"Will they know if you're having boys or girls yet?"

"Yeah, but Nate doesn't want to know. I do, but we've agreed to wait until they're born."

Josie imagined she would too. Not that she was ever going to have the chance. Sadness curled around her like a vine, but she wouldn't let it grab hold.

"I sure wish he'd change his mind," Laurel said.

It took Josie a moment to realize Laurel was talking about the sex of the babies. "Do you have a preference? You always wanted a little girl."

"Honey, at this point, I'm just happy to have a baby. Well, two babies."

"I hope they're identical." An old memory sprang into Josie's mind. "Remember when Dale and Darren Seavers switched identities for those classes my freshman year?"

Dale had been an algebra whiz and Darren loved English, so they took each other's place one semester.

"Oh, man." Laurel laughed. "I'd forgotten. They 'bout got away with it too."

Except Dale's ex-girlfriend had discovered the truth and ratted them out. "They got suspended for two weeks, remember?"

Laurel grimaced. "I've decided I don't want identical twins."

"I'm sure yours would be little angels." It wouldn't be long, and they'd be here, tiny bundles of wiggling joy. It would do this house good to see some little ones again. The thought pressed hard on her heart. Would she even be here to greet them?

"I've been giving some thought to what we talked about on the porch." The change of subject was abrupt.

She was surprised Laurel was bringing it up, but maybe she'd seen the light. Maybe she'd been thinking about life after the babies' arrival.

"I don't know how I thought I was going to manage the orchard and the babies. Would've been hard enough with just one baby, but two'll keep me busy for sure."

"Some parents of twins hire extra help. Of course, Aunt Lola will be here, and it'll be winter when the babies come, so she'll be free to help out."

"Yeah, I'm thankful for that."

Josie realized she wasn't helping her own cause. "But Grady won't be able to prune all the trees himself."

"And once fall comes again, Aunt Lola will have to mind the store, and Grady will still be shorthanded."

"Exactly." A rush of relief flowed through Josie.

"And you're right," Laurel said. "The orchard has never been to me what it was to you and Daddy. I mean, I love the place, and I love the history, but the work of the orchard was never really my thing. I've only done it all these years because I've felt responsible for it."

A prick of guilt stabbed Josie. She'd abandoned her sister here, forcing the load of the orchard on her.

Dad was here when you left. You couldn't have known he'd have a stroke.

But since then, the responsibility had fallen on Laurel. It would do her good to be out from the strain of it, to have the opportunity to pursue her own dreams. She probably didn't even realize the weight of the stress she carried. And once the babies were here, she wouldn't need the extra worries.

". . . So I was wondering if you'd consider coming back."

Josie had missed something important; it was what she got for letting her mind wander. In the kitchen, Aunt Lola dropped something that clanked to the floor.

"What?"

"I know you have a life in Louisville, and I don't want you to think I'm discounting that. But really, the orchard has always been your passion. I always thought you'd stay here and take over when the time came."

Josie didn't like where this was headed. She stared at Laurel, hoping she was wrong, but her sister was studying her stubby fingernails, the pink polish half chipped away.

Josie gathered her courage around her like armor. "What are you saying?"

Laurel wrung her swollen hands and took a deep breath, her chest expanding and deflating in the space of two seconds. "I want you to consider coming back home to stay."

Josie felt her face freeze. This wasn't supposed to be happening. This wasn't why she'd come home. Laurel was supposed to be thinking about selling the orchard, not restructuring Josie's life.

"I've caught you by surprise," Laurel said.

That didn't begin to describe her emotions. How did she explain to Laurel why she couldn't come back? She couldn't tell her everything. It brought her shame just knowing it herself. Shame and guilt.

The feelings welled up inside her, but she pushed them down firmly. No, this wasn't what she wanted. This would spoil everything. Somehow she had to make Laurel see the impossibility of her request so she'd consider the only real solution to their problem: selling the orchard.

"You don't have to answer right away," Laurel was saying.

Unbidden, the image of her and Grady working the fields came to mind. She imagined the spring with the trees in full bloom; the air filled with the fragrance of their white, velvety blossoms; honeybees buzzing through the fields and pollinating the flowers. Spring brought a fresh sense of hope, an expectation for nature's bounty. She could almost feel the excitement building inside her now.

No, no, this was all wrong. What was she doing?

She shook her head. "I don't have to think about it." Josie tucked her hands under her legs, pinning them to the sofa cushion. "My life is in Louisville now. I'm not staying."

"But why?"

"I'm just not, Laurel." Frustration rose like a thermometer under the hot sun. Laurel had always tried to tell her what to do, but Josie was an adult now and her sister wouldn't have her way this time.

"Is this about Daddy? I know the two of you—"

"No. This isn't about that. But now that you mention it, he should've sold this place a long time ago. It would've saved you a lot of trouble."

"What are you talking about?"

"Come on, Laurel. Don't you think it was selfish of him to ask you to drop your life and come nurse him for months on end? To put your family on hold, to run the orchard, give up your house in town—"

"He's our dad. It was my duty—"

"It was his responsibility to look out for your needs. If he'd sold this place, he could've afforded health care and not expected his daughter to drop her whole life to be his nurse. I would never be a burden on my family like that."

"He wasn't a burden. I didn't know you felt that way."

Josie had bitten her tongue through too many phone conversations. She hadn't meant it to come out now—it was too late to change things.

"Well, Daddy's gone now, and the orchard is my responsibility. If you came back, you'd be in charge. You could run the orchard any way you wanted."

Josie imagined Grady overhearing that sentence, imagined her becoming his boss. A wry laugh slipped out. Yeah, that would be the day.

"It's not a ridiculous thought, Josie."

She recognized the tone of Laurel's voice. Her sister was getting frustrated right back at her.

"You always planned to stay here anyway, and it's not like you have anyone waiting for you in Louisville."

The truth hurt, dug down deep into the private places where a Do Not Disturb sign hung on the door.

"You probably don't even have a job anymore, so what is there to return to?"

Josie shook her head.

"You have family here. That used to mean something to you. You have me and nieces or nephews on the way." She lowered her voice. "And Aunt Lola won't be around forever, you know."

Josie needed to take a hard line. She wasn't staying here, couldn't stay here, and she needed to make Laurel understand that whether her sister got her reasons or not.

"I won't do it, Laurel. I *like*"—she forced out the word—"my life in Louisville. It's not much, but it's mine, and I'm going back after harvest." She stood, needing to retreat to her room, needing space.

She left her sister staring after her, her hands laid protectively over her belly. Josie's legs trembled as she took the stairs. In all her thoughts of coming to Shelbyville and convincing her sister to sell, she'd forgotten one major detail that could ruin everything: her sister was capable of digging in like a tick on a rottweiler.

eleven

Josie closed her bedroom door behind her, shutting out the garlicky smell of spaghetti sauce. Nausea worked its way into her throat and lodged there, an acidic lump. She rooted through her purse for the roll of antacids, bumping aside her wallet, checkbook, and a packet of tissues.

A bottle dislodged from the corner of her purse, the pills clacking against its plastic shell. She stilled, her eyes settling on the amber-colored bottle, on her name typed across the label.

She could open the bottle and swallow a pill and be done with it. Her stomach turned, as if in agreement. Her legs shook, the fatigue settling over her like a lead blanket.

Her fingers closed around the bottle. Should she? Was it worth it?

The phone call she'd received from the attorney flitted through her mind. All her planning, all her reasons.

It was that—the reasons—that made her release her death grip. Let the plastic bottle fall with a quiet clack to the bottom of her purse.

She grabbed the antacids and chewed two tablets, then curled up on the bed, wishing it were bedtime so she wouldn't have to face Laurel again.

The sound of a mourning dove beckoned outside her window, calling back all the mornings she'd awakened to that very sound. If only she could go back and change things . . .

But there were no do-overs in life. Not really. Not when death stole them away.

She tried to smother the thought before it had a chance to ignite, but her sister's proposition fueled the flame. The memory came quickly, incinerating everything in its path.

They'd had a particularly cold January her senior year in high school, with more snow than usual and winds that stained her cheeks red.

On that day, they'd had a snowfall, and Josie had talked Laurel into digging their old sled from the barn in an effort to recapture their youth. After supper, they had headed to the best hill at the peak of their driveway. It was almost a mile away, but well worth the walk.

Josie was first, starting from the top. The sled was smaller than she remembered, and her legs were scrunched up, the rubber soles of her boots flat against the steering board. She gripped the rope tightly in her mittened hands and shoved off. The runners coughed up snow that hit her face, burning her skin. She passed Laurel at the turn, pushing hard with her left foot to make the sharp curve and avoid veering off the drive and down the dangerously steep slope toward the creek. Once around the corner, she flew down the second incline, closing her eyes against the snow shower.

Her sled slid to a stop at the bottom and she jumped off, exhilarated by the fast ride. By the time she reached Laurel at the halfway point, she was huffing from the climb.

"You almost didn't make the turn," her sister scolded.

"I always make the turn, and you always say that."

Laurel straddled the sled and sat, choosing to start halfway down for safety's sake.

"Besides," Josie said, "the creek is probably frozen."

"No matter, that hill's too steep even for you."

Laurel pushed off and down she went, screaming all the way. On Laurel's third run, Ian appeared wearing an impossibly thin parka and his old beat-up Nikes that made his feet slide with every step.

He and Laurel shared the sled, making the runs from the middle of the hill. Josie started her runs from the top.

Laurel was first to quit, complaining of frozen fingers and an icy-cold nose. After Laurel left, Josie wished Ian would go home too. Now that he was fifteen, she had to look up at him. He'd had a few growth spurts the past two years, and he towered over her by ten inches. She hated that.

"Why don't you just start from here?" Ian handed her the rope. Snowflakes clung to the long lashes framing his brown eyes, and his freckles stood out on his pasty winter skin.

"Same reason I didn't last time." Josie took the sled and started the steep trek up the hill. Her boots crunched through the packed snow. Ian was such a wuss. He was too cautious, and the way he looked at her dad, like he'd set the moon and stars in orbit, made her sick. Wasn't one father enough for him? He had to claim hers too?

After school her dad had taken Ian to the hardware store. When she'd offered to go, he'd reminded her of her English homework. It rankled to see Ian and her dad leaving together while she was stuck at the table with a number-two pencil and a blank sheet of paper.

It wasn't fair. She didn't have a mom anymore and she may as well not have a dad. He didn't care about her. He was too busy doting on crummy old Ian. She hated the way it made her feel inside, like something black and ugly was swelling up.

Josie reached the top of the hill and turned. It was getting dark. This would have to be her last turn.

Ian stood at the inside of the curve, well out of harm's way, waiting. The thing that swelled up inside her felt like it was going to bust. Why didn't he just go home and leave her alone? Why did he always have to hang around?

"The corner's getting kind of slick," Ian called.

The runners had packed it down good, but she could make the turn. She sat on the sled. A thought buzzed in her mind, begging escape.

"I think I might go down toward the creek this time," she called, just to get under his skin.

"You know that's too dangerous." The edge to his voice fed her mean streak.

"The creek's got to be frozen. It'll be fun." She wasn't going down the slope anyway. Even if she made the bump off the drive and the steep ride down into the gap, there was always a chance the creek wasn't frozen enough to withstand the impact of the sled or the slice of the runners.

She pulled her feet up and set them in place.

"No, Josie!" His words were as firm as she'd ever heard from him, like a parent to a naughty two-year-old.

Who did he think he was, bossing her around? He might have her dad wrapped around his long, skinny fingers, but he didn't have her.

Somewhere between the top of the hill and the curve, she made the decision. Entering the turn, Josie pushed on the right side of the board, and the sled veered toward the hill.

"Josie!"

She barely heard her name through the tornado of snow that whirled around her. She hit the bump at the edge of the drive at an angle and went airborne. The sled tilted crazily, then she landed.

She sped down the impossibly sloped hill. She was falling through a wet, white world. Her breath choked on the cold, her eyes blinked blindly. Where was the bottom?

The runners cut through the snow. She braced her feet against the board, grasped the rope in her gloved hands, leaned back. Gravity pulled her forward, downward. She remembered the big rock that jutted out into the creek. What if she hit it? She looked for it, but the spray of snow blinded her.

Abruptly, the slope leveled, then a bump. She held her breath, pulled hard on the rope. The ground leveled as the sled skated across the ice. The runners sliced through the snow, and the sled came to a gradual stop.

Her heart pumped blood in thumping bursts. Her vision cleared. She was in the middle of the frozen creek. She'd made it!

The scariness of the ride drained away, leaving an aftertaste of exhilaration. She scooted off the sled, onto her knees, screaming, "Woohoo!"

No one had gone down that hill before. No one. And she'd made it. It was better than a roller-coaster ride at Six Flags.

Ian stood at the top of the slope, his gloved hands on top of his head. "That was the dumbest thing you ever did!"

She'd never seen him mad before. That just made the trip even more worthwhile. Josie stood to her feet and reached for the rope. "Oh, just shut up." She was so tired of him. Why couldn't he just—

There was a sickening sound. A sharp crack.

Josie froze, her hands in midair, reaching. A longer sound followed, like a chunk of Styrofoam snapping in half. The sound of ice cracking under her weight.

She stopped breathing, afraid the weight of filled lungs would be all it took to make the ground split beneath her.

"Come on, Josie, stop goofing around. It's time to go home."

Should she lie down flat? Tiptoe off the ice?

She bent her knees slowly, easing down, reaching with her hands.

A loud crack split the night. Then she was falling.

"Josie!"

The water swallowed her, the edge of the ice cut through her mitten and into her fingers. Coldness enveloped her. Her lungs sucked in a mouthful of water.

She kicked hard, and the water opened to air. She coughed, sputtering, reaching for the edge of the ice. The wet cold permeated her clothing. The weight of it dragged her down.

Her hand found the edge of the ice and she braced her body on it.

"I'm coming, Josie!"

The ice in her hand snapped, and she went under a second time. When she came up, her head hit ice. The current had carried her from the hole.

She panicked, sucking in a breath. Her eyes opened wide under the murky water, searched frantically.

There! She was so close. She grabbed for the ice and pulled herself up. The cold air hit her face. Her lungs coughed up the water, stinging her throat.

Her body shivered, her hands moved mechanically across the ice, shaking.

"Josie!"

The shore seemed so far away. Ian stepped toward her, out onto the frozen creek.

Josie grabbed the edge of ice and tried to pull herself up. She grunted with the effort. Her sodden clothes weighed her down. If she could only get a little leverage with her feet. But the bottom was too far down.

She strained, pushing with her arms, trying to get high enough to lay her body across the ice. She groaned and screamed with the effort.

"I'm coming, Josie!" Ian was lying belly-down, slowly moving toward her.

Her arms collapsed under the strain and she sank down until her chin touched the water's surface. Her teeth knocked together. Shivers shook her whole body. How long could she last like this? The water was frigid, and she'd already been cold. Her arms and legs felt numb.

"Help me!"

"Hang on, Josie!"

She tried to pull herself up again, but her arms were weak. *What if I don't make it? What if I die here in the creek?*

Tears tracked down her face, freezing halfway down. Her skin stung. She was helpless. But Ian was coming. He was getting close.

"Hurry!" Her voice betrayed her panic.

Ian scooted to the rim of ice, hand reaching out.

She grasped it, then the other. Ian pulled, grunting. But instead of drawing her from the water, he slid forward, pulled by her weight.

"Wait. Let go," he said.

But he was her lifeline, and she couldn't make her fingers loosen.

"Let go, Josie! I'm not going anywhere."

She straightened her stiff fingers and clutched the ice. She couldn't feel her fingers anymore. Her legs hung limply. They didn't feel cold anymore. She tried to remember what she'd seen about hypothermia on TV last winter when some kid had gone skating on a pond he'd thought was frozen.

"Grab my hands." Ian was sitting now, bracing his feet in front of him. What if the ice cracked under him? Then they would both die.

"Maybe you should get help!" But even as she said the words, Josie wondered if there was time for that.

"Grab on!"

She took his hands and he pulled. Her chest scraped against the edge of the ice. Ian grunted.

Josie strained. "Help me, God!" She kicked as hard as she could. *Don't let me die!*

Then the ice cracked under her torso and she slid back into the water.

Ian scooted back and they tried again.

"Kick your legs! Kick hard!" Ian pulled.

Josie tried to kick, but her legs responded in slow motion as if they were drugged. Her arms felt like they were being ripped from their sockets.

The ice under her gave way again, and she grabbed for the new ledge, a fresh batch of tears clogging her throat.

Ian backed up, gasping. "It's no use."

"Go . . . for . . . help!" The words escaped between chatters. Why was he just sitting there? "Hurry!" Her feet felt funny, all tingly. Her hands weren't doing what she asked of them.

And still, Ian sat.

"Go . . . Ian . . . *please!*" She wouldn't last much longer. Maybe she could hold on long enough for help to arrive. *Please, God! I don't want to die.*

"I have an idea." Ian scooted toward her.

What was he doing? She didn't have the strength to ask. Until he scooted close enough that the ice cracked under him too. And he was falling into the water in front of her.

"Ian!" *No, God!* What hope did they have now? What was he doing?

Then he was beside her, shivering. His eyes had a look she'd never seen. A confidence, almost a resignation. And a strength of will she didn't expect from Ian.

"I'm going under," he said, his teeth knocking together. "Put your feet in my hands and I'll push you up."

"But . . . what about—"

Ian was under the water. She felt movement around her. Somehow he found her feet, and then she was being pushed upward. She used her hands. They pushed against the ice. *Please don't crack. Please don't crack.*

Then she was out of the water. On her belly. Everything hurt, tingling painfully. She scooted like a snake away from the hole, slowly, her muscles not cooperating.

She had to help him! But how? She wasn't strong enough to pull him out, even if the ice didn't give way. She had to go for help, and quick. She crawled, afraid to stand, her knees scraping the ice.

When she reached the shore, she turned, breathing hard. "Ian!" She had to help him, but she could barely move.

"I'm here," he called.

"I'm going for help!"

The slope she'd slid so quickly down was now a formidable

enemy. Even on a good day it would be a difficult climb with its slippery covering.

It was slow going. She didn't know how long it took her to climb the hill. It was dark when she reached the top. She called Ian's name and he didn't answer. She fell several times on the long trek home, stumbling clumsily.

When she got home, Aunt Lola called for help and her dad called Hank. They left Josie at the house, warming up. They were gone a long time. Long enough that feeling had crept back into her limbs and warmth had seeped into her flesh. What was taking so long?

They heard sirens, and Josie told herself that was good. Ian was getting help and he would be okay too. How long had it been? It seemed like hours.

She was wrapped in a blanket on the couch, snuggled between Aunt Lola and Laurel when her dad returned. He didn't even look their way as he removed his coat.

"Is he okay?" Josie asked.

When he turned, she saw the answer on his face. Long lines etched his forehead, but it was his eyes that told her what she didn't want to hear.

Beside her, Laurel began to cry.

"We were just . . . too late." Her dad stood there as if he didn't know what to do next.

There were two full minutes of shocked silence, then Aunt Lola slid off the sofa. "You need something warm in you. Where's Hank?"

Her dad gestured toward the door. "He went to the hospital with—Ian."

Everything in Josie froze up all over again. A different kind of freezing. This one started on the inside and worked its way out.

It was all her fault. All her stupid fault. She just had to go down that dumb hill.

And Ian had saved her life.

If only she hadn't let her temper take over. If only she'd gone the other way. But she hadn't. And now Ian was gone. Gone forever. He'd saved her life.

No, he had sacrificed himself for her.

It should be her body being driven to the hospital. A hollow spot opened up inside her, wide and gaping. Why was she alive and Ian dead?

It was supposed to have been her.

"He should've known better," her dad mumbled.

He never should have jumped in the water. What had he been thinking?

He'd been thinking about saving you.

He should've gone for help.

Now he's dead and it's your fault.

She looked at her father, standing by the door, snow-covered boots dripping all over Aunt Lola's clean floor. He was going to hate her when he found out what her foolishness had done. Hank was going to hate her. They all were.

Laurel was sobbing now, and her dad seemed suddenly aware of it. He turned toward them.

Then his eyes found Josie. "You did the right thing, coming for help."

They didn't know. They didn't know what had happened out there on the frozen creek. They'd seen the sled. They'd assumed

Ian hadn't made the turn, that Josie had tried to help him out of the water.

She tried to find it in her to speak. *Tell them the truth, Josie. Just say it.*

Her tongue stuck to the roof of her mouth.

Ian saved me. She had to tell them the truth.

But she couldn't make herself say the words. Not that night, not the day of the funeral, and not any day afterward. No one had pressed her for details. Seeing the sled, the hole, they assumed they knew what had happened.

The truth had stayed buried inside, a tiny seed that had eaten her alive every day since. Not a day had gone by that she hadn't questioned why Ian was dead while she remained alive. Not a day that she hadn't questioned why he gave himself for her. She was unworthy of such a sacrifice and no one knew it better than she.

twelve

Laurel was taking a bath and Mr. Murphy was on the front porch with Aunt Lola. He'd brought his mandolin and Josie could hear the sweet strains of a hymn as he practiced for his solo performance at the Shelbyville Apple Festival. Her mind filled in the familiar words of "Redeemed" as he played.

> Redeemed and so happy in Jesus,
> No language my rapture can tell.
> I know that the light of his presence
> With me doth continually dwell.

The music halted as Josie walked toward the back door. With everyone else occupied, Josie could finally have a private word with Nate. She found him in the backyard, raking the grass cuttings. "Need help?" Josie hoped he'd say no. She was already shaking with fatigue.

"I'm almost done." He raked the clippings into the burn pile with broad sweeps. Behind him, the laundry waved on the line like horizontal flags.

Josie tested the strength of the tire swing with a hefty tug on the frayed rope. Satisfied, she put her legs through the opening and pushed off.

"Laurel said you two used to spin each other until you were dizzy."

How many hours had they spent under these shade trees, playing and swinging, the pine-scented air rushing through their hair?

"I can't believe it's still here."

He gave the rake one last sweep and leaned against the handle. "I was going to take it down a couple summers ago. But you know Laurel, she's so sentimental."

"Now your kids will swing on it when they're old enough and—"

"Spin each other until they're dizzy. I know, that's what Laurel said." Nate ran his hand through his short clipped hair. He seemed to be taking in the property, probably calculating how many days until he had to mow again.

Now was as good a time as any to ask. "Did Laurel tell you what she asked me?"

"I guess not."

Josie was surprised. Nate and Laurel seemed close. Maybe she figured there was no point unless Josie decided to move back. "She asked if I'd come back for good."

He leaned the rake against a tree and stuffed his hands in his pockets. "What did you say?"

Josie dragged her feet until she came to a stop. She shook her head.

He nodded, not seeming to need further explanation, which was good because she wasn't going to offer one.

"When did she ask you?"

"Yesterday."

He nodded again slowly.

"She has a lot on her mind. Besides, she's probably hoping I'll change my mind."

"That still wouldn't solve much. She'd still fret over every frost, every season. Worry we'll lose another crop."

"It's unending, part of the job." Josie ran her hands across the rough treads of the tire.

"Grady thinks he can turn things around, given time. He has ideas for using a different type of tree, bringing in tours, stuff like that."

"Which would require more workers."

"I know."

Other orchards did it, but ultimately the responsibility would fall on Laurel. She'd always feel a duty toward it, just as she'd felt a duty toward their dad after his stroke. She would always need help, and Laurel had never enjoyed the work the way Josie and her dad had.

"I think she might change her mind after the babies are born. Her focus will shift to them, and she might see she needs to let loose of the place."

Might. After the babies are born. It was all so iffy, all too far away. Josie might not have that much time, and she wanted this albatross off her sister's neck before she was gone. She couldn't leave her sister knowing she'd dumped the entire weight of the orchard on her.

"I think it would be better if we put it up for sale soon. We can't guarantee a good harvest next year or the year after, and no one will pay a premium price for a failing orchard."

Nate nodded, chewed his lip. "I see your point. I'm just worried about Laurel. It's a stressful time for her with the pregnancy. I don't want her upset."

Did he think Josie did? She had a ticking clock motivating her, but there was no way to tell him that. "Selling the orchard will lessen her stress."

"Eventually, yes. Initially, she'll feel guilty though. You know how she is."

"She'll still have the house and acreage around it. It's not as though she'll lose all our history."

"I know. I know. I just think we need to bide our time a bit."

That was where they parted ways then. Because time was one thing Josie didn't have much of.

thirteen

Josie's old Nikon whirred as she pressed the button. After all these years and a change of batteries, it felt like an old friend again, fitting into her palms as if it were made for her.

It was the perfect time of day for photos, when the sky gave off a golden glow leaving no shadows, no harsh highlights on the subject—in this case, the covered bridge on Old Fork Road that spanned the gap over Sweetwater Creek. It was even better light for portraits, but she'd left the orchard to be alone.

She shifted the camera, capturing a leafy twig at the edge to frame the photo, and snapped the shot. The week had dragged so slowly Josie wondered if it would ever end. She would've given her best pair of jeans for a trip to Asheville, but money was tight. She couldn't afford to leave every weekend. Still, that didn't mean she had to stay cooped up at the orchard. Just leaving the property, escaping the ghosts of the past, renewed her.

Especially today, after the tension of the week. She'd avoided the subject of the orchard with Laurel after their argument. Instead, they'd focused on the ultrasound pictures Laurel had brought home the day before. The photos had shifted her sister's attention from their argument.

If Laurel hadn't told her husband about her hopes of Josie running the orchard, Josie was sure she hadn't told Grady. As much as he wanted to keep the orchard, she was sure he didn't want to be under Josie's supervision.

Why are you dwelling on this? You didn't walk all this way for nothing. She drew in a deep breath, relishing the fresh piney smell. The creek trickled under the bridge, punctuated by a dove's occasional call.

She'd snapped two rolls of film when a distant peal of thunder reached her ears. Dark clouds had gathered, capping the hills around her in a smoke-colored haze. She'd best start home. The light was fading anyway.

Josie capped the camera and knelt beside the one-lane road to stow it in its bag. She'd just zipped the case and stood when her eye caught a gray-haired man walking toward her. Worn jeans hung on his thin frame, and a plaid shirt, buttoned crookedly, flapped in the sudden breeze.

He'd aged more years than could be accounted for, but she knew it was Jackie and Boone's dad. As he neared, she saw a layer of gray stubble coating his jaw and neck. His eyes widened, he looked this way and that.

"Mr. Barrow?" She remembered Boone telling her about his Alzheimer's.

He stopped a car's length from her, his house slippers scraping the asphalt.

"It's Josie Mitchell. Remember me?"

There was no flicker of recognition in his eyes. He scanned the hills and road as if looking for an escape.

Another peal of thunder sounded and he jumped. "I can't—I don't know—" He scratched his jaw.

She approached Mr. Barrow slowly, not wanting to frighten him further. "Let's go home, okay, Mr. Barrow?" She took his arm in hers and turned him toward his home. "This way."

They started a slow shuffle up the incline of the winding road, their shoes grinding the loose pebbles into the old pavement. Mr. Barrow moved in slow, stiff movements, his bony arm jerking with each step. He must've wandered off from home. Mrs. Barrow was probably worried sick.

If only she'd brought her cell phone, she could've called and set the woman's mind at ease. But then, reception was spotty around here anyway.

"I don't—" Mr. Barrow worked his jaw but couldn't seem to finish the sentence.

"I know, I know." Josie patted his arm. "It's okay. We're going home."

Thunder roared loudly, closer this time. Gray clouds seemed to have dipped down into the valley. The Barrows lived a good mile away in the opposite direction of the orchard. Josie realized with a start that, at this pace, they'd never beat the storm.

Grady pulled out of the driveway and turned toward town. Darkness was beginning to fall, enough so he'd put on his headlights. The smell of rain was heavy in the air that streamed through his window. He liked the earthy smell, liked to hear the patter of the rain on the truck's metal roof.

Lightning lit the sky south of town. He hoped Peggy didn't close the diner early as sometimes happened when bad weather cleared town. He was hungry, and the only things in his fridge were butter, coke, and a few slices of crusty-edged bologna. He really needed to get to the grocery store.

The first drops of rain came in slow, heavy splashes on his windshield. They were followed by quick pelts of water. He rolled up the window and turned on his wipers. A roll of thunder echoed loudly through the canyon.

At least it had come after work hours. The orchard would dry out tomorrow and the apples would be ready to pick again come Monday.

Rounding a corner, he caught sight of two figures walking on the opposite side of the road. He recognized the bright blue shirt and slowed beside Josie and Mr. Barrow. Josie's head was ducked against the rain, a futile position. Her hair hung in wet strings around her face.

He put the window down. "Get in," he shouted over the rain.

She wasted no time, ushering Mr. Barrow into the middle before climbing in beside him. She pulled the door shut, set her camera bag on the floor, and wiped her wet hands on her jeans.

"'Evening, Mr. Barrow." Grady put the truck in gear.

The man seemed oblivious to his drenched condition. Grady grabbed his hoodie from behind the seat and handed it to Josie. She used it to dry off Mr. Barrow's arms.

"I found him walking along the road. I guess he's lost." She dried the man's face, speaking to him now. "But we're going home, aren't we? Everything's going to be okay now."

Grady accelerated up the gradual incline. He thought of calling Mrs. Barrow on his cell, but there was no reception on this stretch of the road.

Josie was rebuttoning Mr. Barrow's shirt in the dim light of the cab and talking to him softly. The soothing sound of her voice discomforted Grady almost as much as her ministrations did. This wasn't a side of her he'd seen before.

He pulled into the short gravel drive and stopped beside the farmhouse. The rain pummeled him as he made his way around the truck. Josie had already helped Mr. Barrow from the vehicle.

As they walked the man up the porch, Mrs. Barrow burst through the door. "Ted! Where have you been?" Fright ignited an angry tone.

"I'm home," Mr. Barrow said as if it was any ordinary day and he was arriving home from work, sopping slippers and all.

"He was walking along Old Fork Road," Josie said. They ushered him inside.

"You're soaking wet," Mrs. Barrow said to Ted, then addressed Josie and Grady. "Thank you so much. He slipped out while I was fixing supper. Boone went looking for him, but I wanted to stay here in case he came home on his own. I'd better call Boone and let him know he's home."

Grady hadn't known how bad Mr. Barrow had gotten. Or maybe the symptoms came and went. He'd seen the man in the hardware store a couple of months ago and he'd seemed lucid.

"Are y'all hungry?" Mrs. Barrow asked after she made the phone call. "I can heat up some supper for you."

Grady met Josie's eyes, but she must've been thinking the same thing. The Barrows had enough on their minds without having company tonight.

"No, thanks, Mrs. Barrow," Josie said. "We'll be off now. We just wanted to make sure he got home okay."

The woman thanked them profusely as they left, then they darted through the rain into the dry comfort of the truck. Grady started the engine and backed down the drive, his thoughts heavy on the Barrow family and their difficult journey. It was a good thing Mrs. Barrow had Boone's help.

"I'm glad you came along when you did," Josie said.

Her hair was flattened to her head, one wet string strung across her neck like a rope necklace. Inside the house he'd noticed her lashes were wet and spiked. "It's not like you could've gotten any wetter."

She almost smiled. "True. But Mr. Barrow was getting anxious about the thunder. He kept wanting to duck into the woods, to hide or something I guess."

He turned toward town. "They have their hands full."

"I didn't realize it was that bad." Josie looked out the window into the fading daylight.

It was only then he realized he'd turned toward the diner without thought to the fact that he had Josie along now. "I was on my way to get supper at the diner." He checked his watch and saw he had twenty-five minutes until they closed—if they hadn't closed early on account of the storm. "I can take you home first if you want."

"Actually, I'm starving."

Aunt Lola didn't cook on Saturday nights, so they were on their own. Laurel and Nate often went out for a date night in Burnsville, but tonight they'd stayed home, just the two of them.

A part of him was relieved he'd get a decent meal, but another part realized it meant spending the evening with Josie. For some reason, that made him shift uncomfortably on the seat. He told himself it was on account of his rain-soaked jeans.

Josie grabbed the hoodie and ruffled her hair with the cotton material. "I must look like a wet dog."

"I can't look much better." His own hair was dripping after their slow trek up to the porch with Mr. Barrow. The rain had slowed now, and he turned his wipers to low.

Josie pulled at her shirt and it made a sucking sound as it left her skin. He should've taken her home for a change of clothing. Too late now.

He eased the truck into town, the headlights slicing through the fog. The rain-slicked roads reflected their glow as he pulled up to the diner. The windows were darkened, the neon Open sign off.

"They're closed," Josie said.

Grady's empty stomach let out a growl. "Bummer."

Up ahead, Maggie Lou was closing the Curl Up and Dye salon, the red of her dyed hair almost fluorescent under the streetlamp. She waved as she slipped into her retro Volkswagen Beetle.

Grady turned his attention to the problem at hand. The nearest restaurant was in Burnsville, but that was a good twenty minutes away.

"What do you think?" he asked.

"I think they roll up the sidewalks way too early around here."

He glanced at his watch. "It's eight forty-two. Respectable citizens are home in bed by now."

"And hungry ones are out of luck."

"There's always Burnsville."

"Either that or we could grab some snacks at Joe's."

He wasn't taking her to some smoky tavern. "By the time we get to Burnsville everything will be closed. And I need something more than pretzels and peanuts."

"I'd fix something at the house, but I hate to do that. Aunt Lola went over to Mr. Murphy's, and, well, Laurel and Nate don't get much time to themselves."

"You don't even want to see what's in my fridge."

"I'll take your word for it."

In the distance, the shimmering lights of Ingles mocked him. *It's what you get for going three weeks between trips to the grocery.*

Josie's eyes had gone in the same direction. "Are you thinking what I'm thinking?"

"That bachelors don't shop often enough?"

"That the only food in town is over there."

He pulled his eyes from her face and stared at the lit store. They did have a deli. And a few booths tucked away in the corner. If his mom ever found out he'd taken a woman to a grocery store for dinner, she'd have his head.

Saturday night at the grocery deli. "How sad are we?" Grady gave a wry grin.

Josie shrugged. "Look at it as an adventure."

Grady put the truck in gear. "Like I said, how sad are we?"

Josie reached for her fork, then paused when Grady bowed his head in prayer. She quietly set her fork down and tapped her foot under the table.

When he was finished, she popped a bite of grilled chicken into her mouth, then washed it down with a sip of coke. "This isn't bad."

She was warmer and drier after trading her shirt for Grady's hoodie, though her hair was a lost cause.

Grady grunted, slicing into his mashed potatoes with a plastic fork. His hair was just as wet, but somehow it only made him look more Marlboro Man. Life was so unfair.

"It's not Aunt Lola's, but at least it's warm," Grady said.

Their conversation turned to orchard business, then ventured off into new growing techniques and tree varieties.

After a while, Josie's stomach began its quiet churning, and she decided to call it quits. She set the fork on her plate and waited for Grady to finish. There was only a handful of shoppers in the store, and they were the only ones in the eating area.

Josie wiped her mouth with the paper napkin. "Thank you for supper. It was a unique dining experience." He'd insisted on paying since he'd kind of dragged her along.

"You're a cheap date," Grady said, then seemed to realize what he'd said. "Not that this was a date. I mean—you know what I mean." He pressed his lips together, probably figuring they'd gotten him in enough trouble already.

She watched Grady squirm in his seat, amused by his discomfort. Sometimes she wondered if he was as confident as he appeared.

Finally, he put his napkin on his plate. "Are you finished?"

"Yep."

They dropped their trash in the receptacle, but when Grady started for the exit, she grabbed his arm. "Where're you going?"

He looked down at her, his brows tilted. "Home . . ."

"Well, for heaven's sake, you said you needed groceries." Her hands waved, encompassing the store.

He slumped as if all his energy had left his body, leaving him wilted. "Aw, I don't want to shop."

"Men. You can be such babies. We're here, let's just get it over with. We could have it done in half an hour. Besides, with our quick supper, we've hardly given Laurel and Nate time enough for a quiet meal."

"Josie . . ."

She tugged his arm, enjoying the way her name sounded on his lips, the way his thick arm felt in her hand. "Come on, stop being such a man."

"I am a man, in case you haven't noticed."

She felt her lips twitch. "I've noticed."

Fifty-five minutes later, Josie understood Grady's dread. She watched him compare the prices on three packages of popcorn. Cost, price per unit, coupons from the flyer they found in the cart.

"At this rate, Laurel's babies will have graduated from high school before we get back." There was a reason women did the shopping. "Can you just get the generic and be done with it?"

He looked up from his task as if suddenly aware of her presence.

"I'm all for a bargain, but, uh, my clothes are actually dry now."

"Aren't you the one who insisted I shop?"

"That was before I knew you were Mr. Thrifty."

She sighed, leaning on the cart handle. Her feet ached from being on them the past two weeks.

He set the generic brand in the cart. "There's no crime in being careful with your hard-earned money."

"There's careful and then there's—" She stopped at his glare, feeling her lips twitch again. This was almost fun. She couldn't believe she was enjoying Grady's company.

"Okay, I guess I'm done."

"Already?"

He tossed a frown over his shoulder, and she pushed the full cart forward to the register.

"Howdy, Grady," the cashier, Harmony Schneider, purred. She would've been pretty if not for the thick black liner rimming her brown eyes. She was barely into her twenties with a smattering of cute freckles on her nose.

"Evening, Harmony." Grady helped set the groceries on the conveyor belt.

She seemed to notice Josie's presence as she scanned a can of chili beans. "Hey, Josephine."

Josie greeted her, suddenly realizing her mistake. When a man and woman shopped together, it indicated a certain intimacy. Not that Harmony had a big mouth, but a thing like this didn't go unnoticed in Shelbyville. By tomorrow the town would be placing bets on their wedding date.

Grady was loading groceries into plastic bags at warp speed, probably thinking the same thing. Harmony finished scanning the items, gave a total, then took the cash from Grady.

"Y'all have a nice night now," Harmony said, her eyes for Grady only.

He nodded good-bye, and they exited the store in silence. The rain had stopped, thankfully, but they set the groceries in the cab just to be safe.

Darkness swallowed the truck as they turned out of town and up the hill toward home.

"I guess that'll be all over town by daybreak tomorrow," Grady said.

"If not sooner." Oh well, she'd never let what people said stop her from doing what she wanted. She was half sorry she hadn't laid a big wet one on Grady right there at the Ingles checkout counter. Might as well give them something to talk about.

Heat flowed up her neck and settled into her cheeks at the thought. How long had it been since she'd been kissed, much less swept off her feet by passion? Too long.

She'd bet her favorite Birkenstocks Grady was a good kisser. Her eyes traveled to the left where his work-calloused hands gripped the wheel. She imagined what it would feel like to have those hands cup her chin, brush her hair back from her face. What it would feel like to have his lips close over hers.

"Some people and their crazy ideas." Grady was shaking his head at the notion of the two of them as a couple.

Josie closed her eyes, wincing. *Yeah. Some people and their crazy ideas.*

fourteen

$\mathcal{S}$omething was torturing her. Josie moved away, but it followed her, writhing, twisting. She jerked her legs, but they tangled in a knot. She kicked, trying to free them.

Something was ticking. She listened, zoning in on the sound. The alarm clock ticked beside her, bringing her more fully aware. She worked her feet from the sheet and rolled onto her side, pulling her knees toward her stomach.

The clock read twelve seventeen. She'd only been in bed an hour, and she was already regretting that slice of apple pie. She hadn't wanted it, but Aunt Lola was fine-tuning her recipe for the Shelbyville Apple Festival bake-off.

She smothered a moan as the nausea worked into her throat. She tried to swallow it down, but it hung there stubbornly.

Her heart pounded, and she knew she was going to see that apple pie again. She bolted from bed and ran to the connecting bathroom, barely making it in time.

Sweat dotted her upper lip and cooled the back of her neck. She hung there, waiting, wondering if it was over.

She'd felt more nausea the last month, but this was the first time she'd vomited. It was getting worse. There was no denying it.

Josie flushed the toilet, hoping it wouldn't awaken Laurel or Aunt Lola, then sank down on the linoleum, leaning her head against the hard oak cabinets. Was this going to become a regular occurrence? How would she hide it from her sister? From Grady? She was going to be skin and bones by the end of harvest. Already, her jeans hung on her frame. She remembered trying so hard to keep her weight down in high school. She would've given anything for loose jeans then, but this was no way to lose weight.

She grabbed a towel from its hook and wiped her face, then closed her eyes, waiting for her stomach to settle. It had only been three months. She hadn't expected it to progress so quickly. But then, the doctor hadn't expected it to worsen at all.

Her thoughts rewound to that day. How many tests had she had leading up to it? She'd felt like a human guinea pig. And paying the insurance deductible from those tests had wiped out what little savings she'd managed to accrue.

"Have a seat, Josephine," the doctor had said. She was fifty-ish with Carol Brady hair and a warm smile that was currently absent.

Josie sank into the chair across from the desk, feeling like she'd had a four-shot Americano, but in fact she'd skipped coffee altogether today. It was bad news. They never called you in unless it was.

"As the nurse told you on the phone, the results of the ACTH stimulation test are in. The test showed that your output of cortisol in response to synthetic ACTH is blunted."

The words made no sense. Josie swallowed. "What does that mean exactly?"

"It means that your adrenal glands are damaged. They're not

producing sufficient amounts of certain hormones. That's why you've been feeling fatigued and having dizzy spells."

Josie tried to recall anything she could about the adrenal glands from her high school physiology class. She was drawing a blank.

Dr. Nichols continued. "Your adrenal glands are located above your kidneys. They're part of your endocrine system, and they produce cortisol, which gives instructions to practically every tissue and organ. Your body hasn't been making sufficient amounts of this hormone."

Josie's mouth was dry. "That sounds bad."

Dr. Nichols folded her hands atop the manila folder. "Your tests show you have Addison's disease."

Addison's disease? A tremor passed through her. She'd never heard of it. "Is there a cure?" But even as Josie said the words, she knew the answer.

"Not a cure per se, but a treatment. Most people who have Addison's function quite well as long as they follow the treatment. I'll be writing a prescription for a corticosteroid to replace the deficiency. It will mimic the amount of hormone your body would normally be making, thereby minimizing your symptoms."

The doctor's words jumbled into an auditory blur. Oddly though, the news settled into Josie as if it'd always been there.

Dr. Nichols was still talking, and Josie forced herself to listen. "It's especially important to monitor your health when you're facing a stressful situation or a major illness. We may need to increase your dosage during those times."

"What else?" There was more, Josie was certain, though how she knew it, she wasn't sure.

"As I said, it's very important to take your medication, and we'll work closely together to make sure we have you on the optimum dose, which will likely fluctuate from time to time."

She paused and seemed to be gauging Josie's response. "Although the disease can be managed, there is potential for something called an Addisonian Crisis, or acute adrenal insufficiency. This can happen when the symptoms of Addison's suddenly become worse. The condition can result in death if left untreated."

Death.

She tried the word on, draping it over her shoulder, glancing in the three-way mirror to check the fit. She'd always thought of death as being black, but today the color of death didn't seem so dark or ominous. It wasn't white or bright red either, but a subtle hue that suited her.

Maybe she was just numb. Or in denial.

"I'll be writing a prescription for injectable cortisol that you'll need to have with you at all times." Dr. Nichols tilted her head. "I know this is a lot to take in all at once."

That was it. She was numb. It wasn't every day someone told you that you could die—that your body was malfunctioning.

"Here's a pamphlet with more information about the disease, including the symptoms of an Addisonian Crisis. One thing I highly recommend is getting a medical ID bracelet. And we'll need to set up another appointment in two weeks. Do you have any questions?"

She should have dozens of them, but right now, she was swimming in some kind of warm, fuzzy place. "No, I don't think so."

"Well, I'm sure you'll have more questions when you have time to digest this a bit."

Josie walked out of the office with two prescriptions. Mechanically, she drove to the nearest Walgreens and waited in the molded plastic chair while the prescriptions were being filled.

She watched people coming and going, browsing products, loading carts. People going places, buying things, while she waited for medications to treat her disease. It seemed odd this disease had been going on inside her body and she hadn't known.

Disease.

The word sounded foreign in her mind. *I have a disease.*

I have a disease.

This isn't what she thought she'd feel upon hearing such a diagnosis. She did feel stunned, maybe even numb, but there was something else. Something she was sure wasn't normal. As all the information settled in layers inside her, something rose from the midst like a spring of water.

She wasn't unsettled or panic-stricken the way she thought people felt upon such a diagnosis.

She felt something else. She struggled to put a word to the feeling.

It was a sense of inevitability. As if her life had been heading toward this point, none of it making sense until now. A puzzle that had no recognizable image until that one last piece had slid into place.

The disease was that last piece.

For the first time since Ian died, she felt things were . . . *right*. In the years since that night, she'd felt like a person who'd gotten away with a crime. The guilt of surviving had been a heavy load that weighed her down like an anchor.

Now, with the discovery of her illness, she felt like she'd finally been caught. There was relief. Great relief. The penance was easier to bear than the weight of guilt.

"Josephine Mitchell." A voice through the store intercom interrupted her thoughts. "Your prescriptions are ready for pickup."

Mechanically, she went to the window. A man with gray hair and ruddy cheeks took her money, then handed her the crinkly bag with the drug information stapled to it.

"Have a nice day," he said.

As Josie exited the store, she opened her purse and dumped the prescriptions inside, wondering why she'd bothered to fill them at all.

fifteen

*J*osie set the last plate on the table as the family entered through the front door.

"I knew they'd been watered," Aunt Lola was saying. Her matronly black dress swayed with each step.

Laurel ducked her head, laying her hand on her stomach. Josie thought she looked adorable in the white maternity dress that sported an empire waistline and wide collar.

Nate followed his wife, a protective hand on Laurel's back.

"What's going on?" Josie asked as she finished setting the table.

"Little Miss Busy has been at it again," Aunt Lola said. "She weeded the beds and watered my flowers." She shot Laurel a look as she helped get the food on the table. "You keep your black thumb away from my flowers, missy."

"Not to mention, she should be *resting*," Nate added.

Josie had a feeling they were all wasting their breath.

Grady entered the dining room, a surprise. Having been gone the weekend before, she didn't know he ate with the family on Sundays. Josie grabbed another plate from the cupboard, flummoxed by the way her heart betrayed her at the sight of him in beige jeans and a black suit coat.

You'd better watch yourself, girl. It won't do any good to lose your heart to a man you're going to leave behind.

She placed the plate at his spot as he slid into his seat, and he offered her a half grin. Her heart was not cooperating.

"Missed a good service, Josephine," Aunt Lola said, carrying the plate of sliced ham into the dining room.

They'd invited her to church, but after her rough night, she'd slept in. "What was the sermon on?"

"Hellfire and brimstone," Nate said.

Laurel swatted him on the arm as he helped her into her seat. "Was not. Pastor Keeley taught on the Israelites and their grumbling and complaining."

"And the Smiths' new baby let out a wail at just the right time," Grady said.

Josie took her seat as Aunt Lola set the last dish on the table. She'd skipped breakfast, and the smell of baked ham stirred her appetite.

The family joined hands, and Aunt Lola began a prayer. "Heavenly Father, we thank thee for this wonderful Lord's day . . ."

Feeling Grady's hand around hers, Josie's insides fluttered like oak leaves in a summer storm. His hand was warm and strong. It wasn't the first time they'd joined hands, but something had changed. Their time together had shifted something inside her.

Grady had let his guard down, and Josie liked what was beneath it. Her thoughts returned to the night before when he'd dropped her off. After he'd parked and leaned over to open her door, there'd been an awkward pause.

"'Night," he said. He was so close, his breath tickling her drying hair. She hadn't noticed how deep his voice was. In the darkness of the cab, all her other senses came alive. The touch of his breath, the sound of his voice, the musky scent of his cologne.

She found her voice. "Good night." Her legs trembled as she took the porch steps. She tried to tell herself it was fatigue, but her heart didn't quite buy it.

Now she startled as Grady pulled his hand from hers. The prayer had ended and she hadn't heard a word. She raised her head belatedly and grabbed her fork, hoping no one had noticed her daydreaming.

"Mary Beth Keeley said she saw you two at Ingles last night." Aunt Lola regarded Josie, one eyebrow disappearing under her choppy gray bangs.

Josie's gaze skimmed Grady's face. He was busy cutting his ham, but she saw the faintest twitch at the corner of his lips. The rumor mill was operating at full speed. Well, she didn't care what anyone said about her and Grady, or her absence from church. It was none of their business.

"Are you feeling okay?" Laurel asked. "You were up in the middle of the night."

Josie hoped she hadn't heard everything. "I didn't sleep well. It felt good to sleep in this morning." She hated that she felt compelled to make excuses for missing church. She respected her family's desire to attend. Why couldn't they accept her as she was?

"Maybe you can go next week," Aunt Lola said.

"I was thinking about going to Asheville next weekend." Actually, she hadn't thought that far ahead, but now that she'd said it, the idea jelled. She should call Jackie and Ashley and make plans. Her thoughts filled with shopping and fun and gabbing late into the night.

In Asheville there were no reminders of her past, no reminders that she wasn't good enough, no reminders of the guilt that chased her around the orchard like a swarm of angry bees.

Grady watched Josie mentally retreat. He wished Aunt Lola wouldn't press her about church. He didn't know her well, but he had a feeling pushing Josie was about as effective as trying to push a seven-hundred-pound hog into a bathtub.

He watched her slide a bite of potatoes into her mouth, her eyes fixed on her plate. He couldn't get the previous night out of his mind. Pictures of her guiding the cart through Ingles, flopping around in those wet sandals, sending him exasperated looks . . . he'd reviewed it a dozen times in bed, then a dozen more times during church.

They'd talked about the orchard while they'd eaten at Ingles. The woman knew her stuff, and he'd enjoyed talking shop with her. He could see her passion for the business in the way her eyes lit when she talked about new methods versus old, and semidwarfs versus dwarfs. He felt understood in a way he hadn't felt before, certainly not by Danielle, who hadn't even liked the outdoors. It was refreshing and energizing to talk agriculture with someone who shared his zeal.

What is with you, Mackenzie? It wasn't good, this connection with Josie. He had to stop this nonsense. He ticked off all the reasons why.

Josie was leaving in a few months, and even though she seemed to fit in here, she was determined to go back to Louisville. Josie didn't appear to share his faith either, and that was nonnegotiable. On top of that, she wanted to sell the orchard and she was too much like his ex-wife. There was every reason in the world he shouldn't give her a second glance, yet here he was, tripping over thoughts of her.

But was she really like Danielle? She was so at home in the orchard, connected to it in the same way he was. And he remembered the way she'd dealt with Mr. Barrow. The way she'd been content to have a grocery-store supper. Danielle wouldn't have done either of those things, not without complaint.

"The ham was delicious, Aunt Lola." Josie suddenly stood and removed her plate from the table, but not before Grady saw she'd left half her food.

"How are we going to fatten you up if you eat like a bird?" Aunt Lola frowned.

"I'm not interested in being fattened up." A smile softened her words.

Josie carried her plate into the kitchen and he could hear her footsteps as she took the back stairway. The woman didn't eat much.

"She was sick last night," Laurel was saying quietly. "I heard her when I got up to use the bathroom for the hundredth time."

"You mean throwing up?" Nate asked.

"Must've been that food at Ingles last night." Aunt Lola's gaze flittered by Grady.

Prickles of heat climbed the back of his neck. He hoped she didn't have food poisoning from their cheap night out.

"She's been getting tired easily, too, I've noticed," Laurel said a little too casually just before she and Aunt Lola exchanged a look.

Aunt Lola pressed her lips together in a firm line.

Laurel stirred her potatoes, her fork tines screeching against the plate, before she took another bite.

What was that about? The question had no sooner entered his mind than the dots began connecting. Vomiting . . . fatigue . . . Laurel had those symptoms at the beginning of her pregnancy.

Could Josie be pregnant? The thought weighted him like a brick tied to a balloon. Is that why Josie had been working so slowly in the field? Why she took so many breaks? He'd once seen her sway on the ladder and grab the rail, blinking. He'd thought she'd lost her balance, but maybe she'd gotten dizzy the way Laurel did sometimes.

Suddenly he wasn't feeling too well, the food congealing into a solid lump in his stomach. If there was another man in Josie's life, that was just one more thing to add to his list of reasons to get the woman out of his head.

"Can we talk?" Laurel poked her head into Josie's room as she was about to turn off the light.

"Sure." Josie wore the hoodie Grady had loaned her the night before, telling herself it wasn't the smell of the jacket but the warmth that she craved.

Josie pulled the sheet to her chin, covering the sweatshirt. "What's up?"

Laurel perched on the edge of the bed, twisting her wedding band around a finger that looked like a little swollen sausage.

"I'm worried about you," Laurel said. "You don't quite seem yourself."

Josie had thought she'd been covering so well. She shook her head. "I'm fine." If all else fails, change the subject. "Hey, guess what? I found my old camera and took it out for a test run yesterday."

"That's great. You always did have a way with that thing. But don't think you can change the subject." Laurel nailed her with her hazel eyes, and Josie knew this was going to be a direct conversation. She was right.

"I heard you throw up last night."

She'd been afraid of that. Josie cleared her throat. "I guess that deli food from Ingles didn't settle too well. I'm fine now." What was she going to say next time and the time after that? Maybe she could get something for the nausea.

"You haven't been eating much. And you're tired all the time."

Josie pulled her knees to her chest, the pink sheet draped like a tent around them. "I'm not used to working in the heat, and I'm not a teenager anymore, in case you haven't noticed."

"Are you pregnant?" The bold question vibrated the air between them.

"What?"

"I'm intimately acquainted with the symptoms, you know."

She couldn't believe what Laurel was thinking. Josie's laugh was brittle. "Not unless it's an immaculate conception."

Laurel studied her face. "You'd tell me if you were . . ."

"I haven't had a date in months, Laurel, much less . . . anything else."

Her sister's shoulders slumped a fraction of an inch, her back hunched in an arc that left the mound of her stomach resting on her thighs. "Okay. I had to ask."

"One pregnant woman in the house is more than enough, don't you think?"

sixteen

The weather was an accurate reflection of Josie's emotions. The sky, a gray abyss, promised a full day of rain. She could smell the rain in the air already. She'd been relieved when Grady had given the ladders to the others. With her balance problems, she didn't need any help from a wet ladder.

The Red Delicious apples were big and colorful, perfectly ripened and ready for picking. There were many Red and Golden Delicious trees, mostly on the outskirts of the area she'd avoided since her arrival. The creek.

Even now, she kept her eyes on her job, not wanting to see it. *Grab, twist, pull, bag. Grab, twist, pull, bag.*

But the nearness of the creek, the ripple of the current, was a constant reminder of its presence. The rain leaked down her face like misplaced tears.

Focus on your work, Josie. She shook her head as if to jar the memories free, then hitched the rough canvas bag higher on her shoulder. *Only one more day and you get away from here. Focus on that.*

She'd called Jackie early in the week and they were set for the weekend. The girls had even offered to split the gas cost with her. They were going to have friends over to the apartment Saturday night, a casual party that would no doubt result in Jackie trying to set her up with every single man present.

Josie wasn't interested, but that didn't matter. What mattered was getting away from here where the memories smothered her. At least when she was someplace else, there was some relief.

Asheville was her reward for making it another week. Something to look forward to. It was what kept her hands reaching up for the next apple and the one after that.

The migrants sang a jaunty Spanish tune, passing the time. Behind her, Grady pulled the truck and trailer forward, bringing it closer to the next empty bin. The tires bumped over the ground, the chains on the trailer rattling against the hitch as he pulled to a stop.

She wanted to broach the topic of selling the orchard again now that she and Grady were on better terms. Ever since their night out together, he'd softened toward her. She wasn't sure why, but what did it matter?

It matters, and you know it. Okay, so maybe she was crushing on Grady. What harm was there? It felt good to have a man looking out for her, being nice to her. He'd brought her a bottle of water earlier and suggested a break.

Grady walked toward her now, hooking a bag over his shoulder, then began picking the other side of the tree. They picked in silence awhile, though Josie was sure she felt Grady's eyes on her a few times. She was glad for the distraction from her darker thoughts, no matter where it came from.

"These look great," she said, bagging a deep red apple, smooth and supple in her palm.

A limb snapped back in place as he plucked an apple from its branch. "We had plenty of sun this summer. Turned out some nice color."

They bagged in silence, and when she'd filled her bag, she emptied it into the bin and returned.

"I've been thinking about what you said about selling," Grady said.

Josie couldn't believe he'd introduced the subject. "Yeah?"

"I'd like you to consider selling to me." He lowered his hands, peeking around a leafy branch at her.

To him? But Laurel had said he didn't have that kind of money. Why hadn't he said so before?

"It makes sense," he continued. "No outsider knows this place like I do. I'm sure I can keep it going and turn it around. I could make this place into an orchard your father and grandfather would be proud of."

"I'm sure you could. I didn't realize you were in a position to buy us out." Relief breezed through her, whistling a happy song. She never dreamed there was such an easy solution. She smiled at Grady, but he shifted his eyes to an apple as he grabbed it.

"Well," he said, "I'm not exactly, at the moment." He hurried on. "But we could work something out. You want to be rid of the property and I want to buy it. It might take awhile, but I could return the fifteen percent profit to you and Laurel each year."

Her relief deflated like an inner tube with a gaping hole. Fifteen percent of the profits? How many years would it take at that rate? And that wasn't counting the years when there was no profit. Or, like the year before, when there was a loss.

"Plus, I'd give you whatever I manage to save besides. I could get a part-time job during the slow season."

She addressed the most obvious flaw in his plan. "You won't be able to get all the pruning done alone as it is."

"You're not seeing the big picture. As this place grows, we'll be able to afford more help. We could have a self-pick area. I can see school field trips in the autumn, hayrides, campfires. We could have a cider press and sell our cider to local markets—"

"All that costs money."

"A lot of other orchards make it work. It's good extra income for minimal start-up costs."

She could see Grady's passion, had felt it in their conversation at Ingles. She hated to burst his bubble, but this wouldn't work.

Grady's cell phone rang, sparing her a reply, giving her time to think about how to word her rejection.

He took his phone from his pocket and answered, leaving the tree and heading for high ground and better reception. She'd stopped bringing her cell phone to the orchard since she wasn't able to get reception out here anyway.

Maybe he could do everything he said. Shoot, he probably could with his knowledge and determination, but it would take years. Way too long to give her peace of mind. And even if he were buying Laurel out, it would still be her sister's responsibility for years. It would still keep Laurel from pursuing her own dreams. The twins might be in high school before the deal was complete, and that was if Grady managed to make the orchard profitable. Half her sister's life would be gone before the load would be lifted.

She couldn't live with that. She gave a wry laugh. She couldn't die with it either.

She heard Grady's words as he approached. "We'll be right over," he said into the phone.

Something was wrong. She could see it in his eyes.

He closed the phone. "That was Aunt Lola. She's been trying to reach you. Your sister's having contractions and the doctor wants her to go to the hospital."

"Contractions? It's too early."

He shrugged off his bag. "Come on, I'll drive you to the house."

She followed him to the truck and got in. *No, please. Don't let anything happen to the babies.* She didn't know who she was pleading with. God had never listened to her before.

Grady started the truck and pulled away, towing the trailer behind them. The orchard whizzed by as they bumped through the field. What if Laurel lost them? She was almost thirty weeks; were they big enough to survive on their own? The pictures from the sonogram flashed through her mind. Laurel had been so proud, so thrilled when she'd showed them off.

She couldn't shake the bad thoughts, couldn't shake the memory of her mother's difficult pregnancy and the devastating result.

"Aunt Lola thought you should meet Nate at the hospital in Burnsville."

They would save a little time that way. Could the doctors stop labor if it had begun? She knew nothing about this kind of thing.

"I'm sure she's going to be okay," Grady said.

"You can't know that." What if Laurel was doing too much? Heaven knew they'd had an impossible time keeping her off her feet. Maybe Josie should've stayed at the house instead of working the fields. Nothing was more important than Laurel and her babies, certainly not a bunch of apples. Let them fall off the trees and rot on the ground.

But that wouldn't do anything for Laurel's peace of mind.

They pulled onto the gravel drive that led to the house. "Are you going to be okay? Do you want me to drive?"

"I'll be fine. Is Aunt Lola with Laurel?"

"Yeah. Laurel called her at the store." But Aunt Lola didn't have a driver's license.

"Is she in much pain?"

"She didn't say."

A few minutes later, Grady pulled up to the house. They both jumped from the truck and ran inside.

Laurel was sitting on the couch, leaning back, her hands plastered to her belly. "Thanks for coming so quick."

Aunt Lola entered the room with their purses and Josie's keys. "You're all set. I'll be praying hard for you, Laurel. God will see you through this."

Josie and Grady helped her off the couch.

"Is it bad?" Josie asked.

"Not so much. But they're coming every ten minutes." She looked into Josie's eyes. "I'm afraid."

"You listen to me. You're going to be just fine." She was making the same promise Grady had made only moments ago, but the words seemed to strengthen her sister.

Two hours later Josie wished there were words to calm her own nerves. What was taking so long? She twisted the straps of her purse until they were too tight to twist any further. Nate had come out over an hour ago and told her they'd put Laurel on a fluid IV to see if that would stop the contractions, but she hadn't heard anything since.

Was this what her mom and dad had gone through? Or had it been a normal pregnancy up until the tragic birth?

That was a long time ago. Medicine has come a long way since then. This is Laurel and everything's going to be fine.

Meanwhile, Josie watched patient after patient being admitted and taken back through the double doors while she waited, wondering what was happening. The evening news was coming on a TV in the corner, put there, no doubt, to distract relatives from the fact that they were in the ER.

The entrance doors beside her whooshed open and Aunt Lola entered, her purse hanging from the crook of her elbow.

"I couldn't sit around the house all evening. I've been praying up a storm. Any word?"

"No, nothing since we last spoke. I tried to call Nate, but he has to keep his cell off back there."

Aunt Lola sank down in the chair beside her.

"How did you get here?" Josie set down this week's copy of the *Shelbyville Gazette*.

"Grady. He's parking the truck."

Warmth flowed through her, and she told herself she was just grateful for the company. Still, it was nice of him to bring Aunt Lola. He'd practically become a member of the family.

Josie and her aunt stared at the TV in silence until Grady appeared and took a seat on Josie's other side.

His denim-clad leg rested against hers, giving her a feeling of stability and strength. "Any word?"

Josie shook her head. "Nothing for over an hour. I guess it takes awhile to see if the fluids are doing their job."

Grady propped his elbow on the armrest between them and leaned back.

"Thanks for coming." She'd meant to say, "Thanks for bringing Aunt Lola."

His eyes met hers. Golden flecks shone under the bright fluorescent lights. "Sure."

The double doors opened, revealing a tired-looking Nate. He walked toward them. Josie couldn't read his expression.

She and Grady stood as he approached. "How's she doing?" Josie asked.

"Sorry it took so long. I didn't have anything to report until just now. The fluids didn't stop the contractions and her labor was progressing, so they gave her an injection of something that's supposed to stop them. So far it seems to be working."

Relief slumped Josie's shoulders. "That's great news."

"Thank the good Lord," Aunt Lola said.

Nate looked like he'd aged five years since this morning. "Well, keep the prayers coming."

Nate went back to be with Laurel, and she and Grady took their seats again. The medicine might be working, but Josie couldn't help but wonder how Laurel was going to get through the rest of the pregnancy. Would she have to be on bed rest? And if she did, how were they going to manage both Laurel's care and the orchard?

seventeen

$\mathscr{B}$ed rest!" Laurel said. "I can't believe this is happening."

Josie pulled the worn quilt over her sister, then propped her hips on the side of the firm mattress. Laurel was washed out, her makeup long gone, her nose red from crying.

"Everything's going to be fine. You have to take care of those babies."

Laurel closed her eyes. "I know, I know. And I'm so grateful the contractions stopped. I was so afraid—"

"Well, you don't have to be afraid anymore. Your only job is to lie around and do nothing."

"I stink at that."

"No kidding. I'll go to the library and get some books tomorrow." Her weekend trip to Asheville would have to be canceled. Nate had called a family meeting to discuss how they were going to manage. They were waiting for her downstairs.

"I guess I could start cross-stitching and knitting again," Laurel said, a pout outlining her words.

"That's a great idea. I'll run over to Burnsville tomorrow and find some things for you to work on. Hey, you could do bibs or blankets for the babies."

"I guess so." Laurel sank deeper into the feather pillow.

"I'm going to let you get some sleep." Behind the fretting over the bed rest, Josie knew her sister was concerned that the contractions would start again. "No worries, now, all right?"

Laurel sighed deeply. "All right."

Josie flipped out the lamp and left the room. Downstairs, Nate, Aunt Lola, and Grady sat in the living room waiting for her. The clock ticking on the mantel was the only sound breaking the silence. Josie took a seat beside Aunt Lola on the couch. She guessed Grady really had become part of the family.

Nate seemed to read her thoughts. "I asked Grady to come since this is going to affect the orchard."

Josie nodded. "What are we going to do?"

"Someone needs to be here round the clock," Nate said. "The doctor doesn't want Laurel walking around."

Laurel's voice barreled down the stairwell. "I do not need a babysitter!"

Nate rolled his eyes and Grady grinned.

"Go to sleep, darlin'," Nate called, then lowered his voice. "She means well, but I don't trust her to stay down like the doctor told her to do."

"I agree," Aunt Lola said. "Someone needs to keep an eye on her."

"I can't quit my job, obviously," Nate said. "And you can't do it, Aunt Lola. We need the income from the store, so we can't shut that down."

"And I need Josie in the orchard," Grady said.

His statement made Josie feel good. It felt good to be needed, even if it was only for picking apples and helping to manage the crew.

"Right," Nate said. "None of us can drop what we're doing, so that presents a problem."

"Can we pay a high schooler to come stay with her?" Aunt Lola asked.

Laurel would love that. Her own personal babysitter.

"I'd rather not if we can work around it, both for financial reasons and for Laurel's mental health." Nate gave a wry grin.

"How about shifts?" Grady suggested.

If they each gave a little less time to their jobs, they might be able to juggle it all. "That might work," Josie said.

"I could cut back my hours at the shop," Aunt Lola offered. "We're not busy in the mornings. I could open up at noon instead of nine."

"I could cut my day short, not take appointments after two for a while," Nate said. "I could be home around three."

"And I could take the noon-to-three shift." Josie looked to Grady for his approval.

He nodded. "That should work."

"I'm here all weekend," Nate said, "so that won't be an issue. And I can take over payroll, too, if she wants me to."

"What about sales?" Josie asked. Finding markets for their apples was imperative, otherwise they'd go to waste. "Should I take that over?"

"She'll probably want to keep doing those things. It'll give her something productive to do and keep her out of the kitchen," Aunt Lola said.

Josie nodded. "Sounds like a plan." Laurel wasn't going to be happy about it, but that didn't matter. Nothing mattered now but giving those babies a chance at life.

eighteen

Grady watched the family fall into a pattern over the next two weeks. Their shifts became as regular as clockwork. Laurel had taken up residence on the living room couch during the day where she could feel like an active part of the family. Josie had gathered up a basketful of things to keep her occupied.

Laurel had completed a bib for each baby and read enough books to start her own library, or so she said. Her mood had gotten progressively worse and tonight at supper she'd been downright snippy. Not that he could blame her. He wouldn't want to vegetate on the couch for days either.

Josie worked in the orchard from sunup until eleven forty-five when she drove back to the house. At three fifteen, she reappeared, her old car spitting out blue exhaust. She did it all without complaint, even when he could tell she was exhausted.

Sometimes he found himself glancing at her stomach, wondering if Laurel's suspicions were true. She was a little thing, and he couldn't see anything that resembled a lump under her T-shirts. But women didn't show for a while, did they? As the days passed and the symptoms persisted, he became convinced Laurel was right.

The timer on the microwave dinged, and Grady opened the

door and removed the swollen, steamy bag of popcorn. Somewhere outside a cricket chirped. With the microwave silent, the house was too quiet.

With the tension of Laurel's mood, he'd been eager to leave the main house after supper, but now the night stretched ahead of him.

He wished he had something to do.

And someone to do it with.

It was Friday night and his big plans involved the couch, a movie, and a bag of popcorn.

Pathetic, Mackenzie. It wasn't even that he minded a night at home. Shoot, he preferred it. But being alone all the time was getting to him.

He needed some single friends. But all the men his age in Shelbyville were settled down with two kids, three cats, and six chickens.

It was what he missed most about marriage—sharing life with someone. The Mitchells were great and all. They treated him like family, but there was something about that special bond between a husband and wife.

The bond Danielle broke when she cheated on you with your best friend?

Yeah, there was that. Grady filled a glass with ice water and sank into his favorite recliner, the worn leather creaking under him. He wondered what Danielle was doing these days. Last he'd heard she was dating some hotshot Chicago lawyer. He pitied the poor fool who fell for her. Of course, there was always the chance that she'd changed. Life had a way of doing that to you.

He grabbed the remote from the end table and flipped on the

TV. "Looks like it's you and me again." He opened the popcorn bag and steam rolled out.

Maybe he needed a dog. He hadn't had one since he was a boy on the orchard. Barney had been a brown and white mutt they'd found alongside the road after school one day. He'd had him for several years until he disappeared. They never did find out what happened to him.

A knock sounded on the door, pulling him from his thoughts. He set the bag down and padded barefoot across the wood floor, bits of dirt sticking to the bottoms of his feet. He really needed to sweep.

He opened the door and Josie stood on the other side.

"Hey," she said.

"Hey there."

She held out a packet of papers bound by a paper clip. "Laurel forgot to give you these."

Printouts of the hours each employee had worked. "Oh, thanks."

Josie shuffled her feet, then put her hands behind her back. She looked adorable there on the stoop with the golden porch light pouring over her face.

She tucked her hair behind her ears. "Everything going okay with the crew? I feel out of the loop since I'm spending less time in the field."

"Everything's fine." They'd caught up on the schedule since Josie had arrived. The season looked to be the best he'd seen at the orchard.

With the door open, he could hear faint sounds of music coming from the migrant housing. They liked their parties on the weekend.

"Sounds like they're having a good time," she said.

"Not so much in the morning." He gave a wry grin.

She matched it with one of her own. "No, not so much."

An awkward silence ensued. The cricket chirped again. Once. Twice.

Maybe he should invite her in. Was she trying to say something and couldn't find the words?

Her gaze bounced off him. Finally, her shoulders fell and her tongue loosened. "Laurel's in a rotten mood. I know she's my sister, but man, I can't offer her a magazine without getting snapped at. And poor Nate. I think he's at his wits' end. I guess I just needed to get out of the house . . ." Her hands came up in a little shrug.

His own tongue seemed to be inoperable. *Invite her in, stupid. You were wanting company.*

Yeah, but Josie Mitchell? Is that a good idea? She was already pulling on his heartstrings, and time alone with her wouldn't diminish that. *You do not need another Danielle in your life.* He was surprised she hadn't run off to the city to shop or party or whatever she did while she was there.

Not to mention, she was quite probably pregnant.

She stepped back, looking sheepish and vulnerable. "This was stupid. I'm sorry." She turned.

"Wait." That was all he had—he hadn't thought any further. He crossed his arms. "Uh, you're welcome to hang out here awhile if you want. I was just getting ready to put a movie in."

Her face slowly brightened like the sky at dawn, and just as pretty. "You don't mind?"

"I even have an extra bag of popcorn." *What are you doing,*

Mackenzie? He told his inner voice to shut up and opened the door wide enough for her to pass.

"Have a seat." He entered the kitchen and put the last packet of popcorn in the microwave.

"Can I get you a drink?" he called over the noise of the microwave, then opened the refrigerator. "I have—" He surveyed the empty fridge. Shoot. "Well . . . water or water." Why was he always in need of groceries?

"Water's fine," she called.

Grady fixed her a glass of ice water, and when the popcorn finished, he poured it into a big bowl and joined her in the living room.

"You haven't gone to the grocery since that night, have you?" she asked.

"So?"

She shook her head, then held up the DVD case. *"Jaws?"* Her eyebrows disappeared under her bangs.

"It was a busy night at the Pick-a-Flick."

She handed him the DVD and he put it in.

"I don't care what it is," she said. "By the time it's over, Laurel will be asleep, and that's all that matters."

He offered her a consoling grin.

She winced. "I'm awful. Being immobile is hard on her. I should just suck it up."

"Go easy on yourself. You have all weekend to suck it up."

She laughed. "Oh, thanks."

Grady flipped off the lamp, then settled in the recliner as Josie grabbed her bowl of popcorn from the coffee table. The faint glow of the TV lit her face. *I'd rather watch her than the movie.*

He snapped his head toward the screen. *I cannot believe you just thought that. What was it about her?*

She's just here to kill time. She wants to sell the orchard, remember? She is not your friend, much less anything more.

But curled on the sofa, her bare feet tucked under her, her mouth working on a handful of popcorn, she didn't exactly conjure up the picture of an enemy. A few moments later, she set the popcorn on the table and leaned back, resting her hand on her stomach the way he'd seen Laurel do in recent weeks.

He wanted to forget, just for tonight, that she might be pregnant. That she wanted to sell the orchard, that she was a little too much like his ex-wife. It was just a movie, after all.

Josie set down the bowl of popcorn. It had managed to upset her stomach even though it had been the blandest popcorn she'd ever had. She remembered watching Grady select this particular box. He'd vacillated between the store brand and a name brand for several minutes. He'd picked the wrong one.

The screen options came on the TV and Grady selected Play.

He looked at her, meeting her eyes, swallowing a bite of popcorn. "It's kinda bland." His tone was apologetic.

"I wasn't going to say anything."

He fetched the saltshaker and shook it over his bowl, then offered some to her.

"No, thanks."

"I guess taste has to factor in there somewhere."

She shrugged. "Live and learn."

Grady forwarded through the previews as Josie glanced around the dim room. She was suddenly aware that before Grady lived here, it was Ian's house. She never came inside when he and Hank lived here. Their old manager liked his space, fixed his meals here in the house, and didn't come around her family unless he was working.

Ian, on the other hand, was a household fixture, butting in, usurping her father's attention. Every time she turned around, there he was. And her father with him. No wonder she could never please him.

Josie turned back to the screen. *Forget about Ian. Forget about everything else. Just relax and watch the movie.*

But it was impossible to forget Grady, stretched out on the recliner, his body claiming the entire chair. In the light of the TV screen, shadows flickered across his face.

"Have you seen this before?" he asked.

She shook her head. "I'm probably the only person on the planet who hasn't."

"It was a little before your time. Wait until you see the special effects."

The movie started, and Josie soon became wrapped up in the plot. She forgot everything but what was happening on the small screen. The movie was tense, and when the first shark attack came, she shrank back in her seat and closed her eyes. She hadn't expected the blood. And those teeth . . .

From beside her, she heard Grady's chuckle. "Can you believe how fake that—"

Screams screeched from the TV. And that terrible music.

"Are your eyes closed?" Grady asked.

"It's an old seventies movie and it said PG. I didn't think it would be this scary."

"Want me to turn it off?"

She wanted to know what happened next. She just didn't want to watch the scary parts. "No."

A few minutes later, he said, "You can open your eyes now."

She shifted, feeling a little silly under Grady's scrutiny.

"You know Spielberg directed this, right? I saw a documentary on him once. He was only twenty-something at the time, and it was the second film he directed. He wrote most of the—"

"Shhhhh." Now that the scary part was over, she wanted to hear what was going on.

"Yes, ma'am," Grady drawled.

They finished the film in silence, and Josie found several more scenes through which she closed her eyes. She'd never liked scary movies, but she thought an old movie wouldn't have enough realism to terrify her. Wrong.

When the credits rolled, Grady kicked in his footrest and shut off the DVD player.

"I am never going in the ocean again. Actually, the thought of dipping my feet into any body of water is now out of the question."

"I didn't know you were such a chicken."

"Even Laurel on bed rest isn't that scary."

His smile took her breath away. "You can pick next time."

His gaze darted away and his grin slid from his face as if he suddenly realized he'd just invited her over again.

"Deal," she said before he could rescind his offer. Laurel still had weeks to go on her pregnancy. "Maybe a romantic comedy . . ."

He groaned.

"You can close your eyes through the scary parts," she offered.

"Chick flicks are scary all the way through."

"Wimp," she muttered as she stood and stretched. After putting her bowl and glass in the sink, she walked to the door and slipped into her Birkenstocks.

When she turned to say good-bye, Grady was right there, opening the door. The scent of musk and pine overtook her. His face was inches from hers, the door frame at her back. Man, he was good-looking. His bangs hung roguelike over his deep-set eyes. Her breath caught at his closeness, trapping the smell of him in her lungs.

His gaze swept downward to her lips and her heart stuttered. Time suspended, her body froze. *Is he going to kiss me?* He had that look. She'd seen it before.

Do I want him to?

Before she answered the question, he stepped away. An awkward silence fell between them like a heavy curtain.

"Well," she said, then waited for a thought to form. Nothing came. *Say something.*

"Well," he echoed.

Why hadn't he kissed her? She was sure he'd wanted to. *You can reflect on that later, Josie. For now, say something.*

"Good night." "At least—" They spoke at the same time, then laughed nervously.

"What were you going to say?" Josie asked.

"At least Laurel will be in bed when you get back."

She shifted toward the open door. "True. Thanks for letting me hang out." Josie walked outside and crossed her arms against the breeze. It blew across her skin, raising chill bumps and erasing the awkwardness of the moment.

A long path of darkness lay between his house and hers. Not even the moon and stars were out tonight to light her way.

Outside the circle of the porch light lay a darkness so inky black it made her wonder what secrets it held.

The movie's music echoed in her head and the tension of the scenes clung to her like yesterday's nightmare.

He leaned against the door frame. "Good night."

"'Night." She started down the porch steps and exited the glow of the porch light. Her feet tapped along the flagstones, then swished through the damp grass. Darkness enveloped her, and she could hear her own heartbeat. An owl hooted nearby, startling her.

This is why you don't watch scary movies. You know better.

Behind her, Grady mimicked the music from the movie that warned of an impending attack. Brat.

She kept walking, not bothering to turn around.

The staccato music continued, cutting through the darkness.

"Shut up!" she called even as she quickened her pace.

Her only answer was a distant chuckle.

nineteen

"Aunt Lola's making your favorite cake for your birthday," Laurel said.

Josie handed her sister a glass of tea, then sank into the recliner. Her birthday was tomorrow, but she was leaving for Asheville after work for the weekend.

"I smell it baking." She hadn't tasted Mississippi mud cake since her last birthday here, her eighteenth.

"I wish you weren't going into the city tomorrow. We could order pizza and watch movies until late like we used to."

She felt bad for deserting Laurel, but she needed to get away. Especially on her birthday.

"I think I'll head to bed. Do you need help up the stairs?"

She shook her head. "Nate will be in soon. He's at a town council meeting. Peggy Tackett is stirring up the whole parallel parking quandary again."

"It never ends."

Josie went upstairs, shutting her bedroom door behind her. It was early, barely nine o'clock, but the disease had stolen her energy. All she wanted was to crawl under the covers and pull them over

461

her head. At least she'd be working all day, staying busy. Then after supper and the cake, she could leave.

But when she awakened, it would be her birthday. She wished she could sleep through it. When she was away from here, it passed uneventfully.

She changed into her pajamas, washed her face, and flipped off the lamp. The sheets felt cool against her heated skin. Outside her window, an owl's lonely call sounded.

Even with the door closed, she could smell Aunt Lola's cake baking. The rich, chocolaty smell made her stomach turn. She hoped she could hold it down.

Jackie and Ashley wouldn't remember her birthday. She'd always let her birthday pass without a fuss. Especially after her tenth birthday when Aunt Lola had told her about the other baby.

It had been her first birthday without her mom. Aunt Lola had come to live with them, tried to fill the gaping hole her mom had left.

"Happy birthday, Josephine!" Aunt Lola appeared in the dining room doorway with Laurel, carrying a cake ablaze with ten flickering candles.

Josie's taste buds watered at the sight. She only got Mississippi mud cake on her birthday.

She was *ten*. Almost a preteen. Practically a young woman. The scent of chocolate and smoky candles and melted wax filled her nostrils as Aunt Lola set the cake in front of her.

"Make a wish!" Laurel said. At thirteen, Laurel had become a mother figure to Josie as well. When she wasn't bossy, they got along just fine.

She closed her eyes, her thoughts already spinning with wishes, when the scrape of her father's chair snagged her attention. Her eyes popped open.

He was out of the chair and walking away before Josie could say a word. His jaw was set, his shoulders a broad, hard line. She felt the rejection down to her dirty toes. It stirred like a hornet's nest deep in her belly.

Josie looked at Aunt Lola for some explanation. Was he sick? Angry? He'd always been in the background on days like this, her mom leading the celebrations.

But he'd never done this. Just walked away. She watched him now as he reached the top of the stairs, leaving her line of vision. She heard the door to his bedroom shut.

"Hurry up, now," Aunt Lola said. "Make a wish. The wax is melting all over my pretty cake."

With one last glance up the stairs, Josie closed her eyes. *I wish . . . I wish Daddy would . . .*

Josie bit her lip, thinking hard. She couldn't quite finish the sentence. Didn't know how to word what she wanted. *Want me? Accept me? Love me?*

Oh well. Wishes don't come true anyway.

She drew a lungful of air, then released it in a huff, blowing out all the candles.

Afterward, Aunt Lola cut the cake, and Josie ate the gigantic piece that was put on her plate, though she'd forced it down. It didn't taste so good this time.

Aunt Lola gave her a small box wrapped in glossy pink paper. The tag on the card read "From Daddy and Aunt Lola." But it was Aunt Lola's messy scrawl, and Josie had a feeling her dad didn't know what was inside the box any more than she did.

She pulled off the wrapper and opened the lid. Inside, nestled on a velvet pillow, was a silver necklace with a delicate heart pendant.

"Open it," Laurel said, leaning forward until her face was peeking over Josie's shoulder.

Josie pried the heart open with her blunt thumbnails. Inside, a tiny photo of her mom stared back. She gazed at the image. Her dad had removed all the pictures of her mom from the house. Aunt Lola said it was too hard for him to see them. Lately, she'd had trouble remembering what her mom had looked like. Her eyes began to sting.

"Thank you." It was all she could scrape out past her swollen throat.

She clenched the locket tightly in her cold fist. Now, when she had trouble remembering, she could just open the locket.

Aunt Lola blinked fast and began gathering the plates.

"Wait, I have something too." Laurel reached under the table and pulled up a limp package wrapped in the same pink paper.

Josie unwrapped a lavender crocheted hat. "Thanks, Laurel." She wondered how her sister had made it without her knowing.

"It's too hot for it now, but come winter, you'll need it."

"I love the color." She ran her fingers along the soft, fuzzy surface.

"You wanna watch a tape?" Laurel asked. "I got your favorites at Pick-a-Flick today."

"Sure."

Laurel scurried off to the living room to start the movie, and Josie gathered the candles from the table and carried them to the kitchen where Aunt Lola was running water in the sink of dirty dishes.

Her dad hadn't come back. Every now and then she could hear

his footsteps overhead, could hear things banging around like he was angry.

"Aunt Lola?"

Her aunt turned off the faucet and picked up a plate. "What is it?"

She wasn't sure how to ask or even what it was she wanted to know. "Why did Daddy leave?"

Aunt Lola scrubbed hard, then ran clean water over the plate and set it in the strainer. "He's just having a bad day, child."

"He always has a bad day on my birthday." Josie hadn't realized it was true until she said it. But hadn't her father always seemed distracted on her special day? Wasn't he always like a ghost in the corner?

She thought back to Laurel's birthday, only two months ago. He'd taken them all out to Crusty's Pizza and he'd let her have Anna Tackett stay all night. The two had yakked half the night, keeping her awake, the sounds tunneling through their connecting bathroom.

Now Josie looked to her aunt for answers. Aunt Lola's mouth was tight, pressed into a flat line.

"Tell me." Had Josie done something wrong? Is that why her dad didn't like her? The thought drove a sharp peg into her heart. She'd never had that thought, though she realized it sounded true.

"Did I do something wrong?" The ache that had begun behind her eyes when she'd seen the locket formed tears that welled up, blurring her vision. She clutched the locket at her chest.

Aunt Lola turned. "No," she said firmly, then sighed hard. She looked out the window into the darkened yard. "I don't know why they kept it from you," she muttered.

A bad feeling started, swelling slowly, until Josie wasn't sure she wanted to know what Aunt Lola was talking about. She didn't like secrets. Not even good ones.

"It's not your fault. You ain't done a thing wrong, you understand?" Aunt Lola placed a finger under Josie's chin.

"Then what is it?"

Laurel called from the other room, "The movie's ready!"

Josie wanted to go in the living room with Laurel, wanted to go far away from Aunt Lola's answer, but her feet wouldn't move.

Aunt Lola answered Laurel, but her eyes never left Josie's. "She'll be right there." She turned and dried her hands on the towel hanging on the oven door, then scraped her hair off her face.

"All right, I suppose it's time you know. I sure didn't want to tell you on your special day, but now that your mom's gone and—" She shook her head like she needed a do-over.

Josie held the locket tightly, like it might protect her from her aunt's words. And somehow she knew she needed protection from them.

"When your mama was pregnant with you," Aunt Lola said, "there was another baby. Twins."

Twins? *When she was pregnant with me? How can that be?*

"What I mean is, you had a twin. A little boy. Your mama was pregnant with both of you at the same time."

She'd had a twin? Her breath caught. "What happened to him?"

Aunt Lola flinched. "He didn't make it, child. Sometimes these things happen. God knows what he's doing and we just have to trust in his plan. Your mama was almost to term when she went into labor and she lost him. Nearly lost you too."

How had she not known about this? Why had she lived and the other baby died? It didn't seem fair.

"Your daddy's just sad for the baby they lost." Aunt Lola turned and picked up another plate. "I suppose every man wants a son, and your daddy's no different. Especially with the orchard to pass down and all, he always had his heart fixed on a boy. Your daddy— well, it's nothing you did. You see that now."

Josie did see now. Her dad was sadder at the loss of the baby boy than he was happy to have her. And every birthday reminded him of what he'd lost. Kind of the way the pictures of her mom reminded him.

"When your mama got ill and passed away, he lost all hope of having a boy, I suppose. You might have noticed a headstone up at the family cemetery, next to your mom's. That's where your brother's buried."

Josie had only been up there once, for her mom's burial. And she hadn't seen anything that day but the blurry shape of her mom's casket against the frozen grass.

There was a new feeling where her stomach was, like someone had turned it into a heavy, wobbly water balloon.

"Your daddy's just sad today, is all. We need to pray for him." Aunt Lola scrubbed the cake from the plate.

Laurel called out then and Josie somehow found her way to the living room. The movie played, but Josie didn't see it. She wanted to go to bed, wanted her birthday to be over. She didn't want another birthday ever again. Aunt Lola had said it was sadness that drove her dad from the table, but even at ten, Josie knew it was more than that. She knew her dad blamed her for her brother's death.

twenty

Josie escaped the house while it was still quiet and not quite light out. The ground was damp from last night's drizzle and the horizon hinted there might be more coming. Maybe the sky would open up and pour down on them, and she could leave early for Asheville.

As if to mock her, the clouds parted and the sun peeked over the hill. *Happy birthday, Josie.*

She zipped her jacket against the cool air and walked toward Duncan's pen. She'd bought a sack of oats to round out his diet. He'd turned up his nose at the grains at first, but then she'd started putting it out in the evening when he was hungrier.

Now he lumbered toward the trough, bringing his pungent odor with him, as she poured the oats in. "There you go, Duncan." He'd scarf down the donuts, too, but at least he had some grains in him. She'd try wheat after the oats were gone.

Boone's car pulled over the hill, spitting pebbles.

"Looks like your donuts have arrived," she said. Duncan didn't even look up from his meal.

"'Morning," she said when the car pulled to a stop. She opened the back door and withdrew the boxes.

"'Morning, Josie."

Duncan snorted as she dumped the donuts into what was left of the oats. The smell of yeast and chocolate filled her nostrils. "Eat up, Dunky."

When she turned, Boone had joined her. He held out a colorful bouquet of flowers. "Happy birthday."

She couldn't believe he'd remembered—wished he hadn't—but it was awfully sweet of him. "Thanks, Boone."

Josie took the flowers, a spray of yellow daisies, chrysanthemums, purple asters, and miniature hot pink carnations. The wrapper sported a sticker with the Posey Peddler's logo.

He looked as shy as a schoolboy, standing there with his baseball hat in his hand. He'd always been so sweet to her. Spontaneously, she reached up and gave him a peck on the cheek.

His face bloomed as pink as the carnations. She smelled the flowers, breathing in their fresh, sweet scent.

"I heard you were driving down to Asheville today. Didn't know if I'd catch you before you left."

"I'm not going 'til after work." She hoped he hadn't mentioned her birthday to Jackie. But even if he had, her friend wasn't one to take note of things like birthdays.

"Apple Festival's coming up soon," Boone said, shifting his weight.

"Believe me, I know. We've been having apple pie for two weeks straight." And they'd probably be having it for the next month as Aunt Lola refined her recipe.

He grinned. "Aunt Lola took second to Nettie again last year."

"So I heard."

"So everyone in Shelbyville heard. Nettie wore that blue ribbon for a month."

"Aunt Lola's determined this is her year. Her pie is already a big seller for our store. Don't know why she has to have that silly ribbon."

"Well, I hope she gets it. Nettie's head is getting too big for that straw hat of hers."

Duncan snorted down the donuts noisily, and they watched in silence for a moment.

"You sticking around for the festival then?" Boone asked.

Josie shrugged. The good harvest would take them past the festival this year, which was fine since she wanted to be here when the babies were born. She hadn't made plans to attend the festival, but with the cost of gas and her draining funds, she'd probably be trapped here most weekends. "I suppose."

Boone set his cap back on his head. "Well, save me a dance on the square, ya hear?"

"Will do."

Grady pulled the coffee carafe from the maker, poured the brew into the thermos, then took a sip and unplugged the machine.

He'd done more research the night before and was eager to share with Josie how they could utilize the newer method of training the trees on a trellis. Instead of planting trees eight or ten feet apart, they could plant them eighteen inches apart and prune them to grow no higher than they could reach without a ladder.

He'd been wanting to move toward this method for a couple of years, but the orchard hadn't been profitable enough to make it feasible. They could start with a few hundred saplings though, and go from there. It would take several years before they produced apples, but it would be a start.

Grady put on his work boots, grabbed his thermos, and headed to his truck. He was thinking of asking Josie over for a movie. *Just so we can talk about the orchard.*

It wouldn't hurt to soften her with a chick flick before he broached the tricky subject.

Yeah, that's why you want her to come over.

He turned over the truck engine, and it rumbled loudly, breaking the morning silence. *You have all day, minus the afternoon, to talk about the orchard with Josie.*

Dawn was waking the night sky, and when he approached Duncan's pen, he saw Josie and Boone near the fence. They were standing close together, then Josie reached up and kissed Boone. On the cheek? The lips? It was hard to tell from here.

Either way, the gesture filled his gut with lead and something else even less comfortable. Hadn't she been moony-eyed with Grady only a week ago? Now she was getting affectionate with Boone?

Just like Danielle.

Maybe she has an ulterior motive for getting into your head, did you ever think of that?

The thought had nibbled at him before, but he'd dismissed it before letting it settle in. She wanted to sell the orchard, and sure, she could do what she wanted as long as Laurel agreed. But it wouldn't hurt to have him on her side. Is that why she was being so nice to him, why she'd taken refuge in his cabin last week?

That was the thought that was circling his brain when he pulled his truck alongside Josie and Boone.

Josie turned a smile up at him. "Good morning."

He couldn't miss the bouquet she held. He lifted his chin in greeting.

"'Morning," Boone called as he got in his car. "Well, y'all have a good one."

Josie waved, then turned toward Grady, but he was already easing his foot on the accelerator.

"See you in the field." He didn't care if she was put off by his abruptness. He'd been stupid to think she might like him and even more stupid to let a woman like her too close.

twenty-one

I wish you weren't leaving after supper," Laurel said.

Josie finished setting the table and took a seat beside her sister. Grady and Nate hadn't arrived yet. She felt guilty at the sight of Laurel's crestfallen face.

"You know I never cared much for birthdays." The sooner it was over, the happier she would be.

Laurel looked like she wanted to say something, but the door opened and Grady and Nate entered. Her sister knew about her twin who had died, but they never spoke of it. The topic had been avoided throughout her childhood as if the mention of it would be the final straw that broke their dad.

Guilt pressed down hard on her heart, a feeling that had grown so familiar it was a constant companion. A feeling that had only gotten worse when Ian had died. *Died saving you. Saving someone who'd never been meant to live in the first place.*

"Happy birthday, Josie," Nate said, settling into his chair.

Grady's chair grated across the floor. "Oh, I didn't know." His eyes bounced off hers. "Happy birthday." The words were a reluctant concession.

Once they were seated, Aunt Lola started a prayer. "Our dearest heavenly Father, we thank thee for the many blessings . . ."

Grady's hand was warm and rough against hers, his grip just tight enough for their palms to be touching. He'd been distant all day. After their connection at his cabin, they'd been on friendly terms, but he'd been back to his old self in the field, speaking only when necessary.

". . . For it's in your good name we pray, amen."

Josie pulled her hand away, missing the contact. Aunt Lola and Laurel kept the conversation rolling during supper. Grady was quieter than usual, and Josie was counting the minutes until she could leave.

Just after supper was finished, Aunt Lola brought out the Mississippi mud cake with one candle flickering on top. It was like every birthday throughout her childhood. She could almost smell her dad's pipe and his Old Spice cologne. She could almost hear his footsteps as he walked away from the table.

Josie pretended to make a wish, then blew out the candle. Aunt Lola served the cake, and when they were all stuffed from the sweet dessert, Laurel handed her a small, lumpy package.

The paper came off easily, revealing a handmade strap for her camera. Tiny colorful threads were woven tightly in a wide band that would hold her camera securely. A thicker piece cushioned the part that went around the neck.

"I wasn't able to go shopping . . . ," Laurel said.

"Are you kidding? I love it."

"I noticed your camera strap—"

"Is falling apart," Josie finished. "It's beautiful. It must've taken weeks." She fingered the intricate webbing of the threads.

Laurel grinned. "What else do I have to do?"

"You should sell these online. Seriously, you could charge a fortune for custom-made straps."

"She's right, hon," Nate said.

Some of Josie's photographer acquaintances in Louisville would love one of these.

"Well, I may have all the time in the world at the moment." She patted her belly. "But once these two arrive, I won't have time to brush my teeth."

"Don't you worry. You know we'll pitch in," Aunt Lola said. She handed Josie a box wrapped with gold foil and a pretty bow.

"The cake was plenty, Aunt Lola." Josie removed the bow and opened the package. It was a box of chocolate pecan patties from Confectionately Yours, the chocolate shop owned by two of Aunt Lola's church friends.

A smile tugged at her lips. "It's been years since I've bitten into one of these. Thank you."

"You're getting too thin," Aunt Lola said. "And so far, my cooking isn't helping. A man likes a little meat on the bones, doesn't he, Grady?"

Grady pushed his plate back, clearing his throat. "Whatever you say, Aunt Lola."

A change of topic was in order. "Well." Josie scooted her chair back. "Thanks everyone. But I need to get on the road if I want to make it to Asheville before dark."

After kissing Aunt Lola on the cheek, Josie headed up the stairs for her bags, almost giddy with the thought of the weekend trip.

twenty-two

*J*osie wiped the sweat from her forehead with the back of her hand and reached for another apple. The sun was climbing high in the sky and its rays beat down relentlessly. Since she was perched at the top of the ladder, the sun had full access to her back, and she felt a trickle of sweat carve a path between her shoulder blades.

She could even smell the heat. Was it too much to ask for a little breeze? The crew started a slow tune, Hernando's bass voice carrying over all the others. She bagged another apple, grimacing when the branch snapped back and smacked her cheek.

It was one of those days. She'd left Asheville early this morning and made the trek home. Her stomach had felt unsettled all morning. She was hot and tired and drained. She'd enjoyed spending time with her friends, but she'd had a nightmare that clung to her like an itchy wool sweater. In her sleep she'd relived the night Ian had died. But this time, instead of the creek being frozen, it was a watery grave with rippling arms that sucked him under. She could see his face, his eyes.

Josie shook the haunting image from her head. Why had he done it? Why, when all she'd ever done was push him away?

It was an unsolvable riddle that spun around her mind all the time.

The migrants' tune ended and no one started another. It was too hot to sing. Josie pulled a rubber band from her shorts pocket and gathered her hair in a ponytail.

Even so, the air that assaulted her bare neck was thick and heavy with humidity. She longed for the air-conditioning at the house or at least a cool breeze. Her throat was parched, her tongue clinging to the roof of her mouth.

Maybe she needed a water break. Josie checked her watch. It was nearly time to relieve Aunt Lola, but she might as well finish the tree. She reached for a distant apple.

The motion disoriented her, and a wave of dizziness washed over her. Her head swam. She blinked hard and swayed.

Josie grabbed for the ladder, but she was already falling. Her arms reached for the ground even as her feet tangled in the rungs.

She hit the ground with a thud. The ladder crashed beside her, clanging as it landed.

"Josie!"

She heard her name in that instant before her brain registered the pain in her knee and on her palms. She took stock of her body parts.

Does anything else hurt? She rolled over and sat up. Her hands had broken her fall. *You're okay.*

"*Señorita* Josie!" Miguel was the first one to her side.

"I—I'm okay."

Grady was there, kneeling at her side. "Don't move." He poked around her knee, dusting away the grass clippings and dirt.

It was scraped and already red. It hurt like the dickens.

"Does anything hurt?"

My pride? It was sprained at least, possibly fractured.

"I'm fine. Just let me up." She brushed his hands away and pulled herself to her feet.

Miguel was picking up the ladder. Hernando gave her a bottled water.

"*Gracias*, Hernando." She uncapped the bottle and drew from it, feeling sillier by the moment.

"Can you walk?" Grady asked.

Josie capped the bottle. "Of course I can walk." She took a step and her leg nearly buckled under her.

He reached out as if to catch her, but she caught herself and batted away his hands. "I'm fine." She took a few steps. Her knee was fine. Just a little sore.

"You get dizzy, Miss Josie?" Miguel asked. "You need to get out of heat."

Her dizziness wasn't from the heat, but it was a convenient excuse. "Maybe so. It's time to relieve Aunt Lola anyway." Josie started for her car.

Grady caught up to her. "I'll drive you."

What, he was being so nice all of a sudden after ignoring her all day? "I can drive myself." She tried to walk without favoring her good leg and winced.

"Stop being so stubborn." He took her elbow and steered her to his truck and opened the door.

Fine. Have it your way. She didn't understand the man. One week he was distant and brooding, the next he was teasing her, and the week after that he was back to being distant and brooding. *Like I need more complications in my life.*

Grady started the truck and it roared to life, covering the thumping of his heart. Josie had given him the scare of his life.

He'd seen her climbing the ladder over an hour ago and had almost stopped her. A woman in her condition shouldn't be working on a ladder. He'd bit his tongue though, and now look what happened.

When he'd heard the sickening thud of her body hitting the ground, heard the smash of the ladder falling behind her, his stomach was in his throat. He should've said something. He shouldn't have let his foolish pride stop him.

He slapped the steering wheel, then felt Josie's sharp glance.

"I could've driven myself. I'm fine." He couldn't help but notice the way her hand lay protectively over her flat stomach.

"You shouldn't have been on the ladder in the first place."

"It's a little hard to pick the top of the tree without one."

"You're in no condition for that job."

He rounded a bend, then gunned the engine, taking them up the hill. In the rearview mirror, dirt rolled out from the wheels, making a plume of dust.

"Condition?" she asked.

Well, he'd done it now. Stepped right in a pile of cow dung. There was no going back now, and it served her right anyway. How long did she think she could conceal it? She wasn't showing yet, but in another month or two . . .

He unlocked his teeth. "I know about the—the baby." He didn't dare look at her. She might see the things he was working so hard to hide. But, darn it, why didn't the woman take better care of herself?

"The *baby*?"

"I might be a man, but I'm not stupid. I saw Laurel go through all that, remember? The dizziness, the nausea, the fatigue—"

He was interrupted by a bark of laughter. "What is it with everyone?"

He glared at her. She was laughing? Wasn't she the least bit concerned for the—

"I am not pregnant." She pressed her fingers to her temple, mumbling. "Are you kidding me? My last date was . . . too long ago to remember."

"Why the nausea? The dizziness, the fall off the ladder?"

She looked out the window, the smile fading.

"It's hot, in case you haven't noticed. I guess I don't tolerate it very well. And I'm not used to working outside all day in the heat."

"That's all?"

She turned and looked him squarely in the eye. "I am not pregnant. Not now, never have been."

She looked sincere, her eyebrows raised, her head tipping slowly forward, waiting for him to reply.

She held up two fingers, locked together, a sarcastic smile on her lips. "Scout's honor."

He applied his foot to the brake as he slowed for the turn. His lips twitched as he pulled into the drive. She'd probably never been a scout. Even so, he believed her.

A slow whoosh of air drained from Grady's lungs. Relief that she wasn't involved with someone. His reaction should've scared him, but instead left him buoyant and hopeful.

twenty-three

Josie grabbed the tire swing, put her legs through the opening, and pushed off. The scent of lilacs carried on the breeze from the bush at the corner of the house, and she inhaled the familiar smell. Four days after her fall, the pain in her knee had subsided, and even the dizziness and nausea had faded.

Maybe I will make it through harvest. If she could just get the job done, convince Laurel to sell, and get back to Louisville before her health declined further. She didn't want Laurel to see her like that, didn't want to be a burden on her sister. And she didn't want anyone to stand in the way of her decision.

"Hey there." Nate came through the back door and sat on the stoop. He'd shed his dress shirt in favor of a beige T-shirt.

"Hey." The swing's motion was starting to affect her equilibrium. She dragged her feet through the long grass, scraping to a stop.

Nate looked like a dog who'd been kicked to the curb. Laurel hadn't been in the best of moods over supper, and to give Nate credit, he'd spent the evening trying to make her comfortable.

"Needed an escape?" she asked.

"This isn't her best side. Poor thing, she's miserable."

"The hormones don't help."

He nodded thoughtfully. "She enjoyed making that camera strap for you. She showed me her progress every night."

"It's beautiful and unique. She really could sell those, you know." Josie wrapped her arms around the tire and propped her chin on it. The faint smell of worn rubber reached her nose.

"I think it's reviving her dream of selling crafts."

"Really?" Maybe the bed rest was what she needed to remember her passion. She'd been so busy meeting all her obligations that she'd forgotten what she loved. Laurel used to talk all the time about owning a shop where she sold her hats, scarves, and handmade accessories. Maybe she couldn't open a shop for a while, not with the babies coming, but these days selling things was as simple as having an eBay account.

"Maybe it would be a good time for you to mention selling the orchard again," he said. "She might be open to it now."

"Or *you* could mention it . . ."

Nate stood slowly, shoving his hands in his pockets. "Or *you* could . . ."

"Coward." Josie pulled a face. "All right, I'll do it. But I'm waiting for a better mood."

He tossed a sardonic grin over his shoulder. "Smart move."

After he left, Josie closed her eyes. A gentle breeze cooled her skin. The tree above her shimmied, its leaves rustling, and somewhere on the hill two birds tweeted back and forth in conversation.

A distant rumble grew louder until she heard the popping of gravel and the squeal of tired brakes. When she opened her eyes, Grady was pulling his truck to a stop, his elbow protruding from the gaping window.

She hadn't expected to see him after supper. He wore a clean T-shirt and a timid smile.

"That's a precarious place for a nap," he said.

"Not as precarious as in there." She jerked her chin toward the house.

His grin widened. Did he have any idea how handsome he was? No, that was part of his appeal.

"I think I owe you a movie if you're up for it." He reached for something, then held up a white plastic bag.

"Whatcha got? Let me guess. *Jaws 2*."

"Give me some credit. I promised you a chick flick."

This ought to be good. The thought of him facing Berta Combs at the Pick-a-Flick checkout with a chick flick amused her. That must've put a dent in his masculinity. "You picked a movie for me?"

"Three of them. And you'd better say yes because I'm not going through that process again."

She untangled her feet from the swing. "How can a girl refuse an offer like that?"

Josie hopped in the truck, and he drove her to the cabin. Once there, he opened the door for her, then disappeared into the kitchen.

"Popcorn?" he called.

"No, thanks. I'm still full from supper."

A few minutes later, he returned with two glasses of soda.

"Been to the grocery, I see."

He shot her a look and handed her the bag with the DVDs. "Take your pick."

The bag yielded a surprisingly good selection: *The Lake House*, *While You Were Sleeping*, and *You've Got Mail*.

"You totally had help with this." Josie sank onto the sofa.

He perched on the recliner's edge. "I'm in touch with my feminine side."

The remark, a sharp contrast with the bulk of his frame and the manly squareness of his jawline, drew a cynical smile from her.

"Okay, so I had a little help." He flipped on the TV.

"Well, whoever advised you has impeccable taste. I love all three."

"You've seen them all?"

"I could watch any of these a dozen times." Josie shuffled the cases in her hand, deciding.

"We probably have time for two if you want."

She handed him *You've Got Mail*.

He looked at the cover. "Tom Hanks and Meg Ryan, huh?"

"You're in for a treat."

He humphed.

While he put in the DVD, she set her soda on the end table and propped her bare feet on the stuffed ottoman. Her toenails bore the remnants of pale pink polish that Jackie had loaned her upon seeing her neglected feet. When he started the movie, she flipped the light switch and the lamps went dark. Evening light filtered through his bare windows.

He settled in the recliner, but she wished he'd opted for the sofa. He seemed so far away. *Get a grip, Josie. You're here for the movie, to escape the hormonal path of your sister, not to cozy up on the couch with Grady.*

She shifted sideways so the TV was her focus.

Almost two hours later, she'd forgotten everything but the growing romance between Kathleen Kelly and Joe Fox. By the time Brinkley trotted around the bend in the park, Josie was hugging a pillow, wishing the movie wasn't almost over.

Her heart softened as the two came together. *"Don't cry, Shopgirl, don't cry."*

"I wanted it to be you. I wanted it to be you so badly."

The couple embraced, Brinkley jumped on Joe, and the camera floated upward, looking down on them as the soundtrack played "Over the Rainbow."

Ah, what a movie. Josie slowly became aware of her surroundings as the credits rolled. She glanced at Grady, wanting his take on the movie.

Before she could ask, she heard a snort over the soundtrack. The night had colored the sky inky black and only the flickering TV lit the room. Even so, she could see Grady's eyes were closed, his mouth open.

She squeezed the pillow with her fist and hurled it at him Frisbee-style. It hit him square in the chest.

He jumped, opening his eyes, looking around.

"You have got to be kidding me," she said.

"What? Why'd you do that?"

"Have you no shame? *You've Got Mail* is a *classic*, arguably the most romantic movie of all time."

He sat up straight. "I was just resting my eyes."

"You were snoring."

He stood and stretched. "I think I'd better go make some popcorn."

If he was tired, maybe she should leave. "We don't have to watch another one."

"Might as well," he said over his shoulder. "I have to return them tomorrow." She watched him walk to the kitchen, his long denim-clad legs taking their time.

She decided on *The Lake House* and put it in the DVD player. It was more guy friendly.

"Ready for popcorn?" he called.

She remembered the bland variety from last time and was about to turn it down.

"I got the good kind."

She was tempted, especially now that the buttery smell of popping corn wafted into the room. Still, she didn't want to get nauseated. "No, thanks," she called.

When Grady returned he started the movie and settled into the recliner, munching away.

It took her awhile to get caught up in the movie. She was too conscious of Grady sitting across the room. When he finished his popcorn, he thrust his legs out on the leg rest and laced his hands together across his stomach.

Focus on the movie.

Awhile later, she peeked at Grady again. He was still awake, a good sign.

As the movie zinged back and forth through time, Josie felt her limbs getting heavy. It had been especially hot, and she was used to turning in early these days. The sun sapped her energy, and the long days in the orchard were taking a toll on her body.

She sank deeper into the sofa and laid her head back on the soft cushion. She was going to regret staying up late when the alarm sounded in the morning. Still, it was Friday night, and a girl had to have a life. At least it wasn't a scary movie.

Grady still seemed to be watching with interest. It was a movie you had to follow closely or the movements between time became confusing.

Josie curled her legs under her, and when her toes grew cold, she tucked them between the cushions, feeling the nubby material of the sofa against the balls of her feet. She grabbed the other pillow and put it under her cheek. With each breath, she smelled the unique combination of pine and musk that was all Grady.

Before she could stop herself, she inhaled deeply, wanting to hold the air in her lungs for a while longer.

The cushions of the couch seemed to envelop her, and her tired bones sank gratefully into them. The movie played, and out on the porch, a cricket kept time with a hypnotic rhythm.

After a while, a quiet hush replaced the chirping.

Then someone was calling her name, but she didn't want to answer. The soft peace of the world where she lay was not easily abandoned.

"Josie." A man's voice.

Then a whisper of a touch across her cheek.

Her eyes opened and she stared up at Grady. Credits were rolling on the muted TV. She was sprawled on his couch. He was perched on the edge, his hand stretching across her to the sofa's back.

"Resting your eyes?" His words barely broke the silence.

She'd slept so hard she'd forgotten where she was. But now that she remembered, now that Grady was so close, his hip grazing her thigh . . .

Grady watched Josie register her whereabouts. He'd known she was asleep the last thirty minutes of the movie. He'd lost interest in the story, taking the opportunity to observe her unnoticed. He'd watched her breathing, her limbs going loose around the pillow, her face softening. A lock of hair had fallen across her cheek, and he'd wanted to brush it back, tuck it behind her ear.

It was the first thing he'd done when he'd come to wake her up. Now, as she stared at him with those sleepy eyes, he wanted to do more than wake her.

He reached out again and brushed the hair off her shoulder, wanting to feel the soft silkiness between his fingers again.

When he looked back into her eyes, there was a question. He had plenty of his own, but right now, he didn't want to think about that.

Right now he thought about how gentle Josie had been with Ted Barrow. He thought about the way she waited on her sister, the way she sassed him sometimes with her sarcasm.

But underneath it all, in the depths of her eyes, there was an indefinable sadness. Even now, her eyes locked on his, he saw it.

And wanted to eradicate it. He closed the distance between them, brushing her lips with his. The barely-there touch sent a jolt of something electric through him.

She returned the kiss, yielding to him. He pulled her closer. His heart felt like it might explode from the confines of his rib cage. He hadn't felt this way since . . .

Had he ever felt this way? Even in the early days with Danielle?

Danielle.

The memory of her betrayal tainted the moment and he pushed it away.

Josie touched his face, her fingers gliding down his jaw, leaving a hot trail.

Slow down, man. You have got to slow down. Think.

But it felt so good, the way she returned his kiss. Being wanted again, he'd forgotten how heady it could make a man feel.

Danielle made you feel wanted too, remember? Then she slept with your best friend.

Josie wouldn't do that. She's not like that.

Isn't she? How much do you really know about her?

It was true. He'd only known her a matter of weeks. Gathering all the restraint he could muster, he pulled away.

Josie's eyes opened, filled with questions again. Different ones. Ones he didn't want to answer.

He looked away before he could be drawn back in. Somewhere on the porch a cricket chirped, and over the thudding of his heart, he gradually became aware of the faint strains of the crew's music.

He shouldn't have kissed her. They had to work together. She was going to leave in a matter of weeks. She wanted to sell the orchard.

"I'm sorry." He ran his hand over his face, trying to erase her touch. It was the movies, all the romance. It got him thinking wrong.

Josie was still and silent. What was she thinking? God only knew.

twenty-four

Sorry? He's sorry?

Josie lay on the couch, a ball of mortification curling in her gut. Clearly she hadn't been sorry. That had been evident in her feverish response to his kiss.

Sorry?

Not exactly the magical movie ending to their first and probably only kiss.

He stood and distanced himself from her. And that's what he was doing; it didn't take a genius to see it.

She cleared her throat, sitting up, then swung her feet to the floor. She wanted to escape, but the humiliation was going to follow her like the stench of a skunk.

"I shouldn't have done that," he said, apparently not realizing he should quit while he was ahead. Or at least no further behind than he already was. Didn't he know it was the last thing she wanted to hear after he'd kissed her socks off? It was like taking a beautiful Ansel Adams photograph and smearing it with ink.

"It's okay." It was the only thing she could say at a time like this. What else was there? *Really? I'm not.* Pride removed the option of honesty.

Standing, she found her Birkenstocks by the door and slid into them.

"No, really—," he continued, making a halfhearted effort to approach her.

He was going to say it again. *Stupid man.*

"I should be going," she cut in quickly. "It's late. We're tired." Yeah, that's what it was. Fatigue. It made them connect like supercharged magnets and then forced those lame words from Grady's mouth.

"Josie—"

"It's okay. See you in the morning." She slid out the door and pulled it behind her. She took the porch steps quickly and hurried outside the halo of the porch light as if she'd disappear when she reached the darkness. If only.

She hugged herself against the chill in the air. There was no moon to light her way tonight, and her foot hit the corner of a flagstone, tripping her. As her foot caught her weight, her knee buckled, igniting the pain that had nearly healed from her fall off the ladder.

I'm sorry.

What was he sorry about anyway? Sorry he was attracted to her? Sorry he'd shown a little emotion? Sorry their kiss had lit a bonfire under him?

Or maybe it hadn't. Maybe it had only lit a fire under her.

Oh, there's a nice thought.

If that was the case, he had plenty to be sorry about.

It was just a kiss, Josie. Just a stupid, ordinary kiss between two consenting adults. A kiss he was sorry about.

Her feet swished through the grass as she passed the side of the house. The swishes seemed to repeat the word she wanted to forget. *Sor-ry, sor-ry, sor-ry.*

She was relieved when she reached the porch and left the echo of the word in the yard. Upstairs, she readied for bed, tossing aside the hoodie she still hadn't returned to Grady, and flipped off her lamp. Upon closing her eyes, her traitorous mind reviewed the kiss in slow-motion detail. Her breaths thinned at the memory.

Aggravated with herself, Josie flopped over hard, punching down the pillow.

She was the one who should be sorry. Why get attached to Grady? He was tied to a place she wanted to escape—a place she needed to sell.

There was no future here. No future at all.

She was the one who was sorry. She humphed aloud as if the punctuated sound could make the statement a reality, then pulled the sheet over her head.

"Okay, spill," Laurel said the next afternoon, the second the door closed behind Grady. Nate had gone to mow while there was still daylight, and Aunt Lola was cooking supper.

Josie eased onto the couch beside Laurel and flipped on the TV. "What do you mean?"

"Don't play innocent with me. The tension was thicker than a valley fog in here."

"Don't be melodramatic." To the contrary, the day had been anticlimactic. Josie had tossed in bed all night, fretting, yet Grady hadn't said a word about the kiss.

Laurel grabbed the remote and flipped off the TV.

Josie noted the frown lines between her sister's hazel eyes.

"Listen here. I'm stuck in this house all day and night with nothing but my knitting needles for company, and if you have a juicy detail or two, I think you should show a little mercy and share, don't you?"

"When you put it like that . . ."

"Did something happen last night?" Laurel turned toward her, tried to pull her knee up, then gave up when her stomach got in the way. She leaned forward, eager like a cat that just heard a can opener.

"We watched a movie. Two, actually."

"Yeah, yeah. What happened after?"

Josie sighed. "Don't you want to know which movies we watched?"

"Fine. What were they?"

"*You've Got Mail* and *The Lake House*."

She nodded. "Good picks. Go on."

Josie's thoughts went back to the night before for the hundredth time. The way Grady's lips had felt on hers. He'd been so gentle, his touch the barest of whispers. Just the thought of it sent a shiver up her spine.

"Earth to Josie." Laurel wore an expectant grin.

"Sorry. Okay, after the second movie, or actually, during the second movie, I kind of dozed off."

"You fell asleep?"

"Well, he dozed during *You've Got Mail*."

"Never mind. Keep going."

"Well, I'm trying, but you keep interrupting."

Laurel made a zipping motion across her lips.

"Okay, so I dozed off, and next thing I know, I wake up and the movie's over." He'd been perched there, so close, and the look on his face . . . Ah, if she could bottle that look and sell it, she'd be a millionaire.

"Anyway, he's sitting there on the edge of the couch."

"Wait, where are you?"

"On the couch. When I woke, I was lying on my side and he was sitting, like, in the cradle between my arms and knees. Sheesh, you really are desperate."

"Shut up. No, go on."

"He was looking at me like . . . I don't know. I can't explain it. And then he brushed my hair back and kissed me." She shrugged. "That's it."

"That is so not it. Was it just a touch? Or was it more passionate? Where did you put your hands? How long did it last?"

Josie shrugged. There was no way she was going to admit it was the best kiss she'd had. "It was nice." *Liar. It was way more than that.* "*Was* being the key word."

"What do you mean?"

Even now the memory put a hole in her stomach. "Remember when you waited all summer for Evan Rodgers to notice you? Remember when he finally kissed you?"

Laurel's brows knotted. "Yeah . . ."

"Remember what he said afterward?" Her sister had been devastated. Especially when Evan had gotten back with his exgirlfriend the following week.

The lines eased off Laurel's forehead and her mouth tightened. "Grady did not say he was sorry."

Josie nodded.

Laurel leaned back on the cushion and laced her hands over her swollen belly. "Men can be so stupid. What did he say this morning?"

"He acted like it never happened."

Laurel seemed to be digesting this bit of information. Well, if she could figure it out, more power to her.

"He may not have said anything," Laurel finally said. "But I'm telling you, there were vibes bouncing all over the room a minute ago. Trust me, pregnancy has boosted my intuition."

Pregnancy had done more for her moods than her intuition, but Josie wasn't going to be the one to say it.

"No, really," Laurel said. "It's true. Anyway, there ought to be something positive to balance out all this other stuff. Speaking of which, I gotta go to the bathroom again. I swear I have a bladder the size of a peanut. Don't go anywhere, we're not done yet."

Josie helped her off the couch and Laurel waddled across the room and down the hall.

Josie went to the kitchen and offered to help Aunt Lola, but she was shooed away. When she returned to the living room, Laurel was plopping back in her spot next to the end table.

"Need anything? More tea?" Josie asked.

"No, thanks. So, why do you think he was sorry?" Laurel switched gears with the delicacy of a Ford beater.

Josie sighed. "I don't know." *As if I haven't been circling that thought all day.* Circling like a vulture, round and round and round, never finding a spot to land.

"Were you?"

"Was I what?"

Laurel gave her a *hel-lo?* look. "Sorry. Were you sorry, or were you hoping it would lead somewhere?"

Josie gave it some thought. Actually, she'd given it thought all day, picking apples, trying to ignore Grady's presence. Who was she kidding? He was her focus all day, whether she'd wanted him to be or not.

Was she sorry? "It's complicated."

"How so?"

Josie turned so her back was against the armrest and cradled a pillow in her lap. "Part of me is sorry. The part that thinks logically and long-term. The other part of me enjoyed getting my socks knocked off."

A grin widened on Laurel's face. "He knocked your socks off?"

"Both of them," she admitted. "Or would have, if I'd been wearing any." It was a humiliating admission after Grady's lack of enthusiasm.

"So, what's the problem? Other than that he's sorry, I mean."

Josie shot her a thanks-for-the-reminder look. Did she really want to get into this now? She'd told Nate she would, and Laurel wasn't going to get better anytime soon.

"Grady's committed to the orchard, in case you haven't noticed." Josie said the next as gently as she could. "And I don't want to stay here, honey. I know you want me to, but there's just too many . . . too many reasons I can't."

How could Laurel understand? It had been so much easier for her. Her dad had accepted her. And she wasn't the one who lived with the guilt and shame from Ian's death.

"You still want to sell."

Now was her chance to push hard. "We're bringing in a great harvest. The land will go for maximum value if we move quickly."

Laurel looked away.

"You could continue to make your accessories and sell them. I'm telling you, that camera strap you made would be a hit with photographers."

Laurel seemed to be mulling over the idea, and it buoyed Josie's hopes.

"Imagine not having the worries of the orchard. The pruning, the picking, the mowing, the payroll, the hiring of migrants, the uncertainty of the weather . . . you'll have enough on your hands with the twins."

Laurel sighed. "I know."

"You'd still have the house and we could keep a few acres around it. We wouldn't be losing our heritage, you know. It's just land and trees. Our heritage is right here." She placed her hand over her heart.

Josie continued. "You could knit and sew in your spare time and sell things on eBay without having to leave the house."

Laurel ran her hand over her belly. "I don't know."

"Are you at least considering it?"

Laurel's sigh seemed to come from deep inside. "I am, I promise. And I'm sorry if I came across bossy when I asked you to stay before. I know you're a grown woman now, but old habits die hard." She gave a sheepish smile.

"Supper's ready!" Aunt Lola called from the kitchen.

"Apology accepted." Josie stood and pulled Laurel to her feet.

Josie squeezed her sister's hand. "I'll call Nate in." As she went out the back door, she recognized the relief for what it was. Laurel was close to giving in. Little did her sister know that if she insisted on hanging on to the orchard, it would end up being a burden she carried alone.

twenty-five

It was a bad day from the moment Josie awoke. First, it was Monday, which meant she had six days in the orchard to look forward to. Second, her stomach was unsettled before she untangled her feet from the covers. Third, she had to face Grady again.

She took an extra-long shower, noting how dark her skin had become. She'd strived for a tan in her teen years. But this darkness wasn't from her long hours in the sun so much as a symptom of her illness. She knew this because the tan didn't stop at her clothes.

Deciding to skip breakfast, she filled a thermos with coffee and set out to the orchard. On her way out the door, she found Duncan in the yard, standing over Aunt Lola's flowers, and realized she must've left his pen open the night before. The yellow pansies and orange marigolds lining the walk were crushed. It took fifteen minutes and a slice of leftover apple pie to get Duncan corralled. She'd have to worry about Aunt Lola and the flowers later.

The crew was just arriving as she pulled her car into the Winesap grove. They would start and finish that variety this week. The bulk of the remaining apples ripened in mid-October and would be ready for picking next week: Fuji, Goldrush, Granny Smith, Pink

Lady, and Limbertwig. They'd be busy getting those off the trees through November, hoping and praying for the absence of wind and rainy periods that brought fungus.

Josie greeted the crew and grabbed a bag, starting on a semi-dwarf toward the top of the hill, far away from Grady's trailer. The day promised to be cooler. Already a thick layer of clouds hung low in the sky, shadowing the mountains, and the air smelled vaguely of rain.

She picked for two hours before her stomach settled enough for coffee and by then she had a caffeine headache. Taking a break with the others, she dug two Advil from her purse, swallowed them with a gulp of coffee, then perched on the open tailgate of the pickup truck, grateful for the reprieve.

The crew spoke in rapid Spanish. A slow drizzle started as they returned to work, but that didn't stop the men from singing.

Within five minutes Josie's hair hung in limp clumps. The coffee had unsettled her stomach and the Advil wasn't working. Her muscles ached more than usual. She checked her watch, hoping time was going faster than she thought. No such luck. It was three more hours until her turn to stay with Laurel.

She reached for another apple, twisting it from the branch, then she bagged it. Her stomach was not pleased that she'd forced coffee upon it. It churned and cramped, offended.

Was she going to get sick? Her stomach spasmed in response to the thought. Josie scanned the area for a private place just in case. Behind the trailer? She didn't want to be sick in front of everyone. Especially not Grady. He was facing the other direction on a ladder at a semidwarf, the trailer just beyond him.

But if she went over the ridge and down the hill, she'd be out of sight. Hopefully it wouldn't come to that.

She reached for the next apple and the next. Before she got the third apple in the bag, she felt the unmistakable sensation of impending disaster. She shrugged off the bag and scrambled up the hill, then down the other side.

She was ten feet from the top when her stomach expelled its contents. She bent over, heaving.

Her stomach cramped, her pulse pounded at her temples. She caught her breath, hoping it was over. She was out of sight, far enough down the hill, and the migrants' singing had covered the sound of her retching.

Her legs shook like a sapling in a windstorm, and her hands trembled as she straightened and wiped her leaking eyes. That's when she saw Grady standing near the top of the hill.

Grady had tried not to notice Josie all day. He hadn't seen her since Saturday when they'd carefully avoided the subject of the kiss. But no matter how hard he'd tried, he'd been aware of her every movement.

He'd followed her with his eyes so often, it was a wonder he'd gotten any work done. But he couldn't seem to stop. He'd known something was wrong when she dashed up the hill, her shoulders stiff.

Now, as she straightened and turned, her eyes still glassy from her ordeal, apprehension cast a thick shadow over his thoughts.

She swayed slightly and he rushed to her side, taking her elbow.

"Sit down." His voice was gruffer than he intended. He pulled her under the nearest tree and helped her sit.

"I'm fine." Josie wiped the raindrops off her face and turned away.

She wasn't fine. A week ago she fell off a ladder and now she just puked up coffee. Had she lied to him about being pregnant? He squatted beside her, studying her. She was still shaking as she wiped her mouth with the back of her hand. He was torn between fetching her a glass of water and interrogating her.

"You're not fine," he said.

She shrugged. "It's just the—"

"Don't even say it's the heat, Josie. It's seventy-two degrees and raining."

She looked away, her eyes scanning the dozens of trees as if she might pick an answer from one of them.

The migrants ended a tune and started another in the gap of silence.

Josie's head fell against the bark of the tree as if her neck hadn't the strength to support it. Her eyes were bloodshot, tired-looking.

Fatigue, nausea, dizziness. She had all the symptoms, even if she had denied it once. Maybe it was none of his business, but he needed to know the truth. "Are you pregnant?"

That roused her. Her head rolled toward him and her eyes narrowed. "*No.* I already told you I wasn't." Somewhere she'd found the energy for anger.

But if it wasn't that, what was it? He'd seen signs of illness all along. And if the dizzy spells weren't from the heat, what was causing them?

"You need to see a doctor."

She leaned forward, readying to stand. "I don't need a doctor."

"Like heck you don't." He took her elbow, stilling her. "I've watched you get dizzy and fall off a ladder and puke your guts up. Where I come from, that means you're sick."

She pulled her elbow from his grasp. "I'm fine. I was just a little queasy. I should've eaten breakfast."

She had to know something was wrong. He stood and held out his hand. "Come on. I'll take you now."

Josie took his hand and stood, dusting off her damp jeans. "I don't need a doctor." As if belying her words, she swayed suddenly, reaching for the tree.

Grady grabbed for her waist, steadying her. Water dripped from the leaves above onto her face.

"You can walk to my truck, or I'll pick you up and carry you. Your choice."

He saw something in her eyes before she closed them. A flicker of something. He thought he was going to have to follow through on his threat.

A shadow passed over her green eyes, turning them stormy gray. She leaned against the tree. "I'm sick, okay? I already know that."

The words, her tone, planted a seed of fear deep in his bones. Sick? What kind of sick? He watched her, looking for a sign that this illness was some passing food poisoning or harmless virus. The clues he saw, the frown tugging her mouth, the furrow between her brows, weren't reassuring.

"What's wrong?" he asked, suddenly unsure he wanted to know.

He could hear Hernando's deep chuckle in the distance over the rain pattering on the leaves. Wind ruffled the tree branches and he heard the familiar sound of a few apples thunking on the ground nearby.

"I have a disease. It makes me sick sometimes, that's all."

But that wasn't all. He could see it on her face. She wasn't telling him everything; she was a terrible liar.

"How sick?" Dread stilled his heart, made the air catch in his lungs.

Josie pulled away from the tree. "It doesn't matter."

Grady grabbed her arm. "It matters to me." He didn't know how much until now.

She looked at him finally, one corner of her mouth pulling into a wry grin. "Let's just say you don't want to get too attached."

What did that mean? She couldn't mean it the way it sounded. She was going to . . . die? But the sadness he'd seen all along, rooted in her eyes, began to make sense. Grady felt something deep in his gut he hadn't felt since he'd found Danielle cheating with his best friend. An ache that started small and expanded painfully.

"Now you're really sorry about that kiss, huh?"

How could she be so nonchalant? Didn't she know he was coming to care for her?

The disease, whatever it was, angered him. Josie, so flippant and sarcastic, angered him. He wanted to scold her, yell at her.

But the look in her eyes stopped him. For all her bravado, for all the degrees her chin had tipped up, for all her sarcastic words, her hollow eyes gave her away. The rest was just a front. The rebuke that had formed on his tongue slid quietly down his throat.

She crossed her arms over her chest, a defensive gesture that made him want to pull her into his arms.

"Is it cancer?" Maybe there was something she could do. Some rock unturned that he could help her find.

"No. It has to do with the endocrine system." She turned and took a couple of steps away, putting space between them. "I don't want to talk about it."

"Why didn't you say something? Why didn't Laurel or Nate tell me?" This last was a question to himself. What would it have mattered? Would he have kept his distance from her to protect himself?

Josie mumbled something just as the sky opened up and the drizzle turned to a steady shower. She looked small hunched over in the rain.

He wished he had a jacket to drape over her. He took a step closer. "I didn't catch that."

She looked over her shoulder. "They don't know. And I don't want them to, understand?" Her words were firm, set in cement.

He couldn't understand why she'd keep something so important from them. They loved her. They'd be devastated, and even more so knowing that Josie had shouldered this alone.

Josie looked directly at him, looking strong for the first time since he'd found her hunkered over. "This is between you and me."

"Your family deserves to know. It's not fair—"

"It's not up to you to decide what's fair. Laurel is at a tenuous point in her pregnancy. She doesn't need the additional stress."

Maybe she had a point, but still. Family was family, and you didn't hide things like this.

"Promise me you won't say anything," she said.

Could he make such a promise? But what did he know of this illness? She may have years left, and if that was the case, what did a couple of months matter one way or the other?

"Promise," she said again.

Whether he agreed or not, in the end, the decision belonged to her, didn't it? And at least he knew now. Josie had someone to confide in if she needed to. "Promise."

The rain continued steadily. Josie was soaked to the skin.

"You should go on to the house."

She squared her shoulders. "I'm feeling better now."

Stubborn woman. The crew picked in the rain unless it was a downpour. It was just short of that today, but he didn't want her out in this.

"I'm calling it quits for the day." He turned and walked up the hill before she could argue.

twenty-six

*F*or the next few days, Josie watched and waited, worried Grady wouldn't keep his word. At times, she couldn't believe she'd told him. With a few words to her sister, he could ruin everything. Yet, what choice had she had when he'd threatened to put her over his shoulder and take her to the doctor?

Throughout awkward suppers and tense business discussions, he'd kept silent about her illness. She'd told him her secret and nothing had changed.

Except for one thing. She felt him watching her in the orchard. He took her heavy bag from her, brought her water, tended quietly to her. Part of her wanted to reject the hovering, the independent part that wanted no handouts. The other part savored his tender care.

Laurel was getting antsy for the babies' arrival and, in her impatience, her mood worsened. She'd mentioned that their parents' graves needed tending—a job Aunt Lola had been too busy for since Laurel had been put on bed rest.

If Josie didn't get up there and do the job, she was going to come home one day to find her pregnant sister up there on her hands and knees.

Even so, she balked. Maybe she could ask Nate or Aunt Lola to do it, then thought twice about that. Her aunt had enough to do with the housekeeping and the store, and Nate had enough of his own pressures with running his business and taking care of Laurel. *Just suck it up, Josie. It'll be over before you know it.* Besides, there was nothing up there but overgrown plots.

On a Sunday morning after the others had left for church, Josie climbed the hill behind the house with a bag of gardening tools. It was Laurel's first time at church in weeks, the doctor having given her permission for the once-a-week outing.

A layer of gray clouds shrouded the sun and the wind blew in from the west, making the tall grass on the hill bow and shimmy. There was news of a possible windstorm the next afternoon. Grady was keeping a close eye on the weather, and if the storm looked likely, every hand he could find would be out gathering apples later today. Otherwise, many apples would drop and be wasted.

When Josie neared the top of the hill, the cemetery came into view. Surrounded by a split-rail fence, the family markers rested under a giant oak tree whose branches stretched out in an enormous canopy over the area. She walked through the opening, remembering her last visit here.

The sky had been spitting sleet and icy rain on the day of Ian's funeral. He was the only one buried in the cemetery who wasn't a blood relative.

The grounds showed signs of being well tended. Aunt Lola had planted ivy along the fence, and it had climbed and crawled obediently along the split rails. Perennials bordered each tombstone. Yellow roses for Grandma Mitchell, white creeping phlox for Grandpa, and myrtle for Uncle Otis. The flowers' smell thickened the air with sweetness.

She walked toward the back and started there, saving the difficult ones for last. Nate had kept up with the mowing and had even used the Weed Eater recently. Weeds grew in the flower beds though, and dead buds needed plucking.

She worked quickly even though the effort tired her and made her back ache. The sooner she was done, the sooner she could get out of here. When she finished the back rows, she moved on to the front, starting at her mother's plot. Aunt Lola had planted red roses, her mother's favorite, around the tombstone.

Josie pulled the weeds and pruned the bush, then sat back on her heels and read the words on the marble marker.

Katherine Mitchell
Beloved Wife and Mother

She tried to call up a picture of her mom but all that came to mind was the image of the photo in her old locket. Josie had been so young. She wasn't even sure whether the memories she had of her mom were her own or someone else's hand-me-downs.

Her dad's grave was next, and Josie could put it off no longer. Newer shoots of ivy poked from the ground at the base of his tombstone. Her aunt would coax them up toward the marble marker as they grew. The mound of earth over his grave site was sparsely covered with new grass. Aunt Lola was tending his grave as carefully as Laurel had tended him after his stroke—not that he'd deserved it. He'd been so selfish to burden Laurel that way.

Well, Josie wouldn't follow in his footsteps. As soon as the harvest was in, she'd go back to Louisville. Her sister wouldn't see her health decline or be burdened with her care.

Her eyes swung back to her father's grave. The marker matched her mother's.

Warren Mitchell
Beloved Husband and Father

Josie could think of a few adjectives to add to the epitaph. But then, she hadn't been here to help Laurel with the arrangements. Hadn't been here for the funeral either. She reached out and tugged at a dandelion that seemed to have endless roots. She should've come home to help Laurel. Lord knew she'd tried. She'd even packed her bags. But in the end, she couldn't do it. Couldn't face the memory of her disapproving father or the guilt over his disappointment. And her anger. She couldn't face that either.

Now, hunkered over his grave, she was face-to-face with the feelings. Her dad had left, was forever gone, and she'd never told him how she felt, had never even hinted at it.

And now it was too late.

It wasn't fair. She wanted to scream at him for the way he'd made her feel. He deserved to know, and she deserved the chance to say those things.

"Why?" she whispered toward the heavens.

The only answer was a dove's call. *Ooh-OOH. Ooh-ooh-ooh.*

"Why did you make me feel so . . . unwanted?" Josie sat back on her heels. "Why wasn't I enough for you? I was just a little girl and you made me feel . . . like I was nothing."

She was going to have her say now, even if he couldn't hear it.

She raised her voice. "And I still feel that way, Dad. You know that? I'm still not enough. It's ingrained so deeply in me, it can never be changed."

Her eyes connected with the gravestone on the other side of her dad's. Her baby twin brother. She wished he'd lived instead of her—that's what should've happened. Even as she thought it, she realized the idea stemmed from her dad's attitude and the way he treated her.

"That's what you wanted, wasn't it? You wanted him and not me. And then Ian came, and you wanted him and not me."

For so many years she'd tried to prove her worth by working hard, by trying to please her father, by trying to make him proud.

But it had never been enough. *She* had never been enough. Not for him, and not for her.

Then Ian had died. And her dad had grieved over him as if he were his own son, while he ignored the fact that he still had two daughters who were alive and needed him. She wanted to spit it out. She wanted to tell him the truth about Ian's death. It had all been her fault. Ian's death was on her hands. In those days after his death, watching her father walk around half-dead himself, sometimes, deep inside in a place she'd hidden from everyone else, she was glad Ian was gone.

But guilt always came on the heels of those feelings. How could she have such horrible thoughts? What kind of person was glad when someone died? Someone who'd shown her nothing but kindness? Someone who'd willingly given his life for her?

Maybe her father had been right. Maybe she was unworthy. Unworthy of love, unworthy of joy, unworthy of life.

Her breath seemed trapped in her expanded lungs, and her pulse pounded in her head. She had to get out of here. Out of this place full of memories better dead and forgotten.

Josie tugged off the gloves and dropped them at the base of

her dad's tombstone. She wasn't ready to face this. Maybe she never would be. Maybe it needed to stay buried deep in her heart. Maybe she needed to take it to the grave with her.

But it was too late. She'd uprooted the memories and now she stood clutching them in her hands, wishing she could shove them back into the gaping holes.

Her breaths came quickly now, drying her mouth, rushing past the hard ache in her throat.

Josie stood, leaving the tools where they lay. She couldn't face this now. She had to escape. Before she finished the thought, her legs were carrying her away from the place.

twenty-seven

*T*he news had been all over church. Grady changed into his work clothes as soon he got home. Nate had gone to tell Josie and gather the crew.

The windstorm alert had been upgraded to a warning a few minutes before church. It was due in the area the next afternoon with high winds and driving rain. They needed every hour of daylight and every hand they could muster to pick the apples most susceptible to dropping.

Once the wind started, the fruit would fall to the ground at an alarming rate where they would lie bruised and useless. Not even processors accepted drops that could carry E. coli or patchulin. A big windstorm could destroy the remainder of their crop.

Grady shoved his feet into his boots and jogged to his truck. When he reached the orchard, Mr. Murphy and a few other men from church were arriving to help, and Nate was arriving with the crew in tow. Some of them had brought their wives to help.

Grady had been picking for ten minutes before he noticed Josie's absence. When the first bin was full, he used the lift tractor to move it into the trailer. He exited the lift as Nate passed with a bag full of apples.

"Where's Josie?" Grady asked.

Nate emptied his bag into the bin. "Don't know. Her car was gone when we got home. Laurel tried to call her cell, but she left it at home."

Maybe she'd gone to the grocery or something. There were only so many options on a Sunday in Shelbyville. She'd be home soon. Lord knew they could use every hand they could get. It was killing Laurel to be on the sofa when the remainder of their crop was at stake.

Josie must not have watched the news and been aware of the weather update. If she was in town, someone would tell her and she'd be back quickly.

Grady and the crew moved at lightning speed all afternoon, barely pausing for water breaks. Aunt Lola fixed sandwiches for an early supper, and the crew worked on. As the afternoon slipped away and there was still no sign of Josie, Grady began to worry.

No one knew where she'd gone. Aunt Lola said her camera was on the desk where she kept it. They weren't worried as they knew Josie liked to stay busy and frequently went off on the weekend. She'd made more than one last-minute trip into Asheville, and he was told Ashley had called the day before. They'd probably made plans for a visit. Josie was a grown woman; it wasn't like she had to leave a flight plan every time she left the house.

But she'd known about the potential windstorm. Even if she did want to sell the place, she wouldn't take off when they needed her.

Grady grew more concerned as the evening passed. His imagination ran wild even while his hands did their automatic work.

What if she was sick? What if she'd gotten dizzy—or worse,

passed out—behind the wheel? What if her car had careened off the road, and she was even now lying at the bottom of a gorge?

The sun sank lower in the sky until it disappeared behind the hills. The crew began packing up. Grady put the last bin in the trailer and drove them home. Darkness had fallen, and the porch light was on at the Mitchell house. Josie's car was still absent from the driveway.

Grady slowed as he passed Nate on the drive.

"Got a lot done today," Nate said. "Hopefully we'll be okay."

Grady nodded. "Josie's not home yet." He couldn't quell the knot in his gut that told him something was wrong. The heavy weight of responsibility pressed down on him. He was the only one who knew she was ill.

Nate's lips tightened into a flat line before he spoke. "She knew the storm was coming. But then, she's not exactly been dependable in the past. Probably drove to Asheville for the day."

A defense rose in Grady's throat, but he pushed it down. "Probably." They said good night and Grady accelerated, easing down the lane toward his cabin.

Her family might worry later if Josie didn't appear by morning, but they'd be worried now if they knew about the illness. Maybe she had driven to Asheville, but she'd never done a day trip. She always stayed overnight. He wondered if Laurel had thought to check for her overnight bag.

Surely Josie would've left a note if she were planning to stay overnight. And she knew about the windstorm. She knew he'd need her help. Regardless of Nate's assessment of Josie's attitude, Grady knew she wouldn't desert them without good cause.

As he reached the turn toward his cabin, he made a split-second decision and passed it, accelerating up the incline toward the main road. On the way, he dug his cell from his pocket and found Boone's number. He'd call Boone's sister in Asheville and find out if Josie was there. He should've done it earlier when he started worrying.

He stopped when he reached the top of the hill and made the call.

"Yep?" Boone's voice sounded in his ear.

"Hey, Boone, it's Grady."

"Hey, Grady. What's up?"

"I was wondering if I could get your sister's number in Asheville. I need to reach Josie and I think she might be there."

Grady put his window all the way down and rested his elbow on the ledge.

"I can give you Jackie's number, but I don't think Josie's there. I passed her in town coming home from church."

Would she have gone to Asheville that late in the day?

"She wasn't heading toward the highway," Boone said. "Everything okay?"

Last thing he needed was to get Boone suspicious. "Yeah, just needed to talk to her is all. Can I get Jackie's number just the same?"

Boone rattled off his sister's number and they hung up. When Grady reached the end of the driveway, he stopped and punched it in.

Someone answered on the second ring. "Hello?"

"Hi, uh, is Josie there?"

"Josie Mitchell?"

"Yeah, this is Grady from Shelbyville. I thought Josie might be down there this weekend."

"Oh, hey, this is Ashley. No, she didn't come this weekend. Is everything okay?"

Grady assured her it was, then hung up, his stomach tightening as each moment passed.

What are you going to do, Mackenzie? Drive down every dark road in Shelbyville looking for her car?

Where would she go? Would she have gone to a friend's house? He couldn't think of anyone in town she was close to.

There was nothing open on a Sunday night in town except the grocery store and Joe's Tavern. But she'd never gone to the tavern before that he knew of. And she couldn't have been there all day.

When he reached the crossroad, he turned toward town. A light rain had begun to fall. He drove slowly along the main road, looking down each street that he passed. There were hairpin curves and deep ravines off the roadside. What if she'd had an accident? It was too dark to see. *Where is she, Jesus? Help me to find her. Keep her safe.*

Maybe he should call Laurel and tell her about Josie's illness. Her life may depend upon being found. They could call Sheriff Roberts, and he could be on the lookout for Josie.

He entered town. Shelbyville was a mere blip on the map, snuggled between two stop signs and a traffic light the town had been proud to install three years earlier.

It was dark and deserted now. Only the park-style streetlamps were lit, an embellishment that had taken three town meetings to decide upon. The storefronts' darkened windowpanes reflected his headlights.

Across town, the lights of Ingles glowed like a big-city stadium. He'd check the grocery last. Maybe someone in there had seen her.

The only sign of life was the corner of Main and Penny Avenue where Joe's Tavern squatted. Music leaked from the wood-paneled building, and neon beer logos shined through the shaded glass. Parking was behind the building, so Grady swung his truck around the corner and slowed at the gravel lot lit by a single streetlamp. His eyes swung through the haphazard rows of vehicles and stopped when they came to the second row.

Almost hidden, tucked between a pickup and an SUV, was Josie's little brown Celica. He turned his truck into the lot, relief battling with anger. Had she been here all day? Been here drinking and partying when he'd been worried she was in a ditch somewhere?

He exited the truck and reached the rear door of the building with long strides. Inside the tavern, smoke gave the interior a hazy glow. A twangy country song poured from the jukebox in the corner. He'd never been in the place but recognized Ray Blackford behind the varnished bar.

"Hey, Grady." Ray filled a mug from the tap and set it in front of a customer.

Grady nodded. "Ray." His eyes swept the dim confines of the bar. He was surprised there were fifteen people in Shelbyville who wanted to be out on a Sunday night.

Ray leaned on the bar. "Looking for someone?"

It was hard to see around the tall booths. "Josie Mitchell. She around?"

Ray nodded his head toward the back of room. "Thataway."

"Thanks."

Adrenaline still coursed through his veins from the worry, from scouring ravines for her knotted-up car. He'd been worried for her, worried for her family. What would they have done if something had happened to her? He'd been afraid on their behalf.

Who are you kidding? You were afraid on your own behalf. You were worried you'd lost her.

He clenched his teeth together, his jaw working. He tried to deny the thought, but it would be a lie, and what good did it do to lie to yourself? He *had* been worried for her, blast it all. Worried on his own behalf.

He turned the corner and spotted her in a booth, her chin propped on her palm, listening to some guy who sat across from her. She blinked, her eyelids moving in slow motion.

The guy was Hispanic, probably a migrant worker on one of the other orchards. He was leaning forward, smiling, too close.

Grady suppressed the desire to pick him up by the collar and remove him from the booth. Instead, he stopped at the table.

Josie straightened. Or tried to. "Grady." Her smile and diction were sloppy. He noted the empty glass on the table by her elbow.

Grady stared the man down until he squirmed, then slid across the booth, standing. "I will see you later, Josie."

Josie waggled her fingers at him.

Grady was torn between sliding into the vacated spot and hauling Josie up from the booth, tossing her over his shoulder, and carrying her to his truck. Exercising restraint, he lowered himself into the seat.

Josie reached out and took his hands, patting them. "I'm so glad y're here."

Grady pulled his hands from hers. He was disappointed in her, running to the tavern and loading up. And of all the days to get skunked, she'd picked today.

What really rankled wasn't her supreme lack of responsibility, but the fact that he'd had her injured or worse in his own mind. He'd seen her hurt and bleeding, unconscious. The adrenaline rush was gone, leaving him shaky in its wake.

"Do you have any idea how worried we were about you?"

A frown tugged the smile from her face. Confusion knitted her brow. "What?" She strung the word into two syllables.

"We needed you at the orchard. Nobody knew where you were."

Her bloodshot eyes opened wide. "Laurel . . ."

"Laurel's fine. It's the windstorm. It's coming."

She blinked. Then she moved suddenly, scrambling up from the table. "The apples . . ."

Grady grabbed her wrist. "It's ten o'clock, Josie."

He was wasting his breath. She was three sheets to the wind. "Gotta get 'em off the trees . . ." She tried to pull her arm away. He tightened his grip. "It's too late. Sit down."

"Everything okay, Josie?" The Hispanic was back, stretching up to his full five feet three inches. He eyed Grady's hand, wrapped around Josie's wrist.

As if Grady would hurt her. But he was in no mood to explain himself. *Back off,* amigo.

He wasn't going to get anywhere here. Josie needed to sleep it off. Grady slid from the booth. "Let's go home." He thought the man might back off when he saw how Grady dwarfed him.

The man didn't seem to notice. "Josie?"

She swayed a little, and Grady and the other man reached out to steady her. Grady glared at him until he let go.

"I'm fine." She smiled, seemingly forgetting the apples, and linked her arm through Grady's. "He's taking me home." She blinked up at him, squinting. "Y're taking me home?" She looked at him with complete vulnerability, like a child at his mercy.

He softened at her confusion. God help him, she was getting to him. How could a woman frustrate the daylights out of him one minute and break his heart the next?

He led her past her friend and past the jukebox. As they passed the dance floor, a slow country ballad began.

Josie turned abruptly, and he plowed into her. In the moment it took to steady her, she draped her arms around his neck and began swaying. "Love this song."

"Come on, Josie." He tugged at her arms, but they tightened around his neck.

"Dance with me." Her lower lip puckered out. "Please . . ."

The Hispanic was eyeing him from across the room. There was a bit of stubbornness in Grady that wanted to defy the man by marching Josie right out the door. But a little time to sober up wouldn't hurt. Aunt Lola would have a conniption if he brought her home like this. Maybe if he waited awhile everyone at the house would be in bed.

He put his hands at Josie's waist and swayed with her. He wondered if he should call and let them know she was okay. But then they'd wonder why she wasn't calling herself.

Why do you need to protect her anyway? She's the one who went out and got soused. If her family disapproves, that's no fault of yours.

Josie snuggled against him, laying her head on his chest. He was glad she was too drunk to notice the way his heart kicked into high gear. She stepped on his toes, the featherweight of her body barely impeding the movement of his feet.

The country singer crooned about drowning his sorrows in a bottle of beer. Is that what Josie had done? Had the reality of her illness been too much? He thought of her all alone in the house while the others were at church. She needed someone she could count on, someone she could talk to. He tried to imagine what it would feel like to know some illness was going to take his life. Then he imagined going through it alone.

A quick pang of loneliness pricked him, just a taste of what Josie must feel. The residual anger drained away, leaving a heavy sadness in its place. He cradled the back of her head. If only she would open herself to the possibility of God. She didn't have to go through this alone.

God, have mercy on your child. Help her through this. Help me be to her what you want me to be.

He wanted to protect her, to shield her from the pain she was trying to drown out with alcohol. He laid his chin on her head, inhaling the scent of lilacs. He felt the breaths come and go from her lungs. Breaths that drew in life.

How long did she have? How could it be that all this life he held in his arms would soon be snuffed out? He tightened his arms around her.

What are you doing, Mackenzie? Where's this going to lead? You're gonna get hurt again. And there was no way for it to end other than hurt. Did he want to go down this path?

He dug deep for the courage to ask the question. *What do you want from me, God?*

Josie pulled her arms from his neck and wrapped them around his waist. Her hands grazed over his back, leaving a hot trail. The singer held out his last note and the song ended.

Just in time. Grady pulled away, hating the cool curtain of air that fell between them. "Time to go, honey."

He ushered her to the truck and helped her in. By the time he turned the key, she was snuggled into the door, her head on the window ledge.

Grady checked the clock. It was almost eleven. He didn't know if Laurel or Aunt Lola would be up waiting and worried, or whether they'd be sound asleep. He could only hope for the latter. Josie didn't need Aunt Lola's disapproving looks or her sister's pointed questions. She needed someone to take care of her, someone to look out for her.

The truck rumbled down Main Street, then he turned onto Stone Gap Road, his lights cutting a winding path in the darkness. From the other side of the cab, quiet snores escaped from Josie.

Sleep was just what she needed. Heaven knew she was going to feel bad enough come morning.

When they reached the house, he cut off his lights and turned off the ignition. The house was dark except for the porch lights, a good sign. Now if he could only rouse Josie.

He touched her arm. "Josie."

A soft snore was his only answer. He tried again, rubbing her arm. "Josie, we're home."

She didn't move, didn't so much as twitch. The glow of the porch light cast a pale yellow sheen over her face. Relaxed in sleep, her lips were parted. Her eyelashes grazed the tops of her cheeks, reminding him of an innocent child.

She was out cold, and he hated to disturb the peaceful oblivion she'd finally found. He exited the truck, closing his door quietly, and went to her side, opening the door slowly so he didn't jar her awake.

As the door slipped from under her, she turned and curled into the seat.

"Josie?" he whispered.

The wind rustled the branches above him, reminding him of the windstorm due in fifteen hours. They had a long day ahead of them.

Deciding to let her sleep, Grady slipped his hands under her and lifted her. She turned into him with a sigh, nuzzling her face in the cradle between his head and shoulder.

He closed the door softly with his hip, then climbed the porch steps and wrestled with the handle. Unable to stop the screen door in time, it slapped against the frame. He winced, hoping it wasn't as loud as he feared.

What would her family think if they saw him carrying Josie into the house? Drunk, no less. *It's a little late to worry about that, buddy.*

He thought he'd skirted the hall table, but one of Josie's feet connected with it. Her sandal thudded to the wood floor.

Way to go. You've probably woken half of Shelbyville by now.

But not Josie. A long, quiet snore erupted.

The stairs creaked as he carried her to the second floor. If the noise woke someone, hopefully they'd think it was Josie returning and go back to sleep. At the top of the stairs, he reached her door, glad the other rooms were at the far end of the hall. Moonlight shone through the gauzy curtains, enough to see by.

He carried her to the twin bed in the corner and laid her down, then went back to shut the door before he flipped on the tiny lamp.

Josie lay just as he'd left her, a floppy doll, arms and legs askew under the frilly canopy. She jerked, the bed quaking, her intake of breath audible.

He waited, praying she didn't wake. What would she think, finding him here in her room? Her hand lay open next to her face on the pillow. Dirt caked the creases of her palm and he wondered how it had gotten there.

She whimpered and her hand balled into a fist. Her head tossed on the pillow and her brows lowered.

He wanted to wake her now that her oblivion had turned nightmarish, but what would he say?

Josie curled into a ball, her dirty fingers clutching the pillow. She muttered something. A name? Ian?

She quieted, her breaths evening out. The bed was still unmade from the night before, the covers shoved down in a wad. He picked up her foot and eased the other sandal off.

She was in jeans and a T-shirt and would have to stay that way. He lifted her other foot off the covers, eased it back down, then pulled the sheet up to her chin.

But before it settled over her shoulders, her eyes opened wide.

twenty-eight

*I*an was drowning. She could see his face through the crystal ice, looking up at her. His eyes were glacier blue. Cold and dead.

She woke with a start, the image haunting her. Within seconds, her rolling stomach snagged her attention. She was going to throw up. *Oh no.*

She pushed past Grady, barely questioning his presence in her hurry to make it in time. She leaned over the bowl and retched. It seemed to be coming all the way from her intestines. Her stomach cramped down hard, making her double over, even when she'd finished.

The light had come on, and she caught sight of Grady's denim-clad legs at her side. The commode flushed, sounding loud in the cramped room.

Her head throbbed in time with her heart, fast and hard, like blows of a hammer. The acidic taste of bile coated her mouth. She felt a cool washcloth settle at the base of her neck, and a glass of water appeared in front of her.

She took it, then stood, her legs wobbling beneath her. Why had she drunk all that beer? Didn't she feel bad enough without adding a hangover to her list of ailments?

She leaned over the sink and rinsed out her mouth. She felt like death warmed over, and she was sure she looked it too.

"Better?" Grady whispered.

She avoided the mirror as she straightened and nodded. She had a vague recollection of dancing with him at Joe's. Had that really happened or was it the precursor to her nightmare?

He flipped off the bathroom light and ushered her back to her room. *God, please let Aunt Lola sleep through this.* She'd never hear the end of it if her aunt caught Grady in her bedroom, and neither would he.

Her steps were slow, her balance unsure. Grady slipped an arm around her waist.

Why was he doing this? She lowered herself onto the mattress, remembering the windstorm. The entire day rushed back like a film in fast-forward. The cemetery, the long drive, the stop at Joe's.

Then Grady's arrival. That part was blurry. She closed her eyes, not able to think past her pounding head. The windstorm was coming, she remembered that part. They both had a long day ahead. It was late, and they both had to be up early. She couldn't believe he'd hunted her down at Joe's and stayed through this.

"I'm sorry . . ." She didn't know where to go from there. Sorry she'd been stupid enough to drown her pain with alcohol. Sorry she hadn't been there for him today. Sorry he'd seen her retching again.

Was it the beer or the illness? It was hard to know where one began and the other ended.

Grady pulled the covers over her and she turned her face into the pillow, wanting to hide. There would be plenty of time for mortification come morning.

"Go to sleep," he whispered.

She felt him turn the cloth on her neck, felt the coolness of the other side against her skin before she heard the click of the lamp, the sound of his footsteps on the floorboards.

She had a fuzzy flashback of dancing again. Of Grady's arms around her waist and the weight of his head resting on hers. Even drunk, she'd been aware of feeling something she hadn't felt in a very long time. Security.

It was the last thought she had before she sank into oblivion.

twenty-nine

A bluebird jeered outside Josie's window, rousing her earlier than usual. The sound of the bird was like a beak pecking at her forehead.

Her head throbbed and her mouth felt as if it were full of cottonwood fluff. Memories of the night before washed over her like a flash flood.

She closed her eyes, moaning against the inevitable confrontation with Grady. The windstorm was due in the afternoon, she remembered. They had a lot of apples to pick and not much time. They couldn't get them all, but if they could get the ripest ones, they might not lose too many.

Putting a hand to her forehead, she rooted through her purse for Advil and swallowed three of them. After a quick shower, she headed outside, deciding to skip coffee for the time being. The pounding in her head had diminished to a dull ache. The horizon was just now pinking up with the rising sun. A steady wind blew in from the west, a precursor of the coming storm. Already she could imagine the dreaded sound of apples thumping to the ground. Orchards expected some drops—ten to fifteen percent was normal. She wondered how many Grady and the crew had picked the day before.

If you'd been here, you would know. Guilt ate at her, feeding on her like a worm on a rotting apple. Laurel probably had to be tied down to be kept at home and Josie had run off and gotten drunk.

Grady had counted on her, and she hadn't been here. Instead, he'd been there for her. The night before was blurry, especially the part at the bar. She didn't even remember how she'd gotten to her bedroom, but she remembered getting sick. She'd kept Grady up late being her nurse. So much for not being a burden.

He probably felt sorry for her. That thought bothered her as much as the guilt. She didn't want his pity, didn't need him feeling sorry for her.

When Josie turned the corner of the house, the spot where she parked her car was empty. It took a moment to remember. Her car was at Joe's. Before the implications sank in, she heard the roar of Grady's truck rumbling down the drive.

He stopped when he reached her side. "Climb in."

She eyed the door, the memory of the night before blazing across her mind like a forest fire. What did he think of her? Was he still angry that she'd deserted him?

Knowing she had no choice, she opened the door and slid inside, avoiding eye contact.

He put the truck in gear and accelerated. Gravel spit from under his tires. Outside a bluebird called. She needed to say something. Had she apologized last night?

She had an instant flash of snuggling against his chest on the dance floor. Had he called her "honey"? She wished she could remember.

Or maybe she didn't.

"Feeling better this morning?" Grady asked.

He didn't sound angry. She was grateful for that and grateful he'd broken the ice, even if it did refer to the night before.

"Much." She remembered nothing after vomiting and falling into bed. She wondered what she'd said and done that she couldn't remember. How many other ways had she embarrassed herself?

His actions were above and beyond the call of duty. She owed him one. "Thanks for—" *Hunting me down at Joe's? Driving me home? Getting me to bed?* "—for taking care of me."

How long had it been since someone had taken care of her? She was used to being independent. Her father had never taken care of her. Laurel had tried to look after her baby sister, but Josie had bucked her sister's authority every chance she got. She hadn't been cared for like that since her mother had been alive.

"I'm sorry about taking off like that," she continued. "I didn't know they'd upgraded the windstorm." She gripped the crackled leather of the armrest as they rounded the bend toward the migrant housing.

"It worked out." She barely heard his words over the hum of the engine.

Unable to stop herself, she looked at him. His thick hands rested at ten and two on the steering wheel. His eyes still wore the remnants of sleep—and no wonder after she'd kept him up late. His hair was damp at his neck from his shower.

More than fatigue though, his face wore the mask of strain and she knew with certainty he'd been worried about her the night before. It was why he'd come looking for her at Joe's.

As if sensing her scrutiny, he turned. His eyes seemed to drink her in. They held her mesmerized.

His Adam's apple bobbed as he faced forward again. "Don't do that again."

The command should've made her defensive, but it didn't. She wasn't sure if it was the vulnerable tone of his voice or the look on his face.

"I won't."

The day passed in a blur for Josie. Laurel insisted she was fine at home alone, and even Aunt Lola closed the store for the day and helped in the orchard. By four o'clock, the wind picked up in heavy gusts that made ladder work treacherous. They'd done their best and could only hope the remaining apples would weather the storm.

Josie hadn't eaten breakfast or lunch, afraid the food would upset her stomach and interfere with her work. Her stomach gurgled loudly after she and Grady dropped off the workers. She folded her arms over her stomach, hoping he hadn't noticed.

"I told Aunt Lola I'd pick up a pizza from Crusty's. Figured we'd stop and pick up your car afterward."

"That would be great, thanks." She leaned back in the seat as fatigue settled over her like a heavy fog. She'd worked hard—they all had. Hard and fast, and the pace had gotten the best of her.

A gust of wind pushed the truck to the edge of the driveway, and Grady corrected it. The apple tree branches were waving, the apples on them diving like fishing bobbers under the tug of a bass.

"I hope they'll be okay." she said.

He looked out his window as a tree dropped half a dozen apples beside the drive. "We've done all we can. Now we just pray it was enough."

Prayer was mentioned so often in her family that Josie had stopped hearing it. Only after being away for several years did she have a fresh perspective. Did prayer work? Her own prayers had never seemed to accomplish anything. Not that she'd said many of them, but the last one she'd uttered in complete desperation had been ignored. Not ignored exactly, she reminded herself. After all, she'd been saved from the frigid water. But in many ways, she'd been lost there too. A loving God, a God who was capable of miracles, could've done much more if he'd wanted.

Her aunt would be appalled at her thoughts, but seeing as how her life would be ending sooner than later, the question of God was beginning to nag at her. What was there after death? Where was Ian right now? Had his faith gotten him to heaven? She wanted to believe in eternal bliss. But if there were such a place, would she make it in? Was believing in God's existence enough?

Probably not. It might be easier not to believe at all. Grady seemed so sure of his faith. Why couldn't she be that sure? Would it change anything if she were? Would the guilt be easier?

"Do you believe God answers prayers?" The question was on her lips before she could stop it.

He turned the truck onto the street, taking his time with the response. "I wouldn't waste my time with it if I didn't."

"But how do you know he cares? How do you know he hears you?"

Grady's shoulder lifted in a half shrug. "I've seen prayers answered. I feel his presence when I talk to him."

It wasn't enough. She was suddenly desperate for an answer she could live with. And die with. "Feelings are misleading."

He shrugged. "Do you believe in the wind?"

She looked out the window, seeing his point. Was it that simple?

"See how the branches are moving and the grass is swaying? You can't see the wind, but you can see its effects."

At the moment that wind was no doubt tugging countless apples from their trees. Was that how God was? Carelessly wreaking havoc at his whim? She wouldn't voice the thought, but still it was there.

Grady was the one who changed the topic. "You skipped lunch."

She was surprised he'd noticed. She'd taken a break with everyone else and had pushed the coleslaw around her plate while the others ate.

"Do you always get sick?"

She shook her head. "It comes and goes." Lately it had been coming more than going. The fatigue was worse too. She was trying her best to hide it, especially from Laurel and Aunt Lola.

"I wanted to talk to you about something . . . I have a friend back in Chicago—a doctor," he said.

Josie shook her head again. "I'm done with doctors."

"He's an endocrinologist."

She needed to be careful. If he found out it was Addison's, he could find out it was treatable. And then what would she do?

This was hard enough as it was. Who did he think he was coming in and trying to fix everything? She nearly laughed out loud. Her problems were beyond fixing. The disease was the least of it. Her hand tightened on the armrest.

"I know you're trying to help, but just back off, all right?" After the words were out, she realized he might misinterpret them.

She liked having him around, liked the way he looked at her sometimes, so deeply she wanted to sink into the brown depths of his eyes.

She hoped he'd ask what she meant so she could clarify. When several moments passed, Josie realized he wasn't going to, and her own tongue seemed stuck to the roof of her mouth.

thirty

The effects of the windstorm weren't apparent until the next morning at daybreak. They'd lost about forty percent of the remaining apples. Since the bulk of the orchard ripened late, this was significant. The mood was somber the rest of the week. A forty percent loss was heavy. Some of the orders Laurel had gotten would have to be canceled—a difficult thing when she worked hard for each sale.

The sale of the orchard had been on Josie's mind all week, and as Friday arrived, she realized something had turned inside her. Whatever decision was made about the orchard, she was going to do her best to make this season a successful one. No more trips to Asheville. No more running off and getting soused. If she had to strap herself to a tree, she was going to be out here every possible hour until the last apple was plucked. It was the least she could do for Grady and Laurel. Even with the loss of apples, they could still make the season a successful one so long as nothing else happened.

Grady was distant, whether from the apple loss or Josie's careless words, she wasn't sure. All she knew was that she missed him.

The bad week they'd had did nothing for Laurel's mood, and

Friday night found Josie retreating to the tire swing. With Aunt Lola having gone out to eat with Mr. Murphy, Laurel and Nate probably needed time alone anyway.

Since Josie had made the decision to devote herself fully to the orchard, she'd only felt trapped. She had too much time to think while she worked and the evenings were even worse. Not having a trip to Asheville to anticipate pulled her mood even lower.

She needed to stay busy, especially in the evening when her mind was prone to wander places she didn't want to go. Josie shifted as the edge of the tire dug into her thigh. She couldn't just sit around and wait for time to pass.

The windstorm had brought down a thick layer of leaves, a crispy brown blanket that smelled of decay. She saw a rake leaning against the oak and untangled her legs from the tire swing.

She had a pile the size of a small car when Grady's truck rumbled up the drive.

As Grady rounded the curve that brought the house into view, he caught sight of Josie raking leaves. She'd looked half-dead over dinner and hadn't eaten enough to keep a robin alive. Was she trying to kill herself? The yard was Nate's job. Where was he? Grady pushed down the irritation, reminding himself Nate didn't know Josie was ill.

The fishing poles in the truck bed jangled against the metal bed as he hit a bump. He pulled to a stop, the notion of an invitation already sparking in his head. *She'll probably say no.* He'd kept his distance all week, but he figured that was the way she wanted it.

Grady leaned his elbow on the door frame. "Going fishing if

you want to tag along," he said before he could reason himself out of it.

Josie leaned against the rake handle. Probably to keep herself upright. She seemed to be considering the idea as she looked over the pile that was high enough to tell him she'd been at it awhile.

"Got an extra pole?"

The jolt of joy was disconcerting. "Yep." A few leaves floated to the ground, landing in the patch of grass Josie had just raked.

She leaned the rake against the nearest tree. "Where at?"

He wondered why it mattered. "Murphy's pond."

She wiped her hands on her jeans as she approached.

Grady cleared the bench seat. Yesterday's newspaper, a cone wrapper from the Dairy Freeze, and a stray fry. He told himself the stutter of his heart was surprise and nothing more. She climbed in.

"You got permission?" she asked as he put the truck in gear.

"Helped him with a roof leak last year, and he lets me use it whenever I want. Why?"

She shrugged. "He's not real fond of me. I caught his bushes on fire, remember?"

He smiled. "I forgot about that. I thought it was his house though."

"Just the overhang."

"Well, that makes it better. He's still dating Aunt Lola, so he must not hold it against you too much."

She shifted, crossing her legs. The denim hung loosely around her knees. Had she lost weight in the weeks she'd been home? She seemed smaller. Her hands looked tiny all folded up in her lap, her arms actress-skinny.

She wasn't taking care of herself. She probably shouldn't be working in the orchard. Her body could be using all that energy to fight whatever disease she had. He wanted to tell her that. Wanted to insist she stay home and rest with Laurel.

But she'd already told him what she thought of him butting into her health affairs. And she was too stubborn to listen anyway. Maybe the best he could do was make sure she was resting when they weren't working. He already slipped in a couple of extra coffee breaks when he saw she was tired.

He'd thought a lot about the question she'd asked him on the day of the windstorm. Her family would be distraught to know she wasn't sure about God. Especially if they knew about her illness.

If only he could pass his faith to her. If only it were that easy. At least she was searching, and that's where the journey began.

A few minutes later, he pulled into Murphy's drive and passed the farmhouse. The lane turned to a bumpy dirt road beyond the house, winding up a hill and through an evergreen forest. Murphy had a prime piece of land and a pond that was a fisherman's dream come true.

He slowed under the fanned branches of a Norway spruce and cut off the engine. They gathered the tackle and headed down the grassy slope where a flat rock jutted out into the water. His favorite fishing spot.

He grabbed a pole and opened the container of worms, threading one onto the hook for Josie. When he finished, he handed it to her. But she had the other pole and was already threading her own hook. Danielle wouldn't have been caught dead with a squirmy worm in her hands. Shoot, she wouldn't have been caught dead fishing in some backwoods pond.

"What?" She set the pole down, rinsing her hands in the pond's clear water.

"Nothing." They settled on the rock, a tight fit for two. The windy weather had moved out, leaving the surface of the pond as smooth as glass. The evergreens reflected back, casting dark shadows over their bobbers.

The only sound was the rustling of dead leaves and pine needles from a squirrel or bird moving along the forest floor. "Sure is peaceful here."

"The air smells so clean." She closed her eyes, inhaling. "Pine sap and autumn leaves and earth."

Her bobber dipped under the surface. "You got a bite."

She opened her eyes and watched the red and white globe, waiting. When it sank, she gave her pole a swift tug and reeled in.

The line was taut, the end of the pole slightly bowed. "You got him."

She reeled in until the fish cleared the water. A nice-sized largemouth bass. She pulled the hook from his mouth and put him in the mesh basket like a pro.

"I think you earned yourself a fish dinner."

She rinsed her hands in the water, wiped them dry on her jeans, and rebaited her hook. "Is that an invitation?" She tilted an unsure look his way.

His breath caught in his throat. Have mercy, she was beautiful when she looked at him like that, all vulnerable and uncertain.

He cleared his throat. "I'll skin them if you fry them." Frankly, he'd skin *and* fry them if only she'd agree to come over.

She cast back out in the same spot. "Deal."

He watched her from the corner of his eye, remembering how soft her hair had felt the night he kissed her. Remembered how pliable her lips had been, how she'd felt against him.

What are you doing, man? Trying to drive yourself crazy?

"Tell me about you," she said suddenly. "I don't know much other than you were married before and studied agriculture."

Anything to change the direction of his thoughts. "What do you want to know?"

"What was your wife like?"

"Just bring in the heavy artillery, why don't you?"

"You mind?"

What was there to hide? It was Josie. She wouldn't judge, and he had nothing to be ashamed of. But when you were betrayed, it somehow left you feeling as if you did.

"We met in college. She was attractive and dangerous."

She almost smiled. "I can relate."

Now there was a comment to follow up on. He pulled his line in a couple of yards and locked the reel. "That song, 'Maneater'? It was written for her."

She cocked her head. "Not good."

"Sadly, I didn't realize until I found her in bed with my best friend."

Her lips pulled down. There might've been pity in her eyes, but he looked away before he could decide.

"I'm sorry."

"I was too. But that was a long time ago."

They were quiet so long, her bobber had floated close to shore before she spoke again. "We all have our demons. How long were you married?"

Too long. It was on his tongue, but that was sarcasm speaking. It had been pretty good in the very beginning. "Less than two years."

He wondered if Josie had ever been close to marriage. He was sure there'd been no lack of male attention.

"Do you miss her?"

He might have dismissed the question with a laugh, but the seriousness of Josie's tone stopped him. "No. I do miss the companionship though."

He missed coming home and having someone there. Having someone in bed beside him when he woke in the middle of the night. Having someone to call when he had good news.

It was time to move on. "How 'bout you? Serious relationships? Ever engaged?"

She reeled in her line to pick up the slack. "None of the above. Lots of dead-end relationships and broken hearts. Mostly mine."

He found that hard to believe. What kind of man wouldn't want a woman like Josie? "Tell me about your job back in Louisville."

She shrugged. "I work with a small group of photographers, and we're assigned events, birthday bashes, anniversary parties, reunions, and the like."

"You enjoy it?"

"Sure. It's nice to be present for happy events and watch the families interact, try and capture some of that excitement on film."

"Doesn't it make you lonely for your own family?"

Josie's gaze skittered away from his. "It's different when it's other people's families. I'm on the outside looking in, and that's not all bad, you know? It's safer." She bit her lip as if afraid she'd revealed too much.

Through the haze of his vision, he saw Josie's bobber go under again. She jerked the rod and reeled in another bass.

thirty-one

*T*hat's the last time I take you fishing," Grady said.

Josie flipped Grady's bluegill in the frying pan and it sizzled, spitting grease darts, one of them catching her on the wrist. She'd already cooked the four bass and one bluegill she'd caught, and had set the crispy brown fillets on a platter. The aroma of fried fish filled his house. Grady's fish stretched across the sad-looking pan he'd dug from a cabinet.

"At least he's big." Grady set the silverware on the corner table. It wobbled when he leaned against it. "Some might even say huge."

"Let's not get carried away."

"He barely fits in the pan."

"He's shrinking more with each second." She removed the fish with the spatula and turned off the burner.

"I'm trying to be a man about this."

"I didn't mean to wound your fragile male ego. That's the biggest bluegill I've ever seen. Better?" She set the platter on the table, and they seated themselves opposite one another.

"That's more like it."

While she arranged the napkin in her lap, he bowed his head

in a quick prayer, then they dug in. The smell of frying fish hadn't nauseated her, and she was hopeful her stomach wouldn't rebel.

Grady nodded as he chewed. "Not bad."

The fish was tender and mild. She ate small portions and hoped for the best.

"I stopped by Pick-a-Flick earlier if you're up for a movie," Grady said a few minutes into their meal.

It was his turn to pick. But it wasn't the movie that tempted her to stay. "Let me guess. *Rambo*."

"Give me some credit."

"A compromise." He reached for a plastic bag and pulled a DVD from it.

"*Speed*. Oh, that's a good one. Another Sandra Bullock flick."

"You've seen this one too?"

What could she say? She had no life. She'd rented every decent movie available the past few years. What else did she have to do on the weekends? After a while, the nightlife scene had worn thin, and the caliber of men she ended up with made a movie seem like a promising option.

"It's worth watching again."

When they were finished eating, Josie rinsed the plates and placed them in the ancient brown-paneled dishwasher.

Grady leaned around her to stash the silverware in the basket, and his chest brushed her back. When he pulled away, she missed the contact.

Josie cleared her throat. "I'll refill our drinks while you put the movie in."

By the time Josie entered the living room, the movie was ready, and Grady was seated on the sofa. She smiled at him as she settled in next to him.

She couldn't stop the thread of anticipation that worked through her. He wanted to be next to her.

"In case there are scary parts," he said as if his choice of seating required explanation. Even in the dim light, she could see the flush that climbed his neck.

The notion that he wanted to be close made her feel wanted—something she hadn't felt in too long. "It is pretty creepy at the end where the bad guy's on top of a train and—"

"Are you trying to ruin it for me?" He pushed Play, and the movie began.

The story was action-packed and tense, holding her attention most of the time. It had been several years since she'd seen it and she'd forgotten parts of it.

Grady watched intently, giving her an opportunity to study him discreetly. He had a strong profile with a perfectly formed nose and a strong jawline. His bangs, parted in the middle, hung beside his forehead, curling ever so slightly inward, almost touching his eyelashes. She let her gaze wander down the column of his neck to his shoulders and his arms, thick and tan. He was handsome and strong. Any woman would be lucky to have him.

His ex-wife was an idiot. How devastated he must've been when she betrayed him. Josie wondered if that was why he hadn't remarried, why he so seldom dated. Why he'd been sorry he'd kissed her. A thing like betrayal had a way of shaking you. Changing you. Trust was a fragile thing not easily restored. Was he afraid of getting hurt again?

What in the world are you doing, Josie? If he's afraid of getting hurt, you are the last thing he needs.

Grady put his arm across the sofa back, shifting her focus. The movie was coming to its dramatic climax, and the bad guy was on top of the train with Keanu Reeves.

Just before the character's decapitation, she turned from the screen. Grady curled his arm around her shoulder and pulled her in until her face was buried in the soft cotton T-shirt.

Mercy, but he smelled good. All piney and musky and manly. There should be a law. His fingers moved on her arm, drawing circles, making her skin tingle.

This is a bad idea. A very bad idea. And yet it was so nice she couldn't tear herself away. It felt good to be held and protected. Even if just for a little while.

"Bad part's over," he whispered, his lips so close to her ear that she felt the warmth of his breath.

Josie didn't want to leave her safe cocoon, but she lifted her head.

And there he was. So close. So tempting. Her hand itched to run up his chest and behind his head. Then she wanted to pull him toward her until—

Bad, Josie.

Bad, bad, bad. Where is this going? You're going to hurt him. He doesn't deserve that. Hasn't he been through enough?

But he was leaning toward her with that look in his eyes. She had to do something.

Josie turned away. "We can't." Her heart complained loudly, emphatically. *Yeah, yeah, I know. Believe me.*

Grady leaned his forehead against her temple, his warm breath tickling her ear. "Why not?"

Because I'm going to die. Because it will hurt you. Because these feelings confuse me, make me question things, and I've already made up my mind.

"You know why," she said instead.

She felt him trace a trail on her back. Her body responded with a quiet shiver. *Not fair.*

"It's just a kiss."

She drew in a shaky breath. "This from a man who is downright dangerous in that particular department." Didn't it always start with just a kiss? A kiss with Grady was like having just one hit of a potent drug. Impossible. Already she wanted it more than she could bear.

And what then, Josie? Where can it go from there?

Maybe I could let it play out. Maybe there's a way . . .

Grady tilted his head. Or was it her? She didn't know, but suddenly their lips were touching. His were like a dove's wing, feathery and soft. It shook her to the core.

So good. Not only the kiss, but the way he wanted her. She wanted to relish that thought for these few minutes. What could it hurt?

Maybe things could be different. Maybe she could find the will to live if she were loved by a man like Grady.

What about the guilt? What about Ian? That won't go away, Josie. He died because of you, and nothing can change that.

She was exhausted from the weight of reality. Too tired of living a life she didn't deserve, trying to pay penance for a sacrifice she could never be worthy of.

And now she was pulling Grady into her mess. He was going to suffer along with her. Suffer, just as he had when Danielle hurt him. She wasn't going to be another Danielle in his life.

She pulled back, her eyes burning. "No."

He framed her face with his palms. "Yes."

"You don't understand." Was that her voice, all choked and raspy?

"I understand everything I need to."

She shook her head.

He brushed away a tear with his thumb. The tenderness of

the gesture broke her. Everything bubbled up inside, ready to spill out. The desire for Grady, the need to end her life.

The maddening knowledge that she couldn't have both.

Could she live with the past if there was a hint of hope for the future? She didn't know. And how could she allow Grady to wade in deeper? Risking her own heart was one matter, but what right did she have to risk his when she was so confused?

She had to get out of there.

Josie jumped up from the couch. She was sliding her feet into her sandals before Grady spoke. "Wait, Josie."

She didn't dare look. Just the strain of his words was enough to make her want to bury herself in his arms again. To hide from life as she'd hid from the movie. But scary scenes ended. The real-life ones just kept going, and she couldn't stay in the refuge of his arms forever.

"I have to go." She opened the door and escaped. Her feet shuffled across the porch and took the steps, outrunning anything Grady might say to make her stay.

thirty-two

Josie plucked an apple from the Fuji tree and dropped it in her bag. Her muscles ached with the movement, and there was nothing to explain the pain except the disease. It was slowly wreaking havoc on her body. Her knees ached when she walked, her back hurt, and then there was the nausea. How much longer?

The progressive symptoms were a needed reminder that she'd made the right decision the night before. Hard as it had been, it was best for both of them.

Grady had only nodded hello earlier. She felt his eyes on her, burning the back of her neck as she worked. It took all her focus to keep her mind on her job. How could she go on like this for the remaining weeks?

The sooner you get these apples down, the sooner you can go home.

Home to what? An empty apartment? An empty life?

No matter how empty Louisville was, it was easier than being here. Easier than being—

"Can we talk?" Grady's voice startled her.

His tired eyes hinted of a long night and she knew from his expression that he didn't have small talk in mind. She wanted to smooth the frown lines from his forehead with her thumb the way he'd smoothed away a tear the night before.

Stop it, Josie.

She twisted a ripened apple and dropped it in her bag. "What's the point, Grady?" Her tone betrayed her fatigue. She'd had a long night of her own and plenty of time to think. She'd reached a decision and was determined to stick with it. No matter whose love she had, it wouldn't be enough to change anything.

"The point is, I care about you."

Her stomach tightened, her hand paused on the next apple. The words played over in her mind, refreshing her. How could a few words sound so good, feel so good?

But what right did she have to them? Grady deserved better than what she could offer. She freed the apple from the branch with a twist and a snap, bagged it, and reached for another.

He grabbed her arm. *"Josie."*

Could he see her chest rising and falling, heaving as her lungs kept pace with her heart? Why was he making it so hard? What could she say to make him understand what he should already know?

Maybe she needed to make it clear she didn't have much longer. Maybe he thought she had years instead of months. "There's no happily-ever-after here, Grady."

His eyes softened, melting like milk chocolate under the sun's warmth. Did his eyes tear up, or was it a trick of the shimmering shadows dancing across his face?

He swallowed, his Adam's apple bobbing. "I want to be here for you."

He'd already lost one love. Why would he set himself up for another loss? The sweetness of his offer, the selflessness of his desire made her eyes ache.

You could change your mind. Maybe Grady could make life worth living again.

This was the voice that scared her most, the one she was afraid to listen to. Afraid because it made her hope. And hope was a scary thing.

"Josie?"

She bolstered the courage to open the door a crack, just enough to let the idea in. She was a bottle of pills away from becoming healthy again. Put that way, it sounded so easy. Too easy.

What about the guilt? What about the burden of trying to make her life matter and failing over and over again? If only she could make it up to Ian. But he was gone. There was no reconciling that.

And this disease didn't happen on its own, remember? God had given her what she deserved.

"You don't have to go through this alone." Grady's fingers grazed her arm, sending prickles of awareness along every nerve.

What if?

What if she opened herself to the possibility of a new life? Being loved by a man like Grady could make a difference, couldn't it? Maybe it would wash away the guilt, make her forget.

It was possible, wasn't it? Looking into his eyes now, she wanted to believe it. Wanted to so badly. Still, this wasn't a decision to be made lightly. She needed to be sure before she committed to anything. It was only fair.

"I need time," she said. Her eyes fell down the column of his neck where his flesh disappeared beneath the crew-neck T-shirt. His shoulders were broad, the white material stretched across them, narrowing down to the waist of his shorts.

"How much time?"

She wasn't going to be rushed, for their own good. "As much as it takes." She was going to take her time and do the right thing for once, whatever it was. Those brown eyes staring into hers only made it more difficult.

"Hurry up." His tone was a caress. "I miss you."

A loud pounding pulled Josie from a deep sleep. She blinked the haze from her eyes. The clock read nine thirty. It was Sunday, and the others were at church. Most of Shelbyville was at church.

Another knock sounded.

Who in the world?

Josie untangled herself from the covers and threw on a robe. A wave of dizziness assaulted her at the top of the stairs, and she grabbed the railing, pausing on the wood step until it passed. The pounding had stopped.

When she reached the door, she pulled it open, but there was no one there. Strange. She stepped out on the porch, belting her robe, feeling mildly annoyed. A green Buick she didn't recognize was parked beside her Celica.

A tall man in a cap was walking away from the house toward the hill.

Josie clutched her robe at the neckline and walked to the edge of the porch. "Hello?" she called.

The man turned, then lifted a hand. "Didn't think anyone was home." He walked back toward the house.

As he approached, Josie recognized him. Hank, their former manager. Ian's father. Panic welled up inside her. What was he doing here?

Maybe he knows.

But there was no way he could.

He was walking up the hill. He's carrying a cluster of flowers. He's only come to visit the grave.

"Josephine Mitchell." He removed his cap, revealing a hairline that had receded several inches. His face had aged, the tired lines around his eyes a permanent stamp of grief.

"Mr. Leland, how wonderful to see you." The lie slipped out easily.

His booted feet stopped just shy of the porch. His Wranglers hung on his frame. The potbelly she remembered was gone, his jeans held in place by a wide brown belt.

"You're all grown up," he drawled.

As opposed to Ian, who's rotting in his grave. She shook away the thought. It wasn't what he'd meant. "I suppose I am. Laurel told me you moved to Tennessee."

"Yep, that's where I am now." His dark eyes, shaped like almonds and slightly turned up at the corners, were so much like Ian's.

Maybe he'd remarried. Maybe he'd found happiness in the hills of Tennessee. Maybe he'd made peace with his loss and moved on.

"Have a little cabin set back off the road a ways. It's small, but there's just me."

"Sounds nice."

"It's home. I come back here every year on Ian's birthday though." He gestured up the hill. "Put flowers on his grave."

Ian's birthday. She'd forgotten it was in October. How could she have forgotten? It was right before the festival.

How hard this day must be for Hank. Josie cupped her elbows. She should invite him in. It was the hospitable thing to do.

"Your aunt takes good care of his grave. It's a solace for me to come back and see it well tended."

Josie nodded, unsure of what to say. Unable to untangle her thoughts enough to pull a few coherent words from the mess.

"My boy loved you like a sister, Josephine. Hope you know that."

Bile churned in her stomach. She worked to keep a smile on a face that felt more like plastic than flesh. *Speak, Josie. Say something.*

"Thank you. He was—he was a special boy." And yet she'd never felt anything for him except resentment. Never took the time to get to know him at all.

Did Hank know that? Had her adolescent envy been obvious? Ian had never seemed to realize, but he'd been a boy, desperate for a friend. Adults perceived things that children were oblivious to. Was Hank trying to pour salt in her wounds? No, he wasn't that kind of man. But death had a way of changing people.

Maybe he does know.

Josie averted her eyes.

"That he was. He would've been twenty-one today."

An ache swelled inside her, massive and heavy. Twenty-one. Legally an adult. Instead, he'd died on the brink of manhood. *Because of me.*

Hank set the cap back on his head. "Well."

She didn't know what to say. She wanted to beg his forgiveness, tell him it should have been her. Tell him it was all her fault. *I'm so sorry.* Instead, the ache inside swallowed up her words and expanded.

"I'll be on my way. Tell Laurel and your aunt I'll stop by and see them before I head out of town."

He was coming back. The thought brought dread, and she felt guilty for her selfishness. Blue Ridge Orchard was a connection to his only child.

Josie pried her tongue from the dry roof of her mouth. "Will do."

With a wave, he turned toward the hill.

Josie went into the house and shut the door behind her, her breaths coming unnaturally fast. Just when she thought maybe . . .

The reminder of what she'd done and who she was came rushing back. What right did she have to life when she'd taken someone else's? What right did she have to love when she'd yanked away the only thing Mr. Leland had left in this world?

She thought of his face, all sunken and hollow. He looked ill instead of looking like a man enjoying the fruits of his labor. Ill and lonely.

What right did she have to happiness when she'd deprived Ian of it? The disease was justice. God's way of evening the score. And who was she to stand in his way?

She returned to her room, her mind fixed on the thing she should've done weeks ago. Maybe she hadn't had the courage until now. Maybe she'd clung to a futile hope that was buried like a seed deep inside her. Maybe Grady had been all the temptation she'd needed.

But now there was nothing to stop her. She grabbed her purse from the dresser and dug deep until her fingers closed around the injectable cortisol and the two bottles. She went to the bathroom, wrapped the shot with a wad of tissue and tossed it into the waste can, then she twisted off the lids and upended the bottles over the commode. With the flick of her hand, the pills were spinning, spinning, swirling through the water, and then they were gone.

thirty-three

The autumn foliage was Josie's excuse to disappear with her camera for the day. She spent a fortune on film and stayed out until twilight drew its heavy curtains across the hills. She'd left her rolls of film at Ingles to be developed while she was out snapping more photos, then she'd picked them up, eager to see her work.

She sat in the deli booth where she and Grady had sat before and opened the packages, surveying the images she'd captured. A couple of them were blurry, but there were a few she was pleased with. One of them was of the creek water rippling over a rock, the water frozen in time, each drop in perfect focus. Maybe she would enlarge that one. The covered bridge over the gap was also good. The shadow of a tree fell across the entrance, darkening the interior.

She was proud of her work, and she found herself wanting to show someone. Leaving the world of her photos, she looked up and saw she was alone in the deli. She'd been alone all day, wanting to avoid Hank and her family.

It was getting late though, and Hank would surely be on his way by now. She packed her prints and returned to her car.

Within minutes she was pulling into the driveway and longing for her bed. She wanted to erase Hank from her thoughts, and sleep was the only way that was going to happen. She hadn't been able to get his tired, gentle eyes out of her mind all day. Eyes so like Ian's.

She forced the image from her mind as she crested the hill and glided down the slope. Would she ever go down this hill without thinking of that night? Her eyes darted to the left where her sled had gone over, where Ian had trudged down when she'd fallen through the ice.

Stop it, Josie. Stop thinking about it.

How much worse can I feel? How much sorrier can I be? There's nothing I can do to make it right. Nothing.

Yes, there is. You're doing it now, doing the only thing that will make it right.

But Ian was gone and she couldn't bring him back. If she could reverse time, she'd do things differently. She wouldn't go down the hill. Wouldn't let Ian jump into the frigid water. She'd rather she'd died herself. Her father probably would've too.

Josie accelerated down the hill as if she would escape the memory as soon as she left the area. But there would be no escaping the memory until she left this property for good. Once harvest was over, once Laurel had the twins and she could leave, it would be better.

The thought was heartening until she realized it was a lie. Had she been able to forget in Louisville? In Columbus? In Pittsburgh? There was no escaping the memory until life was over.

And what then? What waited for her on the other side? What if she would be eternally punished for what she'd done? Anxiety rose inside her with the speed and force of a hurricane.

Maybe there was no escape at all. Maybe there was a price to be paid for her sin. A price inescapable even through death.

The thought shook her to the core. It was easier to think of death as an end. Oblivion, or at least the cease of existence. But what if her family was right and there was more? What if God punished her eternally for what she'd done, for who she was?

She pulled up to the house, her mind so far from her whereabouts, she didn't notice the Buick until she was beside it.

A heavy sigh filled the car. She was beginning to believe God was hanging around, if only because somebody had to be orchestrating this bad string of events.

She let her head fall against the headrest, looking up to the heavens through her roof. "Are you serious?" Her voice rang out in the darkness.

Her engine hissed and snapped. Apparently so.

When she opened the front door, she heard the sound of chatter from the dining room. If she could just sneak up to her room.

"Got a plate for you, Josie," Aunt Lola called. "Come say hi to Mr. Leland."

So much for that. Josie entered the dining room, avoiding eye contact with Grady. She greeted Mr. Leland again and took a seat.

"We were just talking about the time we went up to Grandfather Mountain and Ian got stuck on the middle of the bridge," Laurel said.

He'd been terrified of heights. It had been Josie who'd convinced him to go across. Dared him. Laurel had been the one to get him.

Mr. Leland laughed. "So much for facing your fears. He wouldn't go past the second rung on a ladder after that."

I was so mean. I wanted him to fail. I wanted him to make a fool of himself.

Josie picked at the meatloaf, wishing she'd turned down supper. Now she was stuck at the table until they were finished.

"Nate said you had a good year, Grady," Hank said.

Grady scooped a bite of peas onto his fork. "Yes, sir. Good crop, our best since I've been here. Would've been even better except for the windstorm, but we'll still turn a profit."

"Good you've moved back home, Josephine. Looks like Grady's making more work for everyone." He smiled.

"Oh. I'm just back 'til the end of harvest. I live in Louisville now." She saw Grady's fork pause on the way to his mouth.

"We're hoping to change her mind," Nate said.

"If only she weren't so stubborn." Laurel poked her with her elbow. "I keep telling her I'll need her for aunt duty." Hank's visit had turned her mood around.

"I'm so happy y'all are being blessed with babies," Hank said.

"Won't be long now," Aunt Lola said.

"How much bigger could I possibly get?" Laurel said.

Josie wondered how long she needed to wait before she could excuse herself without being rude.

"What are you doing up in Louisville, Josephine?"

She cleared her throat. "I'm a photographer."

He nodded. "Always did have that camera around your neck. But I thought sure you'd stick around and run this place. You had a knack for it."

That's what she'd thought too. She'd seen a bumper sticker once: "If you want to make God laugh, make plans."

"Ian had hopes of helping you run it someday. He sure loved this place."

A sharp knife wedged between her ribs, sinking deep into her flesh.

"He'd be proud to see it prospering," Hank continued.

Panic bubbled up inside her, begging escape. She chewed a

mouthful of peas, hoping someone else would speak. Couldn't they talk about something else, someone else? Then she felt guilty for the thought. It must bring Mr. Leland joy to talk to people who knew Ian. Who was she to rob him of that?

Finally, Grady mentioned the vine-style method of growing apple trees, and the two started talking shop. Josie remained quiet for the rest of the meal and excused herself when Aunt Lola brought out another apple pie.

"It's the recipe that's going to win me the grand prize," Aunt Lola tempted.

"Save me a slice, and I'll have it tomorrow." She said good-bye to Hank and slipped from the room, to the stairway, feeling Grady's eyes burning the back of her neck.

He caught her on the second step. "Josie."

So close to escaping. She sighed, turning around. He was eye level.

"You okay?" The concern in his chocolaty eyes was the only thing that stayed her irritation.

Her bed beckoned. She wanted to sink into its quilted softness and pull the covers over her head. "I'm just tired."

A strand of hair brushed the side of his eye and caught in his eyelashes. "Can I get you anything?"

"I just need sleep." Oblivion, really, but sleep would suffice for now.

He nodded. "All right. 'Night, Josie." He touched her chin with his index finger. Just a whisper of a touch, but it melted her. Made her want to sink into his embrace and find her escape there.

"Good night," she said, then bolted up the stairs before her weakness led her further astray.

thirty-four

*You still look tired."

Josie swallowed the sip of hot coffee and scooted across the tailgate to make room for Grady. The others sat a distance away under a shade tree, enjoying a coffee break after a long morning.

"I'm not sleeping well." The illness had its repercussions, but Hank's visit hadn't helped either. When she had slept, visions of Ian had haunted her.

Hank's words echoed in her mind all night. *"He'd be proud to see it prospering."* This year's crop would've made Ian proud. Even with the loss from the windstorm, it was a good year. She could picture Ian now, scanning the orchard, his scrawny shoulders pulled back, a silly grin on his freckled face. He'd taken pride in his work here.

Josie was going to make sure she was doing everything in her power to produce a harvest that would make Ian proud. That's the one good thing she could do with the time she had left. She owed Ian. Maybe she couldn't work off the debt, but she could even the scales a little.

"You're working too hard."

It was the least she could do. And in truth, staying busy was easier on her mind, just harder on her body. Grady's thigh pressed against hers, made her forget there was anything wrong with her body. The contact made her feel whole, connected.

Which was all wrong. She shifted, pulling her knees to her chest.

"We only have a couple of weeks to go on harvest. You could stay with Laurel all day, and Aunt Lola could keep longer hours at the shop."

Did he have to be so concerned for her? It only made it harder. Made her decision to stay away more painful. His suggestion was tempting. Being at the house would mean less contact with Grady, but it would also mean too much time on her hands. Besides, she was determined to see this harvest through, work as hard as Ian would have if he were still here.

"I'd rather stay busy." It was the only thing that would make the time pass quickly. Would keep her mind from filling with thoughts of Ian and Hank and her dad. "Besides, I like it out here." It was the one place she knew what she was doing.

"Your body needs rest."

Why couldn't he just leave her alone? "Don't tell me what my body needs." It felt good, snapping at him. But just for a moment. Then the familiar pang of guilt crept in.

She set the thermos down, then rubbed the back of her neck as if she could massage away her guilt.

Grady let Josie's sharp tone roll off his back. She wasn't feeling well and it made her irritable. She wasn't so different from her sister. Why did she have to be so stubborn about the work?

"Sorry," Josie said, barely meeting his eyes before flickering away. "I know you're just trying to help."

She looked so small tucked into a ball on the edge of the tailgate. He wanted to wrap his arms around her and protect her. But he couldn't protect her from everything. Wasn't sure she wanted him to try.

He wanted to ask why she'd acted so strangely over dinner. There was something she wasn't telling him. Her face had turned ashen when Hank was talking. She'd picked at her thumbnail with her middle finger the way she did when she was upset or anxious. The way she was doing now.

Maybe if he figured out what was worrying her, it would take off some of the pressure. "Hank seems to be faring well."

Josie stopped picking and sipped her coffee. "Mhmm."

"His son was about your age, wasn't he?"

Josie stirred, looking restless. "A few years younger." She checked her watch, let go of her legs, and set them dangling over the end, poised for flight. "Probably should get back to work."

"It's only been three or four minutes." There was something bothering her, and his hunch that it had to do with Hank was right on. It was all starting to make sense. The way she kept busy all the time, never sitting still until she was about to drop. The way she wanted to run off to the city. The way she'd run from the orchard even though she'd always wanted to stay and run it.

He was tired of beating around the bush. "What is it, Josie? What are you running from?"

Her answer was too quick. "I'm not running from anything."

He knew she'd left shortly after Ian's death. Had that factored into her decision? Maybe he shouldn't press her. She had enough problems, didn't she? And yet sometimes talking helped. She kept everything to herself, all bottled up.

He pushed a little harder. "It must have been hard when Ian died."

She froze for an instant, her dangling legs stiff. "Stop it." Her skin had blanched. "All right. We all have our ghosts. And maybe I *am* running from them."

He felt bad for pushing so hard. But running didn't help. He knew it better than anyone. His voice gentled. "How's that working for you?"

She hopped off the truck, a dismount that was surprisingly agile until her legs buckled on the landing.

Grady was off the truck and grabbing her before her knees gave way.

She brushed him away. "I'm fine."

She was so stinking independent. Couldn't she let him in just a little? "You're not fine. You should be at the house."

"And you should mind your own business."

"You are my business."

Her chin went up and she crossed her arms. "How do you figure?"

This wasn't going the way he wanted. Why did he have to get so pushy? And why did she have to be so prickly when all he wanted was to help? When he just wanted to take care of her because he . . .

What? Cared for her? It was what he'd told her two days before. The phrase seemed hollow compared to the feelings she stirred in him. Was he in deeper than that? Had he fallen in love with her?

Did she return those feelings? Is that why her lip quivered for just a moment before she stilled it with her teeth?

Her chin had come down just a notch, though her hands still gripped her own biceps like a lifeline. A strand of hair came loose from her ponytail and a breeze caught it, dragging it across her face.

He reached out to tuck it behind her ear.

She flinched away before he caught the strand. That one movement told him more than anything she'd said. He felt the rejection down to his bones.

"I can't do this," she said.

He didn't have to ask what. Still, he waited for some kind of elaboration. Was it the illness? The certainty of—what was it she'd said? *"There's no happily-ever-after here."*

Or was it something else? That thing from the past—whatever it was—that she ran from?

Hernando's boisterous laugh cut through the silence.

"Harvest is nearly over," she said. "I'll be going home soon, and until then, I just need—"

Her words halted; her lips worked, seeking the right word. He wished he could fill in the blank for her. *You.*

"I just need to be left alone."

The ache in his bones spread. "Left alone?" *It's not complicated, amigo, that makes it pretty clear.*

In the grove, the crew rattled off Spanish faster than he could follow even if he were paying attention.

She let loose of her arm long enough to tuck the wayward strand behind her ear. "A relationship is out of the question right now."

"You've made your decision . . ."

"I hope you understand."

There was understanding, and then there was accepting. But it was her decision, not his.

The words she'd just said rang in his head. *Left alone.* What did that mean? They worked together, they ate supper together. Was he not supposed to talk to her, look at her, help her?

He was only willing to cooperate so far. "I guess I'll have to be content with friendship." Assume the sale. His dad had taught him that.

"Grady . . ." Her head tipped sideways, and he could see another rejection poised on the end of her tongue.

What? A moment ago he was hoping for love, now he had to beg for friendship? It was a little humiliating.

But he was going to fight for whatever he could get. "We have to work together, lead this crew together. Friendship is the bare minimum, don't you think?" He tossed the words out as casually as he could, shamed by how desperate he felt for her consent.

The chatter between the crew wound down as they finished their coffee and made their way back to the trees.

"Friends?" He put out his hand.

She looked at it as if it were a rotten apple. Finally, she extended her own.

"Friends," she said, the word wobbling ever so slightly on her lips.

thirty-five

*W*hat is going on between you and Grady?" Laurel's question made Josie wish she'd retreated to her room after supper instead of taking pity on her sister.

"I don't know what you mean." Denial was the best defense. For the past two days, there'd been tension between her and Grady. She felt every weighted glance he sent her way.

"Baloney. The way he looks at you . . ." Laurel fanned her face, her knitting needle waving. "Heaven have mercy."

Josie felt a need to fan her own face as heat climbed her cheeks. "Your hormones are affecting your reasoning skills."

"On the contrary, my perception has never been sharper. Spill it."

Her sister was easy to talk to, but Laurel didn't know enough to understand why the relationship was impossible. And she couldn't tell Laurel everything.

"You have the hots for our manager, admit it."

The crass expression didn't begin to describe her feelings. Feelings that made everything harder, more complicated. Feelings she had to put from her mind if she was ever going to survive these remaining weeks.

And she hated what this was doing to Grady. Her decision had hurt him, and she regretted that. She wished she could do something for him. Something that would make it—

The orchard. He'd always wanted one of his own, and she could see to it that he could buy it. She weighed the cost, the extra burden on Laurel during the years it would take him to buy her shares. She trusted Grady now. He was a hard worker, and if her family had managed to keep it going for three generations, she was sure he could too.

Maybe she could even sign some of her shares over to him in her will. The thought of leaving Grady something he treasured buoyed her spirits.

Now Laurel's voice startled her from her thoughts. "Are you all right?"

"I'm fine." She lifted the corners of her lips, hoping for a convincing smile. She wanted any idea of a pairing between her and Grady banished from her sister's thoughts. "We're just friends." It was what they'd decided on. Or rather, what she'd reluctantly agreed to.

"I never had a friend look at me the way Grady looks at you . . ."

"We're *friends.*"

Laurel shrugged and her needles clacked together as she worked the yarn. "Whatever you say."

"We're just friends." Grady loaded a crate of Granny Smiths for the farmer's market. They'd hired a high school student to man the stand.

"Sorry to pry." Nate adjusted the crate in the bed of the pickup. "That's what Josie said, but Laurel's concerned. She says Josie doesn't seem herself, and hasn't been since she's come home."

Grady felt a prick of guilt. How could she be herself? He hated that she was going through this alone. He'd hoped that being her friend meant she'd spend time with him, confide in him. He was half tempted to tell Nate about her illness. She needed her family right now, especially since she wasn't letting him in.

But then there was Laurel's condition. Josie was right that she didn't need the stress. She needed to carry those babies as long as possible.

Grady pushed the crate onto the bed and shoved the tailgate closed. "Laurel doing okay?"

"She's bored and uncomfortable, but the babies are healthy. She's got the furniture all picked out, but I need to finish painting the room. Probably ought to do that tomorrow night."

"Must be getting close to delivery time." The closer, the better. Once the babies were born, Josie could tell her sister, and then she'd have the support she needed. Surely she wouldn't go back to Louisville as she'd said. He didn't like the thought of her being alone.

"Her due date is in three and a half weeks, but she'll likely deliver early since it's twins. Still, the longer she carries them, the better."

Every day the delivery was delayed was another day Josie suffered in silence. He knew it was the right thing, but that knowledge didn't make it any easier. In the meantime, he'd just have to see to it that being friends with Josie meant being a shoulder for her to lean on.

thirty-six

Josie was minding her own business, her thoughts far away, when Laurel set her sneaky plan in motion.

". . . So I was wondering if you could pick it up tonight, Josie," Laurel was saying.

Josie chewed a mouthful of green bean casserole. "What?"

"The baby furniture? I just told you it's on sale now and I was wondering if you could pick it up tonight if you don't have plans."

As if she ever had plans. At least it would get her away from the house. "Sure."

Laurel beamed. "Great. It's all settled."

Grady scooted his chair back. "I'm ready whenever you are."

She stared up at him. "What?" *You have got to pay better attention.* Her eyes fell to his trim waist, then she looked away.

"To leave for Asheville . . . ?" Grady said.

Grady was going too? Josie set down her fork and wiped her mouth, stalling. An hour there, an hour back. Lots of time. All alone. "Oh, I thought . . ."

That she was going to haul furniture for twins in her Celica? Of course they'd need Grady's truck.

"Pick you up in ten minutes?"

569

She checked her watch. If they were going to get there before it closed, they'd have to hurry. "Sure." He left, the screen door slapping against the door frame as he exited.

Josie nailed Laurel with a glare, which her sister missed entirely.

"I'll get started on the trim." Nate pecked Laurel on the cheek.

"Chicken," Laurel murmured.

Aunt Lola began gathering plates. "Better get the dishes done." She disappeared into the kitchen.

Josie pushed away from the table and stared her sister down. "I see right through this little plan of yours, missy."

"Don't be paranoid." Laurel rubbed the small of her back, arching. "The furniture I wanted finally went on sale today, and I'm about to pop here, in case you haven't noticed."

"You know perfectly well Grady could've gotten it himself."

Laurel sighed. "I have some female things I need you to get while you're there. I couldn't very well ask him to pick up a few nursing bras, could I?"

As if she couldn't have asked Nate to do that. Her sister was up to no good and Josie knew it.

"Stop looking at me like that. I'm just a bored pregnant lady in need of a little excitement. Humor me."

The thought of a trip alone with Grady was providing a measure of excitement for Josie too.

Twenty minutes later they were on their way. The truck rumbled and bumped down the highway, filling the awkward silence and jarring the contents of Josie's stomach.

Did Grady know they'd been set up? If so, he didn't seem to

mind. He flipped on the radio and whistled along to the country tune. Josie watched the trees, clothed in vibrant autumn hues, march by in the fading light. October was passing quickly, bringing a crisp chill to the air that warned of winter's approach.

Josie leaned back and forced herself to relax. She was finally escaping the orchard, only she wasn't escaping at all. Instead, she was trapped in a vehicle with the man who made her want to throw all caution aside and embrace life.

It was dangerous stuff. *And you've already been down this road, Josie. Already made your decision. Now you just have to stick to it.* This was the easy part, right?

When the song ended, Grady turned down the radio. "Tell me about your life in Louisville. You haven't said much about it."

Because there wasn't much to say. "I lived in an apartment near downtown, second floor. I chose it because it had this wonderful veranda that faced east. I have an impressive garden out there with lavender and strawberry, wisteria . . . Well, I did anyway."

"How long did you live there?"

"Eight months." It was the longest she'd stayed anywhere since she'd left the orchard. She found herself unsettled after staying any one place awhile. Maybe it was time to get a new place anyway.

"What about friends?"

"I've only been in Louisville eight months. I was in Columbus before that. And Pittsburgh before that. I guess I like to move around, experience new things." Running, just like Grady had said. Being on the go was easier. She got stir-crazy when she stayed in one place too long.

"Doesn't sound like you have many roots."

"Roots are overrated. If you aren't careful, they climb right up and strangle you whole."

She felt his eyes on her. "Really? You think so?"

"It's not like you have so many roots yourself."

The singer crooned about a lost love and a dog that died. If Grady had any relatives, he never talked about them. He was as much a loner as she.

"I have my mom, she just lives too far away. But the man she married has a business in Chicago, so she's not moving anytime soon. I guess I'm trying to grow roots in Shelbyville. That's why the orchard is so important to me."

She'd never told him she'd changed her mind about selling. It was the least she could do for him. How could she take away what he'd worked so hard for? She'd called Allen, her attorney, the day before and made sure fifteen percent of her shares would go to him. That would leave Grady with thirty percent and Laurel with seventy. Her sister and Grady could work out the buy from there. Between him and Nate, they'd make things right, make sure Laurel was taken care of after she was gone.

If she asked him to, he would. The song was winding down, and Josie worked up the nerve to ask. "Would you do something for me?"

He looked at her. "What's that?"

She had to think about after. It was the most important thing. "You know the orchard was never Laurel's thing. She assumed the responsibility because I left and then Dad had the stroke."

The song on the radio ended and the DJ started talking. Grady snapped it off.

"Laurel always dreamed of selling her crafts, and I'd like her to have that chance if she still wants it. Either way, I don't want her to worry about the orchard. That's why I was so adamant about selling it."

An ache started in her throat. "At the same time, I respect what you've done with Blue Ridge and the plans you've made for its future success. I wondered if you were still interested in working out a buying arrangement. Something long-term that would give you time to buy it out." She didn't mention the shares she'd left him. She'd let that be a surprise. Her gift to him.

Grady braked at a stoplight. It was what he'd wanted so badly. She didn't expect the long silence that followed. Maybe he didn't want it anymore. Maybe he'd changed his mind. Her gaze found his.

She couldn't quite read the look in his eyes. The shadows were pressing in around them. Something flickered in his eyes before he looked away. The light changed, and he accelerated.

His Adam's apple dipped. "I didn't want it like this."

Something in his tone bothered her. He felt sorry for her. He wanted to buy the orchard, but not because she was dying.

"You wanted to sell it so it wouldn't be a burden to your sister after—" His words choked to a halt.

"She never wanted it to begin with. Not really. It was my fault for leaving." And her dad's fault for dumping it on her.

"You couldn't have known your dad was going to pass."

But she hadn't come home even then. Couldn't face the guilt of Ian, didn't want to face the unresolved issues with her dad. She didn't want to think about this now, much less talk about it.

"Are you still interested in buying it?"

His jaw clenched, the shadows dancing across his face. "I don't want to talk about this."

It wasn't as if she had all the time in the world. "I need to get this settled, Grady."

His hands worked on the steering wheel as if he wanted to

strangle it. He blinked rapidly, emotion drawing his facial muscles into a hard plane.

Maybe he didn't want it anymore and was afraid to tell her. "If you're not, I'll figure something else out." She didn't want to dump the orchard on Grady any more than on Laurel. He deserved to be happy. To find those roots he wanted. A place that was home, someone to keep the loneliness at bay.

The thought tightened her stomach, made it twist painfully. She didn't want to think of him with someone else. It should've been her. If fate hadn't intervened, she would've stayed on the orchard all along and would've met him after Hank retired. She and Grady and Ian would be working the orchard together.

She and Grady would've fallen in love. Maybe they'd be married by now. Maybe they'd be driving to Asheville to pick up their own baby's furniture.

Stop. What are you doing to yourself?

"I'll work something out with Laurel, if she wants to sell," he said. "I won't let the orchard be a burden to her." He placed his hand on hers and met her gaze. "I promise."

The warmth from his fingers enveloped hers as he stared into her eyes. The connection felt good, made her feel whole and healthy and content. She could pretend, if she wanted, that they *were* married. That they *were* picking up their own baby furniture.

That she'd never caused Ian's death and hadn't been on the run from the truth ever since.

"Thank you." She slipped her hand from under his and looked away. She tried to enjoy the relief she should be feeling now that everything was in place. She was sure Laurel would let him buy her out once she got a taste of life after the twins were born. Nate would help convince her.

It was all taken care of. She just wasn't sure why the relief she had expected never came.

By the time they reached The Baby Loft, the mood had lightened. Grady had turned the radio back on, and when he started singing along to a hit tune, she joined in, which only made it sound worse, if that was possible.

Somewhere between Burnsville and Weaverville, her stomach settled, and though her energy level was still low, her spirits were higher.

Grady let her off at the door and got out to shift a few things in the back. Josie grabbed the nursing bras and a few other items Laurel had written on a list while she waited for the worker to load the boxes: a pair of cribs, a changing table, and a matching bureau.

She wished she had time to stop and see Ashley and Jackie, but it was getting late, and they probably had plans anyway. Besides, it would be late by the time she and Grady got home as it was.

Her cell phone rang as she exited the store. A man was helping Grady heft one of the boxes into the truck bed. She pulled out her phone. Ah, five bars of reception. Welcome to the city.

"Hello?"

"It's Nate. You might want to get home as soon as you can. Laurel's in labor."

Josie's feet stopped on the sidewalk outside the store. "But we just left."

"Her back's been hurting all day, but apparently that was the beginning of labor. We're at the hospital and the doctor says she's progressing quickly."

Grady approached. "What's wrong?"

"Laurel's in labor."

Two seconds later he was shoving the other boxes into the truck and slamming the tailgate in place.

"Everything is okay," Nate said. "The babies are positioned right and the doctor expects a smooth delivery." He covered the phone and Josie heard a muffled voice, then he was back on the line. "Laurel said to get your heinie back here."

Josie smothered a smile, excitement building inside. "Tell her it was a fine time to send me after her furniture."

A rustling sounded through the line. "Uh, she's in a bit of pain now. Gotta go."

Josie flipped her phone closed and hopped in the passenger side as Grady turned the key, released the parking brake, and eased onto the street.

"Come on, come on, step on it."

He tossed her a bemused smile. "Patience, Auntie Josie."

She couldn't help it. Somehow the whole baby thing hadn't seemed real until this moment. What if Laurel gave birth before she got there? She didn't want to miss the big event.

Worse, what if something went wrong? What if something happened to one of the babies? Or to Laurel? Nate hadn't said it was too early. He'd even said the doctors expected a smooth delivery. But what if—

"Stop worrying. Everything's going to be fine."

"You can't know that." Grady turned a corner and slowly worked up to the speed limit. "Could we put the pedal to the metal, please?"

Within minutes Grady was accelerating onto the freeway, the distance between Josie and her sister growing shorter by the second.

thirty-seven

*J*osie rushed to the desk, braking only when her hands hit the sharp edge of the counter. "Is Laurel okay? Has she had the babies?"

The woman's hazel eyes peered over a pair of black, heavily framed reading glasses. "Are you a member of the family?"

Josie narrowed her eyes at Aunt Lola's friend. "Verna Mae Pridemore, you know very well I'm Laurel's sister."

The woman pursed her lips, then smoothed her flippy cartoon hair. "Laurel's doing fine. She's in delivery, but you'll have to wait in the lobby just down the hall."

"Thank you." Josie rushed down the hall and found Aunt Lola in the nook of cushioned chairs flanked by tables.

"She's doing fine," her aunt said in greeting, then gave her a sturdy hug. "They took her into delivery about twenty minutes ago."

What a relief. Somehow she didn't quite believe it until she saw Aunt Lola's peaceful countenance.

Josie took a seat on the edge of a chair and set her purse on the table. "I tried to call Nate on the way over, but I guess he turned his cell off."

"I think he's got his hands full with Laurel. Where's Grady?"

"Parking the car."

Aunt Lola filled her in. When Grady appeared and sank into the seat next to Josie, Aunt Lola sat on his other side and caught him up too. As silence settled between them, Aunt Lola bowed her head, her lips moving in a silent prayer.

A moment later, Grady joined hands with Aunt Lola and Josie and bowed his own head.

Josie closed her eyes. It had been so long. She didn't know what to say, how to begin even. It seemed to come so naturally to everyone else. Maybe God wouldn't mind if she just sat here quietly. She was sure Aunt Lola's and Grady's prayers would have more effect anyway.

Grady squeezed her hand and let it go when he was finished, then Josie grabbed a magazine to occupy her mind. She flipped through one after another, looking up each time the doors leading to the delivery rooms opened. An hour passed, then two. At times, the hands on the utilitarian clock seemed stuck.

At one thirty, Josie set down the copy of *Carolina Country* magazine she hadn't been able to read. Grady was slumped in the seat beside her, his arms folded across his chest, his eyes closed.

Aunt Lola watched a rerun of *Judge Judy* on the ancient TV in the corner.

"What's taking so long?" Josie asked. She thought the delivery was the short part of labor.

"She's delivering babies, not mail, Josephine. These things take time."

She only hoped everything was okay. There was always a possibility of a C-section with twins, and she knew Laurel was hoping to avoid that.

"You took twenty-some hours yourself, you know, and as I recall, the delivery part was no walk in the park for your mama."

She hadn't known that. Her mom hadn't said anything, and that wasn't something her dad would've passed on, especially given the memory of her twin's death.

The thought sent a shiver of fear through her. What if it happened to one of Laurel's babies? Was this sort of thing genetic? And why didn't someone come out here and tell them what was going on?

Josie's back ached and she shifted, facing Grady, trying to get comfortable on the chair. She'd already flipped through every magazine on the table. She laid her cheek against the back of the vinyl chair and pulled her knee up, careful not to jostle Grady.

Grady let out a soft snore, drawing her attention. His dark locks fell in waves along his face. He looked serene and vulnerable in sleep.

She let her eyes rest on the planes of his face. The harsh fluorescent lights cut across his features, highlighting pencil-thin shadows that fanned out from his eyes. She noticed a tiny crescent-shaped scar at the corner of his mouth and wondered how he'd come by it.

His skin had darkened under the autumn sun and looked golden brown against his black crew-neck T-shirt. His neck and jaw sported a five o'clock shadow that made him look rugged. She remembered her initial impression of him as Marlboro Man and felt a smile tug at her lips. She'd been attracted to him from the beginning, and that was before she knew the man beneath the handsome exterior.

He was gentle and caring, always watching out for her. He was a man you could count on, a rarity in her experience. Her eyes fell to his lips, slightly parted in sleep. His upper lip had a bow that made her want to dip her finger into the valley of it, and his lower lip had just enough fullness to make him ripe for kissing. She could nearly feel the kiss now, feel the feathery softness of it.

She sensed a change, an awareness, and when her gaze trailed upward, she found Grady's eyes open. Their gazes locked, a steady current of something strong connecting them. She wanted him that moment in a way she'd never wanted a man. She wanted all of him, completely. She wanted to jump inside his mind and curl up with his thoughts. She wanted to love him and let him love her.

The thought startled her, and she broke eye contact, sitting up in the chair. She was weak, so weak! She had to stop thinking about what she wanted. She had to think of Grady, of what was best for him. And she wasn't it.

The delivery door busted open and Nate appeared, a silly grin spread across his face.

Josie shook herself from her thoughts and stood.

"We have two healthy baby girls!" Nate said.

Girls! Josie embraced Nate, relief making her legs go wobbly.

"Laurel okay?" Aunt Lola was right behind her.

"She's fine. Exhausted, but fine."

"Congratulations, Nate." Grady shook his hand.

"Thanks. They're identical, can you believe it? I'm going to have to put their initials on their feet or something."

Josie was so happy for Laurel. She'd always imagined her sister with girls. Now it was a reality. And two of them . . .

"When can we see them?" Josie asked.

"I'm not sure. They're doing all that after-birth stuff, but the girls are breathing just fine and got high scores, whatever that means."

"I think it means those babies will be going home with Laurel," Aunt Lola said.

Nate pushed on the door, clearly eager to return to his wife. "She was worried about that. I'd better get back to her. Just wanted to thank you guys for praying and let you know all is well."

After he left, they sat down and waited again. Any fatigue Josie had felt before had been washed away by the wonderful news. She was almost shaking with it.

"You could probably go on home and get some rest, Grady," Aunt Lola said. "Josephine and I will want to stay awhile."

Grady tossed Josie a look. "I'm not leaving until I get a peek at those future troublemakers."

"Suit yourself. Shouldn't be long anyhow."

I'm an aunt. Josie let the idea soak in. There hadn't been a baby in the family since she'd been born. And now Laurel was a *mom.* Everything was changing.

A wave of dizziness washed over her, and she leaned back in the chair. She laid her head against the wall and closed her eyes a minute, hoping it would pass. Instead, closing her eyes and tipping her head made it worse. Her head felt weighted with lead as she pulled upright and opened her eyes. Her vision swam.

"You're not feeling well," Grady whispered.

I will not pass out. Not here. Not now. She licked her lips and gathered enough breath for an answer. "I'm fine." She could feel his eyes on her. The last thing she needed was for him to call attention to her illness here in the hospital.

"Liar."

The door swung open and a nurse appeared. "All right, family, you can come see your little darlings now."

Josie feared she might faint when she stood, and then what would happen? She had to hide it from her aunt.

Seeming to realize her predicament, Grady reached out and

took Josie's hand. Fortunately, Aunt Lola was in a hurry toward Laurel's room, her sneakers squeaking against the hospital tile.

Grady helped her to her feet. "All right?"

The initial wave of dizziness passed after a few seconds. She nodded, and they followed in Aunt Lola's wake.

Laurel was propped in the bed holding a bundle when they arrived. Her hair was damp around her forehead, her face flushed.

Josie leaned down and placed a kiss on her forehead. "Congratulations, Mommy." She looked down into the tiny face of her niece. Her blue eyes peered into Laurel's face. "Oh, look at her! She's so tiny." An impossibly small fist curled next to her cheek. "I wish I had my camera."

"This one's five pounds two ounces," Laurel said. "And Hefty over there weighs five pounds seven ounces."

Nate transferred the other infant into Aunt Lola's waiting arms.

"I can't believe they're identical," Josie said. Her legs still shaky, she grabbed the handrail for support.

"Want to hold her?" Laurel asked.

Her arms ached to hold the baby, but what if she fainted or fell? Grady pulled a chair from the corner and placed it behind her.

Laurel transferred the baby into her arms and Josie sank into the rocking chair. The infant was so little and helpless. Her eyes were shaped like Nate's, but she had Laurel's dark head of hair. What a little miracle. That Nate and Laurel's love had created a tiny human being full of potential. One day this little one would grow into a full-fledged adult with all her own capabilities and strengths.

And you won't be around for it.

She felt an ache at the back of her eyes and the baby's face blurred.

"Did you finally decide on some names for the little rug rats?" For all her snap, Aunt Lola's voice was choked.

The one in Josie's arms blinked, her eyes opening wide. Josie pulled her close, cradling the back of her head.

"We did," Laurel said. "You're holding Katherine Marie . . ."

"After our mom," Josie explained to Grady.

"I'm sure she would've loved that," Grady said.

"And Josie's holding Corinne Josephine."

"You named her after me?" Josie looked down at the bundle in her arms, feeling awed and proud, and grossly undeserving of the honor.

"Katie and Corie for short," Nate said.

"I like that," Grady said.

"Your mama would be so proud, Laurel," Aunt Lola said.

The words faded as Josie watched her niece suck in her lower lip. "Hey, little Corie," she whispered. "It seems we share a name." She could only hope this one had a brighter future. "You deserve so many good things. Your mama and daddy are going to be the best parents ever. You'll see." A rock lodged in her throat.

Corie blinked up at her with somber eyes as if she heard and understood Josie's words.

Grady peered over her shoulder. "Amazing."

He didn't have to say anything else. She knew exactly what he was feeling because she was feeling it too. New life. New hope. A renewal of all things good, wrapped up in the tiny bundle of a baby. It was enough to renew her hope in a loving God.

God, if you're listening, could you look out after these two? Bless them with a long, happy life and lots of love.

How long had it been since she'd prayed? She wasn't sure, but she had the distinct feeling this prayer made its way past the hospital ceiling, maybe into the very ears of God himself.

thirty-eight

*J*osie slept hard and late, waking to the whirring motor of an electric tool. The clock read ten forty-two. Her body ached all the way to her bones, especially her back, and she was already nauseated.

Today was the apple festival and the orchard work would be put on hold for the biggest event of the year. By now, the parade would be well under way if not over, and the downtown streets would be lined with people. The square would be filled with carnival games for the children, and tonight it would be converted to a dance floor with a live band. A loud and colorful display of fireworks would conclude the big event. Until then, vendors on the sidewalks would sell everything from apple dumplings to crafts, and clusters of neighbors would chat about the harvest, the latest gossip, and the windstorm they'd all survived.

Josie suddenly realized they had no one to man their own apple booth now that the twins had arrived and Nate was otherwise occupied. She needed to get down there fast.

After her shower, Josie followed the whirring sound and found Grady on the nursery floor amid crib rails, tools, and what looked like a million screws of varying lengths. It was sweet of him to assemble the furniture. Nate wasn't too good with tools.

"'Morning." Josie took the rubber band she'd grabbed and pulled her hair into a ponytail.

The drill stopped. "'Morning." His eyes raked over her, and she wished she didn't look so frumpy and tired. "Sorry if I woke you."

She pulled her ponytail tight. "You should've woken me earlier. Someone needs to be at the booth."

"Aunt Lola's got it covered. You needed some sleep."

Aunt Lola had stayed up as late as she. "Where's Nate?"

"He was up around seven and left to check on Laurel and the babies."

Just the mention of the twins made Josie crave them, long to cuddle them against her chest. To smell the sweet baby scent and feel the slight weight of them in her arms. She couldn't wait to photograph them.

She'd love nothing more than to zip over to the hospital, but Laurel and Nate deserved some time alone. This was a huge moment in their lives, and they needed privacy.

Grady shifted the nearly assembled crib, setting it upright, testing its weight. "Good stuff."

"It would've cost a fortune if it hadn't been twenty-five percent off. Need some help?" With the orchard workers off for the day, and the booth at the festival covered, Josie had nothing but time on her hands.

Then she remembered the apple pie bake-off. "Oh no, Aunt Lola's apple pie. She should be here baking." She checked her watch. The judging was at two. "I'll go take over the booth."

Grady checked the time. "I offered to take the booth this

morning, but she said the contest didn't matter. Anyway, by the time you got down there and she got back, she wouldn't have time to make it."

He was right. "She worked so hard on that recipe, and we all agreed it was the best one yet. It means so much to her. And now Nettie Albert will win again and hold it over poor Aunt Lola all year."

Josie wasn't going to let that happen.

"Where you going?" Grady called as she rushed from the room.

"I got a pie to bake."

Josie chewed off the last of her pinkie nail as she watched Sheriff Clem Roberts stroll to the microphone under the big tent.

Beside her, Aunt Lola shifted, wiped her sweaty hands down the legs of her jeans. Grady had taken over the booth so Aunt Lola could be here for the awards.

Across the tent, Nettie Albert straightened her straw hat and smoothed her khaki shorts where the pleats parted to make room for her rounded stomach.

"Look at her," Josie heard Verna Mae whisper into Aunt Lola's ear. "She thinks she's a shoo-in."

"She probably is," Aunt Lola said.

"Stop that." Josie nudged her aunt. "Think positively and have a little faith."

"I'm saying a heartfelt prayer as we speak," Aunt Lola muttered in reply.

Josie wasn't sure God cared about apple pies, but he cared

about Aunt Lola, didn't he? She felt silly as she offered up a silent request. She'd followed Aunt Lola's recipe to a T. The fluted crust wasn't quite as neat as her aunt's work, but she thought it looked pretty good.

Banjo music poured in through the open tent flaps, and the smell of baked apples and fried elephant ears wafted in on a crisp breeze. A fly settled on Josie's arm, and she brushed it away.

Clem tilted the microphone and a loud squeal followed. When he spoke, he made a production of the award announcement, as if the five minutes at the microphone were his five minutes of fame for the year, and he wanted to make the most of it. He thanked everyone from the judges to the hovering flies.

Finally, he got around to the awards. "Third place in the pie category goes to Maggie Lou Sparks." A brief patter of applause accompanied Maggie to the front as she accepted her award. Sometime in the last few days, her hair color had gone from red to black, with chunky blonde highlights.

"Good for her," Aunt Lola said. "It's her first time finishing."

"In second place we have . . ." Clem held the paper arm's length away, tilted his head back, and read over the flat top of his glasses. "Nettie Albert."

Josie smiled. "You won, I just know it."

"Hush, you're getting my hopes up."

Nettie's smile was as flat as a pressed leaf. After accepting her red ribbon, she made her way to the back of the crowd.

"And finally, we have our grand prize winner in the apple pie category . . ." Clem held up the ruffled blue ribbon.

Every muscle Josie had was stiff with anticipation.

"Lola Mitchell!" he said with a flourish.

"You won!" The applause was thunderous as Josie hugged her

aunt, then watched her approach the stage and take her ribbon. The smile on her aunt's face was priceless. It had meant so much to Aunt Lola to win, just once. Josie's eyes burned, threatening to spill over. She remembered the little prayer she'd whispered and wondered if that had any bearing on the outcome.

Aunt Lola returned, showing her ribbon to Josie and Verna Mae. "A little prayer goes a long way, ladies."

"And a great recipe don't hurt either," Verna Mae returned.

thirty-nine

*J*osie took over the booth for Grady so he could go home and finish the furniture. After Aunt Lola showed off her ribbon, she went to check on Laurel and the babies and came back in time to hear Mr. Murphy's performance on the mandolin. He played his sweet-sounding rendition of "Redeemed."

The afternoon sped by as Josie stayed busy selling apples and caramel dip. Boone stopped by the booth and reminded her she'd promised him a dance later.

Once the booth was closed, she went home for her camera, then visited Laurel and the babies. She snapped two rolls of photos and was eager to get them developed. Laurel was rested and antsy to go home and get settled with the babies, but the hospital wanted to keep the three until the next day.

By the time Josie left Nate and Laurel at the hospital, she was exhausted. The excitement from the night before and the hours selling apples had drained her. She hadn't eaten all day, afraid it would only make her sick.

If she had her druthers, she'd drive home and curl up in bed, but she didn't want to miss the best part of the festival and she'd promised Boone a dance. As darkness crept over the hills, they would turn on the string of lantern lights lining the dance floor and gather to catch up with neighbors over a cup of apple cider. She smiled thinking of how little girls would dance with their daddies, and Ray and Connie Blackford would waltz around the floor, bumping into everyone. Some things never changed.

Tired or not, she was in for the long haul. Josie parked her car at the end of Main Street and started the long walk toward the town square. Streetlamps glowed in the darkness, and in the distance, the colorful lantern lights shimmied in the breeze. Strains of a fast country song carried on the breeze. Her body seemed not to have recovered from the excitement of the night before. She felt as if she were moving through quicksand. Her legs trembled as she walked, and she wondered if she had the strength to dance. Maybe best to stick with slow dances tonight.

As she approached town, she walked under the banner that stretched across Main Street: "52nd Annual Shelbyville Apple Festival." Triangular flags, strung from the lampposts, lined the street, dancing in the wind.

When she approached the square, she scanned the crowd and located Aunt Lola on one of their big quilts under a tall oak tree. Josie navigated the lawn chairs and blankets, greeting friends and neighbors as she went. When she reached the quilt, she lowered herself and leaned back on her elbows, stretching out her legs.

Her aunt's blue ribbon was pinned to her floral blouse. Her apple pie would be available at the store and would be the pie of choice to serve at family gatherings and the like. It had been a weekend to remember.

"Quite the weekend, huh, Aunt Lola?"

"I should say."

A breeze sent dried leaves scuttling across the sidewalk and caused a chill to run through Josie. She should've gone home for a sweater.

Mr. Murphy approached, his booted feet stopping at the frayed edge of the quilt. "'Evening, ladies."

Josie complimented him on his performance, then he invited Aunt Lola to dance. Josie watched them go, Mr. Murphy's beefy hand on the small of her aunt's back. Maybe she'd finally found someone to love. Judging by the way her aunt looked at him as he pulled her into his arms, she'd say the answer might be yes. She was happy for Aunt Lola. She'd been alone far too long.

Dancing beside her aunt and Mr. Murphy was Maggie Lou's little girl and Boone. He twirled her around, her sundress ballooning and her thin blonde hair fanning outward. If she were photographing this event, she would capture that moment on film. Boone would make a wonderful father someday. Maggie Lou watched from her lawn chair near the swing set.

Josie's eyes scanned the crowd, skimming along the low stone wall that circled the square. People were perched in groups of two or three. She stopped when her eyes ran across Grady. He leaned against the wall, watching the dancers, his long legs crossed at the ankles.

Beside him, Harmony Schneider said something and laughed, touching his arm. Josie felt a prick of jealousy. She'd known since that night at the grocery that, for a chance with Grady, Harmony would turn in her cashier's apron in a heartbeat.

She watched for Grady's response, but he barely spared Harmony a glance as he crossed his arms and continued watching the action on the dance floor.

As if sensing her scrutiny, he scanned the crowd until he found her. Without breaking eye contact with Josie, he said something to Harmony, then straightened and walked her way, tucking his hands into his jean pockets.

Heaven have mercy, he was handsome. From the top of his dark head to the soles of his booted feet. No wonder Harmony was smitten. She took a mental snapshot and hoped it was imprinted on her brain for later so she could pull it up and linger over it awhile.

The smile he'd saved just for her only reinforced the thought. He lowered himself beside her, and she sat upright, hoping to ease the crick in her back. They sat in silence for a few moments, listening to the band's tune, watching the dancers.

The Apple Queen and King, chosen earlier in the day by a panel of judges, took a spin around the floor. The teenaged girl's tiara tipped sideways and her partner steadied it.

Grady must've been watching them too. "Aunt Lola told me that was you a handful of years ago," he said.

It had been her senior year in high school, just before her world fell apart. "It seems like a lifetime ago."

The tune ended, and Boone approached moments later, still a little winded from his frantic turn around the floor with Maggie's girl. "'Evening, Josie. Grady." He extended his hand to Josie. "May I have the pleasure?"

Josie took his hand, reluctant to leave Grady. Her legs wobbled as she stood, and Grady reached out to steady her, but not before Boone swept her away.

The band was playing a fast tune, much to her dismay. Nonetheless, she put on a smile and let Boone twirl her until she was dizzy—it didn't take much these days.

She was grateful when the band started a slow song. Her heart raced faster than the tempo of the previous song. Boone took one of her hands and set his other at her waist. He looked boyishly cute without his hat, his curls damp at his neck. He'd gone home and spiffed up, changing into a white polo and a crisp pair of jeans.

"Aunt Lola said Laurel and the twins are doing great," he said when they were moving in a slow circle.

"They are." She couldn't help but smile as she thought of her sweet nieces. "So adorable."

"New twins and a blue ribbon all in one weekend. Can you stand it?"

"It's been pretty exciting."

He turned her gracefully. "Mr. Murphy seems pretty taken with Aunt Lola."

"I was noticing that. She deserves someone who'll cherish her."

Many couples joined them until the floor was packed with dancers. Boone's mom and dad danced at the edge of the floor. Mr. Barrow was having a good day, seemed to have come out from under the Alzheimer's enough to recognize his wife. Josie thought how hard it must be for them both.

Josie looked at all the familiar faces. People she'd known since she was old enough to have a thought. People who'd given her lollipops and gum, people who'd looked out for her when she was out of Laurel's sight, people who made this town special.

It was a great place to grow up. A great place to belong.

Boone seemed to read her mind. "Tell me you don't just love Shelbyville."

Once upon a time she had. Now the memory of Ian haunted it. "If you like small-town living."

"Which you do."

"Fine, I do, but I'm still going back to Louisville."

He leaned back. "What? With those new nieces coming home and all?"

"Don't start on me, Boone Barrow. I've been getting enough grief from Laurel and Aunt Lola." Not to mention Grady.

When the band ended the tune, the dancers applauded, then the band started another slow song. Her arms ached, but Boone moved them in a quick circle before swaying in time to the ballad.

"Just 'cause you're so stubborn," Boone said.

"Am not."

"Are so."

She shook her head, giving up. Much as Boone might think they were right for each other, she couldn't think of him as anything more than a brother.

"Cut in?" Grady was beside them, towering over them with his broad shoulders and set jaw.

She was about to suggest a break, but Boone was smiling graciously and stepping back, letting Grady assume his spot.

His right hand held hers the same way Boone's had. His left hand rested in the same spot. How come it felt entirely different? Why did she have these impossible feelings? Why did he have to be so difficult to resist?

Grady's feet shuffled, landing partly on her toes. He winced. "Sorry. Not much of a dancer."

Her legs trembled against his. These feelings he evoked were exhausting. "Why'd you cut in then?" She stared into the vee of his shirt where tiny dark hairs peeked out.

"Couldn't stand seeing you in Barrow's arms."

Why did he have to say things like that? Things that made her stomach go all tight and hard?

"He's just a friend," Josie said. And that was a fact.

Grady squeezed her hand the tiniest bit. "I know the feeling."

She breathed a wry laugh because Grady didn't know at all. There was nothing the same in her feelings for the two men.

She watched the other couples swirling around them. Boone passed on the other side of the floor with Harmony Schneider. Her head tilted back in a deep laugh at something he'd said, and Josie thought they looked good together.

Her stomach gave a growl loud enough to be heard over the music.

"Have you eaten?"

Since when? And what was the point when she'd only feel sick for hours? "I'm not hungry."

Grady studied her, seeing right through her. "You can't stop eating. Maybe the doctor can give you something for the nausea."

She didn't want to talk about this tonight. She was weak and chilly, and getting very tempted to lean into his chest and let him hold her. They were barely swaying now, which was more in keeping with Grady's skill level.

She was leaving in a week anyway, once the harvest was complete. It wasn't as if she was going to kiss him or lead him on. She just wanted to snuggle against the cool night air. He wouldn't mind that, would he?

When his hand moved to the small of her back, she lowered her own aching arm and wrapped it around his waist.

He pulled her close, and she didn't resist. She laid her head on his chest, letting the thud of his heart drown out the band's bass. His embrace was warm and safe.

He rubbed her back in small circles, sending a shiver up her spine. She felt his chin resting atop her head, and had a brief flashback of dancing at Joe's the night before the windstorm. But she was fully sober this time and in way deeper than she had been then.

As weary as she felt, she no longer wanted to go home. She wanted to stay here, to linger in his embrace as long as she could. *Keep playing the slow ones, guys,* she instructed the band.

His thighs swept against hers as they shuffled. Josie closed her eyes and inhaled the scent of him. She wanted to embed it in her memory so she could carry it home to Louisville and unpack it like a favorite pillow. Pine. Musk. Man.

Utterly intoxicating. As she shifted her weight, her knee buckled.

Grady grasped her elbows, a frown catching between his brows.

"I'm fine." She just wanted him close again. But as she moved toward him, he held her away so he could look into her eyes.

"You're shaking."

Maybe her hands trembled a little. Maybe her legs were a little wobbly.

"Let's take a break," he said.

She wanted to whine like a tired three-year-old, but he was leading her through the throng and back to the blanket. He sat, propping his back against the tree, then pulled her into his side. One tug of the quilt, and she was covered to her waist.

"Better?" he asked.

She nodded against the material of his shirt. By morning there'd be bets on how long until they walked the aisle, but even that thought didn't deter her.

She was giving in, but she couldn't seem to stop herself. *I'm not feeling well. Can't a girl weaken a little at times like this?* She closed her eyes and let her head rise and fall with each of his breaths, breathing in the scent that was all Grady.

But the motion made her dizzy and she opened her eyes until the world stilled again.

"You want to go home?"

She should. But what was there but an empty house, an empty bed? "No." She knew she could use the sleep, but tomorrow's light would bring the realization of her foolishness, and she wasn't ready to give up the fantasy just yet.

"Want something to eat?" His voice rumbled through his chest cavity and into her ear. "I could run to The Corner Café and grab something bland like dinner rolls from Peggy."

Her stomach twisted at the mention of food. Another thing that would keep until morning. "Un-uh." She turned her head into him. The softness of his T-shirt contrasted with the hardened muscles beneath it. A delectable combination.

"It's getting worse, isn't it." It wasn't a question.

And it was true. The decline seemed sudden, but maybe it was only the excitement of the weekend. The doctor had said something about stress, and even good moments brought a kind of stress.

"All the excitement from last night, I think," she said. "It's been a long day." They sounded like excuses. She'd slept late this morning and baking an apple pie was hardly as wearing as working in the field.

"At least you won't have to hide it much longer."

She could make it another week until harvest was over. Once she was back in Louisville, she wouldn't have to pretend anymore.

"When are you going to tell them?"

She realized he wasn't talking about her going home. He was talking about telling her family. She'd used Laurel's pregnancy as an excuse, but the twins had arrived safely and there was no reason, from his perspective, to keep the illness a secret any longer.

But Laurel wasn't even home from the hospital yet. Plus, there would be raging hormones and feeding schedules. Her sister didn't need this right now.

"I'm going to wait a bit," she said finally.

He shifted so he could look at her. "Wait for what?"

She could see it wasn't going to go down so easily this time. "For things to settle. Laurel has enough going on right now without dumping this on her." Feeling Grady stiffen, Josie sat up and instantly missed the closeness.

"*You* have enough going on right now without having your family's support."

She felt suddenly alone. A cold wind enveloped her in a frosty hug. Josie wrapped her arms around her waist, shivering. "I'm fine."

"Do you realize the absurdity of that statement?"

He looked as if he wanted to shake her. "Don't be angry." She didn't want his wrath. She wanted the warmth of his arms, but that was lost now. Like so many other things.

"How's Laurel going to feel when she finds out? How's she going to feel knowing you kept this from her? She might understand about the pregnancy, but there's no reason now, Josie. No reason at all that justifies you keeping the truth from her."

What was she going to do? She couldn't tell her family. They'd want to know all the details, and then they'd find out her disease was treatable. They couldn't know that. It would ruin everything.

"Look at me," Grady implored.

But she didn't want to look at him. Didn't want to get caught up in those eyes that cared too much, that did things to her reasoning skills.

She couldn't tell her family and she couldn't explain why. And Grady wasn't going to let her off the hook.

"Your family needs to know. Not just for you, but for them."

Who was he to tell her what she needed? What her family needed? It was *her* illness, her life. In a week, she'd be back home, and he could wash her from his memory. The thought disturbed her. *That's what you want, isn't it?* She was so confused. And the way her head was spinning wasn't helping.

"Mind your own business, Grady."

She pulled her feet under her, poised for flight.

He leaned toward her, adamant. "You need their support."

She gave a half smile. "How much support can they be from three hundred and fifty miles away?"

Her reply stopped him cold, made him freeze in place. Not so much as a blink. Finally, he straightened and his brows slowly knotted together. "You're going back?"

His confusion baffled her, annoyed her. It had been the plan all along. Why did everyone seem to think she'd changed her mind? Why did she feel as if she were continually explaining herself to everyone? And to Grady of all people, whom she hadn't even known three months ago.

"You're going back?" His voice was louder this time.

Well, she could be snippy too. "Yes, I'm going home. Louisville is my *home*, remember?"

"You pretty much said before that there's no one and nothing there, that about right? What's there to go home to? You have family here. People who—" His face twisted, shadows dancing in the hollows of his cheeks. "People who love you."

She looked away before she could drown in the depths of those eyes, before she could let herself believe he was talking about his own feelings. She had to get out of there.

"I want to go home." She made to stand.

He held her with a firm hand. "You are not going through this alone. I won't let you." His eyes locked on hers, held her every bit as tightly as his grasp did. "If I have to tell them myself, I will."

Panic swelled inside, pushing the air from her lungs. There were boundaries, and he was overstepping them. She never should've told him about the illness, never should've let herself get involved with him at all. Now he was usurping her right to choose, forcing her hand.

How dare he think he had a right to force her into this. He had no right. No right at all. She jerked her arm away and was on her feet before he could say a word. And then she was walking as fast as her feet would carry her across the darkened square.

forty

Josie made her way blindly through the square, navigating chairs and blankets and people she didn't really see. What was she going to do now? What was she going to do if he told them?

Why are you doing this to me, God? This is what you want, isn't it? For me to die like Ian?

She couldn't even die right. Her dad was right. She really was pathetic.

The throng of people opened to a spacious field of grass. The sound of the band faded. Her legs trembled, buckling every few steps on the uneven ground. She had to keep going, had to reach her car. Why had she gone this way? The street would've been faster.

Maybe she should drive all the way back to Louisville tonight. She wouldn't have to face Grady and his unfair ultimatum.

It was a grand fantasy, but there were too many obstacles. Her body would never make the trip without a night's rest, and there was her family to consider.

Besides, what would it change? Grady would tell them anyway, and he would be forced to do so sooner than later as an explanation of why she'd up and left.

The creek gurgled beside her, running as fast as she was, chasing her. Above the whoosh of the wind, a voice called her name.

Grady.

Go away. She didn't know whether to hide behind a tree, turn around and tell him off, or quicken her steps. Who was she kidding? She couldn't walk any faster if she wanted. Her lungs choked on the oxygen that rushed in and out, burning her chest.

The toe of her sandal caught a tree root, and she tumbled in the darkness. The impact forced the air from her lungs, making her grunt. She pushed against the ground, damp and spongy, fringed with long grass.

"Josie!" He was there quick as the snap of a flag.

She rolled over, sat up, heaving from exertion. She felt the ache of frustration clogging her throat in a massive lump.

She batted away his hands, striking him. "Go away! Just leave me alone." Why was this happening? Why now when she was so close to leaving? "You have no right to make my decisions for me. You don't understand anything!"

He sat back on his haunches, giving her space.

She gulped in air, the dampness of the earth seeped into her jeans. In the distance, the bass of the band kept tempo with her heart.

Beside them, the creek trickled, whispering secrets as it had that night. She could almost feel the cold, steely fingers pulling her under. Could see Ian's face disappearing under the watery grave as she'd seen so many nights in her sleep.

"Then tell me. Make me understand."

Her eyes burned, ached. All of her ached, from the inside out. She was so tired. So tired of carrying this impossible burden. She just wanted it to be over.

"It was my fault," she whispered. Her hands clutched at the fringe of grass. Some of the strands snapped in her fist.

"What was, honey?"

The gentleness of his voice was her undoing. She could tell one person, couldn't she? She could unload this burden on Grady; maybe it would alleviate the pressure building in her.

"We were sledding," she said. *Just get it out. Say it, and get it over with.* "I—I did something stupid. I went down the hill into the gap, toward the creek. I thought it was frozen."

The night crashed in on her. The frosty smell of cold, the slice of the runners cutting through the snow. The sickening crack of splitting ice.

"The ice gave way with this horrible sound, and then I was falling. I was so cold and I couldn't reach the bottom and I couldn't get out. He couldn't get me out."

"Who couldn't?"

She didn't want to say his name. As if saying it aloud had some kind of power that would pull her under as easily as the creek.

"Ian?"

She nodded, grateful he'd spared her that one thing. "He kept trying, but the ice kept giving way and I was getting so cold. Too cold." She didn't want to say the next part. The hard part. Her throat closed up, refusing to surrender the words.

"What happened?" He ran his thumb across her face, smearing the wetness.

Just say it, Josie. Saying it won't make it any truer. "I was panicking. I didn't think I would make it much longer. He jumped in." She looked Grady in the eye, needing him, needing someone, to understand what Ian had done. "He knew. He knew he wouldn't make it. He gave his life to save mine."

Once the words were out, there was no stopping the rest. "He had to have known. We were so far from home and the water was so cold. I was numb. He jumped in and lifted me out. He saved me and he knew—there was a look on his face—" She covered her own face as if she could hide from the memory of it. She would never forget the look on his face.

"He knew he was going to die. Why did he do it?" *Why?* She screamed the question in her mind as she never had before.

Grady took her wrists, pulled her hands away from her face. "It was an accident. That's all. You didn't mean for him to die."

"It should've been *me.*" She jabbed her finger into her sternum. "I was supposed to die."

"*No.*"

"Yes! It was my foolishness and it should've been me. Ian was—good. He didn't deserve to die."

Grady was shaking his head. "Neither did you."

"How can I ever be worthy of his sacrifice? Grady, answer me that. I can't. There's nothing I can do to earn it." God knew she'd tried, tried so hard. Some debts were too big to pay off.

"You don't have to be worthy—"

He thought he had all the answers. "You don't know what you're talking about, what I've lived with since it happened. You don't know how it feels to be so utterly, completely unworthy." How could he? He was Grady, whom everyone loved and respected. So good, so worthy.

"You're wrong, Josie. Someone gave his life for me too."

She cleared her vision with a blink. Was it true? And if it was, how had he coped? She searched his face for answers.

He wetted his lips. "'While we were still sinners, Christ died for us.'"

It took a moment for the words to sink in, for the words to ring the bell of her memory. He was quoting Scripture? She didn't need a Sunday school lesson, she needed someone to understand.

She backed away from him, angry. "That's not the same."

"Isn't it?"

"No." She knew it wasn't. But all the reasons, the words, twisted around in her mind unassembled. She tried but couldn't make sense of her thoughts, much less express them.

She said what she did know, what she'd come to understand through the whole ordeal. "That God you worship gave me this disease, Grady. He's punishing me for—"

"No, honey."

She looked away so she couldn't see the look on his face, so she wasn't tempted to believe what he was saying.

"He's punishing me for what I did. I should've died then and I didn't, so he's making sure I die now." She felt the weight of the penalty crushing her, so heavy she thought it might press her flat on the ground.

"God doesn't work like that. He loves you."

She shook her head, wanting to cover her ears.

"He does." Grady pulled her into his arms.

She pushed at him, but he was too strong. And she was too weak. She finally stopped fighting and crumpled in his lap, crying. She was so tired. Tired of fighting, tired of feeling unworthy.

He brushed wet strands of hair off her cheek, off her forehead.

"Shhh. He loves you," Grady whispered in her ear. His fingers brushed the soft flesh of her cheeks. "And God help me, so do I."

She opened her eyes, staring up at him. He looked as tortured as she felt. Her precious Grady. He loved her? She could scarcely believe she could stir those kinds of feelings in a man like Grady.

But if he really could love her . . .

If he could love her, maybe God could too. It was possible, wasn't it? She wanted to believe it so badly.

"I don't know the purpose for this disease," he said. "But it's not his punishment, honey. He wants you to find him. He wants you to let him love you through it. He wants you to find peace."

Peace. A foreign word. Something she hadn't felt in so long. Maybe never. Why was it so hard to believe what Grady said? To stop fighting and surrender? What was the worst that could happen?

What do you want with me, God?

She closed her eyes, her chest aching with each rise and fall. Her heart beat slow and hard against her ribs. Grady believed what he said, she knew that with certainty. But was it true? Did God really love her and want her to find peace? Could it be as easy as surrendering to him?

Why not? She'd tried everything else. She'd fought, she'd run, she'd given up.

All right. All right, Jesus, you win.

You win.

Josie opened her eyes and stared into Grady's. Her head felt as if it were filled with helium. She tried to lift her hand, steady her head, but she couldn't seem to make it move. The world still tilted and swayed. Grady blurred.

"Josie?"

Everything was going dark, tapering down to a pinpoint of light. She blinked, trying to regain her vision.

"*Josie.*"

She opened her mouth. *I'm not feeling so good.* Her head floated, spinning, spinning. And then the tiny pinpoint of light was swallowed by darkness.

forty-one

*G*rady paced across the waiting area in the ER where he'd sat with Josie when Laurel had gone into early labor. It seemed so long ago, much longer than a couple of months.

The blue carpet swallowed the thud of each step. In the corner, a news program carried on as if his world hadn't just come to an abrupt and jarring halt.

The ambulance had arrived within minutes of his 911 call, and they'd let him ride with Josie as they assessed her situation and questioned him. The paramedics hadn't detected a blood pressure or a pulse.

He'd told them all he knew. "She has an endocrine disease of some kind. No, I don't know what it is. She's been sick. Nausea, some vomiting. She's been achy and tired. Can't you do something?"

Once they arrived at the hospital, they'd wheeled her still body on the gurney through the double doors, and he hadn't heard a thing since. He checked his watch and saw it had only been twenty-eight minutes. It seemed like much more. He'd called Nate once he'd arrived and left a voice mail. Aunt Lola didn't own a cell, so he'd called Mr. Murphy and asked him to bring her over.

He ran his hands through his hair, then jumped when his cell rang.

He fished it from his pocket. "Yeah?"

"It's Nate . . . your message, and I'm . . . way down. Any word?"

The signal was breaking up and Grady struggled to hear. "No, nothing." Couldn't they at least send someone out with an update?

"Shoot. I . . . give Laurel something positive . . . on to . . . wanting to keep her upstairs . . . hear something."

"You're breaking up."

Nate said he'd be down in a minute and Grady pocketed his phone.

Maybe it was his fault. Maybe it was the stress of reliving those memories she'd been running from. *She's already sick, Mackenzie, did you have to go and push her like that?*

Maybe the stress was all she'd needed to send her body over the edge. He ran a cold palm over his face. *Oh, God, please save her. Please. She can't die this way.*

He reminded himself that he'd known she was dying. But knowing it and living through it were two separate things. And now that he'd seen the full weight of the burden she carried, he wished for more time. If nothing else, he wanted her to find peace, to find God before the arms of death carried her away.

"Not getting a pulse."

"No blood pressure either."

The paramedics' words rang in his ears. Were they trying to pull her back from the clutches of death even now?

Please, God.

He hoped the plea was enough. He couldn't formulate more words, couldn't get them untangled from the snarl in his mind.

Nate appeared, running toward him, his shoes squeaking on the hospital tile.

"Still nothing," Grady said as Nate slowed.

Before he could respond, the exit doors opened and Aunt Lola whooshed in, her face drawn, Mr. Murphy on her heels. Aunt Lola looked as if she'd aged ten years since this morning. "How is she?"

"No word yet," Nate said, then caught her up on what Grady had told him. He heard Aunt Lola's gasp when he told her there'd been no pulse in the ambulance. Mr. Murphy set a hand on her shoulder.

Grady turned and walked away, ran a hand through his hair. *You've got to tell them about the disease. They need to know.* It was the right thing to do. Maybe he should've told them long ago, Laurel's pregnancy notwithstanding.

Yeah, and look what happened to Josie when you forced her hand. Guilt rode him long and hard. He'd never forgive himself if—

He turned back to Aunt Lola, saw her wilted shoulders and glazed eyes. Her blue ribbon hung askew on her shirt like a forgotten painting on a wall. He had to tell them, forewarn them.

He walked toward them, reluctance paving the way for his slow steps.

The double doors behind him swung open, and they all turned to face a small middle-aged woman in teal scrubs. Grady recognized her as one of Peggy Tackett's daughters. She barely came up to Grady's chest as she approached.

"Lola, Nate." She nodded, tucking her mouse brown hair behind her ears. "Grady." She wore concern between her clear blue eyes.

"How is she?" Aunt Lola asked.

"She's holding her own."

Grady released a breath he didn't know he'd held and closed his eyes. *Thank you.*

"We've given her hydrocortisone and saline through an IV, and she's starting to come around."

"Thank God," Aunt Lola said. "Do you know what's wrong with her?"

She glanced at Grady. "You mentioned to the paramedics that Josie has an endocrine disease."

He could feel the heavy weight of Aunt Lola's appraisal. He didn't even want to look her way. She was going to give it to him later, and he probably deserved it. But right now, he was too thankful Josie was still alive to worry about it.

"She has a disease?" Aunt Lola asked.

"It's called Addison's," the doctor continued. "It's a disease that results in your body producing insufficient amounts of cortisol and sometimes another hormone called aldosterone."

"Is it serious?" Nate asked.

Grady wished he could protect them from the truth, but he'd already done that too long and it wouldn't change the facts. He was glad Aunt Lola had Mr. Murphy there for support.

"Left untreated, the disease culminates in what's called an Addisonian Crisis, which is fatal if the patient doesn't seek medical treatment. This happens when there's a severe adrenal deficiency. It's difficult to diagnose," she said, addressing Grady, "but your knowledge that she's suffering from an endocrine disorder helped me to diagnose quickly."

He remembered Josie's lack of a pulse in the ambulance. "Did you have to revive her?"

The doctor shook her head. "During a crisis, patients can present with no pulse or blood pressure. It's quite strange, really, and rare. I've only diagnosed one other case in my career."

"But she's going to be okay?" Aunt Lola asked.

"We need to run more tests, but she's coming around. We'd

like to keep her a couple of days. Addison's patients have to take replacement hormones orally and have to be vigilant about their health. Otherwise, they can lead a pretty normal life."

It took Grady's fuzzy mind a minute to digest the words. Where was the bad news? Where was the prognosis Josie told him about? Maybe this doctor had it all wrong.

"Wait," Grady said. "Are you sure that's what she has? Addison's disease?"

"Josie confirmed the test results when she was awakening."

He didn't understand. Josie was going to be okay? The disease wasn't a death sentence?

"Can we see her?" Aunt Lola asked.

"We're getting her into a room now. I'll send a nurse out with the room number in a few minutes."

It was quiet as the doctor exited through the doors.

"Thank you, Jesus," Aunt Lola whispered.

"I need to tell Laurel the good news," Nate said.

"I'll go with you," Aunt Lola said, with a look toward Grady that promised she wasn't finished with him. "Give us a call when they have a room number."

Grady nodded, then they walked toward the hallway leading to the elevators.

He sank into a chair, his legs giving way under the pressure of his discovery. He turned the information around in his head, seeing it from every possible angle, trying to make sense of it.

Josie knew she had Addison's and had told him the disease was fatal. The doctor said it was easily treated. Which was the truth?

What had the doctor said? Something about the disease leading to a crisis if left untreated. She'd used the word *fatal* in there somewhere.

Fatal. Left untreated.

Why hadn't Josie been taking her medication if it were as simple as that? She knew she had the disease, the doctor had confirmed it with her. Surely her doctor had prescribed those hormones she needed.

Josie's words from earlier played in his head. *"God gave me this disease, Grady. He's punishing me."*

Reality hit like a solid sudden punch to the gut.

Oh, God.

Is she letting this disease take her life because she—because she doesn't want to live anymore? Because she thinks you gave it to her? The slow suicide of a woman who thought she deserved to die?

He closed his eyes against the thought. Why didn't she tell him? Why didn't she tell him the truth so he could tell her how special she was? *This isn't your will for her, God. Let her know how much you love her.*

He tried to imagine the tremendous guilt and pressure she'd lived under. Thinking she was to blame for Ian's death and carrying that burden alone. Feeling unworthy of the sacrifice. Had anything he'd said helped, or had his words only weakened her body and nearly killed her?

Josie's eyes fluttered open. She squinted against the too-bright light. An IV bag hung on a stand at her side, its cord disappearing beneath the bandage on the back of her hand.

The metal bed railing was cold against her arm. She wore an ugly, speckled blue hospital gown. A monitor beeped beside her. She had a vague recollection of people bustling around her bed, of a doctor asking her questions.

Then she remembered the last moments before she'd passed out. Feeling dizzy and sick and . . . peaceful.

She remembered Grady's voice calling her name.

Grady. Where was he? She turned her head on the pillow, but she was alone. The door was open and a girl wearing peach scrubs passed by. She sucked in a breath, let it fill her lungs, and released it in a deep sigh.

Where was her family? Did they know about the disease? Did it matter?

Caroline Tackett appeared in the doorway. She picked up the chart and gave Josie a smile. "How are you feeling?"

"Better." Her throat was raspy and dry. "My family . . ."

"Is downstairs wearing a hole in the carpet." Her eyes crinkled at the corners.

She felt bad for making them worry. She had just come through the crisis she'd anticipated all these months. Only she hadn't expected to survive it. What would her family be going through if she'd had her way?

"Am I okay?" Did she want to be? Did she want to get better, go on? She felt different now that she'd come through the other side. She felt herself holding her breath, waiting for Caroline's answer.

"You'll be right as rain in a couple days." Dr. Tackett asked her questions related to her disease, then told her she was scheduling some tests for the next day.

When she left, Josie looked out the window where darkness swallowed everything but the lights in the parking lot. It was late. She was so tired. She'd just been through an ordeal, had barely come through, according to Caroline.

She closed her eyes, but instead of being claimed by sleep, she found herself remembering the moments leading up to the crisis. Grady's words, her decision. And it had been a decision. Not the "sinner's prayer" she'd heard so many times in church, but a real decision.

Is this your answer, God? Do you want me to live after all?

It seemed unfathomable after so many months of believing she was going to die, was meant to die. Could she readjust her thinking and accept whatever God wanted? The notion was scary. Strange that life could be a scarier proposition than death.

And what of Ian and the guilt? What of the pain that his death had left her with? Could she find a way to deal with that? Would having God in her life make it bearable?

A shuffling sound awakened her. The doorway was filled with a sight more beautiful than the Blue Ridge Mountains on an October morning.

Grady.

Every nerve in her body sung with awareness. He stopped just inside the door, pocketing his hands, unsure. She wanted to grab him and pull him closer.

"He loves you. And God help me, so do I."

Were sweeter words ever spoken? Josie wet her lips. "Come 'ere."

Eyes locked, he took three steps and was at her side. Now that he was closer, she saw the fatigue that lined his eyes, rimmed his taut lips.

There was a somber look in his dark eyes, and Josie knew that he knew everything. That her disease wasn't fatal. That she'd been killing herself one day at a time. The thought shamed her now. Humiliated her. Why hadn't she considered how her actions would affect others? Wouldn't she have left them with the same kind of guilt she'd been trying to escape? She looked away.

Did her family know what she'd done? The thought made her want to pull the hospital sheets over her head.

"Look at me," Grady whispered.

Ashamed as she was, she was hungry for him, too hungry to resist his request.

His mouth opened and closed. He tried again. "You're okay. We're going to get you through this." He took her hand, the one with the IV, and held it, his warmth seeping into her cold flesh.

She drank in everything his eyes, his touch, his words said.

"I'm so sorry I upset you," he said.

She shook her head. "No—"

"It wasn't my place to—"

"Everything happened just as it was meant to." She didn't realize the truth until she verbalized it. She'd meant to be back in Louisville before the crisis happened. But God had different plans.

Her words left him speechless.

"Does my family know about the disease? About—" She couldn't put words to her actions.

He smoothed his thumb across her knuckles. "They know you have the disease and they know I knew about it." His smile wobbled. "I don't think Aunt Lola's too happy with me right about now."

She would have to tell them what she'd done. They wouldn't understand unless she told them everything.

And maybe it was high time she did.

"I guess I have a lot of explaining to do."

He pressed a soft kiss against her knuckles. "Later. Right now you need your rest."

She didn't want rest. She wanted to hear those words again, the ones that made her heart sing just thinking about them.

But he was leaning over, placing a soft kiss to her forehead. "One day at a time, honey."

forty-two

*J*osie crested the hill, then began the descent, her feet swishing through the tall grass. When she reached the bottom, winded, she stepped onto the rock that jutted into the water—the one she'd barely missed on that treacherous night.

Sweetwater Creek was running slowly today, a peaceful pool of water cradled in the gap. On both sides, the hills, clothed in vibrant autumn hues, rose majestically toward the heavens.

The air smelled like ripened apples and autumn, and the cloudless sky was a shade of blue that matched the twins' eyes. Those two little dolls had stolen Josie's heart, and she was wearing the role of Auntie Josie quite well if she did say so herself. Laurel had taken to motherhood as naturally as a fish to water, just as she'd figured.

Josie sank onto the rock, her legs aching as she stretched them out. The harvest was complete; it was a day of celebration. They'd picked the last of the apples, finishing in midafternoon. Tonight they'd have a barbecue, then tomorrow they'd say goodbye to the crew.

When Josie had come home from the hospital two days before, she'd been ready to work, but Grady would have none of it. Only because today was the final day had he reluctantly given in.

"No ladder, no lifting. And lots of breaks. More breaks than work, actually, and if you get tired, you'll tell me right away."

A smile curled the corners of her mouth as she remembered his unwavering conditions. She had gotten tired today. And hot. It was unseasonably warm and she wasn't as recovered as she'd thought, though she wasn't about to admit it.

The water babbled against the rock, whispering an invitation. She slipped off her shoes and socks and lowered her feet into the creek. The water bubbled over them, washing, refreshing.

She'd had a lot of time to reflect at the hospital between the testing and poking and prodding. She thought about Ian and that night and she thought about God.

Grady's scripture had replayed until it was etched into the recesses of her brain. *"While we were still sinners, Christ died for us."*

His comparison between Ian's sacrifice and God's hadn't been so far off target. They were all guilty of something, weren't they? There was no way to earn some gifts. At some point, you just had to receive it.

Why had it taken so long to realize it? She waved her feet in the water, feeling the current tug at her legs as if to say, *Come along, Josie. There's more work to do.*

She'd told her family about Ian the day after she'd come home. Laurel's eyes had filled with tears when she found out what Ian had done for Josie. It had been a shock for them to realize Josie had wanted to die, but Laurel and Aunt Lola were taking it in one day at a time. They all were. She would call Hank in a day or two, as soon as she found the nerve. Ian's father deserved to know how selfless his son had been.

Last night she'd had a long overdue conversation with Aunt Lola about her father. There was still a lot of healing to be done there, a lot of feelings to process and hurt to work through. But she was beginning to understand that it was his flaws that had caused him to treat her as he did, and not her own. That would have to sink in a little at a time until she fully believed it.

Above her, she heard a voice calling her name.

"Down here!" she called, her eyes scanning the top of the hill for Grady's form.

When he appeared at the crest, she watched him take the incline, watched his long legs eat up the distance.

He stopped on the fringe of grass that edged the creek, tucking his hands in his back pockets. The sun hit the flesh of his arms, carving shadows under the muscles.

"Wondered where you'd gotten off to," he said.

She should've told him, but he'd been talking to Hernando when they'd finished, and she hadn't wanted to interrupt.

"Saved a seat for you." She patted the rock ledge beside her.

He tucked a smile into the corner of his mouth. "Best invitation I've had all week."

When he was beside her, pants rolled to his knees, feet in the water, they sat in comfortable silence. His thigh moved against hers, slow, subtle movements, as he swung his feet in the current.

Above them, a dove called from a tree on the hillside, and Josie tracked it to a maple, where its round gray body contrasted against the vibrant red leaves.

The dove called again. *Ooo-OOH. Ooh-ooh-ooh.* The sound reminded her of home. Of mornings in bed when she was young and her mother was alive. Of swinging on the tire swing after she finished her homework and was free for the evening. There

were good memories here too. Those were the ones she needed
to remember.

Grady's voice broke into her thoughts. "I do believe this is the
first time we've been alone since Saturday night."

Half the town of Shelbyville had been to the hospital, usually
outside visiting hours, much to Verna Mae's frustration. Ashley
and Jackie had even driven from Asheville one evening to check
on her.

"That right?" She'd been hungry for time alone with him, but
even when she'd gotten home, there were her family and the babies.
And much to her frustration, she was exhausted by dinnertime. It
didn't help that two certain squallers were keeping her up nights.

"You've changed." He was staring at her, and her flesh warmed
under his appraisal.

"How so?"

"You tell me."

She was different. She hadn't felt like running once since she'd
left the hospital. Her mind hadn't been bogged down with guilt.
Her focus was not on the past, but the future.

"I have peace." Such a simple word, yet what joy was there in
life without it? Not much, as she'd discovered.

"That's a good thing."

"It really is." The lazy sounds of the water, the dove calling,
and the warmth of the sun made her sleepy. She lay back against
the flat surface of the rock, keeping her feet in the water.

"You're tired."

Josie closed her eyes against the sun. "Little bit. It's going to
take time." She hadn't fallen asleep until eleven the night before,
then she'd woken every two hours to the twins' cries.

"I'll tell you one thing," she said. "When I'm fully recovered,

I'm going to help Laurel with the twins' feedings. Poor thing's going to be a walking zombie in a matter of weeks."

Grady's thigh stilled against hers, and she sensed a change in the quiet that followed.

She opened her eyes, shielding the light with her hand. "What?"

He was looking at her as if trying to read the fine print. "You're staying then?"

They'd never exactly had the conversation. The family had tiptoed around her the last few days, keeping the mood light, avoiding stressful topics, even when she tried to broach them. Probably doctor's orders, but completely unnecessary. As if she could convince them of that.

But yeah, she was staying. This was home, and the bad memories no longer had her in their grip. She was free, and planned to enjoy it.

"Think you can stand working with me every day?" she asked.

His mouth twitched at the corner. A sign of nervousness or pleasure, she wasn't sure. Learning things like that took time, but they'd have plenty of that. If he was willing.

"Are you going to be stubborn and sassy?"

"Probably."

He smiled. "What I figured. I guess I can put up with you."

She remembered his dream of owning an orchard. His plans to buy Laurel out. She wanted his dreams to come true too. "We can still work something out with Laurel's shares."

"Maybe I can work something out with the other owner." He reached over and touched her arm, drawing his finger down it.

A shiver ran up her spine at the contact. Heavens to Betsy,

what he did to her. She closed her eyes and wondered if he could see her heart trying to burst from the confines of her rib cage.

"I don't mean to rush you. We can go slow as you like."

It had only been one harvest, after all, but it seemed like longer. They'd spent so many hours together, working.

"Shoot," Grady said, the word riding a nervous chuckle. "We can start over if you want."

She felt him shift and opened her eyes.

He was extending his hand. "Hi. I'm Grady." There was vulnerability in his eyes, the kind that made her want to kiss him silly. He gave a tiny one-shoulder shrug. "I'm kind of in love with you."

His words were a balm to her battered heart.

And she didn't want to start over. Not when there was so much to look forward to. "No." Her voice was barely audible over nature's sounds.

His smile fell, pulling the corners of his eyes with it. His hand fell to his side.

Josie pulled herself upright until her face was inches from his. She looked into the rich brown pool of his eyes. "I'd rather we pick up right where we left off." She found the courage to say the words. "'Cause I'm kind of in love with you too."

His face transformed, softening. His gaze was like a caress on her face, so powerful she could almost feel it.

When his lips brushed hers, it was like coming home. The tiredness she'd felt moments before evaporated like a rain puddle under an August sun.

He made her feel alive. Loved. So much more than she would've expected from a man she'd once thought of as Marlboro Man. How could a first impression be so wrong?

A moment later, he drew back.

She laughed with joy.

"What?" The seriousness of his expression only tickled her more.

This was going to be an adventure, so much fun. She looked forward to every last bit of it.

"What?" he asked again. "I'm trying to be all romantic here, you know."

Heaven forbid she should stand in the way of romance, especially with the likes of Grady. "Shut up and kiss me, Marlboro Man."

One of his brows disappeared beneath his bangs. "What?"

"Oh, never mind." Before he could press her for an answer, she brushed her lips across his and Grady returned the favor with eagerness, the subject seemingly forgotten. There would be time to talk later, but for now she wanted to savor the moment there in the cradle of Sweetwater Gap.

acknowledgments

$\mathcal{I}$ owe many people a debt of gratitude for their contributions toward this novel.

To Karen Solem for her support and encouragement.

To Ami McConnell, editor extraordinaire. I am amazed by your insight, skill, and wisdom. All writers should be so blessed as to have an editor like you!

I am privileged to work with the entire Thomas Nelson Fiction team led by Allen Arnold: Amanda Bostic, Jocelyn Bailey, Jennifer Deshler, Natalie Hanemann, Ami McConnell, Becky Monds, Katie Schroder, Lisa Young, the creative cover design team led by Mark Ross, and all the copy editors.

Thanks to the Thomas Nelson sales force who make sure my books make it to the bookstore shelves.

Maureen Kercher from Kercher's Sunrise Orchards took time from her busy schedule to educate me on the workings of an apple orchard. Any errors are mine alone.

Thanks also to Dr. Ronda Wells who educated me on the symptoms, treatments, and diagnosis of Addison's disease.

Thanks to Kristi Etter for Aunt Lola's fabulous apple pie recipe which can be downloaded from my website.

Every story I write evolves from a brainstorming session with my dear friends and fellow authors from the Girls Write Out blog (www.GirlsWriteOut.blogspot.com), Kristin Billerbeck, Colleen Coble, and Diann Hunt. Love you, girls!

To Jessica Alvarez for helping me hone the story and fine-tune the wording. My readers thank you!

Thanks to my husband, Kevin, whose support and encouragement mean the world to me.

Thanks most of all to God who, twelve years ago, took my modest dream of finishing a novel-length manuscript and turned it into so much more than I imagined.

I love to hear from my readers! Feel free to send me an e-mail at denise@denisehunterbooks.com or visit my website at www.DeniseHunterBooks.com.

reading group guide

1. What role did each of these characters play in Josie's life: Aunt Lola, Laurel, Josie's dad, Grady?

2. How did the attitude of Josie's father toward her shape the way Josie felt about herself?

3. What characteristics of Grady appealed to Josie?

4. Josie didn't feel she could live with the guilt of Ian's sacrifice. What are some things she did to assuage the guilt?

5. How was Ian's sacrifice like Christ's? How are Josie's responses to Ian's sacrifice similar to our response to Christ's sacrifice?

6. How did Grady's love for Josie demonstrate selflessness? How did his love for Josie lead her toward God?

7. Josie reached a point of despair where she felt there was
   only one way out. What could you say to a friend in
   desperate straits that would give him or her hope?

8. The gospel seed had been planted in Josie from the time
   she was young. Why do you think it took her so long to
   accept it? What was it about her present situation that
   made her ready?

9. What meaning do you think the title *Sweetwater Gap* has?

*Download the recipe for "Aunt Lola's Dutch Apple Pie" at Denise's
website: www.DeniseHunterBooks.com*

A note from the author

Dear Friend,

I hope you enjoyed your time in Shelbyville, North Carolina, with Grady, Josie, and her family. This story was birthed when my editor sent me an article about a soldier who suffered from survivor guilt after his friend literally jumped on a grenade to save his life. I began thinking about the parallels with Christ's sacrifice and a story was born.

Guilt is a complicated emotion that can affect the things we do and our relationships with those we love. If you struggle with guilt in your life, I hope you'll find peace and healing as Josie did, through the redeeming work of Christ.

Whether you're currently struggling through life or peacefully sailing through your spiritual journey, I hope you'll make time to attend a Women of Faith conference soon. The hours spent at one of these extraordinary events will refresh your spirit and bless you in ways you cannot imagine. I know these conferences have blessed me tremendously.

In His grace,
Denise

On the beautiful island of Nantucket,
salt and roses scent the air,
waves sparkle over hidden currents,
and a storm-tossed soul seeks safe harbor.

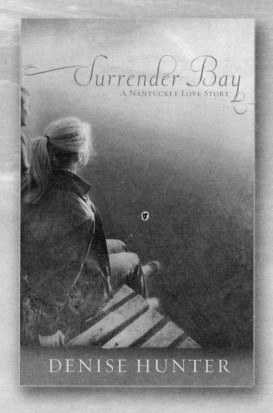

A Nantucket Love Story

THOMAS NELSON
Since 1798

She wrote the book—literally—
on finding the right mate. But does she really
understand what love's about?

A Nantucket Love Story

THOMAS NELSON
Since 1798

*"No matter where you are
or how long it takes until we can be together,
I'll keep searching for you."*—Tucker

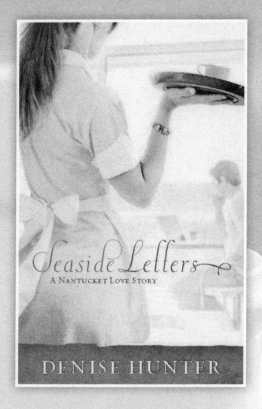

A Nantucket Love Story

THOMAS NELSON
Since 1798